THE
WORKS OF
HENRY FIELDING

Edited by

GEORGE SAINTSBURY

ONE OF HER FATHER'S FAVORITE TUNES

The Works of
HENRY FIELDING

VOLUME II

THE ADVENTURES OF
TOM JONES
PARTS ONE AND TWO

BIGELOW, BROWN & CO., Inc.
NEW YORK

THE HISTORY OF TOM JONES

VOL. I.

CONTENTS OF VOL. I

BOOK I.

CONTAINING AS MUCH OF THE BIRTH OF THE FOUNDLING AS IS
NECESSARY OR PROPER TO ACQUAINT THE READER WITH IN THE
BEGINNING OF THIS HISTORY.

BOOK II.

CONTENTS

CONTENTS

BOOK III.

BOOK V.

CONTAINING A PORTION OF TIME SOMEWHAT LONGER THAN HALF A YEAR.

CONTENTS

INTRODUCTION

THE *orbis terrarum* of literary criticism has not had much difficulty in deciding that *Tom Jones* is, in something else than mere size, Fielding's greatest work. If both Johnson and Thackeray seem to have preferred *Amelia*, enough allowance has been made in the General Introduction for any expression of the former, while the latter was evidently biased at the particular moment. The characteristics of *Amelia* were well suited to contrast with and atone for the rather exaggerated delineation of Fielding's Bohemianism which it had suited Thackeray to give; and, speaking to a mixed audience, he no doubt felt it easier to dwell on the later than on the earlier book. The extreme condemnation of Tom the hero as distinct from *Tom* the book, which is put elsewhere in the mouth of Colonel Newcome, is at least partly dramatic; and I am not sure that the indirect eulogy in *Pendennis*— that *Tom Jones* was the last book in which an English novelist was allowed to depict a man— does not make up for any censure expressed or implied elsewhere. It is, without the grandiloquence, nearly as lofty a eulogy as Gibbon's. What that great writer said is universally known, and no comment on it is necessary, except a reminder that in many ways Gibbon's tastes were rather Continental or cosmopolitan than English, and that he was by no means likely to be bribed by the intensely national flavor of the novel. Of late there has been a disposition to demur to Coleridge's hardly less lofty eulogy of the mere craftsmanship shown in the novel. But Scott, a practiced critic, a novelist of unsurpassed competence, and not always a very enthusiastic encomiast of Fielding, has endorsed it in the Introduction to the *Fortunes of Nigel.* After such names it is unnecessary to cite any others by way of authority, and we may pass to the direct consideration of the book itself.

Tom Jones, then, is a novel which differs from almost all other novels both in the range and the precision of its scale and scheme. Its personages are extremely numerous, and there is justice in the half-humorous protestation of the author, in reference to the apparent repetition in the two landladies, that they are "most carefully differentiated from each other." Its scenes are extremely varied, and each has its local color adjusted with perfect propriety. Of the actions and passions represented it is indeed possible for the *advocatus diaboli* to urge that, whatever their range and truth to nature within their limits, there is a certain want of height and depth in them. But this is only saying in other words that the middle of the eighteenth century was not the beginning of the sixteenth; that Fielding had not the tragic touch; and that though he was most emphatically a "maker," he was not in the transferred and specialized sense a poet. Lastly, all these varying excellences and excellent variations are adjusted together in so cunning an arrangement of dramatic narrative, that some have found it absolutely impeccable, while few have done more than protest against the Man of the Hill, question whether we do not see more than we need of Mrs. Fitzpatrick, and ask whether the catastrophe is not, especially considering the very leisurely movement of the earlier scenes, somewhat hurried and huddled. As for the characters, exception, so far as I know, has not been seriously taken to any save on the score of art and nature to Allworthy and Blifil, on the score of morality to Mr. Jones himself. Some have indeed expressed their desire for something with more air and fire than the heroine; but there are always people who grumble thus. Let us try to sweep the negatives aside before attempting the affirmative.

I have already in the General Introduction attempted to disable the objection to the "Man of the Hill," and I need say no more on that head except that he, like all his kind, is distinctly a *hors-d'œuvre,* to be taken or left at choice. Nor do the other objections to construction seem to me much more valid. The famous preliminary observations have had extended to them by severe judges the indulgence which I myself claim for the episodes, and while they cannot be said in any way to delay the action, they provide the book with an additional element of interest—an element with which, to the same extent and in the same intensity, no other novel in the world is furnished. As for the end, a certain "quickening-up at the finish" hath invariably been allowed, and even prescribed, to artists, and I do not know that it can be said to be greatly exceeded here.

It is, however, undeniable that the defects of Allworthy and Blifil appear at this point more than elsewhere, and indeed to some extent produce the effect complained of. And I shall further admit that these two characters, especially Blifil, seem to me almost the only spots in Fielding's sun. For Allworthy we can indeed make some excuse—lame after its kind, for your excuse invariably *claudicat*. There is little doubt that Fielding was hampered and misled by his intention to glorify a particular person, his benefactor Allworthy. Nature, when you cannot take liberties with her, is always a clog on Art, and gratitude constrains the license of the will of men more than malevolence, inasmuch as there is a greater difficulty in disguising particulars. But Allworthy is not so unnatural as he is unsatisfactory; for a very benevolent and very unsuspicious man, whose head was not quite so good as his heart, might act in the way here described. Moreover, his folly and injustice (for his action towards Tom really deserves these words) are not only useful, but almost necessary to the course of the action—a defense rather technical than convincing, but technically good. And here it may be sufficient to say a few words about the effect of Fielding's long practice in drama before he took to fiction. The order has not been usual, for obvious reasons, though the contrary process, the corruption of a good novelist into a dramatist not so good, is, for reasons equally obvious, quite common. But Fielding and Dumas are eminent instances of the happy effect which dramatic practice exercises on the novelist. Dumas, a better dramatist than Fielding, cannot touch him as a novelist; but, like him, he owes to his dramatic practice the singular freedom of even his most hastily cobbled-up stories from what is really otiose. His playwright's eye kept him from the commonest and worst fault of novel-writing, the introduction of matter irrelevant to the story. But it may be somewhat questioned whether the same playwright's habit did not in Fielding's case induce the fault of being contented, in rare instances, with what *was* necessary for the story.

This operated, I think, even more strongly in the case of Blifil. I do not know that even he can be pronounced wholly unnatural. "A prig, and a bad prig," is not, I fear, an unnatural character in itself. But for this or that reason, Fielding has not made this young wretch alive, as he has made every one else, great and small, among his personages. He seems almost to have deliberately abstained from doing so. We see very little of Blifil in action; he is generally recounted to us. The "messengers," to use the term familiar to readers of the Greek drama, do his business; the author hangs back to tell his misdeeds; himself is seldom in much evidence on the actual stage. It may be that Fielding could not trust himself with him; that he felt that if he had allowed his figure to appear more actively, something of the dread-

ful greatness of Jonathan Wild would have passed
into Blifil, and have dwarfed and eclipsed the
healthier and lighter characters. It may be that
he disliked him too much, and shoveled him as
quickly as possible out of his hands, as a little
later he may have done with a particularly loath-
some rogue at Bow Street. But here again these
are weak excuses. If Thackeray has one great
advantage over his master, I think it is when we
compare Barnes Newcome with Blifil. They are
very much alike; indeed, as Mr. Blifil, we are expressly told, "retired to the North," it may possibly have happened that some of his blood was
in the veins of that most respectable family. But
Barnes is much more human, much completer,
much more alive. The late Mr. G. S. Venables,
an excellent lawyer and an excellent critic, used,
I am told, to remark in connection with some puzzling passages at the end of *Oliver Twist,* that
"Dickens hanged Fagin for being the villain of a
novel." I am inclined to think that Fielding exacted a more terrible penalty from this his one
odious child for the same offense. He deprived
him of life to start with.

Nobody can say this of Blifil's brother by the
mother's side. "Mr. Thomas" is exceedingly human; and the objections which have been lodged
against him have been and must be quite different. With one of them—the anathema launched
by Colonel Newcome—there is some slight difficulty in dealing. But the Colonel, though one of
the best, was not one of the wisest of men, and
he was decidedly weak in history. It might be al-

most sufficient to say that Scott, the paragon of
manly chivalry, and not always a very lenient or
sympathetic judge of Fielding, does not seem to
have taken any special objection to the Lady
Bellaston episode. And I frankly admit that I
do not see why he should. In the first place, it
must be remembered that the point of honor
which decrees that a man must not under any circumstances accept money from a woman with
whom he is on certain terms, is of very modern
growth, and is still tempered by the proviso that
he may take as much as he likes or can get from
his wife. In Fielding's days, or but a very little
earlier, this moral had simply not been invented.
Marlborough, his father's great commander, notoriously took a large sum from the Duchess of
Cleveland in precisely Tom Jones' circumstances;
and though Marlborough's enemies included the
bitterest and brightest wits of his time, they seem
to have objected, when they objected at all, rather
to his careful investment of this money than to
his acceptance of it. No easy-going gentleman
of the late seventeenth and early eighteenth centuries in France or England—and it must be remembered that to compare Tom Jones with the
grave and precise ones is absurd—would have
thought the worse of himself for accepting a present of money from his mistress, any more than
he would have thought the worse of her for accepting one from him. During Tom's youth not
a few of the finest gentlemen in Europe found a
Lady Bellaston in the Czarina Elizabeth, and during his age many more found one in the Czarina

Catherine. I have myself a great admiration for nice fine points of honor—I don't think you can make them too nice or too fine; but the person who has not been taught them—nay, in whose time they scarcely exist—cannot justly be said to violate them. It seemed perfectly natural to Tom that, when he had money, he should dress out Molly Seagrim, who had none: I do not suppose that it seemed much less natural to him that Lady Bellaston should dress him out when she had money and he had none. A shocking blindness, doubtless; but all blindness is more or less relative.

The more general objections to Mr. Thomas's character seem to me to proceed from one of the commonest but most uncritical faults of criticism —the refusal to consider what it is that the author intended to give us. It is most certain that Fielding did not intend to give us an Æneas or an Amadis, a Galahad or an Artegal. He meant to give us an extremely ordinary young man in all respects except good luck, good looks, fair understanding, and generous impulses—a young man incapable of doing anything cruel, or, as far as he understood it, mean, but of no very exceptional abilities, rather thoughtless, fond of pleasure, and not extraordinarily nice about its sources and circumstances—*a jeune homme sensuel moyen,* in short. His concessions to heroic needs consisted in making Tom not only—

"Like Paris handsome, and like Hector brave,"

but a much better fellow than Paris and a much
luckier one than Hector.

It seems to me that we have absolutely no business to go beyond these limits and insist that
Tom shall be a Joseph or even a Percivale; still
less to demand that he shall be a young man of
literary and artistic sympathies; least of all that
he shall be troubled about his soul either in the
manner of Launcelot Smith or in the manner of
Francis Neyrac.   The late Mr. Kingsley was, and
the living M. Bourget is, a very clever man.   To
them too, especially to the first, fell something of
the faculty of creative observation, and neither
mixes with it more ephemeral matter than he had
a right to mix.   But if, when the eighteenth and
nineteenth centuries are to some future generation what the first before and the first after Christ
are to us, some competent critic turns out of a
new Herculaneum or Pompeii a box containing
Tom Jones, Yeast, and *La Terre Promise,* I know
what his verdict will be.

A very little of the same injustice which has
thus weighed upon Tom has involved the divine
Sophia; but with this we need hardly concern ourselves at all.   It is not necessary that she should
be our ideal, or any one's ideal.   But if any one
has read and digested the great and famous first
chapter of the Sixth Book, which, if not exactly
exhaustive of its difficult subject, contains more
practical wisdom than the *Phædrus* and more
honest passion than all Stendhal's treatise *De
l' Amour,* he will admit that she was a worthy ob-

ject of the feelings it discusses. Perhaps Mr. Jones was not quite worthy of her; it is not the least of her own worthinesses that the fact is extremely unlikely ever to have occurred to her.

For all the rest we have few vituperators. I think indeed with Scott, rather than with my friend Mr. Dobson, that Squire Western ought not to have taken that beating from the Captain; but then I own myself, as Scott probably was, jealous for the honor of the Tory party, to which Mr. Western also belonged. Nobody else is "out" for a moment during the whole of this long and delightful story. Everybody does what he or she ought to have done—I do not mean morally, which might subject me to the censures of the Church and the Schools alike, but according to the probabilities of human nature and the requirements of great art. Fielding cannot introduce the most insignificant character who makes a substantial appearance without finishing the drawing; he cannot send on the merest scene-shifters, the veriest candle-snuffers, and "population of Cyprus," without impressing upon them natural and distinct personalities. As you turn the pages, the long silent world becomes alive again in all its varied scenes, very much as the old Coachyard did when the Bagman's Uncle took that walk from Edinburgh to Leith after supper. The whole thing is perfectly real, and real without effort. Indeed this extraordinary vitality belongs to the minor characters in almost a greater degree than to the major. There is Miss Western, with her perpetual and yet not the least

overdone politics; and her niece Mrs. Fitzpatrick
—very ripe and real she; and Mrs. Waters, for
whom she was mistaken, and who was mistaken
for her and also for other people; and Partridge
the immortal; and the pair of named hand-
maidens, Deborah and Honour, who come only
short of Mrs. Slipslop; and the pair of unnamed
landladies; and their chambermaids, who if they
are not always virtuous or beautiful, possess that
charm which an old poet thought the highest, that
they "never will say no," and are generally good-
natured and charitable souls. There is no mistake about Lady Bellaston, and not much about
Lord Fellamar. But no possible space could
suffice for this sort of talk. Let it be enough to
add to the old and well-deserved praise of the
"fresh air" and healthy atmosphere of the whole
piece, that these effects, so often acknowledged,
are due first of all to the vitality of which we have
been speaking. *Tom Jones* is an epic of life—not
indeed of the highest, the rarest, the most impas-
sioned of life's scenes and phases, but of the
healthy average life of the average natural man;
not faultless nor perfect by any means, but human and actual as no one else but Shakespeare
has shown him in the mimic world.

To the Honorable

GEORGE LYTTLETON, ESQ;

One of the Lords Commissioners of the Treasury.

Sir,

NOTWITHSTANDING your constant refusal, when I have asked leave to prefix your name to this dedication, I must still insist on my right to desire your protection of this work.

To you, Sir, it is owing that this history was ever begun. It was by your desire that I first thought of such a composition. So many years have since past, that you may have, perhaps, forgotten this circumstance: but your desires are to me in the nature of commands; and the impression of them is never to be erased from my memory.

Again, Sir, without your assistance this history had never been completed. Be not startled at the assertion. I do not intend to draw on you the suspicion of being a romance writer. I mean no more than that I partly owe to you my existence during great part of the time which I have employed in composing it: another matter which it may be necessary to remind you of; since there are certain actions of which you are apt to be extremely forgetful; but of these I hope I shall always have a better memory than yourself.

Lastly, It is owing to you that the history appears what it now is. If there be in this work, as some have been pleased to say, a stronger picture of a truly benevolent mind than is to be found in any other, who that knows you, and a particular acquaintance of yours, will doubt whence that benevolence hath been copied? The world will not, I believe, make me the compliment of thinking I took it from myself. I care not: this they shall own, that the two persons from whom I have taken it, that is to say, two of the best and worthiest men in the world, are strongly and zealously my friends. I might be contented with this, and yet my vanity will add a third to the number; and him one of the greatest and noblest, not only in his rank, but in every public and private virtue. But here, whilst my gratitude for the princely benefactions of the Duke of Bedford bursts from my heart, you must forgive my reminding you that it was you who first recommended me to the notice of my benefactor.

And what are your objections to the allowance of the honor which I have solicited? Why, you have commended the book so warmly, that you should be ashamed of reading your name before the dedication. Indeed, sir, if the book itself doth not make you ashamed of your commendations, nothing that I can here write will, or ought. I am not to give up my right to your protection and patronage, because you have commended my book:

for though I acknowledge so many obligations to you, I do not add this to the number; in which friendship, I am convinced, hath so little share: since that can neither bias your judgment, nor pervert your integrity. An enemy may at any time obtain your commendation by only deserving it; and the utmost which the faults of your friends can hope for, is your silence; or, perhaps, if too severely accused, your gentle palliation.

In short, sir, I suspect, that your dislike of public praise is your true objection to granting my request. I have observed that you have, in common with my two other friends, an unwillingness to hear the least mention of your own virtues; that, as a great poet says of one of you, (he might justly have said it of all three), you

Do good by stealth, and blush to find it fame.

If men of this disposition are as careful to shun applause, as others are to escape censure, how just must be your apprehension of your character falling into my hands; since what would not a man have reason to dread, if attacked by an author who had received from him injuries equal to my obligations to you!

And will not this dread of censure increase in proportion to the matter which a man is conscious of having afforded for it? If his whole life, for instance, should have been one continued subject of satire, he may well tremble when an incensed satirist takes him in hand. Now, sir, if we apply this to your modest aversion to panegyric, how reasonable will your fears of me appear!

Yet surely you might have gratified my ambition, from this single confidence, that I shall always prefer the indulgence of your inclinations to the satisfaction of my own. A very strong instance of which I shall give you in this address, in which I am determined to follow the example of all other dedicators, and will consider not what my patron really deserves to have written, but what he will be best pleased to read.

Without further preface then, I here present you with the labors of some years of my life. What merit these labors have is already known to yourself. If, from your favorable judgment, I have conceived some esteem for them, it cannot be imputed to vanity; since I should have agreed as implicitly to your opinion, had it been given in favor of any other man's production. Negatively, at least, I may be allowed to say, that had I been sensible of any great demerit in the work, you are the last person to whose protection I would have ventured to recommend it.

From the name of my patron, indeed, I hope my reader will be convinced, at his very entrance on this work, that he will find in the whole course of it nothing prejudicial to the cause of religion and virtue, nothing inconsistent with the strictest rules of decency, nor which can offend even the chastest eye in the perusal. On the contrary, I declare, that to recommend goodness and innocence hath been my sincere endeavor in this history. This honest purpose you have been pleased to think I have attained: and to say the truth, it is likeliest to be attained in books of this kind; for an example is a kind of picture, in which virtue becomes, as it were, an object of sight, and strikes us with an idea of that loveliness, which Plato asserts there is in her naked charms.

Besides displaying that beauty of virtue which may attract the admiration of mankind, I have attempted to engage a stronger motive to human action in her favor, by convincing men, that their true interest directs them to a pursuit of her. For this purpose I have shown that no acquisitions of guilt can compensate the loss of that solid inward comfort of mind, which is the sure companion of innocence and virtue; nor can in the least balance the evil of that horror and anxiety which, in their room, guilt introduces into our bosoms. And again, that as these acquisitions are in themselves generally worthless, so are the means to attain them not only base and infamous, but at best uncertain, and always full of danger. Lastly, I have endeavored strongly to inculcate, that virtue and innocence can scarce ever be injured but by indiscretion; and that it is this alone which often betrays them into the snares that deceit and villainy spread for them. A moral which I have the more industriously labored, as the teaching it is, of all others, the likeliest to be attended with success; since, I believe, it is much easier to make good men wise, than to make bad men good.

For these purposes I have employed all the wit and humor of which I am master in the following history; wherein I have endeavored to laugh mankind out of their favorite follies and vices. How far I have succeeded in this good attempt, I shall submit to the candid reader, with only two requests: First, that he will not expect to find perfection in this work; and Secondly, that he will excuse some parts of it, if they fall short of that little merit which I hope may appear in others.

I will detain you, sir, no longer. Indeed I have run into a preface, while I professed to write a dedication. But how can it be otherwise? I dare not praise you; and the only means I know of to avoid it, when you are in my thoughts, are either to be entirely silent, or to turn my thoughts to some other subject.

Pardon, therefore, what I have said in this epistle, not only without your consent, but absolutely against it; and give me at least leave, in this public manner, to declare that I am, with the highest respect and gratitude,—

    Sir,

        Your most obliged,

          Obedient, humble servant,

            HENRY FIELDING

THE HISTORY OF TOM JONES,

A FOUNDLING

BOOK I

CONTAINING AS MUCH OF THE BIRTH OF THE FOUND-
LING AS IS NECESSARY OR PROPER TO ACQUAINT
THE READER WITH IN THE BEGINNING OF THIS
HISTORY.

CHAPTER I

The introduction to the work, or bill of fare to the feast.

AN author ought to consider himself, not as
a gentleman who gives a private or
eleemosynary treat, but rather as one
who keeps a public ordinary, at which all persons
are welcome for their money. In the former case,
it is well known that the entertainer provides
what fare he pleases; and though this should be
very indifferent, and utterly disagreeable to the
taste of his company, they must not find any
fault; nay, on the contrary, good breeding forces
them outwardly to approve and to commend whatever is set before them. Now the contrary of this
happens to the master of an ordinary. Men who
pay for what they eat will insist on gratifying
their palates, however nice and whimsical these

may prove; and if everything is not agreeable to
their taste, will challenge a right to censure, to
abuse, and to d—n their dinner without control.

To prevent, therefore, giving offense to their
customers by any such disappointment, it hath
been usual with the honest and well-meaning host
to provide a bill of fare which all persons may
peruse at their first entrance into the house; and
having thence acquainted themselves with the entertainment which they may expect, may either
stay and regale with what is provided for them,
or may depart to some other ordinary better accommodated to their taste.

As we do not disdain to borrow wit or wisdom
from any man who is capable of lending us either,
we have condescended to take a hint from these
honest victualers, and shall prefix not only a general bill of fare to our whole entertainment, but
shall likewise give the reader particular bills to
every course which is to be served up in this and
the ensuing volumes.

The provision, then, which we have here made
is no other than *Human Nature*. Nor do I fear
that my sensible reader, though most luxurious in
his taste, will start, cavil, or be offended, because
I have named but one article. The tortoise—as
the alderman of Bristol, well learned in eating,
knows by much experience—besides the delicious
calipash and calipee, contains many different
kinds of food; nor can the learned reader be ignorant, that in human nature, though here collected
under one general name, is such prodigious variety, that a cook will have sooner gone through all

the several species of animal and vegetable food in the world, than an author will be able to exhaust so extensive a subject.

An objection may perhaps be apprehended from the more delicate, that this dish is too common and vulgar; for what else is the subject of all the romances, novels, plays, and poems, with which the stalls abound? Many exquisite viands might be rejected by the epicure, if it was a sufficient cause for his contemning of them as common and vulgar, that something was to be found in the most paltry alleys under the same name. In reality, true nature is as difficult to be met with in authors, as the Bayonne ham, or Bologna sausage, is to be found in the shops.

But the whole, to continue the same metaphor, consists in the cookery of the author; for, as Mr. Pope tells us—

"True wit is nature to advantage drest;
What oft was thought, but ne'er so well exprest."

The same animal which hath the honor to have some part of his flesh eaten at the table of a duke, may perhaps be degraded in another part, and some of his limbs gibbeted, as it were, in the vilest stall in town. Where, then, lies the difference between the food of the nobleman and the porter, if both are at dinner on the same ox or calf, but in the seasoning, the dressing, the garnishing, and the setting forth? Hence the one provokes and incites the most languid appetite, and the other turns and palls that which is the sharpest and keenest.

In like manner, the excellence of the mental entertainment consists less in the subject than in the author's skill in well dressing it up. How pleased, therefore, will the reader be to find that we have, in the following work, adhered closely to one of the highest principles of the best cook which the present age, or perhaps that of Heliogabalus, hath produced. This great man, as is well known to all lovers of polite eating, begins at first by setting plain things before his hungry guests, rising afterwards by degrees as their stomachs may be supposed to decrease, to the very quintessence of sauce and spices. In like manner, we shall represent human nature at first to the keen appetite of our reader, in that more plain and simple manner in which it is found in the country, and shall hereafter hash and ragoo it with all the high French and Italian seasoning of affectation and vice which courts and cities afford. By these means, we doubt not but our reader may be rendered desirous to read on for ever, as the great person just above-mentioned is supposed to have made some persons eat.

Having premised thus much, we will now detain those who like our bill of fare no longer from their diet, and shall proceed directly to serve up the first course of our history for their entertainment.

CHAPTER II

A short description of squire Allworthy, and a fuller account
of Miss Bridget Allworthy, his sister.

IN that part of the western division of this
kingdom which is commonly called Somersetshire, there lately lived, and perhaps lives
still, a gentleman whose name was Allworthy, and
who might well be called the favorite of both nature and fortune; for both of these seem to have
contended which should bless and enrich him
most. In this contention, nature may seem to
some to have come off victorious, as she bestowed
on him many gifts, while fortune had only one gift
in her power; but in pouring forth this, she was
so very profuse, that others perhaps may think
this single endowment to have been more than
equivalent to all the various blessings which he
enjoyed from nature. From the former of these,
he derived an agreeable person, a sound constitution, a solid understanding, and a benevolent
heart; by the latter, he was decreed to the inheri-
tance of one of the largest estates in the county.

This gentleman had in his youth married a very
worthy and beautiful woman, of whom he had
been extremely fond: by her he had three children,
all of whom died in their infancy. He had likewise had the misfortune of burying this beloved
wife herself, about five years before the time in

which this history chooses to set out. This loss, however great, he bore like a man of sense and constancy, though it must be confessed he would often talk a little whimsically on this head; for he sometimes said he looked on himself as still married, and considered his wife as only gone a little before him, a journey which he should most certainly, sooner or later, take after her; and that he had not the least doubt of meeting her again in a place where he should never part with her more —sentiments for which his sense was arraigned by one part of his neighbors, his religion by a second, and his sincerity by a third.

He now lived, for the most part, retired in the country, with one sister, for whom he had a very tender affection. This lady was now somewhat past the age of thirty, an era at which, in the opinion of the malicious, the title of old maid may with no impropriety be assumed. She was of that species of women whom you commend rather for good qualities than beauty, and who are generally called, by their own sex, very good sort of women—as good a sort of woman, madam, as you would wish to know. Indeed, she was so far from regretting want of beauty, that she never mentioned that perfection, if it can be called one, without contempt; and would often thank God she was not as handsome as Miss Such-a-one, whom perhaps beauty had led into errors which she might have otherwise avoided. Miss Bridget Allworthy (for that was the name of this lady) very rightly conceived the charms of person in a woman to be no better than snares for herself, as well as for others; and yet so discreet was she in her conduct, that her prudence was as much on the guard as if she had all the snares to apprehend which were ever laid for her whole sex. Indeed, I have observed, though it may seem unaccountable to the reader, that this guard of prudence, like the trained bands, is always readiest to go on duty where there is the least danger. It often basely and cowardly deserts those paragons for whom the men are all wishing, sighing, dying, and spreading every net in their power; and constantly attends at the heels of that higher order of women for whom the other sex have a more distant and awful respect, and whom (from despair, I suppose, of success) they never venture to attack.

Reader, I think proper, before we proceed any farther together, to acquaint thee that I intend to digress, through this whole history, as often as I see occasion, of which I am myself a better judge than any pitiful critic whatever; and here I must desire all those critics to mind their own business, and not to intermeddle with affairs or works which no ways concern them; for till they produce the authority by which they are constituted judges, I shall not plead to their jurisdiction.

CHAPTER III

An odd accident which befel Mr. Allworthy at his return
home. The decent behavior of Mrs. Deborah Wilkins,
with some proper animadversions on bastards.

I HAVE told my reader, in the preceding
chapter, that Mr. Allworthy inherited a
large fortune; that he had a good heart, and
no family. Hence, doubtless, it will be concluded
by many that he lived like an honest man, owed
no one a shilling, took nothing but what was his
own, kept a good house, entertained his neighbors
with a hearty welcome at his table, and was charitable to the poor, *i. e.,* to those who had rather
beg than work, by giving them the offals from it;
that he died immensely rich and built an hospital.

And true it is that he did many of these things;
but had he done nothing more I should have left
him to have recorded his own merit on some fair
freestone over the door of that hospital. Matters
of a much more extraordinary kind are to be the
subject of this history, or I should grossly mis-
spend my time in writing so voluminous a work;
and you, my sagacious friend, might with equal
profit and pleasure travel through some pages
which certain droll authors have been facetiously
pleased to call *The History of England.*

Mr. Allworthy had been absent a full quarter
of a year in London, on some very particular busi-

ness, though I know not what it was; but judge
of its importance by its having detained him so
long from home, whence he had not been absent a
month at a time during the space of many years.
He came to his house very late in the evening, and
after a short supper with his sister, retired much
fatigued to his chamber. Here, having spent
some minutes on his knees—a custom which he
never broke through on any account—he was preparing to step into bed, when, upon opening the
clothes, to his great surprise he beheld an infant,
wrapped up in some coarse linen, in a sweet and
profound sleep, between his sheets. He stood some
time lost in astonishment at this sight; but, as
good nature had always the ascendant in his mind,
he soon began to be touched with sentiments of
compassion for the little wretch before him. He
then rang his bell, and ordered an elderly woman-
servant to rise immediately, and come to him; and
in the meantime was so eager in contemplating
the beauty of innocence, appearing in those lively
colors with which infancy and sleep always display it, that his thoughts were too much engaged
to reflect that he was in his shirt when the matron
came in. She had indeed given her master sufficient time to dress himself; for out of respect to
him, and regard to decency, she had spent many
minutes in adjusting her hair at the looking-glass,
notwithstanding all the hurry in which she had
been summoned by the servant, and though her
master, for aught she knew, lay expiring in an
apoplexy, or in some other fit.

It will not be wondered at that a creature who

had so strict a regard to decency in her own person, should be shocked at the least deviation from it in another. She therefore no sooner opened the door, and saw her master standing by the bedside in his shirt, with a candle in his hand, than she started back in a most terrible fright, and might perhaps have swooned away, had he not now recollected his being undressed, and put an end to her terrors by desiring her to stay without the door till he had thrown some clothes over his back, and was become incapable of shocking the pure eyes of Mrs. Deborah Wilkins, who, though in the fifty-second year of her age, vowed she had never beheld a man without his coat. Sneerers and profane wits may perhaps laugh at her first fright; yet my graver reader, when he considers the time of night, the summons from her bed, and the situation in which she found her master, will highly justify and applaud her conduct, unless the prudence which must be supposed to attend maidens at that period of life at which Mrs. Deborah had arrived, should a little lessen his admiration.

When Mrs. Deborah returned into the room, and was acquainted by her master with the finding the little infant, her consternation was rather greater than his had been; nor could she refrain from crying out, with great horror of accent as well as look, "My good sir! what's to be done?" Mr. Allworthy answered, she must take care of the child that evening, and in the morning he would give orders to provide it a nurse. "Yes, sir," says she; "and I hope your worship will

send out your warrant to take up the hussy its
mother, for she must be one of the neighborhood;
and I should be glad to see her committed to
Bridewell, and whipped at the cart's tail.   Indeed,
such wicked sluts cannot be too severely punished.
I'll warrant 'tis not her first, by her impudence
in laying it to your worship.''   ''In laying it to
me, Deborah!'' answered Allworthy: ''I can't
think she hath any such design.   I suppose she
hath only taken this method to provide for her
child; and truly I am glad she hath not done
worse.''   ''I don't know what is worse,'' cries
Deborah, ''than for such wicked strumpets to lay
their sins at honest men's doors; and though your
worship knows your own innocence, yet the world
is censorious; and it hath been many an honest
man's hap to pass for the father of children he
never begot; and if your worship should provide
for the child, it may make the people the apter to
believe; besides, why should your worship provide for what the parish is obliged to maintain?
For my own part, if it was an honest man's child,
indeed—but for my own part, it goes against me
to touch these misbegotten wretches, whom I
don't look upon as my fellow-creatures.   Faugh!
how it stinks!   It doth not smell like a Christian.
If I might be so bold to give my advice, I would
have it put in a basket, and sent out and laid at
the churchwarden's door.   It is a good night,
only a little rainy and windy; and if it was well
wrapped up, and put in a warm basket, it is two to
one but it lives till it is found in the morning.
But if it should not, we have discharged our duty

in taking proper care of it; and it is, perhaps, better for such creatures to die in a state of innocence, than to grow up and imitate their mothers; for nothing better can be expected of them.''

There were some strokes in this speech which perhaps would have offended Mr. Allworthy, had he strictly attended to it; but he had now got one of his fingers into the infant's hand, which, by its gentle pressure, seeming to implore his assistance, had certainly outpleaded the eloquence of Mrs. Deborah, had it been ten times greater than it was. He now gave Mrs. Deborah positive orders to take the child to her own bed, and to call up a maid-servant to provide it pap, and other things, against it waked. He likewise ordered that proper clothes should be procured for it early in the morning, and that it should be brought to himself as soon as he was stirring.

Such was the discernment of Mrs. Wilkins, and such the respect she bore her master, under whom she enjoyed a most excellent place, that her scruples gave way to his peremptory commands; and she took the child under her arms, without any apparent disgust at the illegality of its birth; and declaring it was a sweet little infant, walked off with it to her own chamber.

Allworthy here betook himself to those pleasing slumbers which a heart that hungers after goodness is apt to enjoy when thoroughly satisfied. As these are possibly sweeter than what are occasioned by any other hearty meal, I should take more pains to display them to the reader, if I knew any air to recommend him to for the procuring such an appetite.

CHAPTER IV

The reader's neck brought into danger by a description; his escape; and the great condescension of Miss Bridget Allworthy.

THE Gothic style of building could produce nothing nobler than Mr. Allworthy's house. There was an air of grandeur in it that struck you with awe, and rivaled the beauties of the best Grecian architecture; and it was as commodious within as venerable without.

It stood on the south-east side of a hill, but nearer the bottom than the top of it, so as to be sheltered from the north-east by a grove of old oaks which rose above it in a gradual ascent of near half a mile, and yet high enough to enjoy a most charming prospect of the valley beneath.

In the midst of the grove was a fine lawn, sloping down towards the house, near the summit of which rose a plentiful spring, gushing out of a rock covered with firs, and forming a constant cascade of about thirty feet, not carried down a regular flight of steps, but tumbling in a natural fall over the broken and mossy stones till it came to the bottom of the rock, then running off in a pebbly channel, that with many lesser falls winded along, till it fell into a lake at the foot of the hill, about a quarter of a mile below the house on the south side, and which was seen from every room in the front. Out of this lake, which filled the center of a beautiful plain, embellished with groups of beeches and elms, and fed with sheep, issued a river, that for several miles was seen to meander through an amazing variety of meadows and woods till it emptied itself into the sea, with a large arm of which, and an island beyond it, the prospect was closed.

On the right of this valley opened another of less extent, adorned with several villages, and terminated by one of the towers of an old ruined abby, grown over with ivy, and part of the front, which remained still entire.

The left-hand scene presented the view of a very fine park, composed of very unequal ground, and agreeably varied with all the diversity that hills, lawns, wood, and water, laid out with admirable taste, but owing less to art than to nature, could give. Beyond this, the country gradually rose into a ridge of wild mountains, the tops of which were above the clouds.

It was now the middle of May, and the morning was remarkably serene, when Mr. Allworthy walked forth on the terrace, where the dawn opened every minute that lovely prospect we have before described to his eye; and now having sent forth streams of light, which ascended the blue firmament before him, as harbingers preceding his pomp, in the full blaze of his majesty rose the sun, than which one object alone in this lower creation could be more glorious, and that Mr. Allworthy himself presented—a human being re-

plete with benevolence, meditating in what manner he might render himself most acceptable to
his Creator, by doing most good to his creatures.

Reader, take care. I have unadvisedly led thee
to the top of as high a hill as Mr. Allworthy's,
and how to get thee down without breaking thy
neck, I do not well know. However, let us e'en
venture to slide down together; for Miss Bridget
rings her bell, and Mr. Allworthy is summoned to
breakfast, where I must attend, and, if you please,
shall be glad of your company.

The usual compliments having past between
Mr. Allworthy and Miss Bridget, and the tea
being poured out, he summoned Mrs. Wilkins,
and told his sister he had a present for her, for
which she thanked him—imagining, I suppose, it
had been a gown, or some ornament for her person. Indeed, he very often made her such presents; and she, in complacence to him, spent much
time in adorning herself. I say in complacence
to him because she always expressed the greatest
contempt for dress, and for those ladies who
made it their study.

But if such was her expectation, how was she
disappointed when Mrs. Wilkins, according to the
order she had received from her master, produced the little infant? Great surprises, as hath
been observed, are apt to be silent; and so was
Miss Bridget, till her brother began, and told her
the whole story, which, as the reader knows it
already, we shall not repeat.

Miss Bridget had always expressed so great a
regard for what the ladies are pleased to call vir-

tue, and had herself maintained such a severity
of character, that it was expected, especially by
Wilkins, that she would have vented much bitterness on this occasion, and would have voted for
sending the child, as a kind of noxious animal, immediately out of the house; but, on the contrary,
she rather took the good-natured side of the question, intimated some compassion for the helpless
little creature, and commended her brother's charity in what he had done.

Perhaps the reader may account for this behavior from her condescension to Mr. Allworthy,
when we have informed him that the good man
had ended his narrative with owning a resolution
to take care of the child, and to breed him up as
his own; for, to acknowledge the truth, she was
always ready to oblige her brother, and very seldom, if ever, contradicted his sentiments. She
would, indeed, sometimes make a few observations, as that men were headstrong, and must
have their own way, and would wish she had been
blessed with an independent fortune; but these
were always vented in a low voice, and at the most
amounted only to what is called muttering.

However, what she withheld from the infant,
she bestowed with the utmost profuseness on the
poor unknown mother, whom she called an impudent slut, a wanton hussy, an audacious harlot,
a wicked jade, a vile strumpet, with every other
appellation with which the tongue of virtue never
fails to lash those who bring a disgrace on the
sex.

A consultation was now entered into how to

proceed in order to discover the mother. A scrutiny was first made into the characters of the female servants of the house, who were all acquitted by Mrs. Wilkins, and with apparent merit; for she had collected them herself, and perhaps it would be difficult to find such another set of scarecrows.

The next step was to examine among the inhabitants of the parish; and this was referred to Mrs. Wilkins, who was to enquire with all imaginable diligence, and to make her report in the afternoon.

Matters being thus settled, Mr. Allworthy withdrew to his study, as was his custom, and left the child to his sister, who, at his desire, had undertaken the care of it.

I—2

CHAPTER V

Containing a few common matters, with a very uncommon observation upon them.

WHEN her master was departed, Mrs. Deborah stood silent, expecting her cue from Miss Bridget; for as to what had past before her master, the prudent housekeeper by no means relied upon it, as she had often known the sentiments of the lady in her brother's absence to differ greatly from those which she had expressed in his presence. Miss Bridget did not, however, suffer her to continue long in this doubtful situation; for having looked some time earnestly at the child, as it lay asleep in the lap of Mrs. Deborah, the good lady could not forbear giving it a hearty kiss, at the same time declaring herself wonderfully pleased with its beauty and innocence. Mrs. Deborah no sooner observed this than she fell to squeezing and kissing, with as great raptures as sometimes inspire the sage dame of forty and five towards a youthful and vigorous bridegroom, crying out, in a shrill voice, "O, the dear little creature!—The dear, sweet, pretty creature! Well, I vow it is as fine a boy as ever was seen!"

These exclamations continued till they were interrupted by the lady, who now proceeded to execute the commission given her by her brother, and

18

gave orders for providing all necessaries for the child, appointing a very good room in the house for his nursery. Her orders were indeed so liberal, that, had it been a child of her own, she could not have exceeded them; but, lest the virtuous reader may condemn her for showing too great regard to a base-born infant, to which all charity is condemned by law as irreligious, we think proper to observe that she concluded the whole with saying, "Since it was her brother's whim to adopt the little brat, she supposed little master must be treated with great tenderness. For her part, she could not help thinking it was an encouragement to vice; but that she knew too much of the obstinacy of mankind to oppose any of their ridiculous humors."

With reflections of this nature she usually, as has been hinted, accompanied every act of compliance with her brother's inclinations; and surely nothing could more contribute to heighten the merit of this compliance than a declaration that she knew, at the same time, the folly and unreasonableness of those inclinations to which she submitted. Tacit obedience implies no force upon the will, and consequently may be easily, and without any pains, preserved; but when a wife, a child, a relation, or a friend, performs what we desire, with grumbling and reluctance, with expressions of dislike and dissatisfaction, the manifest difficulty which they undergo must greatly enhance the obligation.

As this is one of those deep observations which very few readers can be supposed capable of making themselves, I have thought proper to lend them my assistance; out this is a favor rarely to be expected in the course of my work.   Indeed, I shall seldom or never so indulge him, unless in such instances as this, where nothing but the inspiration with which we writers are gifted, can possibly enable any one to make the discovery.

CHAPTER VI

Mrs. Deborah is introduced into the parish with a simile. A short account of Jenny Jones, with the difficulties and discouragements which may attend young women in the pursuit of learning.

MRS. Deborah, having disposed of the child according to the will of her master, now prepared to visit those habitations which were supposed to conceal its mother.

Not otherwise than when a kite, tremendous bird, is beheld by the feathered generation soaring aloft, and hovering over their heads, the amorous dove, and every innocent little bird, spread wide the alarm, and fly trembling to their hiding-places. He proudly beats the air, conscious of his dignity, and meditates intended mischief.

So when the approach of Mrs. Deborah was proclaimed through the street, all the inhabitants ran trembling into their houses, each matron dreading lest the visit should fall to her lot. She with stately steps proudly advances over the field: aloft she bears her towering head, filled with conceit of her own pre-eminence, and schemes to effect her intended discovery.

The sagacious reader will not from this simile imagine these poor people had any apprehension of the design with which Mrs. Wilkins was now

coming towards them; but as the great beauty of
the simile may possibly sleep these hundred years,
till some future commentator shall take this work
in hand, I think proper to lend the reader a little
assistance in this place.

It is my intention, therefore, to signify, that, as
it is the nature of a kite to devour little birds, so
is it the nature of such persons as Mrs. Wilkins
to insult and tyrannize over little people. This
being indeed the means which they use to recom-
pense to themselves their extreme servility and
condescension to their superiors; for nothing can
be more reasonable, than that slaves and flatterers
should exact the same taxes on all below them,
which they themselves pay to all above them.

Whenever Mrs. Deborah had occasion to exert
any extraordinary condescension to Mrs. Bridget,
and by that means had a little soured her natural
disposition, it was usual with her to walk forth
among these people, in order to refine her temper,
by venting, and, as it were, purging off all ill
humors; on which account she was by no means a
welcome visitant: to say the truth, she was universally dreaded and hated by them all.

On her arrival in this place, she went immediately to the habitation of an elderly matron; to
whom, as this matron had the good fortune to resemble herself in the comeliness of her person, as
well as in her age, she had generally been more
favorable than to any of the rest. To this woman
she imparted what had happened, and the design
upon which she was come thither that morning.
These two began presently to scrutinize the char-

acters of the several young girls who lived in any of those houses, and at last fixed their strongest suspicion on one Jenny Jones, who, they both agreed, was the likeliest person to have committed this fact.

This Jenny Jones was no very comely girl, either in her face or person; but nature had somewhat compensated the want of beauty with what is generally more esteemed by those ladies whose judgment is arrived at years of perfect maturity, for she had given her a very uncommon share of understanding. This gift Jenny had a good deal improved by erudition. She had lived several years a servant with a schoolmaster, who, discovering a great quickness of parts in the girl, and an extraordinary desire of learning—for every leisure hour she was always found reading in the books of the scholars—had the good-nature, or folly—just as the reader pleases to call it—to instruct her so far, that she obtained a competent skill in the Latin language, and was, perhaps, as good a scholar as most of the young men of quality of the age. This advantage, however, like most others of an extraordinary kind, was attended with some small inconveniences: for as it is not to be wondered at, that a young woman so well accomplished should have little relish for the society of those whom fortune had made her equals, but whom education had rendered so much her inferiors; so is it matter of no greater astonishment, that this superiority in Jenny, together with that behavior which is its certain consequence, should produce among the rest some little envy and ill-

will towards her; and these had, perhaps, secretly
burnt in the bosoms of her neighbors ever since
her return from her service.

Their envy did not, however, display itself
openly, till poor Jenny, to the surprise of everybody, and to the vexation of all the young women
in these parts, had publicly shone forth on a Sunday in a new silk gown, with a laced cap, and other
proper appendages to these.

The flame, which had before lain in embryo, now
burst forth. Jenny had, by her learning, increased her own pride, which none of her neighbors were kind enough to feed with the honor she
seemed to demand; and now, instead of respect
and adoration, she gained nothing but hatred and
abuse by her finery. The whole parish declared
she could not come honestly by such things; and
parents, instead of wishing their daughters the
same, felicitated themselves that their children
had them not.

Hence, perhaps, it was, that the good woman
first mentioned the name of this poor girl to Mrs.
Wilkins; but there was another circumstance that
confirmed the latter in her suspicion; for Jenny
had lately been often at Mr. Allworthy's house.
She had officiated as nurse to Miss Bridget, in a
violent fit of illness, and had sat up many nights
with that lady; besides which, she had been seen
there the very day before Mr. Allworthy's return,
by Mrs. Wilkins herself, though that sagacious
person had not at first conceived any suspicion of
her on that account: for, as she herself said, "She
had always esteemed Jenny as a very sober girl

(though indeed she knew very little of her), and had rather suspected some of those wanton trollops, who gave themselves airs, because, forsooth, they thought themselves handsome.''

Jenny was now summoned to appear in person before Mrs. Deborah, which she immediately did. When Mrs. Deborah, putting on the gravity of a judge, with somewhat more than his austerity, began an oration with the words, ''You audacious strumpet!'' in which she proceeded rather to pass sentence on the prisoner than to accuse her.

Though Mrs. Deborah was fully satisfied of the guilt of Jenny, from the reasons above shown, it is possible Mr. Allworthy might have required some stronger evidence to have convicted her; but she saved her accusers any such trouble, by freely confessing the whole fact with which she was charged.

This confession, though delivered rather in terms of contrition, as it appeared, did not at all mollify Mrs. Deborah, who now pronounced a second judgment against her, in more opprobrious language than before; nor had it any better success with the bystanders, who were now grown very numerous. Many of them cried out, ''They thought what madam's silk gown would end in;'' others spoke sarcastically of her learning. Not a single female was present but found some means of expressing her abhorrence of poor Jenny, who bore all very patiently, except the malice of one woman, who reflected upon her person, and tossing up her nose, said, ''The man must have a good stomach who would give silk gowns for such sort

of trumpery!'' Jenny replied to this with a bitterness which might have surprised a judicious
person, who had observed the tranquillity with
which she bore all the affronts to her chastity;
but her patience was perhaps tired out, for this is
a virtue which is very apt to be fatigued by exercise.

Mrs. Deborah having succeeded beyond her
hopes in her inquiry, returned with much triumph,
and, at the appointed hour, made a faithful report
to Mr. Allworthy, who was much surprised at the
relation; for he had heard of the extraordinary
parts and improvements of this girl, whom he intended to have given in marriage, together with a
small living, to a neighboring curate. His concern, therefore, on this occasion, was at least equal
to the satisfaction which appeared in Mrs. Deborah, and to many readers may seem much more
reasonable.

Miss Bridget blessed herself, and said, ''For
her part, she should never hereafter entertain a
good opinion of any woman.'' For Jenny before
this had the happiness of being much in her good
graces also.

The prudent housekeeper was again dispatched
to bring the unhappy culprit before Mr. Allworthy, in order, not as it was hoped by some, and
expected by all, to be sent to the house of correction, but to receive wholesome admonition and re-
proof; which those who relish that kind of instructive writing may peruse in the next chapter.

CHAPTER VII

Containing such grave matter, that the reader cannot laugh once through the whole chapter, unless peradventure he should laugh at the author.

WHEN Jenny appeared, Mr. Allworthy took her into his study, and spoke to her as follows: "You know, child, it is in my power as a magistrate, to punish you very rigorously for what you have done; and you will, perhaps, be the more apt to fear I should execute that power, because you have in a manner laid your sins at my door.

"But, perhaps, this is one reason which hath determined me to act in a milder manner with you: for, as no private resentment should ever influence a magistrate, I will be so far from considering your having deposited the infant in my house as an aggravation of your offense, that I will suppose, in your favor, this to have proceeded from a natural affection to your child, since you might have some hopes to see it thus better provided for than was in the power of yourself, or its wicked father to provide for it. I should indeed have been highly offended with you had you exposed the little wretch in the manner of some inhuman mothers, who seem no less to have abandoned their humanity, than to have parted with their chastity. It is the other part of your of-

27

fense, therefore, upon which I intend to admonish you, I mean the violation of your chastity;—a crime, however lightly it may be treated by debauched persons, very heinous in itself, and very dreadful in its consequences.

"The heinous nature of this offense must be sufficiently apparent to every Christian, inasmuch as it is committed in defiance of the laws of our religion, and of the express commands of Him who founded that religion.

"And here its consequences may well be argued to be dreadful; for what can be more so, than to incur the divine displeasure, by the breach of the divine commands; and that in an instance against which the highest vengeance is specifically denounced?

"But these things, though too little, I am afraid, regarded, are so plain, that mankind, however they may want to be reminded, can never need information on this head. A hint, therefore, to awaken your sense of this matter, shall suffice; for I would inspire you with repentance, and not drive you to desperation.

"There are other consequences, not indeed so dreadful or replete with horror as this; and yet such, as, if attentively considered, must, one would think, deter all of your sex at least from the commission of this crime.

"For by it you are rendered ‚infamous, and driven, like lepers of old, out of society; at least, from the society of all but wicked and reprobate persons; for no others will associate with you.

"If you have fortunes, you are hereby rendered

incapable of enjoying them; if you have none, you are disabled from acquiring any, nay almost of procuring your sustenance; for no persons of character will receive you into their houses. Thus you are often driven by necessity itself into a state of shame and misery, which unavoidably ends in the destruction of both body and soul.

"Can any pleasure compensate these evils? Can any temptation have sophistry and delusion strong enough to persuade you to so simple a bargain? Or can any carnal appetite so overpower your reason, or so totally lay it asleep, as to prevent your flying with affright and terror from a crime which carries such punishment always with it?

"How base and mean must that woman be, how void of that dignity of mind, and decent pride, without which we are not worthy the name of human creatures, who can bear to level herself with the lowest animal, and to sacrifice all that is great and noble in her, all her heavenly part, to an appetite which she hath in common with the vilest branch of the creation! For no woman, sure, will plead the passion of love for an excuse. This would be to own herself the mere tool and bubble of the man. Love, however barbarously we may corrupt and pervert its meaning, as it is a laudable, is a rational passion, and can never be violent but when reciprocal; for though the Scripture bids us love our enemies, it means not with that fervent love which we naturally bear towards our friends; much less that we should sacrifice to them our lives, and what ought to be dearer to

us, our innocence. Now in what light, but that of
an enemy, can a reasonable woman regard the
man who solicits her to entail on herself all the
misery I have described to you, and who would
purchase to himself a short, trivial, contemptible
pleasure, so greatly at her expense! For, by the
laws of custom, the whole shame, with all its
dreadful consequences, falls entirely upon her.
Can love, which always seeks the good of its object, attempt to betray a woman into a bargain
where she is so greatly to be the loser? If such
corrupter, therefore, should have the impudence
to pretend a real affection for her, ought not the
woman to regard him not only as an enemy, but
as the worst of all enemies, a false, designing,
treacherous, pretended friend, who intends not
only to debauch her body, but her understanding
at the same time?"

Here Jenny expressing great concern, Allworthy paused a moment, and then proceeded:
"I have talked thus to you, child, not to insult you
for what is past and irrevocable, but to caution
and strengthen you for the future. Nor should
I have taken this trouble, but from some opinion
of your good sense, notwithstanding the dreadful
slip you have made; and from some hopes of your
hearty repentance, which are founded on the openness and sincerity of your confession. If these
do not deceive me, I will take care to convey you
from this scene of your shame, where you shall,
by being unknown, avoid the punishment which, as
I have said, is allotted to your crime in this world;
and I hope, by repentance, you will avoid the much

heavier sentence denounced against it in the other. Be a good girl the rest of your days, and want shall be no motive to your going astray; and, believe me, there is more pleasure, even in this world, in an innocent and virtuous life, than in one debauched and vicious.

"As to your child, let no thoughts concerning it molest you; I will provide for it in a better manner than you can ever hope. And now nothing remains but that you inform me who was the wicked man that seduced you; for my anger against him will be much greater than you have experienced on this occasion."

Jenny now lifted her eyes from the ground, and with a modest look and decent voice thus began:—

"To know you, sir, and not love your goodness, would be an argument of total want of sense or goodness in any one. In me it would amount to the highest ingratitude, not to feel, in the most sensible manner, the great degree of goodness you have been pleased to exert on this occasion. As to my concern for what is past, I know you will spare my blushes the repetition. My future conduct will much better declare my sentiments than any professions I can now make. I beg leave to assure you, sir, that I take your advice much kinder than your generous offer with which you concluded it; for, as you are pleased to say, sir, it is an instance of your opinion of my understanding."—Here her tears flowing apace, she stopped a few moments, and then proceeded thus:—"Indeed, sir, your kindness overcomes me; but I will endeavor to deserve this good opinion: for if I

have the understanding you are so kindly pleased
to allow me, such advice cannot be thrown away
upon me. I thank you, sir, heartily, for your intended kindness to my poor helpless child: he is
innocent, and I hope will live to be grateful for all
the favors you shall show him. But now, sir, I
must on my knees entreat you not to persist in
asking me to declare the father of my infant. I
promise you faithfully you shall one day know;
but I am under the most solemn ties and engage-
ments of honor, as well as the most religious vows
and protestations, to conceal his name at this
time. And I know you too well to think you would
desire I should sacrifice either my honor or my
religion.''

Mr. Allworthy, whom the least mention of those
sacred words was sufficient to stagger, hesitated
a moment before he replied, and then told her,
she had done wrong to enter into such engage-
ments to a villain; but since she had, he could not
insist on her breaking them. He said, it was not
from a motive of vain curiosity he had inquired,
but in order to punish the fellow; at least, that he
might not ignorantly confer favors on the undeserving.

As to these points, Jenny satisfied him by the
most solemn assurances, that the man was entirely
out of his reach; and was neither subject to his
power, nor in any probability of becoming an object of his goodness.

The ingenuity of this behavior had gained Jenny
so much credit with this worthy man, that he
easily believed what she told him; for as she had

disdained to excuse herself by a lie, and had hazarded his further displeasure in her present situation, rather than she would forfeit her honor or
integrity by betraying another, he had but little
apprehensions that she would be guilty of falsehood towards himself.

He therefore dismissed her with assurances
that he would very soon remove her out of the
reach of that obloquy she had incurred; concluding with some additional documents, in which he
recommended repentance, saying, "Consider,
child, there is one still to reconcile yourself to,
whose favor is of much greater importance to
you than mine."

I—3

CHAPTER VIII

A dialogue between Mesdames Bridget and Deborah; containing more amusement, but less instruction, than the former.

WHEN Mr. Allworthy had retired to his study with Jenny Jones, as hath been seen, Mrs. Bridget, with the good housekeeper, had betaken themselves to a post next adjoining to the said study; whence, through the conveyance of a keyhole, they sucked in at their ears the instructive lecture delivered by Mr. Allworthy, together with the answers of Jenny, and indeed every other particular which passed in the last chapter.

This hole in her brother's study-door was indeed as well known to Mrs. Bridget, and had been as frequently applied to by her, as the famous hole in the wall was by Thisbe of old. This served to many good purposes. For by such means Mrs. Bridget became often acquainted with her brother's inclinations, without giving him the trouble of repeating them to her. It is true, some inconveniences attended this intercourse, and she had sometimes reason to cry out with Thisbe, in Shakespeare, "O, wicked, wicked wall!" For as Mr. Allworthy was a justice of peace, certain things occurred in examinations concerning bastards, and such like, which are apt

34

to give great offense to the chaste ears of virgins, especially when they approach the age of forty, as was the case of Mrs. Bridget. However, she had, on such occasions, the advantage of concealing her blushes from the eyes of men; and *De non apparentibus, et non existentibus eadem est ratio*—in English, "When a woman is not seen to blush, she doth not blush at all."

Both the good women kept strict silence during the whole scene between Mr. Allworthy and the girl; but as soon as it was ended, and that gentleman was out of hearing, Mrs. Deborah, could not help exclaiming against the clemency of her master, and especially against his suffering her to conceal the father of the child, which she swore she would have out of her before the sun set.

At these words Mrs. Bridget discomposed her features with a smile (a thing very unusual to her). Not that I would have my reader imagine, that this was one of those wanton smiles which Homer would have you conceive came from Venus, when he calls her the laughter-loving goddess; nor was it one of those smiles which Lady Seraphina shoots from the stage-box, and which Venus would quit her immortality to be able to equal. No, this was rather one of those smiles which might be supposed to have come from the dimpled cheeks of the august Tisiphone, or from one of the misses, her sisters.

With such a smile then, and with a voice sweet as the evening breeze of Boreas in the pleasant month of November, Mrs. Bridget gently reproved the curiosity of Mrs. Deborah; a vice with which it seems the latter was too much tainted, and which the former inveighed against with great bitterness, adding, ''That, among all her faults, she thanked Heaven her enemies could not accuse her of prying into the affairs of other people.''

She then proceeded to commend the honor and spirit with which Jenny had acted. She said, she could not help agreeing with her brother, that there was some merit in the sincerity of her confession, and in her integrity to her lover: that she had always thought her a very good girl, and doubted not but she had been seduced by some rascal, who had been infinitely more to blame than herself, and very probably had prevailed with her by a promise of marriage, or some other treacherous proceeding.

This behavior of Mrs. Bridget greatly surprised Mrs. Deborah; for this well-bred woman seldom opened her lips, either to her master or his sister, till she had first sounded their inclinations, with which her sentiments were always consonant. Here, however, she thought she might have launched forth with safety; and the sagacious reader will not perhaps accuse her of want of sufficient forecast in so doing, but will rather admire with what wonderful celerity she tacked about, when she found herself steering a wrong course.

''Nay, madam,'' said this able woman, and truly great politician, ''I must own I cannot help admiring the girl's spirit, as well as your ladyship. And, as your ladyship says, if she was deceived by some wicked man, the poor wretch is to be pitied. And to be sure, as your ladyship says, the girl hath always appeared like a good, honest, plain girl, and not vain of her face, forsooth, as some wanton hussies in the neighborhood are."

"You say true, Deborah," said Miss Bridget. "If the girl had been one of those vain trollops, of which we have too many in the parish, I should have condemned my brother for his lenity towards her. I saw two farmers' daughters at church, the other day, with bare necks. I protest they shocked me. If wenches will hang out lures for fellows, it is no matter what they suffer. I detest such creatures; and it would be much better for them that their faces had been seamed with the smallpox; but I must confess, I never saw any of this wanton behavior in poor Jenny: some artful villain, I am convinced, hath betrayed, nay perhaps forced her; and I pity the poor wretch with all my heart."

Mrs. Deborah approved all these sentiments, and the dialogue concluded with a general and bitter invective against beauty, and with many compassionate considerations for all honest plain girls who are deluded by the wicked arts of deceitful men.

CHAPTER IX

Containing matters which will surprise the reader.

JENNY returned home well pleased with the reception she had met with from Mr. Allworthy, whose indulgence to her she industriously made public; partly perhaps as a sacrifice to her own pride, and partly from the more prudent motive of reconciling her neighbors to her, and silencing their clamors.

But though this latter view, if she indeed had it, may appear reasonable enough, yet the event did not answer her expectations; for when she was convened before the justice, and it was universally apprehended that the house of correction would have been her fate, though some of the young women cried out "It was good enough for her," and diverted themselves with the thoughts of her beating hemp in a silk gown; yet there were many others who began to pity her condition: but when it was known in what manner Mr. Allworthy had behaved, the tide turned against her. One said, "I'll assure you, madam hath had good luck." A second cried, "See what it is to be a favorite!" A third, "Ay, this comes of her learning." Every person made some malicious comment or other on the occasion, and reflected on the partiality of the justice.

The behavior of these people may appear impolitic and ungrateful to the reader, who considers the power and benevolence of Mr. Allworthy. But as to his power, he never used it; and as to his benevolence, he exerted so much, that he had thereby disobliged all his neighbors; for it is a secret well known to great men, that, by conferring an obligation, they do not always procure a friend, but are certain of creating many enemies.

Jenny was, however, by the care and goodness of Mr. Allworthy, soon removed out of the reach of reproach; when malice being no longer able to vent its rage on her, began to seek another object of its bitterness, and this was no less than Mr. Allworthy, himself; for a whisper soon went abroad, that he himself was the father of the foundling child.

This supposition so well reconciled his conduct to the general opinion, that it met with universal assent; and the outcry against his lenity soon began to take another turn, and was changed into an invective against his cruelty to the poor girl. Very grave and good women exclaimed against men who begot children, and then disowned them. Nor were there wanting some, who, after the departure of Jenny, insinuated that she was spirited away with a design too black to be mentioned, and who gave frequent hints that a legal inquiry ought to be made into the whole matter, and that some people should be forced to produce the girl.

These calumnies might have probably produced ill consequences, at the least might have occasioned some trouble. to a person of a more doubtful and suspicious character than Mr. Allworthy was blessed with; but in his case they had no such effect; and, being heartily despised by him, they served only to afford an innocent amusement to the good gossips of the neighborhood.

But as we cannot possibly divine what complexion our reader may be of, and as it will be some time before he will hear any more of Jenny, we think proper to give him a very early intimation, that Mr. Allworthy was, and will hereafter appear to be, absolutely innocent of any criminal intention whatever. He had indeed committed no other than an error in politics, by tempering justice with mercy, and by refusing to gratify the good-natured disposition of the mob,[1] with an object for their compassion to work on in the person of poor Jenny, who in order to pity, they desired to have seen sacrificed to ruin and infamy, by a shameful correction in Bridewell.

So far from complying with this their inclination, by which all hopes of reformation would have been abolished, and even the gate shut against her if her own inclinations should ever hereafter lead her to choose the road of virtue, Mr. Allworthy rather chose to encourage the girl to return thither by the only possible means; for too true I am afraid it is, that many women have become abandoned, and have sunk to the last degree of vice, by being unable to retrieve the first slip. This will be, I am afraid, always the case while they remain among their former ac-

---

[1] Whenever this word occurs in our writings, it intends persons without virtue or sense, in all stations; and many of the highest rank are often meant by it.

quaintance; it was therefore wisely done by Mr. Allworthy, to remove Jenny to a place where she might enjoy the pleasure of reputation, after having tasted the ill consequences of losing it.

To this place therefore, wherever it was, we will wish her a good journey, and for the present take leave of her, and of the little foundling her child, having matters of much higher importance to communicate to the reader.

CHAPTER X

The hospitality of Allworthy; with a short sketch of the characters of two brothers, a doctor and a captain, who were entertained by that gentleman.

NEITHER Mr. Allworthy's house, nor his heart, were shut against any part of mankind, but they were both more particularly open to men of merit. To say the truth, this was the only house in the kingdom where you was sure to gain a dinner by deserving it.

Above all others, men of genius and learning shared the principal place in his favor; and in these he had much discernment: for though he had missed the advantage of a learned education, yet, being blessed with vast natural abilities, he had so well profited by a vigorous though late application to letters, and by much conversation with men of eminence in this way, that he was himself a very competent judge in most kinds of literature.

It is no wonder that in an age when this kind of merit is so little in fashion, and so slenderly provided for, persons possessed of it should very eagerly flock to a place where they were sure of being received with great complaisance; indeed, where they might enjoy almost the same advantages of a liberal fortune as if they were entitled to it in their own right; for Mr. Allworthy was not one of those generous persons who are ready most bountifully to bestow meat, drink, and lodging on men of wit and learning, for which they expect no other return but entertainment, instruction, flattery, and subserviency; in a word, that such persons should be enrolled in the number of domestics, without wearing their master's clothes, or receiving wages.

On the contrary, every person in this house was perfect master of his own time: and as he might at his pleasure satisfy all his appetites within the restrictions only of law, virtue, and religion; so he might, if his health required, or his inclination prompted him to temperance, or even to abstinence, absent himself from any meals, or retire from them, whenever he was so disposed, without even a solicitation to the contrary: for, indeed, such solicitations from superiors always savor very strongly of commands. But all here were free from such impertinence, not only those whose company is in all other places esteemed a favor from their equality of fortune, but even those whose indigent circumstances make such an eleemosynary abode convenient to them, and who are therefore less welcome to a great man's table because they stand in need of it.

Among others of this kind was Dr. Blifil, a gentleman who had the misfortune of losing the advantage of great talents by the obstinacy of a father, who would breed him to a profession he disliked. In obedience to this obstinacy the doctor had in his youth been obliged to study physic, or rather to say he studied it; for in reality books of this kind were almost the only ones with which he was unacquainted; and unfortunately for him, the doctor was master of almost every other science but that by which he was to get his bread; the consequence of which was, that the doctor at the age of forty had no bread to eat.

Such a person as this was certain to find a welcome at Mr. Allworthy's table, to whom misfortunes were ever a recommendation, when they were derived from the folly or villainy of others, and not of the unfortunate person himself. Besides this negative merit, the doctor had one positive recommendation;—this was a great appearance of religion. Whether his religion was real, or consisted only in appearance, I shall not presume to say, as I am not possessed of any touchstone which can distinguish the true from the false.

If this part of his character pleased Mr. Allworthy, it delighted Miss Bridget. She engaged him in many religious controversies; on which occasions she constantly expressed great satisfaction in the doctor's knowledge, and not much less in the compliments which he frequently bestowed on her own. To say the truth, she had read much English divinity, and had puzzled more than one of the neighboring curates. Indeed, her conversation was so pure, her looks so sage, and her whole deportment so grave and solemn, that she seemed to deserve the name of saint equally with her namesake, or with any other female in the Roman calendar.

As sympathies of all kinds are apt to beget

love, so experience teaches us that none have a
more direct tendency this way than those of a religious kind between persons of different sexes.
The doctor found himself so agreeable to Miss
Bridget, that he now began to lament an unfortunate accident which had happened to him about
ten years before; namely, his marriage with another woman, who was not only still alive, but,
what was worse, known to be so by Mr. Allworthy.
This was a fatal bar to that happiness which he
otherwise saw sufficient probability of obtaining
with this young lady; for as to criminal indul-
gences, he certainly never thought of them.   This
was owing either to his religion, as is most probable, or to the purity of his passion, which was
fixed on those things which matrimony only, and
not criminal correspondence, could put him in
possession of, or could give him any title to.

He had not long ruminated on these matters,
before it occurred to his memory that he had a
brother who was under no such unhappy incapac-
ity.   This brother he made no doubt would succeed; for he discerned, as he thought, an inclination to marriage in the lady; and the reader perhaps, when he hears the brother's qualifications,
will not blame the confidence which he entertained
of his success.

This gentleman was about thirty-five years of
age. He was of a middle size, and what is called
well-built. He had a scar on his forehead, which
did not so much injure his beauty as it denoted his
valor (for he was a half-pay officer). He had
good teeth, and something affable, when he

pleased, in his smile; though naturally his countenance, as well as his air and voice, had much
of roughness in it: yet he could at any time deposit this, and appear all gentleness and good-
humor. He was not ungenteel, nor entirely devoid of wit, and in his youth had abounded in
sprightliness, which, though he had lately put on
a more serious character, he could, when he
pleased, resume.

He had, as well as the doctor, an academic education; for his father had, with the same paternal
authority we have mentioned before, decreed him
for holy orders; but as the old gentleman died before he was ordained, he chose the church military, and preferred the king's commission to the
bishop's.

He had purchased the post of lieutenant of
dragoons, and afterwards came to be a captain;
but having quarreled with his colonel, was by his
interest obliged to sell; from which time he had
entirely rusticated himself, had betaken himself
to studying the Scriptures, and was not a little
suspected of an inclination to Methodism.

It seemed, therefore, not unlikely that such a
person should succeed with a lady of so saint-like
a disposition, and whose inclinations were no
otherwise engaged than to the marriage state in
general; but why the doctor, who certainly had no
great friendship for his brother, should for his
sake think of making so ill a return to the hospitality of Allworthy, is a matter not so easy to
be accounted for.

Is it that some natures delight in evil, as others

are thought to delight in virtue? Or is there a pleasure in being accessory to a theft when we cannot commit it ourselves? Or lastly (which experience seems to make probable), have we a satisfaction in aggrandizing our families, even though we have not the least love or respect for them?

Whether any of these motives operated on the doctor, we will not determine; but so the fact was. He sent for his brother, and easily found means to introduce him at Allworthy's as a person who intended only a short visit to himself.

The captain had not been in the house a week before the doctor had reason to felicitate himself on his discernment. The captain was indeed as great a master of the art of love as Ovid was formerly. He had besides received proper hints from his brother, which he failed not to improve to the best advantage.

CHAPTER XI

Containing many rules, and some examples, concerning falling in love: descriptions of beauty, and other more prudential inducements to matrimony.

IT hath been observed, by wise men or women, I forget which, that all persons are doomed to be in love once in their lives. No particular season is, as I remember, assigned for this; but the age at which Miss Bridget was arrived, seems to me as proper a period as any to be fixed on for this purpose: it often, indeed, happens much earlier; but when it doth not, I have observed it seldom or never fails about this time. Moreover, we may remark that at this season love is of a more serious and steady nature than what sometimes shows itself in the younger parts of life. The love of girls is uncertain, capricious, and so foolish that we cannot always discover what the young lady would be at; nay, it may almost be doubted whether she always knows this herself.

Now we are never at a loss to discern this in women about forty; for as such grave, serious, and experienced ladies well know their own meaning, so it is always very easy for a man of the least sagacity to discover it with the utmost certainty.

Miss Bridget is an example of all these observations. She had not been many times in the captain's company before she was seized with this passion. Nor did she go pining and moping about the house, like a puny, foolish girl, ignorant of her distemper: she felt, she knew, and she enjoyed, the pleasing sensation, of which, as she was certain it was not only innocent but laudable, she was neither afraid nor ashamed.

And to say the truth, there is, in all points, great difference between the reasonable passion which women at this age conceive towards men, and the idle and childish liking of a girl to a boy, which is often fixed on the outside only, and on things of little value and no duration; as on cherry-cheeks, small, lily-white hands, sloe-black eyes, flowing locks, downy chins, dapper shapes; nay, sometimes on charms more worthless than these, and less the party's own; such are the outward ornaments of the person, for which men are beholden to the tailor, the laceman, the periwig-maker, the hatter, and the milliner, and not to nature. Such a passion girls may well be ashamed, as they generally are, to own either to themselves or others.

The love of Miss Bridget was of another kind. The captain owed nothing to any of these fop-makers in his dress, nor was his person much more beholden to nature. Both his dress and person were such as, had they appeared in an assembly or a drawing-room, would have been the contempt and ridicule of all the fine ladies there. The former of these was indeed neat, but plain, coarse, ill-fancied, and out of fashion. As for the latter, we have expressly described it above. So

I—4

far was the skin on his cheeks from being cherry-
colored, that you could not discern what the
natural color of his cheeks was, they being totally
overgrown by a black beard, which ascended to
his eyes. His shape and limbs were indeed exactly proportioned, but so large that they denoted the strength rather of a plowman than
any other. His shoulders were broad beyond all
size, and the calves of his legs larger than those
of a common chairman. In short, his whole person wanted all that elegance and beauty which is
the very reverse of clumsy strength, and which so
agreeably sets off most of our fine gentlemen; being partly owing to the high blood of their ances-
tors, viz., blood made of rich sauces and generous
wines, and partly to an early town education.

Though Miss Bridget was a woman of the
greatest delicacy of taste, yet such were the
charms of the captain's conversation, that she
totally overlooked the defects of his person. She
imagined, and perhaps very wisely, that she
should enjoy more agreeable minutes with the
captain than with a much prettier fellow; and
forewent the consideration of pleasing her eyes,
in order to procure herself much more solid satisfaction.

The captain no sooner perceived the passion of
Miss Bridget, in which discovery he was very
quick-sighted, than he faithfully returned it. The
lady, no more than her lover, was remarkable for
beauty. I would attempt to draw her picture, but
that is done already by a more able master, Mr.
Hogarth himself, to whom she sat many years ago,

and hath been lately exhibited by that gentleman
in his print of a winter's morning, of which she
was no improper emblem, and may be seen walking (for walk she doth in the print) to Covent
Garden church, with a starved foot-boy behind
carrying her prayer-book.

The captain likewise very wisely preferred the
more solid enjoyments he expected with this lady,
to the fleeting charms of person. He was one of
those wise men who regard beauty in the other
sex as a very worthless and superficial qualification; or, to speak more truly, who rather choose
to possess every convenience of life with an ugly
woman, than a handsome one without any of those
conveniences. And having a very good appetite,
and but little nicety, he fancied he should play his
part very well at the matrimonial banquet, without the sauce of beauty.

To deal plainly with the reader, the captain,
ever since his arrival, at least from the moment
his brother had proposed the match to him, long
before he had discovered any flattering symptoms
in Miss Bridget, had been greatly enamored; that
is to say, of Mr. Allworthy's house and gardens,
and of his lands, tenements, and hereditaments;
of all which the captain was so passionately fond,
that he would most probably have contracted marriage with them, had he been obliged to have taken
the witch of Endor into the bargain.

As Mr. Allworthy, therefore, had declared to
the doctor that he never intended to take a second
wife, as his sister was his nearest relation, and
as the doctor had fished out that his intentions

were to make any child of hers his heir, which indeed the law, without his interposition, would have done for him; the doctor and his brother thought it an act of benevolence to give being to a human creature, who would be so plentifully provided with the most essential means of happiness. The whole thoughts, therefore, of both the brothers were how to engage the affections of this amiable lady.

But fortune, who is a tender parent, and often doth more for her favorite offspring than either they deserve or wish, had been so industrious for the captain, that whilst he was laying schemes to execute his purpose, the lady conceived the same desires with himself, and was on her side contriving how to give the captain proper encouragement, without appearing too forward; for she was a strict observer of all rules of decorum. In this, however, she easily succeeded; for as the captain was always on the look-out, no glance, gesture, or word escaped him.

The satisfaction which the captain received from the kind behavior of Miss Bridget, was not a little abated by his apprehensions of Mr. Allworthy; for, notwithstanding his disinterested professions, the captain imagined he would, when he came to act, follow the example of the rest of the world, and refuse his consent to a match so disadvantageous, in point of interest, to his sister. From what oracle he received this opinion, I shall leave the reader to determine: but however he came by it, it strangely perplexed him how to regulate his conduct so as at once to convey his affection to

the lady, and to conceal it from her brother. He
at length resolved to take all private opportunities of making his addresses; but in the presence
of Mr. Allworthy to be as reserved and as much
upon his guard as was possible; and this conduct
was highly approved by the brother.

He soon found means to make his addresses, in
express terms, to his mistress, from whom he received an answer in the proper form, viz.: the
answer which was first made some thousands of
years ago, and which hath been handed down by
tradition from mother to daughter ever since. If
I was to translate this into Latin, I should render
it by these two words, *Nolo Episcopari:* a phrase
likewise of immemorial use on another occasion.

The captain, however he came by his knowledge,
perfectly well understood the lady, and very soon
after repeated his application with more warmth
and earnestness than before, and was again, according to due form, rejected; but as he had increased in the eagerness of his desires, so the
lady, with the same propriety, decreased in the
violence of her refusal.

Not to tire the reader, by leading him through
every scene of this courtship (which, though in
the opinion of a certain great author, it is the
pleasantest scene of life to the actor, is, perhaps,
as dull and tiresome as any whatever to the audience), the captain made his advances in form, the
citadel was defended in form, and at length, in
proper form, surrendered at discretion.

During this whole time, which filled the space
of near a month, the captain preserved great dis-

tance of behavior to his lady in the presence of the brother; and the more he succeeded with her in private, the more reserved was he in public. And as for the lady, she had no sooner secured her lover than she behaved to him before company with the highest degree of indifference; so that Mr. Allworthy must have had the insight of the devil (or perhaps some of his worse qualities) to have entertained the least suspicion of what was going forward.

CHAPTER XII

Containing what the reader may, perhaps, expect to find in it.

IN all bargains, whether to fight or to marry, or concerning any other such business, little previous ceremony is required to bring the matter to an issue when both parties are really in earnest. This was the case at present, and in less than a month the captain and his lady were man and wife.

The great concern now was to break the matter to Mr. Allworthy; and this was undertaken by the doctor.

One day, then, as Allworthy was walking in his garden, the doctor came to him, and, with great gravity of aspect, and all the concern which he could possibly affect in his countenance, said, "I am come, sir, to impart an affair to you of the utmost consequence; but how shall I mention to you what it almost distracts me to think of!" He then launched forth into the most bitter invectives both against men and women; accusing the former of having no attachment but to their interest, and the latter of being so addicted to vicious inclinations that they could never be safely trusted with one of the other sex. "Could I," said he, "sir, have suspected that a lady of such prudence, such

55

judgment, such learning, should indulge so indiscreet a passion! or could I have imagined that my
brother—why do I call him so? he is no longer a
brother of mine——"

"Indeed but he is," said Allworthy, "and a
brother of mine too."

"Bless me, sir!" said the doctor, "do you know
the shocking affair?"

"Look'ee, Mr. Blifil," answered the good man,
"it hath been my constant maxim in life to make
the best of all matters which happen. My sister,
though many years younger than I, is at least old
enough to be at the age of discretion. Had he
imposed on a child, I should have been more averse
to have forgiven him; but a woman upwards of
thirty must certainly be supposed to know what
will make her most happy. She hath married a
gentleman, though perhaps not quite her equal
in fortune; and if he hath any perfections in her
eye which can make up that deficiency, I see no
reason why I should object to her choice of her
own happiness; which I, no more than herself,
imagine to consist only in immense wealth. I
might, perhaps, from the many declarations I have
made of complying with almost any proposal,
have expected to have been consulted on this occasion; but these matters are of a very delicate nature, and the scruples of modesty, perhaps, are
not to be overcome. As to your brother, I have
really no anger against him at all. He hath no
obligations to me, nor do I think he was under
any necessity of asking my consent, since the
woman is, as I have said, *sui juris,* and of a proper

age to be entirely answerable only to herself for her conduct.''

The doctor accused Mr. Allworthy of too great lenity, repeated his accusations against his brother, and declared that he should never more be brought either to see, or to own him for his relation. He then launched forth into a panegyric on Allworthy's goodness; into the highest encomiums on his friendship; and concluded by saying, he should never forgive his brother for having put the place which he bore in that friendship to a hazard.

Allworthy thus answered: ''Had I conceived any displeasure against your brother, I should never have carried that resentment to the innocent: but I assure you I have no such displeasure. Your brother appears to me to be a man of sense and honor. I do not disapprove the taste of my sister; nor will I doubt but that she is equally the object of his inclinations. I have always thought love the only foundation of happiness in a married state, as it can only produce that high and tender friendship which should always be the cement of this union; and, in my opinion, all those marriages which are contracted from other motives are greatly criminal; they are a profanation of a most holy ceremony, and generally end in disquiet and misery: for surely we may call it a profanation to convert this most sacred institution into a wicked sacrifice to lust or avarice: and what better can be said of those matches to which men are induced merely by the consideration of a beautiful person, or a great fortune?

"To deny that beauty is an agreeable object to the eye, and even worthy some admiration, would be false and foolish. Beautiful is an epithet often used in Scripture, and always mentioned with honor. It was my own fortune to marry a woman whom the world thought handsome, and I can truly say I liked her the better on that account. But to make this the sole consideration of marriage, to lust after it so violently as to overlook all imperfections for its sake, or to require it so absolutely as to reject and disdain religion, virtue, and sense, which are qualities in their nature of much higher perfection, only because an elegance of person is wanting: this is surely inconsistent, either with a wise man or a good Christian. And it is, perhaps, being too charitable to conclude that such persons mean anything more by their marriage than to please their carnal appetites; for the satisfaction of which, we are taught, it was not ordained.

"In the next place, with respect to fortune. Worldly prudence, perhaps, exacts some consideration on this head; nor will I absolutely and altogether condemn it. As the world is constituted, the demands of a married state, and the care of posterity, require some little regard to what we call circumstances. Yet this provision is greatly increased, beyond what is really necessary, by folly and vanity, which create abundantly more wants than nature. Equipage for the wife, and large fortunes for the children, are by custom enrolled in the list of necessaries; and to procure these, everything truly solid and sweet, and virtuous and religious, are neglected and overlooked.

"And this in many degrees; the last and greatest of which seems scarce distinguishable from madness;—I mean where persons of immense fortunes contract themselves to those who are, and must be, disagreeable to them—to fools and knaves—in order to increase an estate already larger even than the demands of their pleasures. Surely such persons if they will not be thought mad, must own, either that they are incapable of tasting the sweets of the tenderest friendship, or that they sacrifice the greatest happiness of which they are capable to the vain, uncertain, and senseless laws of vulgar opinion, which owe as well their force as their foundation to folly."

Here Allworthy concluded his sermon, to which Blifil had listened with the profoundest attention, though it cost him some pains to prevent now and then a small discomposure of his muscles. He now praised every period of what he had heard with the warmth of a young divine, who hath the honor to dine with a bishop the same day in which his lordship hath mounted the pulpit.

CHAPTER XIII

Which concludes the first book; with an instance of ingratitude, which, we hope, will appear unnatural.

THE reader, from what hath been said, may imagine that the reconciliation (if indeed it could be so called) was only matter of form; we shall therefore pass it over, and hasten to what must surely be thought matter of substance.

The doctor had acquainted his brother with what had passed between Mr. Allworthy and him; and added with a smile, "I promise you I paid you off; nay, I absolutely desired the good gentleman not to forgive you: for you know after he had made a declaration in your favor, I might with safety venture on such a request with a person of his temper; and I was willing, as well for your sake as for my own, to prevent the least possibility of a suspicion."

Captain Blifil took not the least notice of this, at that time; but he afterwards made a very notable use of it.

One of the maxims which the devil, in a late visit upon earth, left to his disciples, is, when once you are got up, to kick the stool from under you. In plain English, when you have made your fortune by the good offices of a friend, you are advised to discard him as soon as you can.

Whether the captain acted by this maxim, I will not positively determine: so far we may confidently say, that his actions may be fairly derived from this diabolical principle; and indeed it is difficult to assign any other motive to them: for no sooner was he possessed of Miss Bridget, and reconciled to Allworthy, than he began to show a coldness to his brother which increased daily; till at length it grew into rudeness, and became very visible to every one.

The doctor remonstrated to him privately concerning this behavior, but could obtain no other satisfaction than the following plain declaration: "If you dislike anything in my brother's house, sir, you know you are at liberty to quit it." This strange, cruel, and almost unaccountable ingratitude in the captain, absolutely broke the poor doctor's heart; for ingratitude never so thoroughly pierces the human breast as when it proceeds from those in whose behalf we have been guilty of transgressions. Reflections on great and good actions, however they are received or returned by those in whose favor they are performed, always administer some comfort to us; but what consolation shall we receive under so biting a calamity as the ungrateful behavior of our friend, when our wounded conscience at the same time flies in our face, and upbraids us with having spotted it in the service of one so worthless!

Mr. Allworthy himself spoke to the captain in

his brother's behalf, and desired to know what offense the doctor had committed; when the hardhearted villain had the baseness to say that he should never forgive him for the injury which he had endeavored to do him in his favor; which, he said, he had pumped out of him, and was such a cruelty that it ought not to be forgiven.

Allworthy spoke in very high terms upon this declaration, which, he said, became not a human creature. He expressed, indeed, so much resentment against an unforgiving temper, that the captain at last pretended to be convinced by his arguments, and outwardly professed to be reconciled.

As for the bride, she was now in her honeymoon, and so passionately fond of her new husband that he never appeared to her to be in the wrong; and his displeasure against any person was a sufficient reason for her dislike to the same.

The captain, at Mr. Allworthy's instance, was outwardly, as we have said, reconciled to his brother; yet the same rancor remained in his heart; and he found so many opportunities of giving him private hints of this, that the house at last grew insupportable to the poor doctor; and he chose rather to submit to any inconveniences which he might encounter in the world, than longer to bear these cruel and ungrateful insults from a brother for whom he had done so much.

He once intended to acquaint Allworthy with the whole; but he could not bring himself to submit to the confession, by which he must take to his share so great a portion of guilt. Besides, by how much the worse man he represented his brother to be, so much the greater would his own offense appear to Allworthy, and so much the greater, he had reason to imagine, would be his resentment.

He feigned, therefore, some excuse of business for his departure, and promised to return soon again; and took leave of his brother with so well-dissembled content, that, as the captain played his part to the same perfection, Allworthy remained well satisfied with the truth of the reconciliation.

The doctor went directly to London, where he died soon after of a broken heart; a distemper which kills many more than is generally imagined, and would have a fair title to a place in the bill of mortality, did it not differ in one instance from all other diseases—viz., That no physician can cure it.

Now, upon the most diligent inquiry into the former lives of these two brothers, I find, besides the cursed and hellish maxim of policy above mentioned, another reason for the captain's conduct: the captain, besides what we have before said of him, was a man of great pride and fierceness, and had always treated his brother, who was of a different complexion, and greatly deficient in both these qualities, with the utmost air of superiority. The doctor, however, had much the larger share of learning, and was by many reputed to have the better understandng. This the captain knew, and could not bear; for though envy is at best a very malignant passion, yet is its bitterness greatly heightened by mixing with contempt towards the same object; and very much afraid I am, that whenever an obligation is joined to these two, indignation and not gratitude will be the product of all three.

BOOK II

CONTAINING SCENES OF MATRIMONIAL FELICITY IN DIF-
FERENT DEGREES OF LIFE; AND VARIOUS OTHER
TRANSACTIONS DURING THE FIRST TWO YEARS AF-
TER THE MARRIAGE BETWEEN CAPTAIN BLIFIL AND
MISS BRIDGET ALLWORTHY.

CHAPTER I

Showing what kind of a history this is; what it is like, and
what it is not like.

THOUGH we have properly enough entitled this our work, a history, and not a
life; nor an apology for a life, as is more
in fashion; yet we intend in it rather to pursue the
method of those writers, who profess to disclose
the revolutions of countries, than to imitate the
painful and voluminous historian, who, to preserve the regularity of his series, thinks himself
obliged to fill up as much paper with the detail of
months and years in which nothing remarkable
happened, as he employs upon those notable eras
when the greatest scenes have been transacted on
the human stage.

Such histories as these do, in reality, very much
resemble a newspaper, which consists of just the
same number of words, whether there be any news
in it or not. They may likewise be compared to
a stage coach, which performs constantly the same
course, empty as well as full. The writer, indeed,

seems to think himself obliged to keep even pace with time, whose amanuensis he is; and, like his master, travels as slowly through centuries of monkish dullness, when the world seems to have been asleep, as through that bright and busy age so nobly distinguished by the excellent Latin poet—

Ad confligendum venientibus undique pœnis,
Omnia cum belli trepido concussa tumultu
Horrida contremuere sub altis ætheris auris;
In dubioque fuit sub utrorum regna cadendum
Omnibus humanis esset, terraque marique.

Of which we wish we could give our readers a more adequate translation than that by Mr. Creech—

When dreadful Carthage frighted Rome with arms,
And all the world was shook with fierce alarms;
Whilst undecided yet, which part should fall,
Which nation rise the glorious lord of all.

Now it is our purpose in the ensuing pages, to pursue a contrary method. When any extraordinary scene presents itself (as we trust will often be the case), we shall spare no pains nor paper to open it at large to our reader; but if whole years should pass without producing anything worthy his notice, we shall not be afraid of a chasm in our history; but shall hasten on to matters of consequence, and leave such periods of time totally unobserved.

These are indeed to be considered as blanks in the grand lottery of time. We therefore, who are the registers of that lottery, shall imitate those sagacious persons who deal in that which is drawn at Guildhall, and who never trouble the public with the many blanks they dispose of; but when a great prize happens to be drawn, the newspapers are presently filled with it, and the world is sure to be informed at whose office it was sold: indeed, commonly two or three different offices lay claim to the honor of having disposed of it; by which, I suppose, the adventurers are given to understand that certain brokers are in the secrets of Fortune, and indeed of her cabinet council.

My reader then is not to be surprised, if, in the course of this work, he shall find some chapters very short, and others altogether as long; some that contain only the time of a single day, and others that comprise years; in a word, if my history sometimes seems to stand still, and sometimes to fly. For all which I shall not look on myself as accountable to any court of critical jurisdiction whatever: for as I am, in reality, the founder of a new province of writing, so I am at liberty to make what laws I please therein. And these laws, my readers, whom I consider as my subjects, are bound to believe in and to obey; with which that they may readily and cheerfully comply, I do hereby assure them that I shall principally regard their ease and advantage in all such institutions: for I do not like a *jure divino* tyrant, imagine that they are my slaves, or my commodity. I am, indeed, set over them for their own good only, and was created for their use, and not they for mine. Nor do I doubt, while I make their interest the great rule of my writings, they will unanimously concur in supporting my dignity, and in rendering me all the honor I shall deserve or desire.

CHAPTER II

Religious cautions against showing too much favor to bastards; and a great discovery made by Mrs. Deborah Wilkins.

EIGHT months after the celebration of the nuptials between Captain Blifil and Miss Bridget Allworthy, a young lady of great beauty, merit, and fortune, was Miss Bridget, by reason of a fright, delivered of a fine boy. The child was indeed to all appearances perfect; but the midwife discovered it was born a month before its full time.

Though the birth of an heir by his beloved sister was a circumstance of great joy to Mr. Allworthy, yet it did not alienate his affections from the little foundling, to whom he had been godfather, had given his own name of Thomas, and whom he had hitherto seldom failed of visiting, at least once a day, in his nursery.

He told his sister, if she pleased, the new-born infant should be bred up together with little Tommy; to which she consented, though with some little reluctance: for she had truly a great complacence for her brother; and hence she had always behaved towards the foundling with rather more kindness than ladies of rigid virtue can sometimes bring themselves to show to these children, who, however innocent, may be truly called the living monuments of incontinence.

The captain could not so easily bring himself to bear what he condemned as a fault in Mr. Allworthy. He gave him frequent hints, that to adopt the fruits of sin, was to give countenance to it. He quoted several texts (for he was well read in Scripture), such as, *He visits the sins of the fathers upon the children; and the fathers have eaten sour grapes, and the children's teeth are set on edge, &c.* Whence he argued the legality of punishing the crime of the parent on the bastard. He said, "Though the law did not positively allow the destroying such base-born children, yet it held them to be the children of nobody; that the Church considered them as the children of nobody; and that at the best, they ought to be brought up to the lowest and vilest offices of the commonwealth."

Mr. Allworthy answered to all this and much more, which the captain had urged on this subject, "That, however guilty the parents might be, the children were certainly innocent: that as to the texts he had quoted, the former of them was a particular denunciation against the Jews, for the sin of idolatry, of relinquishing and hating their heavenly King; and the latter was parabolically spoken, and rather intended to denote the certain and necessary consequences of sin, than any express judgment against it. But to represent the Almighty as avenging the sins of the guilty on the innocent, was indecent, if not blasphemous, as it was to represent him acting against the first principles of natural justice, and against the original notions of right and wrong, which he himself had implanted in our minds; by which we were to judge not only in all matters which were not revealed, but even of the truth of revelation itself. He said he knew many held the same principles with the captain on this head; but he was himself firmly convinced to the contrary, and would provide in the same manner for this poor infant, as if a legitimate child had had the fortune to have been found in the same place.

While the captain was taking all opportunities to press these and such like arguments, to remove the little foundling from Mr. Allworthy's, of whose fondness for him he began to be jealous, Mrs. Deborah had made a discovery, which, in its event, threatened at least to prove more fatal to poor Tommy than all the reasonings of the captain.

Whether the insatiable curiosity of this good woman had carried her on to that business, or whether she did it to confirm herself in the good graces of Mrs. Blifil, who, notwithstanding her outward behavior to the foundling, frequently abused the infant in private, and her brother too, for his fondness to it, I will not determine; but she had now, as she conceived, fully detected the father of the foundling.

Now, as this was a discovery of great consequence, it may be necessary to trace it from the fountain-head. We shall therefore very minutely lay open those previous matters by which it was produced; and for that purpose we shall be obliged to reveal all the secrets of a little family with which my reader is at present entirely unacquainted; and of which the economy was so rare and extraordinary, that I fear it will shock the utmost credulity of many married persons.

CHAPTER III

The description of a domestic government founded upon rules
directly contrary to those of Aristotle.

MY reader may please to remember he hath been informed that Jenny Jones had lived some years with a certain schoolmaster, who had at her earnest desire, instructed her in Latin, in which, to do justice to her genius, she had so improved herself, that she was become a better scholar than her master.

Indeed, though this poor man had undertaken a profession to which learning must be allowed necessary, this was the least of his commendations. He was one of the best-natured fellows in the world, and was, at the same time, master of so much pleasantry and humor, that he was reputed the wit of the country; and all the neighboring gentlemen were so desirous of his company, that as denying was not his talent, he spent much time at their houses, which he might, with more emolument, have spent in his school.

It may be imagined that a gentleman so qualified and so disposed, was in no danger of becoming formidable to the learned seminaries of Eton or Westminster. To speak plainly, his scholars were divided into two classes: in the upper of which was a young gentleman, the son of a neighboring squire, who, at the age of seventeen, was

72

just entered into his Syntaxis; and in the lower
was a second son of the same gentleman, who,
together with seven parish-boys, was learning to
read and write.

The stipend arising hence would hardly have indulged the schoolmaster in the luxuries of life,
had he not added to this office those of clerk and
barber, and had not Mr. Allworthy added to the
whole an annuity of ten pounds, which the poor
man received every Christmas, and with which he
was enabled to cheer his heart during that sacred
festival.

Among his other treasures, the pedagogue had
a wife, whom he had married out of Mr. Allworthy's kitchen for her fortune, viz., twenty
pounds, which she had there amassed.

This woman was not very amiable in her person.
Whether she sat to my friend Hogarth, or no, I
will not determine; but she exactly resembled the
young woman who is pouring out her mistress's
tea in the third picture of the Harlot's Progress.
She was, besides, a professed follower of that noble sect founded by Xantippe of old; by means of
which she became more formidable in the school
than her husband; for, to confess the truth, he
was never master there, or anywhere else, in her
presence.

Though her countenance did not denote much
natural sweetness of temper, yet this was, perhaps, somewhat soured by a circumstance which
generally poisons matrimonial felicity; for children are rightly called the pledges of love; and
her husband, though they had been married nine

years, had given her no such pledges; a default
for which he had no excuse, either from age or
health, being not yet thirty years old, and what
they call a jolly brisk young man.

Hence arose another evil, which produced no
little uneasiness to the poor pedagogue, of whom
she maintained so constant a jealousy, that he
durst hardly speak to one woman in the parish;
for the least degree of civility, or even correspondence, with any female, was sure to bring his wife
upon her back, and his own.

In order to guard herself against matrimonial
injuries in her own house, as she kept one maid-
servant, she always took care to choose her out of
that order of females whose faces are taken as a
kind of security for their virtue; of which number
Jenny Jones, as the reader hath been before informed, was one.

As the face of this young woman might be called
pretty good security of the before-mentioned kind,
and as her behavior had been always extremely
modest, which is the certain consequence of understanding in women; she had passed above four
years at Mr. Partridge's (for that was the schoolmaster's name) without creating the least suspicion in her mistress. Nay, she had been treated
with uncommon kindness, and her mistress had
permitted Mr. Partridge to give her those instructions which have been before commemorated.

But it is with jealousy as with the gout: when
such distempers are in the blood, there is never
any security against their breaking out; and that

often on the slightest occasions, and when least
suspected.

Thus it happened to Mrs. Partridge, who had
submitted four years to her husband's teaching
this young woman, and had suffered her often to
neglect her work in order to pursue her learning.
For, passing by one day, as the girl was reading,
and her master leaning over her, the girl, I know
not for what reason, suddenly started up from her
chair: and this was the first time that suspicion
ever entered into the head of her mistress.

This did not, however, at that time discover
itself, but lay lurking in her mind, like a concealed
enemy, who waits for a reinforcement of additional strength before he openly declares himself
and proceeds upon hostile operations: and such
additional strength soon arrived to corroborate
her suspicion; for not long after, the husband and
wife being at dinner, the master said to his maid,
Da mihi aliquid potum: upon which the poor girl
smiled, perhaps at the badness of the Latin, and,
when her mistress cast her eyes on her, blushed,
possibly with a consciousness of having laughed
at her master. Mrs. Partridge, upon this, immediately fell into a fury, and discharged the
trencher on which she was eating, at the head of
poor Jenny, crying out, "You impudent whore, do
you play tricks with my husband before my face?"
and at the same instant rose from her chair with
a knife in her hand, with which, most probably,
she would have executed very tragical vengeance,
had not the girl taken the advantage of being

nearer the door than her mistress, and avoided
her fury by running away: for, as to the poor husband, whether surprise had rendered him motionless, or fear (which is full as probable) had restrained him from venturing at any opposition, he
sat staring and trembling in his chair; nor did he
once offer to move or speak, till his wife, returning from the pursuit of Jenny, made some defensive measures necessary for his own preservation;
and he likewise was obliged to retreat, after the
example of the maid.

This good woman was, no more than Othello, of
a disposition

> To make a life of jealousy,
> And follow still the changes of the moon
> With fresh suspicions———

With her, as well as him,

> ———To be once in doubt,
> Was once to be resolv'd———

she therefore ordered Jenny immediately to pack
up her alls and begone, for that she was determined she should not sleep that night within her
walls.

Mr. Partridge had profited too much by experience to interpose in a matter of this nature. He
therefore had recourse to his usual receipt of patience; for, though he was not a great adept in
Latin, he remembered, and well understood, the
advice contained in these words:

> ———*Leve fit, quod bene fertur onus.*

in English:

A burden becomes lightest when it is well borne—

which he had always in his mouth; and of which, to say the truth, he had often occasion to experience the truth.

Jenny offered to make protestations of her innocence; but the tempest was too strong for her to be heard. She then betook herself to the business of packing, for which a small quantity of brown paper sufficed; and, having received her small pittance of wages, she returned home.

The schoolmaster and his consort passed their time unpleasantly enough that evening; but something or other happened before the next morning, which a little abated the fury of Mrs. Partridge; and she at length admitted her husband to make his excuses: to which she gave the readier belief, as he had, instead of desiring her to recall Jenny, professed a satisfaction in her being dismissed, saying, she was grown of little use as a servant, spending all her time in reading, and was become, moreover, very pert and obstinate; for, indeed, she and her master had lately had frequent disputes in literature; in which as hath been said, she was become greatly his superior. This, however, he would by no means allow; and as he called her persisting in the right, obstinacy, he began to hate her with no small inveteracy.

CHAPTER IV

Containing one of the most bloody battles, or rather duels,
that were ever recorded in domestic history.

FOR the reasons mentioned in the preceding
chapter, and from some other matrimonial
concessions, well known to most husbands,
and which, like the secrets of freemasonry, should
be divulged to none who are not members of that
honorable fraternity, Mrs. Partridge was pretty
well satisfied that she had condemned her husband
without cause, and endeavored by acts of kindness
to make him amends for her false suspicion. Her
passions were indeed equally violent, whichever
way they inclined; for as she could be extremely
angry, so could she be altogether as fond.

But though these passions ordinarily succeed
each other, and scarce twenty-four hours ever
passed in which the pedagogue was not, in some
degree, the object of both; yet, on extraordinary
occasions, when the passion of anger had raged
very high, the remission was usually longer: and
so was the case at present, for she continued
longer in a state of affability, after this fit of jealousy was ended, than her husband had ever known
before: and, had it not been for some little exercises, which all the followers of Xantippe are
obliged to perform daily, Mr. Partridge would
have enjoyed a perfect serenity of several months.

Perfect calms at sea are always suspected by the experienced mariner to be the forerunners of a storm: and I know some persons, who, without being generally the devotees of superstition, are apt to apprehend that great and unusual peace or tranquillity will be attended with its opposite. For which reason the ancients used, on such occasions, to sacrifice to the goddess Nemesis, a deity who was thought by them to look with an invidious eye on human felicity, and to have a peculiar delight in overturning it.

As we are very far from believing in any such heathen goddess, or from encouraging any superstition, so we wish Mr. John Fr——, or some other such philosopher, would bestir himself a little, in order to find out the real cause of this sudden transition from good to bad fortune, which hath been so often remarked, and of which we shall proceed to give an instance; for it is our province to relate facts, and we shall leave causes to persons of much higher genius.

Mankind have always taken great delight in knowing and descanting on the actions of others. Hence there have been, in all ages and nations, certain places set apart for public rendezvous, where the curious might meet and satisfy their mutual curiosity. Among these, the barbers' shops have justly borne the pre-eminence. Among the Greeks, barbers' news was a proverbial expression; and Horace, in one of his epistles, makes honorable mention of the Roman barbers in the same light.

Those of England are known to be no wise in-

ferior to their Greek or Roman predecessors.
You there see foreign affairs discussed in a manner little inferior to that with which they are
handled in the coffee-houses; and domestic occurrences are much more largely and freely treated
in the former than in the latter. But this serves
only for the men. Now, whereas the females of
this country, especially those of the lower order,
do associate themselves much more than those of
other nations, our polity would be highly deficient,
if they had not some place set apart likewise for
the indulgence of their curiosity, seeing they are
in this no way inferior to the other half of the
species.

In enjoying, therefore, such place of rendezvous, the British fair ought to esteem themselves
more happy than any of their foreign sisters; as
I do not remember either to have read in history,
or to have seen in my travels, anything of the like
kind.

This place then is no other than the chandler's
shop, the known seat of all the news; or, as it is
vulgarly called, gossiping, in every parish in England.

Mrs. Partridge being one day at this assembly
of females, was asked by one of her neighbors, if
she had heard no news lately of Jenny Jones? To
which she answered in the negative. Upon this
the other replied, with a smile, That the parish
was very much obliged to her for having turned
Jenny away as she did.

Mrs. Partridge, whose jealousy, as the reader
well knows, was long since cured, and who had no

other quarrel to her maid, answered boldly, She did not know any obligation the parish had to her on that account; for she believed Jenny had scarce left her equal behind her.

"No, truly," said the gossip, "I hope not, though I fancy we have sluts enow too. Then you have not heard, it seems, that she hath been brought to bed of two bastards? but as they are not born here, my husband and the other overseer says we shall not be obliged to keep them."

"Two bastards!" answered Mrs. Partridge hastily: "you surprise me! I don't know whether we must keep them; but I am sure they must have been begotten here, for the wench hath not been nine months gone away."

Nothing can be so quick and sudden as the operations of the mind, especially when hope, or fear, or jealousy, to which the two others are but journeymen, set it to work. It occurred instantly to her, that Jenny had scarce ever been out of her own house while she lived with her. The leaning over the chair, the sudden starting up, the Latin, the smile, and many other things, rushed upon her all at once. The satisfaction her husband expressed in the departure of Jenny, appeared now to be only dissembled; again, in the same instant, to be real; but yet to confirm her jealousy, proceeding from satiety, and a hundred other bad causes. In a word, she was convinced of her husband's guilt, and immediately left the assembly in confusion.

As fair Grimalkin, who, though the youngest of the feline family, degenerates not in ferocity from
I—6

the elder branches of her house, and though inferior in strength, is equal in fierceness to the
noble tiger himself, when a little mouse, whom it
hath longed tormented in sport, escapes from her
clutches for a while, frets, scolds, growls, swears;
but if the trunk, or box, behind which the mouse
lay hid be again removed, she flies like lightning
on her prey, and, with envenomed wrath, bites,
scratches, mumbles, and tears the little animal.

Not with less fury did Mrs. Partridge fly on the
poor pedagogue. Her tongue, teeth, and hands,
fell all upon him at once. His wig was in an instant torn from his head, his shirt from his back,
and from his face descended five streams of blood,
denoting the number of claws with which nature
had unhappily armed the enemy.

Mr. Partridge acted for some time on the defensive only; indeed he attempted only to guard
his face with his hands; but as he found that his
antagonist abated nothing of her rage, he thought
he might, at least, endeavor to disarm her, or
rather to confine her arms; in doing which her cap
fell off in the struggle, and her hair being too
short to reach her shoulders, erected itself on her
head; her stays likewise, which were laced through
one single hole at the bottom, burst open; and her
breasts, which were much more redundant than
her hair, hung down below her middle; her face
was likewise marked with the blood of her husband: her teeth gnashed with rage; and fire, such
as sparkles from a smith's forge, darted from her
eyes. So that, altogether, this Amazonian heroine

might have been an object of terror to a much bolder man than Mr. Partridge.

He had, at length, the good fortune, by getting possession of her arms, to render those weapons which she wore at the ends of her fingers useless; which she no sooner perceived, than the softness of her sex prevailed over her rage, and she presently dissolved in tears, which soon after concluded in a fit.

That small share of sense which Mr. Partridge had hitherto preserved through this scene of fury, of the cause of which he was hitherto ignorant, now utterly abandoned him. He ran instantly into the street, hallowing out that his wife was in the agonies of death, and beseeching the neighbors to fly with the utmost haste to her assistance. Several good women obeyed his summons, who entering his house, and applying the usual remedies on such occasions, Mrs. Partridge was at length, to the great joy of her husband, brought to herself.

As soon as she had a little recollected her spirits, and somewhat composed herself with a cordial, she began to inform the company of the manifold injuries she had received from her husband; who, she said, was not contented to injure her in her bed; but, upon her upbraiding him with it, had treated her in the cruelest manner imaginable; had tore her cap and hair from her head, and her stays from her body, giving her, at the same time, several blows, the marks of which she should carry to the grave.

The poor man, who bore on his face many more visible marks of the indignation of his wife, stood in silent astonishment at this accusation; which the reader will, I believe, bear witness for him, had greatly exceeded the truth; for indeed he had not struck her once; and this silence being interpreted to be a confession of the charge by the whole court, they all began at once, *una voce,* to rebuke and revile him, repeating often, that none but a coward ever struck a woman.

Mr. Partridge bore all this patiently; but when his wife appealed to the blood on her face, as an evidence of his barbarity, he could not help laying claim to his own blood, for so it really was; as he thought it very unnatural, that this should rise up (as we are taught that of a murdered person often doth) in vengeance against him.

To this the women made no other answer, than that it was a pity it had not come from his heart, instead of his face; all declaring, that, if their husbands should lift their hands against them, they would have their hearts' bloods out of their bodies.

After much admonition for what was past, and much good advice to Mr. Partridge for his future behavior, the company at length departed, and left the husband and wife to a personal conference together, in which Mr. Partridge soon learned the cause of all his sufferings.

CHAPTER V

Containing much matter to exercise the judgment and reflection of the reader.

I BELIEVE it is a true observation, that few
secrets are divulged to one person only; but
certainly, it would be next to a miracle that
a fact of this kind should be known to a whole
parish, and not transpire any farther.

And, indeed, a very few days had past, before
the country, to use a common phrase, rung of the
schoolmaster of Little Baddington; who was said
to have beaten his wife in the most cruel manner.
Nay, in some places it was reported he had murdered her; in others, that he had broke her arms;
in others, her legs: in short, there was scarce an
injury which can be done to a human creature, but
what Mrs. Partridge was somewhere or other affirmed to have received from her husband.

The cause of this quarrel was likewise variously reported; for as some people said that Mrs.
Partridge had caught her husband in bed with his
maid, so many other reasons, of a very different
kind, went abroad. Nay, some transferred the
guilt to the wife, and the jealousy to the husband.

Mrs. Wilkins had long ago heard of this quarrel;
but, as a different cause from the true one had
reached her ears, she thought proper to conceal it;
and the rather, perhaps, as the blame was univer-

sally laid on Mr. Partridge; and his wife, when she was servant to Mr. Allworthy, had in something offended Mrs. Wilkins, who was not of a very forgiving temper.

But Mrs. Wilkins, whose eyes could see objects at a distance, and who could very well look forward a few years into futurity, had perceived a strong likelihood of Captain Blifil's being hereafter her master; and as she plainly discerned that the captain bore no great goodwill to the little foundling, she fancied it would be rendering him an agreeable service, if she could make any discoveries that might lessen the affection which Mr. Allworthy seemed to have contracted for this child, and which gave visible uneasiness to the captain, who could not entirely conceal it even before Allworthy himself; though his wife, who acted her part much better in public, frequently recommended to him her own example, of conniving at the folly of her brother, which, she said, she at least as well perceived, and as much resented, as any other possibly could.

Mrs. Wilkins having therefore, by accident, gotten a true scent of the above story, though long after it had happened, failed not to satisfy herself thoroughly of all the particulars; and then acquainted the captain, that she had at last discovered the true father of the little bastard, which she was sorry, she said, to see her master lose his reputation in the country, by taking so much notice of.

The captain chid her for the conclusion of her speech, as an improper assurance in judging of her master's actions: for if his honor, or his understanding, would have suffered the captain to make an alliance with Mrs. Wilkins, his pride would by no means have admitted it. And to say the truth, there is no conduct less politic, than to enter into any confederacy with your friend's servants against their master: for by these means you afterwards become the slave of these very servants; by whom you are constantly liable to be betrayed. And this consideration, perhaps it was, which prevented Captain Blifil from being more explicit with Mrs. Wilkins, or from encouraging the abuse which she had bestowed on Allworthy.

But though he declared no satisfaction to Mrs. Wilkins at this discovery, he enjoyed not a little from it in his own mind, and resolved to make the best use of it he was able.

He kept this matter a long time concealed within his own breast, in hopes that Mr. Allworthy might hear it from some other person; but Mrs. Wilkins, whether she resented the captain's behavior, or whether his cunning was beyond her, and she feared the discovery might displease him, never afterwards opened her lips about the matter.

I have thought it somewhat strange, upon reflection, that the housekeeper never acquainted Mrs. Blifil with this news, as women are more inclined to communicate all pieces of intelligence to their own sex, than to ours. The only way, as it appears to me, of solving this difficulty, is, by imputing it to that distance which was now grown between the lady and the housekeeper: whether this arose from a jealousy in Mrs. Blifil, that Wilkins showed too great a respect to the foundling; for while she was endeavoring to ruin the little infant, in order to ingratiate herself with the captain, she was every day more and more commending it before Allworthy, as his fondness for it every day increased. This, notwithstanding all the care she took at other times to express the direct contrary to Mrs. Blifil, perhaps offended that delicate lady, who certainly now hated Mrs. Wilkins; and though she did not, or possibly could not, absolutely remove her from her place, she found, however, the means of making her life very uneasy. This Mrs. Wilkins, at length, so resented, that she very openly showed all manner of respect and fondness to little Tommy, in opposition to Mrs. Blifil.

The captain, therefore, finding the story in danger of perishing, at last took an opportunity to reveal it himself.

He was one day engaged with Mr. Allworthy in a discourse on charity: in which the captain, with great learning, proved to Mr. Allworthy, that the word charity in Scripture nowhere means beneficence or generosity.

"The Christian religion," he said, "was instituted for much nobler purposes, than to enforce a lesson which many heathen philosophers had taught us long before, and which, though it might perhaps be called a moral virtue, savored but little of that sublime, Christian-like disposition, that vast elevation of thought, in purity approaching to angelic perfection, to be attained, expressed, and felt only by grace. Those," he said, "came nearer to the Scripture meaning, who understood

by it candor, or the forming of a benevolent
opinion of our brethren, and passing a favorable
judgment on their actions; a virtue much higher,
and more extensive in its nature, than a pitiful
distribution of alms, which, though we would never
so much prejudice, or even ruin our families,
could never reach many; whereas charity, in the
other and truer sense, might be extended to all
mankind.''

He said, ''Considering who the disciples were,
it would be absurd to conceive the doctrine of generosity, or giving alms, to have been preached to
them. And, as we could not well imagine this
doctrine should be preached by its Divine Author
to men who could not practice it, much less should
we think it understood so by those who can practice it, and do not.

''But though,'' continued he, ''there is, I am
afraid, little merit in these benefactions, there
would, I must confess, be much pleasure in them
to a good mind, if it was not abated by one consideration. I mean, that we are liable to be imposed
upon, and to confer our choicest favors often on
the undeserving, as you must own was your case
in your bounty to that worthless fellow Partridge:
for two or three such examples must greatly lessen
the inward satisfaction which a good man would
otherwise find in generosity; nay, may even make
him timorous in bestowing, lest he should be guilty
of supporting vice, and encouraging the wicked;
a crime of a very black dye, and for which it will
by no means be a sufficient excuse, that we have
not actually intended such an encouragement; un-

less we have used the utmost caution in choosing the objects of our beneficence. A consideration which, I make no doubt, hath greatly checked the liberality of many a worthy and pious man."

Mr. Allworthy answered, "He could not dispute with the captain in the Greek language, and therefore could say nothing as to the true sense of the word which is translated charity; but that he had always thought it was interpreted to consist in action, and that giving alms constituted at least one branch of that virtue.

"As to the meritorious part," he said, "he readily agreed with the captain; for where could be the merit of barely discharging a duty? which," he said, "let the word charity have what construction it would, it sufficiently appeared to be from the whole tenor of the New Testament. And as he thought it an indispensable duty, enjoined both by the Christian law, and by the law of nature itself; so was it withal so pleasant, that if any duty could be said to be its own reward, or to pay us while we are discharging it, it was this.

"To confess the truth," said he, "there is one degree of generosity (of charity I would have called it), which seems to have some show of merit, and that is, where, from a principle of benevolence and Christian love, we bestow on another what we really want ourselves; where, in order to lessen the distresses of another, we condescend to share some part of them, by giving what even our own necessities cannot well spare. This is, I think, meritorious; but to relieve our brethren only with our superfluities; to be charitable (I must use the word) rather at the expense of our coffers than ourselves; to save several families from misery rather than hang up an extraordinary picture in our houses or gratify any other idle ridiculous vanity—this seems to be only being human creatures. Nay, I will venture to go farther, it is being in some degree epicures: for what could the greatest epicure wish rather than to eat with many mouths instead of one? which I think may be predicated of any one who knows that the bread of many is owing to his own largesses.

"As to the apprehension of bestowing bounty on such as may hereafter prove unworthy objects, because many have proved such; surely it can never deter a good man from generosity. I do not think a few or many examples of ingratitude can justify a man's hardening his heart against the distresses of his fellow-creatures; nor do I believe it can ever have such effect on a truly benevolent mind. Nothing less than a persuasion of universal depravity can lock up the charity of a good man; and this persuasion must lead him, I think, either into atheism, or enthusiasm; but surely it is unfair to argue such universal depravity from a few vicious individuals; nor was this, I believe, ever done by a man, who, upon searching his own mind, found one certain exception to the general rule." He then concluded by asking, "who that Partridge was, whom he had called a worthless fellow?"

"I mean," said the captain, "Partridge the barber, the schoolmaster, what do you call him?

Partridge, the father of the little child which you found in your bed.''

Mr. Allworthy expressed great surprise at this account, and the captain as great at his ignorance of it; for he said he had known it above a month: and at length recollected with much difficulty that he was told it by Mrs. Wilkins.

Upon this, Wilkins was immediately summoned; who having confirmed what the captain had said, was by Mr. Allworthy, by and with the captain's advice, dispatched to Little Baddington, to inform herself of the truth of the fact: for the captain expressed great dislike at all hasty proceedings in criminal matters, and said he would by no means have Mr. Allworthy take any resolution either to the prejudice of the child or its father, before he was satisfied that the latter was guilty; for though he had privately satisfied himself of this from one of Partridge's neighbors, yet he was too generous to give any such evidence to Mr. Allworthy.

CHAPTER VI

The trial of Partridge, the schoolmaster, for incontinency; the
evidence of his wife; a short reflection on the wisdom of
our law; with other grave matters, which those will like
best who understand them most.

IT may be wondered that a story so well known,
and which had furnished so much matter of
conversation, should never have been mentioned to Mr. Allworthy himself, who was perhaps the only person in that country who had
never heard of it.

To account in some measure for this to the
reader, I think proper to inform him, that there
was no one in the kingdom less interested in opposing that doctrine concerning the meaning of
the word charity, which hath been seen in the pre-
ceeding chapter, than our good man. Indeed, he
was equally entitled to this virtue in either sense;
for as no man was ever more sensible of the
wants, or more ready to relieve the distresses of
others, so none could be more tender of their characters, or slower to believe anything to their disadvantage.

Scandal, therefore, never found any access to
his table; for as it hath been long since observed
that you may know a man by his companions, so I
will venture to say, that, by attending to the conversation at a great man's table, you may satisfy.

yourself of his religion, his politics, his taste, and indeed of his entire disposition: for though a few odd fellows will utter their own sentiments in all places, yet much the greater part of mankind have enough of the courtier to accommodate their conversation to the taste and inclination of their superiors.

But to return to Mrs. Wilkins, who, having executed her commission with great dispatch, though at fifteen miles distance, brought back such a confirmation of the schoolmaster's guilt, that Mr. Allworthy determined to send for the criminal, and examine him *viva voce*. Mr. Partridge, therefore, was summoned to attend, in order to his defense (if he could make any) against this accusation.

At the time appointed, before Mr. Allworthy himself, at Paradise-hall, came as well the said Partridge, with Anne, his wife, as Mrs. Wilkins his accuser.

And now Mr. Allworthy being seated in the chair of justice, Mr. Partridge was brought before him. Having heard his accusation from the mouth of Mrs. Wilkins, he pleaded not guilty, making many vehement protestations of his innocence.

Mrs. Partridge was then examined, who, after a modest apology for being obliged to speak the truth against her husband, related all the circumstances with which the reader hath already been acquainted; and at last concluded with her husband's confession of his guilt.

Whether she had forgiven him or no, I will not

venture to determine; but it is certain she was an unwilling witness in this cause; and it is probable from certain other reasons, would never have been brought to depose as she did, had not Mrs. Wilkins, with great art, fished all out of her at her own house, and had she not indeed made promises, in Mr. Allworthy's name, that the punishment of her husband should not be such as might anywise affect his family.

Partridge still persisted in asserting his innocence, though he admitted he had made the above-mentioned confession; which he however endeavored to account for, by protesting that he was forced into it by the continued importunity she used: who vowed, that as she was sure of his guilt, she would never leave tormenting him till he had owned it; and faithfully promised, that, in such case, she would never mention it to him more. Hence, he said, he had been induced falsely to confess himself guilty, though he was innocent; and that he believed he should have confessed a murder from the same motive.

Mrs. Partridge could not bear this imputation with patience; and having no other remedy in the present place but tears, she called forth a plentiful assistance from them, and then addressing herself to Mr. Allworthy, she said (or rather cried), "May it please your worship, there never was any poor woman so injured as I am by that base man; for this is not the only instance of his falsehood to me. No, may it please your worship, he hath injured my bed many's the good time and often. I could have put up with his drunkenness and neg-

lect of his business, if he had not broke one of the
sacred commandments. Besides, if it had been
out of doors I had not mattered it so much; but
with my own servant, in my own house, under my
own roof, to defile my own chaste bed, which to be
sure he hath, with his beastly stinking whores.
Yes, you villain, you have defiled my own bed, you
have; and then you have charged me with bullock-
ing you into owning the truth. It is very likely,
an't please your worship, that I should bullock
him? I have marks enow about my body to show
of his cruelty to me. If you had been a man, you
villain, you would have scorned to injure a woman
in that manner. But you an't half a man, you
know it. Nor have you been half a husband to
me. You need run after whores, you need, when
I'm sure—— And since he provokes me, I am
ready, an't please your worship, to take my bodily
oath that I found them a-bed together. What,
you have forgot, I suppose, when you beat me into
a fit, and made the blood run down my forehead,
because I only civilly taxed you with adultery! but
I can prove it by all my neighbors. You have almost broke my heart, you have, you have.''

Here Mr. Allworthy interrupted, and begged
her to be pacified, promising her that she should
have justice; then turning to Partridge, who stood
aghast, one half of his wits being hurried away by
surprise and the other half by fear, he said he was
sorry to see there was so wicked a man in the
world. He assured him that his prevaricating
and lying backward and forward was a great aggravation of his guilt; for which the only atone-

ment he could make was by confession and repentance.   He exhorted him, therefore, to begin by
immediately confessing the fact, and not to persist in denying what was so plainly proved against
him even by his own wife.

Here, reader, I beg your patience a moment,
while I make a just compliment to the great wisdom and sagacity of our law, which refuses to admit the evidence of a wife for or against her husband.   This, says a certain learned author, who,
I believe, was never quoted before in any but a
law-book, would be the means of creating an
eternal dissension between them.   It would, indeed, be the means of much perjury, and of much
whipping, fining, imprisoning, transporting, and
hanging.

Partridge stood a while silent, till, being bid to
speak, he said he had already spoken the truth,
and appealed to Heaven for his innocence, and
lastly to the girl herself, whom he desired his worship immediately to send for; for he was ignorant,
or at least pretended to be so, that she had left
that part of the country.

Mr. Allworthy, whose natural love of justice,
joined to his coolness of temper, made him always
a most patient magistrate in hearing all the witnesses which an accused person could produce in
his defense, agreed to defer his final determination
of this matter till the arrival of Jenny, for whom
he immediately dispatched a messenger; and then
having recommended peace between Partridge and
his wife (though he addressed himself chiefly to
the wrong person), he appointed them to attend

I—7

again the third day; for he had sent Jenny a whole day's journey from his own house.

At the appointed time the parties all assembled, when the messenger returning brought word, that Jenny was not to be found; for that she had left her habitation a few days before, in company with a recruiting officer.

Mr. Allworthy then declared that the evidence of such a slut as she appeared to be would have deserved no credit; but he said he could not help thinking that, had she been present, and would have declared the truth, she must have confirmed what so many circumstances, together with his own confession, and the declaration of his wife that she had caught her husband in the fact, did sufficiently prove. He therefore once more exhorted Partridge to confess; but he still avowing his innocence, Mr. Allworthy declared himself satisfied of his guilt, and that he was too bad a man to receive any encouragement from him. He therefore deprived him of his annuity, and recommended repentance to him on account of another world, and industry to maintain himself and his wife in this.

There were not, perhaps, many more unhappy persons than poor Partridge. He had lost the best part of his income by the evidence of his wife, and yet was daily upbraided by her for having, among other things, been the occasion of depriving her of that benefit; but such was his fortune, and he was obliged to submit to it.

Though I called him poor Partridge in the last paragraph, I would have the reader rather im-

pute that epithet to the compassion in my temper
than conceive it to be any declaration of his innocence. Whether he was innocent or not will perhaps appear hereafter; but if the historic muse
hath entrusted me with any secrets, I will by no
means be guilty of discovering them till she shall
give me leave.

Here therefore the reader must suspend his
curiosity. Certain it is that, whatever was the
truth of the case, there was evidence more than
sufficient to convict him before Allworthy; indeed,
much less would have satisfied a bench of justices
on an order of bastardy; and yet, notwithstanding
the positiveness of Mrs. Partridge, who would
have taken the sacrament upon the matter, there
is a possibility that the schoolmaster was entirely
innocent: for though it appeared clear on comparing the time when Jenny departed from Little
Baddington with that of her delivery that she had
there conceived this infant, yet it by no means followed of necessity that Partridge must have been
its father; for, to omit other particulars, there was
in the same house a lad near eighteen, between
whom and Jenny there had subsisted sufficient intimacy to found a reasonable suspicion; and yet,
so blind is jealousy, this circumstance never once
entered into the head of the enraged wife.

Whether Partridge repented or not, according
to Mr. Allworthy's advice, is not so apparent.
Certain it is that his wife repented heartily of the
evidence she had given against him: especially
when she found Mrs. Deborah had deceived her,
and refused to make any application to Mr. All-

worthy on her behalf. She had, however, somewhat better success with Mrs. Blifil, who was, as
the reader must have perceived, a much better-
tempered woman, and very kindly undertook to
solicit her brother to restore the annuity; in which,
though good-nature might have some share, yet
a stronger and more natural motive will appear in
the next chapter.

These solicitations were nevertheless unsuccessful: for though Mr. Allworthy did not think, with
some late writers, that mercy consists only in punishing offenders; yet he was as far from thinking
that it is proper to this excellent quality to pardon great criminals wantonly, without any reason
whatever. Any doubtfulness of the fact, or any
circumstance of mitigation, was never disre-
garded: but the petitions of an offender, or the intercessions of others, did not in the least affect
him. In a word, he never pardoned because the
offender himself, or his friends, were unwilling
that he should be punished.

Partridge and his wife were therefore both
obliged to submit to their fate; which was indeed
severe enough: for so far was he from doubling
his industry on the account of his lessened income,
that he did in a manner abandon himself to despair; and as he was by nature indolent, that vice
now increased upon him, by which means he lost
the little school he had; so that neither his wife
nor himself would have had any bread to eat, had
not the charity of some good Christian interposed,
and provided them with what was just sufficient
for their sustenance.

As this support was conveyed to them by an unknown hand, they imagined, and so, I doubt not, will the reader, that Mr. Allworthy himself was their secret benefactor; who, though he would not openly encourage vice, could yet privately relieve the distresses of the vicious themselves, when these became too exquisite and disproportionate to their demerit. In which light their wretchedness appeared now to Fortune herself; for she at length took pity on this miserable couple, and considerably lessened the wretched state of Partridge, by putting a final end to that of his wife, who soon after caught the small-pox, and died.

The justice which Mr. Allworthy had executed on Partridge at first met with universal approbation; but no sooner had he felt its consequences, than his neighbors began to relent, and to compassionate his case; and presently after, to blame that as rigor and severity which they before called justice. They now exclaimed against punishing in cold blood, and sang forth the praises of mercy and forgiveness.

These cries were considerably increased by the death of Mrs. Partridge, which, though owing to the distemper above mentioned, which is no consequence of poverty or distress, many were not ashamed to impute to Mr. Allworthy's severity, or, as they now termed it, cruelty.

Partridge having now lost his wife, his school, and his annuity, and the unknown person having now discontinued the last-mentioned charity, resolved to change the scene, and left the country, where he was in danger of starving, with the universal compassion of all his neighbors.

CHAPTER VII

A short sketch of that felicity which prudent couples may extract from hatred: with a short apology for those people who overlook imperfections in their friends.

THOUGH the captain had effectually demolished poor Partridge, yet had he not reaped the harvest he hoped for, which was to turn the foundling out of Mr. Allworthy's house.

On the contrary, that gentleman grew every day fonder of little Tommy, as if he intended to counterbalance his severity to the father with extraordinary fondness and affection towards the son.

This a good deal soured the captain's temper, as did all the other daily instances of Mr. Allworthy's generosity; for he looked on all such largesses to be diminutions of his own wealth.

In this, we have said, he did not agree with his wife; nor, indeed, in anything else: for though an affection placed on the understanding is, by many wise persons, thought more durable than that which is founded on beauty, yet it happened otherwise in the present case. Nay, the understandings of this couple were their principal bone of contention, and one great cause of many quarrels, which from time to time arose between them; and which at last ended, on the side of the lady, in a sovereign contempt for her husband; and on the husband's, in an utter abhorrence of his wife.

As these had both exercised their talents chiefly in the study of divinity, this was, from their first acquaintance, the most common topic of conversation between them. The captain, like a well-bred man, had, before marriage, always given up his opinion to that of the lady; and this, not in the clumsy awkward manner of a conceited blockhead, who, while he civilly yields to a superior in an argument, is desirous of being still known to think himself in the right. The captain, on the contrary, though one of the proudest fellows in the world, so absolutely yielded the victory to his antagonist, that she, who had not the least doubt of his sincerity, retired always from the dispute with an admiration of her own understanding and a love for his.

But though this complacence to one whom the captain thoroughly despised, was not so uneasy to him as it would have been had any hopes of preferment made it necessary to show the same submission to a Hoadley, or to some other of great reputation in the science, yet even this cost him too much to be endured without some motive. Matrimony, therefore, having removed all such motives, he grew weary of this condescension, and began to treat the opinions of his wife with that haughtiness and insolence, which none but those who deserve some contempt themselves can bestow, and those only who deserve no contempt can bear.

When the first torrent of tenderness was over, and when, in the calm and long interval between the fits, reason began to open the eyes of the lady, and she saw this alteration of behavior in the captain, who at length answered all her arguments only with pish and pshaw, she was far from enduring the indignity with a tame submission. Indeed, it at first so highly provoked her, that it might have produced some tragical event, had it not taken a more harmless turn, by filling her with the utmost contempt for her husband's understanding, which somewhat qualified her hatred towards him; though of this likewise she had a pretty moderate share.

The captain's hatred to her was of a purer kind; for as to any imperfections in her knowledge or understanding, he no more despised her for them, than for her not being six feet high. In his opinion of the female sex, he exceeded the moroseness of Aristotle himself: he looked on a woman as on an animal of domestic use, of somewhat higher consideration than a cat, since her offices were of rather more importance; but the difference between these two was, in his estimation so small, that, in his marriage contracted with Mr. Allworthy's lands and tenements, it would have been pretty equal which of them he had taken into the bargain. And yet so tender was his pride, that it felt the contempt which his wife now began to express towards him; and this, added to the surfeit he had before taken of her love, created in him a degree of disgust and abhorrence, perhaps hardly to be exceeded.

One situation only of the married state is excluded from pleasure: and that is, a state of indifference: but as many of my readers, I hope, know what an exquisite delight there is in conveying pleasure to a beloved object, so some few, I am afraid, may have experienced the satisfaction of tormenting one we hate. It is, I apprehend, to come at this latter pleasure, that we see both sexes often give up that ease in marriage which they might otherwise possess, though their mate was never so disagreeable to them. Hence the wife often puts on fits of love and jealousy, nay, even denies herself any pleasure, to disturb and prevent those of her husband; and he again, in return, puts frequent restraints on himself, and stays at home in company which he dislikes, in order to confine his wife to what she equally detests. Hence, too, must flow those tears which a widow sometimes so plentifully sheds over the ashes of a husband with whom she led a life of constant disquiet and turbulency, and whom now she can never hope to torment any more.

But if ever any couple enjoyed this pleasure, it was at present experienced by the captain and his lady. It was always a sufficient reason to either of them to be obstinate in any opinion, that the other had previously asserted the contrary. If the one proposed any amusement, the other constantly objected to it: they never loved or hated, commended or abused, the same person. And for this reason, as the captain looked with an evil eye on the little foundling, his wife began now to caress it almost equally with her own child.

The reader will be apt to conceive, that this behavior between the husband and wife did not greatly contribute to Mr. Allworthy's repose, as it tended so little to that serene happiness which he had designed for all three from this alliance; but the truth is, though he might be a little disappointed in his sanguine expectations, yet he was far from being acquainted with the whole matter; for, as the captain was, from certain obvious reasons, much on his guard before him, the lady was obliged, for fear of her brother's displeasure, to pursue the same conduct. In fact, it is possible for a third person to be very intimate, nay even to live long in the same house, with a married couple, who have any tolerable discretion, and not even guess at the sour sentiments which they bear to each other: for though the whole day may be sometimes too short for hatred, as well as for love; yet the many hours which they naturally spend together, apart from all observers, furnish people of tolerable moderation with such ample opportunity for the enjoyment of either passion, that, if they love, they can support being a few hours in company without toying, or if they hate, without spitting in each other's faces.

It is possible, however, that Mr. Allworthy saw enough to render him a little uneasy; for we are not always to conclude, that a wise man is not hurt, because he doth not cry out and lament himself, like those of a childish or effeminate temper. But indeed it is possible he might see some faults in the captain without any uneasiness at all; for men of true wisdom and goodness are contented to take persons and things as they are, without complaining of their imperfections, or attempting

to amend them. They can see a fault in a friend,
a relation, or an acquaintance, without ever mentioning it to the parties themselves, or to any
others; and this often without lessening their affection. Indeed, unless great discernment be tempered with this overlooking disposition, we ought
never to contract friendship but with a degree of
folly which we can deceive; for I hope my friends
will pardon me when I declare, I know none of
them without a fault; and I should be sorry if I
could imagine I had any friend who could not see
mine. Forgiveness of this kind we give and demand in turn. It is an exercise of friendship, and
perhaps none of the least pleasant. And this forgiveness we must bestow, without desire of amendment. There is, perhaps, no surer mark of folly,
than an attempt to correct the natural infirmities
of those we love. The finest composition of human nature, as well as the finest china, may have a
flaw in it; and this, I am afraid, in either case, is
equally incurable; though, nevertheless, the pattern may remain of the highest value.

Upon the whole, then, Mr. Allworthy certainly
saw some imperfections in the captain; but as this
was a very artful man, and eternally upon his
guard before him, these appeared to him no more
than blemishes in a good character, which his
goodness made him overlook, and his wisdom prevented him from discovering to the captain himself. Very different would have been his sentiments had he discovered the whole; which perhaps
would in time have been the case, had the husband
and wife long continued this kind of behavior to

each other; but this kind Fortune took effectual means to prevent, by forcing the captain to do that which rendered him again dear to his wife, and restored all her tenderness and affection towards him.

CHAPTER VIII

A receipt to regain the lost affections of a wife, which hath
never been known to fail in the most desperate cases.

THE captain was made large amends for the
unpleasant minutes which he passed in
the conversation of his wife (and which
were as few as he could contrive to make them),
by the pleasant meditations he enjoyed when
alone.

These meditations were entirely employed on
Mr. Allworthy's fortune; for, first, he exercised
much thought in calculating, as well as he could,
the exact value of the whole: which calculations
he often saw occasion to alter in his own favor:
and, secondly and chiefly, he pleased himself with
intended alterations in the house and gardens, and
in projecting many other schemes, as well for the
improvement of the estate as of the grandeur of
the place: for this purpose he applied himself to
the studies of architecture and gardening, and
read over many books on both these subjects; for
these sciences, indeed, employed his whole time,
and formed his only amusement. He at last completed a most excellent plan: and very sorry we
are, that it is not in our power to present it to
our reader, since even the luxury of the present
age, I believe, would hardly match it. It had, indeed, in a superlative degree, the two principal in-

gredients which serve to recommend all great and noble designs of this nature; for it required an immoderate expense to execute, and a vast length of time to bring it to any sort of perfection. The former of these, the immense wealth of which the captain supposed Mr. Allworthy possessed, and which he thought himself sure of inheriting, promised very effectually to supply; and the latter, the soundness of his own constitution, and his time of life, which was only what is called middle-aged, removed all apprehension of his not living to accomplish.

Nothing was wanting to enable him to enter upon the immediate execution of this plan, but the death of Mr. Allworthy; in calculating which he had employed much of his own algebra, besides purchasing every book extant that treats of the value of lives, reversions, &c. From all which he satisfied himself, that as he had every day a chance of this happening, so had he more than an even chance of its happening within a few years.

But while the captain was one day busied in deep contemplations of this kind, one of the most unlucky as well as unseasonable accidents happened to him. The utmost malice of Fortune could, indeed, have contrived nothing so cruel, so mal-a-propos, so absolutely destructive to all his schemes. In short, not to keep the reader in long suspense, just at the very instant when his heart was exulting in meditations on the happiness which would accrue to him by Mr. Allworthy's death, he himself—died of an apoplexy.

This unfortunately befel the captain as he was

taking his evening walk by himself, so that nobody was present to lend him any assistance, if
indeed, any assistance could have preserved him.
He took, therefore, measure of that proportion of
soil which was now become adequate to all his future purposes, and he lay dead on the ground, a
great (though not a living) example of the truth
of that observation of Horace:

> *Tu secanda marmora*
> *Locas sub ipsum funus; et sepulchri*
> *Immemor, struis domos.*

Which sentiment I shall thus give to the English
reader: "You provide the noblest materials for
building, when a pickaxe and a spade are only necessary: and build houses of five hundred by a
hundred feet, forgetting that of six by two."

CHAPTER IX

A proof of the infallibility of the foregoing receipt, in the lamentations of the widow; with other suitable decorations of death, such as physicians, &c., and an epitaph in the true style.

MR. Allworthy, his sister, and another lady, were assembled at the accustomed hour in the supper-room, where, having waited a considerable time longer than usual, Mr. Allworthy first declared he began to grow uneasy at the captain's stay (for he was always most punctual at his meals); and gave orders that the bell should be rung without the doors, and especially towards those walks which the captain was wont to use.

All these summons proving ineffectual (for the captain had, by perverse accident, betaken himself to a new walk that evening), Mrs. Blifil declared she was seriously frightened. Upon which the other lady, who was one of her most intimate acquaintance, and who well knew the true state of her affections, endeavored all she could to pacify her, telling her—To be sure she could not help being uneasy; but that she should hope the best. That, perhaps the sweetness of the evening had inticed the captain to go farther than his usual walk: or he might be detained at some neighbor's. Mrs. Blifil answered, No; she was sure some accident had befallen him; for that he would never stay out without sending her word, as he must know how uneasy it would make her. The other lady, having no other arguments to use, betook herself to the entreaties usual on such occasions, and begged her not to frighten herself, for it might be of very ill consequence to her own health; and, filling out a very large glass of wine, advised, and at last prevailed with her to drink it.

Mr. Allworthy now returned into the parlor; for he had been himself in search after the captain. His countenance sufficiently showed the consternation he was under, which, indeed, had a good deal deprived him of speech; but as grief operates variously on different minds, so the same apprehension which depressed his voice, elevated that of Mrs. Blifil. She now began to bewail herself in very bitter terms, and floods of tears accompanied her lamentations; which the lady, her companion, declared she could not blame, but at the same time dissuaded her from indulging; attempting to moderate the grief of her friend by philosophical observations on the many disappointments to which human life is daily subject, which, she said, was a sufficient consideration to fortify our minds against any accidents, how sudden or terrible soever. She said her brother's example ought to teach her patience, who, though indeed he could not be supposed as much concerned as herself, yet was, doubtless, very uneasy, though his resignation to the Divine will had restrained his grief within due bounds.

"Mention not my brother," said Mrs. Blifil;

I—8

"I alone am the object of your pity. What are the terrors of friendship to what a wife feels on these occasions? Oh, he is lost! Somebody hath murdered him—I shall never see him more!"—Here a torrent of tears had the same consequence with what the suppression had occasioned to Mr. Allworthy, and she remained silent.

At this interval a servant came running in, out of breath, and cried out, The captain was found; and before he could proceed farther, he was followed by two more, bearing the dead body between them.

Here the curious reader may observe another diversity in the operations of grief: for as Mr. Allworthy had been before silent, from the same cause which had made his sister vociferous; so did the present sight, which drew tears from the gentleman, put an entire stop to those of the lady; who first gave a violent scream, and presently after fell into a fit.

The room was soon full of servants, some of whom, with the lady visitant, were employed in care of the wife; and others, with Mr. Allworthy, assisted in carrying off the captain to a warm bed; where every method was tried, in order to restore him to life.

And glad should we be, could we inform the reader that both these bodies had been attended with equal success; for those who undertook the care of the lady succeeded so well, that, after the fit had continued a decent time, she again revived, to their great satisfaction: but as to the captain, all experiments of bleeding, chafing, dropping,

&c., proved ineffectual. Death, that inexorable judge, had passed sentence on him, and refused to grant him a reprieve, though two doctors who arrived, and were fee'd at one and the same instant, were his counsel.

These two doctors, whom, to avoid any malicious applications, we shall distinguish by the names of Dr. Y. and Dr. Z., having felt his pulse; to wit, Dr. Y. his right arm, and Dr. Z. his left; both agreed that he was absolutely dead; but as to the distemper, or cause of his death, they differed; Dr. Y. holding that he died of an apoplexy, and Dr. Z. of an epilepsy.

Hence arose a dispute between the learned men, in which each delivered the reasons of their several opinions. These were of such equal force, that they served both to confirm either doctor in his own sentiments, and made not the least impression on his adversary.

To say the truth, every physician almost hath his favorite disease, to which he ascribes all the victories obtained over human nature. The gout, the rheumatism, the stone, the gravel, and the consumption, have all their several patrons in the faculty; and none more than the nervous fever, or the fever on the spirits. And here we may account for those disagreements in opinion, concerning the cause of a patient's death, which sometimes occur, between the most learned of the college; and which have greatly surprised that part of the world who have been ignorant of the fact we have above asserted.

The reader may perhaps be surprised, that, in-

stead of endeavoring to revive the patient, the
learned gentlemen should fall immediately into a
dispute on the occasion of his death; but in reality
all such experiments had been made before their
arrival: for the captain was put into a warm bed,
had his veins scarified, his forehead chafed, and
all sorts of strong drops applied to his lips and
nostrils.

The physicians, therefore, finding themselves
anticipated in everything they ordered, were at a
loss how to apply that portion of time which it is
usual and decent to remain for their fee, and
were therefore necessitated to find some subject
or other for discourse; and what could more naturally present itself than that before mentioned?

Our doctors were about to take their leave, when
Mr. Allworthy, having given over the captain, and
acquiesced in the Divine will, began to enquire
after his sister, whom he desired them to visit before their departure.

This lady was now recovered of her fit, and, to
use the common phrase, as well as could be expected for one in her condition. The doctors,
therefore, all previous ceremonies being complied
with, as this was a new patient, attended, according to desire, and laid hold on each of her hands,
as they had before done on those of the corpse.

The case of the lady was in the other extreme
from that of her husband: for as he was past all
the assistance of physic, so in reality she required
none.

There is nothing more unjust than the vulgar
opinion, by which physicians are misrepresented,

as friends to death. On the contrary, I believe, if the number of those who recover by physic could be opposed to that of the martyrs to it, the former would rather exceed the latter. Nay, some are so cautious on this head, that, to avoid a possibility of killing the patient, they abstain from all methods of curing, and prescribe nothing but what can neither do good nor harm. I have heard some of these, with great gravity, deliver it as a maxim, "That Nature should be left to do her own work, while the physician stands by as it were to clap her on the back, and encourage her when she doth well."

So little then did our doctors delight in death, that they discharged the corpse after a single fee; but they were not so disgusted with their living patient; concerning whose case they immediately agreed, and fell to prescribing with great diligence.

Whether, as the lady had at first persuaded her physicians to believe her ill, they had now, in return, persuaded her to believe herself so, I will not determine; but she continued a whole month with all the decorations of sickness. During this time she was visited by physicians, attended by nurses, and received constant messages from her acquaintance to inquire after her health.

At length the decent time for sickness and immoderate grief being expired, the doctors were discharged, and the lady began to see company; being altered only from what she was before, by that color of sadness in which she had dressed her person and countenance.

The captain was now interred, and might, perhaps, have already made a large progress towards oblivion, had not the friendship of Mr. Allworthy taken care to preserve his memory, by the following epitaph, which was written by a man of as great genius as integrity, and one who perfectly well knew the captain.

HERE LIES,

IN EXPECTATION OF A JOYFUL RISING,

THE BODY OF

CAPTAIN JOHN BLIFIL.

LONDON

HAD THE HONOR OF HIS BIRTH,

OXFORD

OF HIS EDUCATION.

HIS PARTS

WERE AN HONOR TO HIS PROFESSION

AND TO HIS COUNTRY:

HIS LIFE, TO HIS RELIGION

AND HUMAN NATURE.

HE WAS A DUTIFUL SON,

A TENDER HUSBAND,

AN AFFECTIONATE FATHER,

A MOST KIND BROTHER,

A SINCERE FRIEND,

A DEVOUT CHRISTIAN,

AND A GOOD MAN.

HIS INCONSOLABLE WIDOW

HATH ERECTED THIS STONE,

THE MONUMENT OF

HIS VIRTUES

AND OF HER AFFECTION,

BOOK III

CONTAINING THE MOST MEMORABLE TRANSACTIONS WHICH PASSED IN THE FAMILY OF MR. ALL-WORTHY, FROM THE TIME WHEN TOMMY JONES ARRIVED AT THE AGE OF FOURTEEN, TILL HE AT-TAINED THE AGE OF NINETEEN. IN THIS BOOK THE READER MAY PICK UP SOME HINTS CONCERN-ING THE EDUCATION OF CHILDREN.

CHAPTER I

Containing little or nothing.

THE reader will be pleased to remember, that, at the beginning of the second book of this history, we gave him a hint of our intention to pass over several large periods of time, in which nothing happened worthy of being recorded in a chronicle of this kind.

In so doing, we do not only consult our own dignity and ease, but the good and advantage of the reader: for besides that by these means we prevent him from throwing away his time, in reading without either pleasure or emolument, we give him, at all such seasons, an opportunity of employing that wonderful sagacity, of which he is master, by filling up these vacant spaces of time with his own conjectures; for which purpose we

119

have taken care to qualify him in the preceding
pages.

For instance, what reader but knows that Mr.
Allworthy felt, at first, for the loss of his friend,
those emotions of grief, which on such occasions
enter into all men whose hearts are not composed
of flint, or their heads of as solid materials?
Again, what reader doth not know that philosophy
and religion in time moderated, and at last extinguished, this grief? The former of these teach-
ings the folly and vanity of it, and the latter correcting it as unlawful, and at the same time as-
suaging it, by raising future hopes and assurances,
which enable a strong and religious mind to take
leave of a friend, on his deathbed, with little less
indifference than if he was preparing for a long
journey; and, indeed, with little less hope of seeing him again.

Nor can the judicious reader be at a greater loss
on account of Mrs. Bridget Blifil, who, he may
be assured, conducted herself through the whole
season in which grief is to make its appearance on
the outside of the body, with the strictest regard
to all the rules of custom and decency, suiting the
alterations of her countenance to the several alterations of her habit: for as this changed from
weeds to black, from black to gray, from gray to
white, so did her countenance change from dismal
to sorrowful, from sorrowful to sad, and from sad
to serious, till the day came in which she was allowed to return to her former serenity.

We have mentioned these two, as examples only
of the task which may be imposed on readers of

the lowest class. Much higher and harder exercises of judgment and penetration may reasonably be expected from the upper graduates in criticism. Many notable discoveries will, I doubt not, be made by such, of the transactions which happened in the family of our worthy man, during all the years which we have thought proper to pass over: for though nothing worthy of a place in this history occurred within that period, yet did several incidents happen of equal importance with those reported by the daily and weekly historians of the age; in reading which great numbers of persons consume a considerable part of their time, very little, I am afraid, to their emolument. Now, in the conjectures here proposed, some of the most excellent faculties of the mind may be employed to much advantage, since it is a more useful capacity to be able to foretell the actions of men, in any circumstance, from their characters, than to judge of their characters from their actions. The former, I own, requires the greater penetration; but may be accomplished by true sagacity with no less certainty than the latter.

As we are sensible that much the greatest part of our readers are very eminently possessed of this quality, we have left them a space of twelve years to exert it in; and shall now bring forth our hero, at about fourteen years of age, not questioning that many have been long impatient to be introduced to his acquaintance.

CHAPTER II.

The hero of this great history appears with very bad omens. A little tale of so LOW a kind that some may think it not worth their notice. A word or two concerning a squire, and more relating to a gamekeeper and a schoolmaster.

AS we determined, when we first sat down to write this history, to flatter no man, but to guide our pen throughout by the directions of truth, we are obliged to bring our hero on the stage in a much more disadvantageous manner than we could wish; and to declare honestly, even at his first appearance, that it was the universal opinion of all Mr. Allworthy's family that he was certainly born to be hanged.

Indeed, I am sorry to say there was too much reason for this conjecture; the lad having from his earliest years discovered a propensity to many vices, and especially to one which hath as direct a tendency as any other to that fate which we have just now observed to have been prophetically denounced against him: he had been already convicted of three robberies, viz., of robbing an orchard, of stealing a duck out of a farmer's yard, and of picking Master Blifil's pocket of a ball.

The vices of this young man were, moreover, heightened by the disadvantageous light in which they appeared when opposed to the virtues of

122

Master Blifil, his companion; a youth of so different a cast from little Jones, that not only the family but all the neighborhood resounded his praises.
He was, indeed, a lad of a remarkable disposition;
sober, discreet, and pious beyond his age; qualities which gained him the love of every one who
knew him: while Tom Jones was universally disliked; and many expressed their wonder that Mr.
Allworthy would suffer such a lad to be educated
with his nephew, lest the morals of the latter
should be corrupted by his example.

An incident which happened about this time will
set the characters of these two lads more fairly
before the discerning reader than is in the power
of the longest dissertation.

Tom Jones, who, bad as he is, must serve for the
hero of this history, had only one friend among
all the servants of the family; for as to Mrs. Wilkins, she had long since given him up, and was
perfectly reconciled to her mistress. This friend
was the gamekeeper, a fellow of a loose kind of
disposition, and who was thought not to entertain
much stricter notions concerning the difference of
meum and *tuum* than the young gentleman himself. And hence this friendship gave occasion to
many sarcastical remarks among the domestics,
most of which were either proverbs before, or at
least are become so now; and, indeed, the wit of
them all may be comprised in that short Latin
proverb, *"Noscitur a socio;"* which, I think, is
thus expressed in English, "You may know him
by the company he keeps."

To say the truth, some of that atrocious wickedness in Jones, of which we have just mentioned three examples, might perhaps be derived from the encouragement he had received from this fellow, who, in two or three instances, had been what the law calls an accessory after the fact: for the whole duck, and great part of the apples, were converted to the use of the gamekeeper and his family; though, as Jones alone was discovered, the poor lad bore not only the whole smart, but the whole blame; both which fell again to his lot on the following occasion.

Contiguous to Mr. Allworthy's estate was the manor of one of those gentlemen who are called preservers of the game. This species of men, from the great severity with which they revenge the death of a hare or partridge, might be thought to cultivate the same superstition with the Bannians in India; many of whom, we are told, dedicate their whole lives to the preservation and protection of certain animals; was it not that our English Bannians, while they preserve them from other enemies, will most unmercifully slaughter whole horse-loads themselves; so that they stand clearly acquitted of any such heathenish superstition.

I have, indeed, a much better opinion of this kind of men than is entertained by some, as I take them to answer the order of Nature, and the good purposes for which they were ordained, in a more ample manner than many others. Now, as Horace tells us that there are a set of human beings

Fruges consumere nati,

"Born to consume the fruits of the earth;" so I make no manner of doubt but that there are others

Feras consumere nati,

"Born to consume the beasts of the field;" or, as it is commonly called, the game; and none, I believe, will deny but that those squires fulfill this end of their creation.

Little Jones went one day a shooting with the gamekeeper; when happening to spring a covey of partridges near the border of that manor over which Fortune, to fulfill the wise purposes of Nature, had planted one of the game consumers, the birds flew into it, and were marked (as it is called) by the two sportsmen, in some furze bushes, about two or three hundred paces beyond Mr. Allworthy's dominions.

Mr. Allworthy had given the fellow strict orders, on pain of forfeiting his place, never to trespass on any of his neighbors; no more on those who were less rigid in this matter than on the lord of this manor. With regard to others, indeed, these orders had not been always very scrupulously kept; but as the disposition of the gentleman with whom the partridges had taken sanctuary was well known, the gamekeeper had never yet attempted to invade his territories. Nor had he done it now, had not the younger sportsman, who was excessively eager to pursue the flying game, over-persuaded him; but Jones being very importunate, the other, who was himself keen enough after the sport, yielded to his persuasions, entered the manor, and shot one of the partridges.

The gentleman himself was at that time on horseback, at a little distance from them; and hearing the gun go off, he immediately made towards the place, and discovered poor Tom; for the gamekeeper had leaped into the thickest part of the furze-brake, where he had happily concealed himself.

The gentleman having searched the lad, and found the partridge upon him, denounced great vengeance, swearing he would acquaint Mr. Allworthy. He was as good as his word: for he rode immediately to his house, and complained of the trespass on his manor in as high terms and as bitter language as if his house had been broken open, and the most valuable furniture stole out of it. He added, that some other person was in his company, though he could not discover him; for that two guns had been discharged almost in the same instant. And, says he, "We have found only this partridge, but the Lord knows what mischief they have done."

At his return home, Tom was presently convened before Mr. Allworthy. He owned the fact, and alleged no other excuse but what was really true, viz., that the covey was originally sprung in Mr. Allworthy's own manor.

Tom was then interrogated who was with him, which Mr. Allworthy declared he was resolved to know, acquainting the culprit with the circumstance of the two guns, which had been deposed by the squire and both his servants; but Tom stoutly persisted in asserting that he was alone; yet, to say the truth, he hesitated a little at first, which would have confirmed Mr. Allworthy's belief, had what the squire and his servants said wanted any further confirmation.

The gamekeeper, being a suspected person, was now sent for, and the question put to him; but he, relying on the promise which Tom had made him, to take all upon himself, very resolutely denied being in company with the young gentleman, or indeed having seen him the whole afternoon.

Mr. Allworthy then turned towards Tom with more than usual anger in his countenance, and advised him to confess who was with him; repeating, that he was resolved to know. The lad, however, still maintained his resolution, and was dismissed with much wrath by Mr. Allworthy, who told him he should have to the next morning to consider of it, when he should be questioned by another person, and in another manner.

Poor Jones spent a very melancholy night; and the more so, as he was without his usual companion; for Master Blifil was gone abroad on a visit with his mother. Fear of the punishment he was to suffer was on this occasion his least evil; his chief anxiety being, lest his constancy should fail him, and he should be brought to betray the gamekeeper, whose ruin he knew must now be the consequence.

Nor did the gamekeeper pass his time much better. He had the same apprehensions with the youth; for whose honor he had likewise a much tenderer regard than for his skin.

In the morning, when Tom attended the reverend Mr. Thwackum, the person to whom Mr. All-

worthy had committed the instruction of the two
boys, he had the same questions put to him by that
gentleman which he had been asked the evening
before, to which he returned the same answers.
The consequence of this was, so severe a whipping,
that it possibly fell little short of the torture with
which confessions are in some countries extorted
from criminals.

Tom bore his punishment with great resolution;
and though his master asked him, between every
stroke, whether he would not confess, he was contented to be flayed rather than betray his friend,
or break the promise he had made.

The gamekeeper was now relieved from his anxiety, and Mr. Allworthy himself began to be concerned at Tom's sufferings: for besides that Mr.
Thwackum, being highly enraged that he was not
able to make the boy say what he himself pleased,
had carried his severity much beyond the good
man's intention, this latter began now to suspect
that the squire had been mistaken; which his extreme eagerness and anger seemed to make probable; and as for what the servants had said in
confirmation of their master's account, he laid no
great stress upon that. Now, as cruelty and injustice were two ideas of which Mr. Allworthy
could by no means support the consciousness a
single moment, he sent for Tom, and after many
kind and friendly exhortations, said, "I am convinced, my dear child, that my suspicions have
wronged you; I am sorry that you have been so
severely punished on this account." And at last
gave him a little horse to make him amends;

again repeating his sorrow for what had passed.

Tom's guilt now flew in his face more than any severity could make it. He could more easily bear the lashes of Thwackum, than the generosity of Allworthy. The tears burst from his eyes, and he fell upon his knees, crying, "Oh, sir, you are too good to me. Indeed you are. Indeed I don't deserve it." And at that very instant, from the fullness of his heart, had almost betrayed the secret; but the good genius of the gamekeeper suggested to him what might be the consequence to the poor fellow, and this consideration sealed his lips.

Thwackum did all he could to persuade Allworthy from showing any compassion or kindness to the boy, saying, "He had persisted in an untruth;" and gave some hints that a second whipping might probably bring the matter to light.

But Mr. Allworthy absolutely refused to consent to the experiment. He said, the boy had suffered enough already for concealing the truth, even if he was guilty, seeing that he could have no motive but a mistaken point of honor for so doing.

"Honor!" cried Thwackum, with some warmth, "mere stubbornness and obstinacy! Can honor teach any one to tell a lie, or can any honor exist independent of religion?"

This discourse happened at table when dinner was just ended; and there were present Mr. Allworthy, Mr. Thwackum, and a third gentleman, who now entered into the debate, and whom, before we proceed any further, we shall briefly introduce to our reader's acquaintance.

CHAPTER III

The character of Mr. Square the philosopher, and of Mr. Thwackum the divine; with a dispute concerning——

THE name of this gentleman, who had then resided some time at Mr. Allworthy's house, was Mr. Square. His natural parts were not of the first rate, but he had greatly improved them by a learned education. He was deeply read in the ancients, and a professed master of all the works of Plato and Aristotle. Upon which great models he had principally formed himself; sometimes according with the opinion of the one, and sometimes with that of the other. In morals he was a professed Platonist, and in religion he inclined to be an Aristotelian.

But though he had, as we have said, formed his morals on the Platonic model, yet he perfectly agreed with the opinion of Aristotle, in considering that great man rather in the quality of a philosopher or a speculatist, than as a legislator. This sentiment he carried a great way; indeed, so far, as to regard all virtue as matter of theory only. This, it is true, he never affirmed, as I have heard, to any one; and yet upon the least attention to his conduct, I cannot help thinking it was his real opinion, as it will perfectly reconcile some contradictions which might otherwise appear in his character.

This gentleman and Mr. Thwackum scarce ever met without a disputation; for their tenets were indeed diametrically opposite to each other. Square held human nature to be the perfection of all virtue, and that vice was a deviation from our nature, in the same manner as deformity of body is. Thwackum, on the contrary, maintained that the human mind, since the fall, was nothing but a sink of iniquity, till purified and redeemed by grace. In one point only they agreed, which was, in all their discourses on morality never to mention the word goodness. The favorite phrase of the former, was the natural beauty of virtue; that of the latter, was the divine power of grace. The former measured all actions by the unalterable rule of right, and the eternal fitness of things; the latter decided all matters by authority; but in doing this, he always used the scriptures and their commentators, as the lawyer doth his Coke upon Lyttleton, where the comment is of equal authority with the text.

After this short introduction, the reader will be pleased to remember, that the parson had concluded his speech with a triumphant question, to which he had apprehended no answer; viz., Can any honor exist independent on religion?

To this Square answered; that it was impossible to discourse philosophically concerning words, till their meaning was first established: that there were scarce any two words of a more vague and uncertain signification, than the two he had mentioned; for that there were almost as many different opinions concerning honor, as concerning reli-

gion. "But," says he, "if by honor you mean the
true natural beauty of virtue, I will maintain it
may exist independent of any religion whatever.
Nay," added he, "you yourself will allow it may
exist independent of all but one: so will a Ma-
hometan, a Jew, and all the maintainers of all the
different sects in the world."

Thwackum replied, this was arguing with the
usual malice of all the enemies to the true Church.
He said, he doubted not but that all the infidels
and heretics in the world would, if they could, confine honor to their own absurd errors and
damnable deceptions; "but honor," says he, "is
not therefore manifold, because there are many
absurd opinions about it; nor is religion manifold,
because there are various sects and heresies in the
world. When I mention religion, I mean the
Christian religion; and not only the Christian religion, but the Protestant religion; and not only
the Protestant religion, but the Church of England. And when I mention honor, I mean that
mode of Divine grace which is not only consistent
with, but dependent upon, this religion; and is
consistent with and dependent upon no other.
Now to say that the honor I here mean, and which
was, I thought, all the honor I could be supposed
to mean, will uphold, much less dictate an untruth,
is to assert an absurdity too shocking to be conceived."

"I purposely avoided," says Square, "drawing
a conclusion which I thought evident from what
I have said; but if you perceived it, I am sure you
have not attempted to answer it. However, to

drop the article of religion, I think it is plain, from what you have said, that we have different ideas of honor; or why do we not agree in the same terms of its explanation? I have asserted, that true honor and true virtue are almost synonymous terms, and they are both founded on the unalterable rule of right, and the eternal fitness of things; to which an untruth being absolutely repugnant and contrary, it is certain that true honor cannot support an untruth. In this, therefore, I think we are agreed; but that this honor can be said to be founded on religion, to which it is antecedent, if by religion be meant any positive law——"

"I agree," answered Thwackum, with great warmth, "with a man who asserts honor to be antecedent to religion! Mr. Allworthy did I agree——?"

He was proceeding when Mr. Allworthy interposed, telling them very coldly, they had both mistaken his meaning; for that he had said nothing of true honor.—It is possible, however, he would not have easily quieted the disputants, who were growing equally warm, had not another matter now fallen out, which put a final end to the conversation at present.

CHAPTER IV

Containing a necessary apology for the author; and a childish
incident, which perhaps requires an apology likewise.

BEFORE I proceed farther, I shall beg leave
to obviate some misconstructions into
which the zeal of some few readers may
lead them; for I would not willingly give offense
to any, especially to men who are warm in the
cause of virtue or religion.

I hope, therefore, no man will, by the grossest
misunderstanding or perversion of my meaning,
misrepresent me, as endeavoring to cast any ridicule on the greatest perfections of human nature;
and which do, indeed, alone purify and ennoble
the heart of man, and raise him above the brute
creation. This, reader, I will venture to say (and
by how much the better man you are yourself, by
so much the more will you be inclined to believe
me), that I would rather have buried the sentiments of these two persons in eternal oblivion,
than have done any injury to either of these glorious causes.

On the contrary, it is with a view to their service, that I have taken upon me to record the lives
and actions of two of their false and pretended
champions. A treacherous friend is the most
dangerous enemy; and I will say boldly, that both
religion and virtue have received more real dis-

134

credit from hypocrites than the wittiest profligates or infidels could ever cast upon them: nay, farther, as these two, in their purity, are rightly called the bands of civil society, and are indeed the greatest of blessings; so when poisoned and corrupted with fraud, pretense, and affectation, they have become the worst of civil curses, and have enabled men to perpetrate the most cruel mischiefs to their own species.

Indeed, I doubt not but this ridicule will in general be allowed: my chief apprehension is, as many true and just sentiments often came from the mouths of these persons, lest the whole should be taken together, and I should be conceived to ridicule all alike. Now the reader will be pleased to consider, that, as neither of these men were fools, they could not be supposed to have holden none but wrong principles, and to have uttered nothing but absurdities; what injustice, therefore, must I have done to their characters, had I selected only what was bad! And how horribly wretched and maimed must their arguments have appeared!

Upon the whole, it is not religion or virtue, but the want of them, which is here exposed. Had not Thwackum too much neglected virtue, and Square, religion, in the composition of their several systems, and had not both utterly discarded all natural goodness of heart, they had never been represented as the objects of derision in this history; in which we will now proceed.

This matter then, which put an end to the debate mentioned in the last chapter, was no other

than a quarrel between Master Blifil and Tom
Jones, the consequence of which had been a bloody
nose to the former; for though Master Blifil, notwithstanding he was the younger, was in size
above the other's match, yet Tom was much his
superior at the noble art of boxing.

Tom, however, cautiously avoided all engage-
ments with that youth; for besides that Tommy
Jones was an inoffensive lad amidst all his
roguery, and really loved Blifil, Mr. Thwackum
being always the second of the latter, would have
been sufficient to deter him.

But well says a certain author, No man is wise
at all hours; it is therefore no wonder that a boy
is not so. A difference arising at play between
the two lads, Master Blifil called Tom a beggarly
bastard. Upon which the latter, who was somewhat passionate in his disposition, immediately
caused that phenomenon in the face of the former,
which we have above remembered.

Master Blifil now, with his blood running from
his nose, and the tears galloping after from his
eyes, appeared before his uncle and the tremendous Thwackum. In which court an indictment of
assault, battery, and wounding, was instantly preferred against Tom; who in his excuse only
pleaded the provocation, which was indeed all the
matter that Master Blifil had omitted.

It is indeed possible that this circumstance
might have escaped his memory; for, in his reply,
he positively insisted, that he had made use of no
such appellation; adding, "Heaven forbid such

naughty words should ever come out of his mouth!''

Tom, though against all form of law, rejoined in affirmance of the words. Upon which Master Blifil said, ''It is no wonder. Those who will tell one fib, will hardly stick at another. If I had told my master such a wicked fib as you have done, I should be ashamed to show my face.''

''What fib, child?'' cries Thwackum pretty eagerly.

''Why, he told you that nobody was with him a shooting when he killed the partridge; but he knows'' (here he burst into a flood of tears), ''yes, he knows, for he confessed it to me, that Black George the gamekeeper was there. Nay, he said —yes you did—deny it if you can, that you would not have confessed the truth, though master had cut you to pieces.''

At this the fire flashed from Thwackum's eyes, and he cried out in triumph—''Oh! ho! this is your mistaken notion of honor! This is the boy who was not to be whipped again!'' But Mr. Allworthy, with a more gentle aspect, turned towards the lad, and said, ''Is this true, child? How came you to persist so obstinately in a falsehood?''

Tom said, ''He scorned a lie as much as any one: but he thought his honor engaged him to act as he did; for he had promised the poor fellow to conceal him: which,'' he said, ''he thought himself farther obliged to, as the gamekeeper had begged him not to go into the gentleman's manor, and had at last gone himself, in compliance with his persuasions.'' He said, ''This was the whole truth of the matter, and he would take his oath of it;'' and concluded with very passionately begging Mr. Allworthy ''to have compassion on the poor fellow's family, especially as he himself only had been guilty, and the other had been very difficultly prevailed on to do what he did. Indeed, sir,'' said he, ''it could hardly be called a lie that I told; for the poor fellow was entirely innocent of the whole matter. I should have gone alone after the birds; nay, I did go at first, and he only followed me to prevent more mischief. Do, pray, sir, let me be punished; take my little horse away again; but pray, sir, forgive poor George.''

Mr. Allworthy hesitated a few moments, and then dismissed the boys, advising them to live more friendly and peaceably together.

CHAPTER V

IT is probable, that by disclosing this secret, which had been communicated in the utmost confidence to him, young Blifil preserved his companion from a good lashing; for the offense of the bloody nose would have been of itself sufficient cause for Thwackum to have proceeded to correction; but now this was totally absorbed in the consideration of the other matter; and with regard to this, Mr. Allworthy declared privately, he thought the boy deserved reward rather than punishment, so that Thwackum's hand was withheld by a general pardon.

Thwackum, whose meditations were full of birch, exclaimed against this weak, and, as he said he would venture to call it, wicked lenity. To remit the punishment of such crimes was, he said, to encourage them. He enlarged much on the correction of children, and quoted many texts from Solomon, and others; which being to be found in so many other books, shall not be found here. He then applied himself to the vice of lying, on which head he was altogether as learned as he had been on the other.

Square said, he had been endeavoring to recon-

139

cile the behavior of Tom with his idea of perfect virtue, but could not. He owned there was something which at first sight appeared like fortitude in the action; but as fortitude was a virtue, and falsehood a vice, they could by no means agree or unite together. He added, that as this was in some measure to confound virtue and vice, it might be worth Mr. Thwackum's consideration, whether a larger castigation might not be laid on upon the account.

As both these learned men concurred in censuring Jones, so were they no less unanimous in applauding Master Blifil. To bring truth to light, was by the parson asserted to be the duty of every religious man; and by the philosopher this was declared to be highly conformable with the rule of right, and the eternal and unalterable fitness of things.

All this, however, weighed very little with Mr. Allworthy. He could not be prevailed on to sign the warrant for the execution of Jones. There was something within his own breast with which the invincible fidelity which that youth had preserved, corresponded much better than it had done with the religion of Thwackum, or with the virtue of Square. He therefore strictly ordered the former of these gentlemen to abstain from laying violent hands on Tom for what had passed. The pedagogue was obliged to obey those orders; but not without great reluctance, and frequent mutterings that the boy would be certainly spoiled.

Towards the gamekeeper the good man behaved with more severity. He presently summoned that

poor fellow before him, and after many bitter re-
monstrances, paid him his wages, and dismissed
him from his service; for Mr. Allworthy rightly
observed, that there was a great difference between being guilty of a falsehood to excuse yourself, and to excuse another. He likewise urged,
as the principal motive to his inflexible severity
against this man, that he had basely suffered Tom
Jones to undergo so heavy a punishment for his
sake, whereas he ought to have prevented it by
making the discovery himself.

When this story became public, many people
differed from Square and Thwackum, in judging
the conduct of the two lads on the occasion. Master Blifil was generally called a sneaking rascal,
a poor-spirited wretch, with other epithets of the
like kind; whilst Tom was honored with the appel-
lations of a brave lad, a jolly dog, and an honest
fellow. Indeed, his behavior to Black George
much ingratiated him with all the servants; for
though that fellow was before universally disliked, yet he was no sooner turned away than he
was as universally pitied; and the friendship and
gallantry of Tom Jones was celebrated by them
all with the highest applause; and they condemned
Master Blifil as openly as they durst, without in-
curring the danger of offending his mother. For
all this, however, poor Tom smarted in the flesh;
for though Thwackum had been inhibited to exercise his arm on the foregoing account, yet, as the
proverb says, It is easy to find a stick, &c. So
was it easy to find a rod; and, indeed, the not being able to find one was the only thing which could

have kept Thwackum any longer time from chastising poor Jones.

Had the bare delight in the sport been the only inducement to the pedagogue, it is probable Master Blifil would likewise have had his share; but though Mr. Allworthy had given him frequent orders to make no difference between the lads, yet was Thwackum altogether as kind and gentle to this youth, as he was harsh, nay even barbarous, to the other. To say the truth, Blifil had greatly gained his master's affection; partly by the profound respect he always showed his person, but much more by the decent reverence with which he received his doctrine; for he had got by heart, and frequently repeated, his phrases, and maintained all his master's religious principles with a zeal which was surprising in one so young, and which greatly endeared him to the worthy preceptor.

Tom Jones, on the other hand, was not only deficient in outward tokens of respect, often forgetting to pull off his hat, or to bow at his master's approach; but was altogether as unmindful both of his master's precepts and example. He was indeed a thoughtless, giddy youth, with little sobriety in his manners, and less in his countenance; and would often very impudently and indecently laugh at his companion for his serious behavior.

Mr. Square had the same reason for his preference of the former lad; for Tom Jones showed no more regard to the learned discourses which this gentleman would sometimes throw away upon him, than to those of Thwackum. He once ventured to make a jest of the rule of right; and at another time said, he believed there was no rule in the world capable of making such a man as his father (for so Mr. Allworthy suffered himself to be called).

Master Blifil, on the contrary, had address enough at sixteen to recommend himself at one and the same time to both these opposites. With one he was all religion, with the other he was all virtue. And when both were present, he was profoundly silent, which both interpreted in his favor and in their own.

Nor was Blifil contented with flattering both these gentlemen to their faces; he took frequent occasions of praising them behind their backs to Allworthy; before whom, when they two were alone, and his uncle commended any religious or virtuous sentiment (for many such came constantly from him) he seldom failed to ascribe it to the good instructions he had received from either Thwackum or Square; for he knew his uncle repeated all such compliments to the persons for whose use they were meant; and he found by experience the great impressions which they made on the philosopher, as well as on the divine: for, to say the truth, there is no kind of flattery so irresistible as this, at second hand.

The young gentleman, moreover, soon perceived how extremely grateful all those panegyrics on his instructors were to Mr. Allworthy himself, as they so loudly resounded the praise of that singular plan of education which he had laid down; for this worthy man having observed the imperfect institution of our public schools, and the many

vices which boys were there liable to learn, had resolved to educate his nephew, as well as the other
lad, whom he had in a manner adopted, in his own
house; where he thought their morals would escape all that danger of being corrupted to which
they would be unavoidably exposed in any public
school or university.

Having, therefore, determined to commit these
boys to the tuition of a private tutor, Mr.
Thwackum was recommended to him for that office, by a very particular friend, of whose understanding Mr. Allworthy had a great opinion, and
in whose integrity he placed much confidence.
This Thwackum was fellow of a college, where he
almost entirely resided; and had a great reputation for learning, religion, and sobriety of manners.   And these were doubtless the qualifications
by which Mr. Allworthy's friend had been induced
to recommend him; though indeed this friend had
some obligations to Thwackum's family, who were
the most considerable persons in a borough which
that gentleman represented in parliament.

Thwackum, at his first arrival, was extremely
agreeable to Allworthy; and indeed he perfectly
answered the character which had been given of
him. Upon longer acquaintance, however, and
more intimate conversation, this worthy man saw
infirmities in the tutor, which he could have
wished him to have been without; though as those
seemed greatly overbalanced by his good qualities,
they did not incline Mr. Allworthy to part with
him: nor would they indeed have justified such a

proceeding; for the reader is greatly mistaken, if he conceives that Thwackum appeared to Mr. Allworthy in the same light as he doth to him in this history; and he is as much deceived, if he imagines that the most intimate acquaintance which he himself could have had with that divine, would have informed him of those things which we, from our inspiration, are enabled to open and discover. Of readers who, from such conceits as these, condemn the wisdom or penetration of Mr. Allworthy, I shall not scruple to say, that they make a very bad and ungrateful use of that knowledge which we have communicated to them.

These apparent errors in the doctrine of Thwackum served greatly to palliate the contrary errors in that of Square, which our good man no less saw and condemned. He thought, indeed, that the different exuberancies of these gentlemen would correct their different imperfections; and that from both, especially with his assistance, the two lads would derive sufficient precepts of true religion and virtue. If the event happened contrary to his expectations, this possibly proceeded from some fault in the plan itself; which the reader hath my leave to discover, if he can: for we do not pretend to introduce any infallible characters into this history; where we hope nothing will be found which hath never yet been seen in human nature.

To return therefore: the reader will not, I think, wonder that the different behavior of the two lads above commemorated, produced the different ef-

I—10

fects of which he hath already seen some instance; and besides this, there was another reason for the conduct of the philosopher and the pedagogue; but this being matter of great importance, we shall reveal it in the next chapter.

CHAPTER VI

Containing a better reason still for the before-mentioned opinions.

IT is to be known then, that those two learned personages, who have lately made a considerable figure on the theater of this history, had, from their first arrival at Mr. Allworthy's house, taken so great an affection, the one to his virtue, the other to his religion, that they had meditated the closest alliance with him.

For this purpose they had cast their eyes on that fair widow, whom, though we have not for some time made any mention of her, the reader, we trust, hath not forgot. Mrs. Blifil was indeed the object to which they both aspired.

It may seem remarkable, that, of four persons whom we have commemorated at Mr. Allworthy's house, three of them should fix their inclinations on a lady who was never greatly celebrated for her beauty, and who was, moreover, now a little descended into the vale of years; but in reality bosom friends, and intimate acquaintance, have a kind of natural propensity to particular females at the house of a friend—viz., to his grandmother, mother, sister, daughter, aunt, niece, or cousin, when they are rich; and to his wife, sister, daughter, niece, cousin, mistress, or servant-maid, if they should be handsome.

We would not, however, have our reader imagine, that persons of such characters as were supported by Thwackum and Square, would undertake a matter of this kind, which hath been a little censured by some rigid moralists, before they had thoroughly examined it, and considered whether it was (as Shakespeare phrases it) "Stuff o' th' conscience," or no. Thwackum was encouraged to the undertaking by reflecting that to covet your neighbor's sister is nowhere forbidden: and he knew it was a rule in the construction of all laws, that *"Expressum facit cessare tacitum."* The sense of which is, "When a lawgiver sets down plainly his whole meaning, we are prevented from making him mean what we please ourselves." As some instances of women, therefore, are mentioned in the divine law, which forbids us to covet our neighbor's goods, and that of a sister omitted, he concluded it to be lawful. And as to Square, who was in his person what is called a jolly fellow, or a widow's man, he easily reconciled his choice to the eternal fitness of things.

Now, as both of these gentlemen were industrious in taking every opportunity of recommending themselves to the widow, they apprehended one certain method was, by giving her son the constant preference to the other lad; and as they conceived the kindness and affection which Mr. Allworthy showed the latter, must be highly disagreeable to her, they doubted not but the laying hold on all occasions to degrade and vilify him, would be highly pleasing to her; who, as she hated the boy, must love all those who did him any hurt. In

this Thwackum had the advantage; for while
Square could only scarify the poor lad's reputation, he could flay his skin; and, indeed, he considered every lash he gave him as a compliment
paid to his mistress; so that he could, with the
utmost propriety, repeat this old flogging line.
"Castigo te non quod odio habeam, sed quod
AMEM.   I chastise thee not out of hatred, but out
of love."   And this, indeed, he often had in his
mouth, or rather, according to the old phrase,
never more properly applied, at his fingers' ends.

For this reason, principally, the two gentlemen
concurred, as we have seen above, in their opinion
concerning the two lads; this being, indeed, almost
the only instance of their concurring on any point;
for, beside the difference of their principles, they
had both long ago strongly suspected each other's
design, and hated one another with no little degree of inveteracy.

This mutual animosity was a good deal increased by their alternate successes; for Mrs. Blifil knew what they would be at long before they
imagined it; or, indeed, intended she should: for
they proceeded with great caution, lest she should
be offended, and acquaint Mr. Allworthy.   But
they had no reason for any such fear; she was
well enough pleased with a passion, of which she
intended none should have any fruits but herself.
And the only fruits she designed for herself were,
flattery and courtship; for which purpose she
soothed them by turns, and a long time equally.
She was, indeed, rather inclined to favor the parson's principles: but Square's person was more

agreeable to her eye, for he was a comely man; whereas the pedagogue did in countenance very nearly resemble that gentleman, who, in the Harlot's Progress, is seen correcting the ladies in Bridewell.

Whether Mrs. Blifil had been surfeited with the sweets of marriage, or disgusted by its bitters, or from what other cause it proceeded, I will not determine; but she could never be brought to listen to any second proposals. However, she at last conversed with Square with such a degree of intimacy that malicious tongues began to whisper things of her, to which, as well for the sake of the lady, as that they were highly disagreeable to the rule of right and the fitness of things, we will give no credit, and therefore shall not blot our paper with them. The pedagogue, 'tis certain, whipped on, without getting a step nearer to his journey's end.

Indeed he had committed a great error and that Square discovered much sooner than himself. Mrs. Blifil (as, perhaps, the reader may have formerly guessed) was not over and above pleased with the behavior of her husband; nay, to be honest, she absolutely hated him, till his death at last a little reconciled him to her affections. It will not be therefore greatly wondered at, if she had not the most violent regard to the offspring she had by him. And, in fact, she had so little of this regard, that in his infancy she seldom saw her son, or took any notice of him; and hence she acquiesced, after a little reluctance, in all the favors which Mr. Allworthy showered on the foundling; whom the good man called his own boy, and in all things put on an entire equality with Master Blifil. This acquiescence in Mrs. Blifil was considered by the neighbors, and by the family, as a mark of her condescension to her brother's humor, and she was imagined by all others, as well as Thwackum and Square, to hate the foundling in her heart; nay, the more civility she showed him, the more they conceived she detested him, and the surer schemes she was laying for his ruin: for as they thought it her interest to hate him, it was very difficult for her to persuade them she did not.

Thwackum was the more confirmed in his opinion, as she had more than once slyly caused him to whip Tom Jones, when Mr. Allworthy, who was an enemy to this exercise, was abroad; whereas she had never given any such orders concerning young Blifil. And this had likewise imposed upon Square. In reality, though she certainly hated her own son—of which, however monstrous it appears, I am assured she is not a singular instance—she appeared, notwithstanding all her outward compliance, to be in her heart sufficiently displeased with all the favor shown by Mr. Allworthy to the foundling. She frequently complained of this behind her brother's back, and very sharply censured him for it, both to Thwackum and Square; nay, she would throw it in the teeth of Allworthy himself, when a little quarrel, or miff, as it is vulgarly called, arose between them.

However, when Tom grew up, and gave tokens

of that gallantry of temper which greatly recommends men to women, this disinclination which
she had discovered to him when a child, by degrees abated, and at last she so evidently demonstrated her affection to him to be much stronger
than what she bore her own son, that it was
impossible to mistake her any longer. She was
so desirous of often seeing him, and discovered such satisfaction and delight in his company,
that before he was eighteen years old he was become a rival to both Square and Thwackum; and
what is worse, the whole country began to talk as
loudly of her inclination to Tom, as they had be.
fore done of that which she had shown to Square:
on which account the philosopher conceived the
most implacable hatred for our poor hero.

CHAPTER VII

In which the author himself makes his appearance on the stage.

THOUGH Mr. Allworthy was not of himself hasty to see things in a disadvantageous light, and was a stranger to the public voice, which seldom reaches to a brother or a husband, though it rings in the ears of all the neighborhood; yet was this affection of Mrs. Blifil to Tom, and the preference which she too visibly gave him to her own son, of the utmost disadvantage to that youth.

For such was the compassion which inhabited Mr. Allworthy's mind, that nothing but the steel of justice could ever subdue it. To be unfortunate in any respect was sufficient, if there was no demerit to counterpoise it, to turn the scale of that good man's pity, and to engage his friendship and his benefaction.

When therefore he plainly saw Master Blifil was absolutely detested (for that he was) by his own mother, he began, on that account only, to look with an eye of compassion upon him; and what the effects of compassion are, in good and benevolent minds, I need not here explain to most of my readers.

Henceforward he saw every appearance of virtue in the youth through the magnifying end, and viewed all his faults with the glass inverted, so

153

that they became scarce perceptible. And this perhaps the amiable temper of pity may make commendable; but the next step the weakness of human nature alone must excuse; for he no sooner perceived that preference which Mrs. Blifil gave to Tom, than that poor youth (however innocent) began to sink in his affections as he rose in hers. This, it is true, would of itself alone never have been able to eradicate Jones from his bosom; but it was greatly injurious to him, and prepared Mr. Allworthy's mind for those impressions which afterwards produced the mighty events that will be contained hereafter in this history; and to which, it must be confessed, the unfortunate lad, by his own wantonness, wildness, and want of caution, too much contributed.

In recording some instances of these, we shall, if rightly understood, afford a very useful lesson to those well-disposed youths who shall hereafter be our readers; for they may here find, that goodness of heart, and openness of temper, though these may give them great comfort within, and administer to an honest pride in their own minds, will by no means, alas! do their business in the world. Prudence and circumspection are necessary even to the best of men. They are indeed, as it were, a guard to Virtue, without which she can never be safe. It is not enough that your designs, nay, that your actions, are intrinsically good; you must take care they shall appear so. If your inside be never so beautiful, you must preserve a fair outside also. This must be constantly looked to, or malice and envy will take care to blacken it so, that the sagacity and goodness of an Allworthy will not be able to see through it, and to discern the beauties within. Let this, my young readers, be your constant maxim, that no man can be good enough to enable him to neglect the rules of prudence; nor will Virtue herself look beautiful, unless she be bedecked with the outward ornaments of decency and decorum. And this precept, my worthy disciples, if you read with due attention, you will, I hope, find sufficiently enforced by examples in the following pages.

I ask pardon for this short appearance, by way of chorus, on the stage. It is in reality for my own sake, that, while I am discovering the rocks on which innocence and goodness often split, I may not be misunderstood to recommend the very means to my worthy readers, by which I intend to show them they will be undone. And this, as I could not prevail on any of my actors to speak, I myself was obliged to declare.

CHAPTER VIII

A childish incident, in which, however, is seen a good-natured
disposition in Tom Jones.

THE reader may remember that Mr. Allworthy gave Tom Jones a little horse, as
a kind of smart-money for the punishment
which he imagined he had suffered innocently.

This horse Tom kept above half a year, and
then rode him to a neighboring fair, and sold him.

At his return, being questioned by Thwackum
what he had done with the money for which the
horse was sold, he frankly declared he would not
tell him.

"Oho!" says Thwackum, "you will not! then I
will have it out of your br——h;" that being the
place to which he always applied for information
on every doubtful occasion.

Tom was now mounted on the back of a footman, and everything prepared for execution, when
Mr. Allworthy, entering the room, gave the criminal a reprieve, and took him with him into another apartment; where, being alone with Tom, he
put the same question to him which Thwackum
had before asked him.

Tom answered, he could in duty refuse him
nothing; but as for that tyrannical rascal, he
would never make him any other answer than

156

with a cudgel, with which he hoped soon to be able to pay him for all his barbarities.

Mr. Allworthy very severely reprimanded the lad for his indecent and disrespectful expressions concerning his master; but much more for his avowing an intention of revenge. He threatened him with the entire loss of his favor, if he ever heard such another word from his mouth; for, he said, he would never support or befriend a reprobate. By these and the like declarations, he extorted some compunction from Tom, in which that youth was not over-sincere; for he really meditated some return for all the smarting favors he had received at the hands of the pedagogue. He was, however, brought by Mr. Allworthy to express a concern for his resentment against Thwackum; and then the good man, after some wholesome admonition, permitted him to proceed, which he did as follows:—

"Indeed, my dear sir, I love and honor you more than all the world: I know the great obligations I have to you, and should detest myself if I thought my heart was capable of ingratitude. Could the little horse you gave me speak, I am sure he could tell you how fond I was of your present; for I had more pleasure in feeding him than in riding him. Indeed, sir, it went to my heart to part with him; nor would I have sold him upon any other account in the world than what I did. You yourself, sir, I am convinced in my case, would have done the same: for none ever so sensibly felt the misfortunes of others. What would you feel, dear sir, if you thought yourself the occasion of them? Indeed, sir, there never was any misery like theirs."

"Like whose, child?" says Allworthy: "What do you mean?"

"Oh, sir!" answered Tom, "your poor game-keeper, with all his large family, ever since your discarding him, have been perishing with all the miseries of cold and hunger: I could not bear to see these poor wretches naked and starving, and at the same time know myself to have been the occasion of all their sufferings. I could not bear it, sir; upon my soul, I could not." [Here the tears ran down his cheeks, and he thus proceeded.] "It was to save them from absolute destruction I parted with your dear present, notwithstanding all the value I had for it: I sold the horse for them, and they have every farthing of the money."

Mr. Allworthy now stood silent for some moments, and before he spoke the tears started from his eyes. He at length dismissed Tom with a gentle rebuke, advising him for the future to apply to him in cases of distress, rather than to use extraordinary means of relieving them himself.

This affair was afterwards the subject of much debate between Thwackum and Square. Thwackum held, that this was flying in Mr. Allworthy's face, who had intended to punish the fellow for his disobedience. He said, in some instances, what the world called charity appeared to him to be opposing the will of the Almighty, which had marked some particular persons for destruction; and that this was in like manner acting in opposition to Mr. Allworthy; concluding, as usual, with a hearty recommendation of birch.

Square argued strongly on the other side, in opposition perhaps to Thwackum, or in compliance with Mr. Allworthy, who seemed very much to approve what Jones had done. As to what he urged on this occasion, as I am convinced most of my readers will be much abler advocates for poor Jones, it would be impertinent to relate it. Indeed it was not difficult to reconcile to the rule of right an action which it would have been impossible to deduce from the rule of wrong.

CHAPTER IX

Containing an incident of a more heinous kind, with the comments of Thwackum and Square.

IT hath been observed by some man of much greater reputation for wisdom than myself, that misfortunes seldom come single. An instance of this may, I believe, be seen in those gentlemen who have the misfortune to have any of their rogueries detected; for here discovery seldom stops till the whole is come out. Thus it happened to poor Tom; who was no sooner pardoned for selling the horse, than he was discovered to have some time before sold a fine Bible which Mr. Allworthy gave him, the money arising from which sale he had disposed of in the same manner. This Bible Master Blifil had purchased, though he had already such another of his own, partly out of respect for the book, and partly out of friendship to Tom, being unwilling that the Bible should be sold out of the family at half-price. He therefore deposited the said half-price himself; for he was a very prudent lad, and so careful of his money, that he had laid up almost every penny which he had received from Mr. Allworthy.

Some people have been noted to be able to read in no book but their own. On the contrary, from

the time when Master Blifil was first possessed of
this Bible, he never used any other. Nay, he was
seen reading in it much oftener than he had before been in his own. Now, as he frequently asked
Thwackum to explain difficult passages to him,
that gentleman unfortunately took notice of Tom's
name, which was written in many parts of the
book. This brought on an inquiry, which obliged
Master Blifil to discover the whole matter.

Thwackum was resolved a crime of this kind,
which he called sacrilege, should not go unpun-
ished. He therefore proceeded immediately to
castigation: and not contented with that he acquainted Mr. Allworthy, at their next meeting,
with this monstrous crime, as it appeared to him:
inveighing against Tom in the most bitter terms,
and likening him to the buyers and sellers who
were driven out of the temple.

Square saw this matter in a very different light.
He said, he could not perceive any higher crime
in selling one book than in selling another. That
to sell Bibles was strictly lawful by all laws both
Divine and human, and consequently there was no
unfitness in it. He told Thwackum, that his great
concern on this occasion brought to his mind the
story of a very devout woman, who, out of pure
regard to religion, stole Tillotson's Sermons from
a lady of her acquaintance.

This story caused a vast quantity of blood to
rush into the parson's face, which of itself was
none of the palest; and he was going to reply with
great warmth and anger, had not Mrs. Blifil, who
was present at this debate, interposed. **That lady**
I—11

declared herself absolutely of Mr. Square's side. She argued, indeed, very learnedly in support of his opinion; and concluded with saying, if Tom had been guilty of any fault, she must confess her own son appeared to be equally culpable; for that she could see no difference between the buyer and the seller; both of whom were alike to be driven out of the temple.

Mrs. Blifil having declared her opinion, put an end to the debate. Square's triumph would almost have stopped his words, had he needed them; and Thwackum, who, for reasons before-mentioned, durst not venture at disobliging the lady, was almost choked with indignation. As to Mr. Allworthy, he said, since the boy had been already punished he would not deliver his sentiments on the occasion; and whether he was or was not angry with the lad, I must leave to the reader's own conjecture.

Soon after this, an action was brought against the gamekeeper by Squire Western (the gentleman in whose manor the partridge was killed), for depredations of the like kind. This was a most unfortunate circumstance for the fellow, as it not only of itself threatened his ruin, but actually prevented Mr. Allworthy from restoring him to his favor: for as that gentleman was walking out one evening with Master Blifil and young Jones, the latter slyly drew him to the habitation of Black George; where the family of that poor wretch, namely, his wife and children, were found in all the misery with which cold, hunger, and nakedness, can affect human creatures: for as to the money they had received from Jones, former debts had consumed almost the whole.

Such a scene as this could not fail of affecting the heart of Mr. Allworthy. He immediately gave the mother a couple of guineas, with which he bid her clothe her children. The poor woman burst into tears at this goodness, and while she was thanking him, could not refrain from expressing her gratitude to Tom; who had, she said, long preserved both her and hers from starving. "We have not," says she, "had a morsel to eat, nor have these poor children had a rag to put on, but what his goodness hath bestowed on us." For, indeed, besides the horse and the Bible, Tom had sacrificed a night-gown, and other things, to the use of this distressed family.

On their return home, Tom made use of all his eloquence to display the wretchedness of these people, and the penitence of Black George himself; and in this he succeeded so well, that Mr. Allworthy said, he thought the man had suffered enough for what was past; that he would forgive him, and think of some means of providing for him and his family.

Jones was so delighted with this news, that, though it was dark when they returned home, he could not help going back a mile, in a shower of rain, to acquaint the poor woman with the glad tidings; but, like other hasty divulgers of news, he only brought on himself the trouble of contradicting it: for the ill fortune of Black George made use of the very opportunity of his friend's absence to overturn all again.

CHAPTER X

In which Master Blifil and Jones appear in different lights.

MASTER Blifil fell very short of his companion in the amiable quality of mercy; but he as greatly exceeded him in one of a much higher kind, namely, in justice: in which he followed both the precepts and example of Thwackum and Square; for though they would both make frequent use of the word mercy, yet it was plain that in reality Square held it to be inconsistent with the rule of right; and Thwackum was for doing justice, and leaving mercy to heaven. The two gentlemen did indeed somewhat differ in opinion concerning the objects of this sublime virtue; by which Thwackum would probably have destroyed one half of mankind, and Square the other half.

Master Blifil then, though he had kept silence in the presence of Jones, yet, when he had better considered the matter, could by no means endure the thought of suffering his uncle to confer favors on the undeserving. He therefore resolved immediately to acquaint him with the fact which we have above slightly hinted to the readers. The truth of which was as follows:

The gamekeeper, about a year after he was dismissed from Mr. Allworthy's service, and before Tom's selling the horse, being in want of bread, either to fill his own mouth or those of his family, as he passed through a field belonging to Mr. Western espied a hare sitting in her form. This hare he had basely and barbarously knocked on the head, against the laws of the land, and no less against the laws of sportsmen.

The higgler to whom the hare was sold, being unfortunately taken many months after with a quantity of game upon him, was obliged to make his peace with the squire, by becoming evidence against some poacher. And now Black George was pitched upon by him, as being a person already obnoxious to Mr. Western, and one of no good fame in the country. He was, besides, the best sacrifice the higgler could make, as he had supplied him with no game since; and by this means the witness had an opportunity of screening his better customers: for the squire, being charmed with the power of punishing Black George, whom a single transgression was sufficient to ruin, made no further inquiry.

Had this fact been truly laid before Mr. Allworthy, it might probably have done the gamekeeper very little mischief. But there is no zeal blinder than that which is inspired with the love of justice against offenders. Master Blifil had forgot the distance of the time. He varied likewise in the manner of the fact: and by the hasty addition of the single letter S he considerably altered the story; for he said that George had wired hares. These alterations might probably have been set right, had not Master Blifil unluckily insisted on a promise of secrecy from Mr. Allworthy before he revealed the matter to him; but by that means the poor gamekeeper was condemned without having an opportunity to defend himself: for as the fact of killing the hare, and of the action brought, were certainly true, Mr. Allworthy had no doubt concerning the rest.

Short-lived then was the joy of these poor people; for Mr. Allworthy the next morning declared he had fresh reason, without assigning it, for his anger, and strictly forbade Tom to mention George any more: though as for his family, he said he would endeavor to keep them from starving; but as to the fellow himself, he would leave him to the laws, which nothing could keep him from breaking.

Tom could by no means divine what had incensed Mr. Allworthy, for of Master Blifil he had not the least suspicion. However, as his friendship was to be tired out by no disappointments, he now determined to try another method of preserving the poor gamekeeper from ruin.

Jones was lately grown very intimate with Mr. Western. He had so greatly recommended himself to that gentleman, by leaping over five-barred gates, and by other acts of sportsmanship, that the squire had declared Tom would certainly make a great man if he had but sufficient encouragement. He often wished he had himself a son with such parts; and one day very solemnly asserted at a drinking bout, that Tom should hunt a pack of hounds for a thousand pound of his money, with any huntsman in the whole country.

By such kind of talents he had so ingratiated

himself with the squire, that he was a most welcome guest at his table, and a favorite companion in his sport: everything which the squire held most dear, to wit, his guns, dogs, and horses, were now as much at the command of Jones, as if they had been his own.   He resolved therefore to make use of this favor on behalf of his friend Black George, whom he hoped to introduce into Mr. Western's family, in the same capacity in which he had before served Mr. Allworthy.

The reader, if he considers that this fellow was already obnoxious to Mr. Western, and if he considers farther the weighty business by which that gentleman's displeasure had been incurred, will perhaps condemn this as a foolish and desperate undertaking; but if he should totally condemn young Jones on that account, he will greatly applaud him for strengthening himself with all imaginable interest on so arduous an occasion.

For this purpose, then, Tom applied to Mr. Western's daughter, a young lady of about seventeen years of age, whom her father, next after those necessary implements of sport just before mentioned, loved and esteemed above all the world. Now, as she had some influence on the squire, so Tom had some little influence on her.   But this being the intended heroine of this work, a lady with whom we ourselves are greatly in love, and with whom many of our readers will probably be in love too, before we part, it is by no means proper she should make her appearance at the end of a book.

BOOK IV

CHAPTER I

Containing five pages of paper.

AS truth distinguishes our writings from those idle romances which are filled with monsters, the productions, not of nature, but of distempered brains; and which have been therefore recommended by an eminent critic to the sole use of the pastry-cook; so, on the other hand, we would avoid any resemblance to that kind of history which a celebrated poet seems to think is no less calculated for the emolument of the brewer, as the reading it should be always attended with a tankard of good ale—

> While—history with her comrade ale,
> Soothes the sad series of her serious tale.

For as this is the liquor of modern historians, nay, perhaps their muse, if we may believe the opinion of Butler, who attributes inspiration to ale, it ought likewise to be the potation of their readers, since every book ought to be read with the same spirit and in the same manner as it is written. Thus the famous author of Hurlothrumbo told a learned bishop, that the reason his

168

lordship could not taste the excellence of his piece was, that he did not read it with a fiddle in his hand; which instrument he himself had always had in his own, when he composed it.

That our work, therefore, might be in no danger of being likened to the labors of these historians, we have taken every occasion of interspersing through the whole sundry similes, descriptions, and other kind of poetical embellishments. These are, indeed, designed to supply the place of the said ale, and to refresh the mind, whenever those slumbers, which in a long work are apt to invade the reader as well as the writer, shall begin to creep upon him. Without interruptions of this kind, the best narrative of plain matter of fact must overpower every reader; for nothing but the everlasting watchfulness, which Homer has ascribed only to Jove himself, can be proof against a newspaper of many volumes.

We shall leave to the reader to determine with what judgment we have chosen the several occasions for inserting those ornamental parts of our work. Surely it will be allowed that none could be more proper than the present, where we are about to introduce a considerable character on the scene; no less, indeed, than the heroine of this heroic, historical, prosaic poem. Here, therefore, we have thought proper to prepare the mind of the reader for her reception, by filling it with every pleasing image which we can draw from the face of nature. And for this method we plead many precedents. First, this is an art well known to, and much practiced by, our tragic poets, who seldom fail to prepare their audience for the reception of their principal characters.

Thus the hero is always introduced with a flourish of drums and trumpets, in order to rouse a martial spirit in the audience, and to accommodate their ears to bombast and fustian, which Mr. Locke's blind man would not have grossly erred in likening to the sound of a trumpet. Again, when lovers are coming forth, soft music often conducts them on the stage, either to soothe the audience with the softness of the tender passion, or to lull and prepare them for that gentle slumber in which they will most probably be composed by the ensuing scene.

And not only the poets, but the masters of these poets, the managers of playhouses, seem to be in this secret; for, besides the aforesaid kettle-drums, &c., which denote the hero's approach, he is generally ushered on the stage by a large troop of half a dozen scene-shifters; and how necessary these are imagined to his appearance, may be concluded from the following theatrical story :—

King Pyrrhus was at dinner at an ale-house bordering on the theater, when he was summoned to go on the stage. The hero, being unwilling to quit his shoulder of mutton, and as unwilling to draw on himself the indignation of Mr. Wilks (his brother-manager) for making the audience wait, had bribed these his harbingers to be out of the way. While Mr. Wilks, therefore, was thundering out, "Where are the carpenters to walk on before King Pyrrhus?" that monarch very quietly eat his mutton, and the audience, however impatient, were obliged to entertain themselves with music in his absence.

To be plain, I much question whether the politician, who hath generally a good nose, hath not scented out somewhat of the utility of this practice. I am convinced that awful magistrate my lord-mayor contracts a good deal of that reverence which attends him through the year, by the several pageants which precede his pomp. Nay, I must confess, that even I myself, who am not remarkably liable to be captivated with show, have yielded not a little to the impressions of much preceding state. When I have seen a man strutting in a procession, after others whose business was only to walk before him, I have conceived a higher notion of his dignity than I have felt on seeing him in a common situation. But there is one instance, which comes exactly up to my purpose. This is the custom of sending on a basket-woman, who is to precede the pomp at a coronation, and to strew the stage with flowers, before the great personages begin their procession. The ancients would certainly have invoked the goddess Flora for this purpose, and it would have been no difficulty for their priests, or politicians to have persuaded the people of the real presence of the deity, though a plain mortal had personated her and performed her office. But we have no such design of imposing on our reader; and therefore those who object to the heathen theology, may, if they please, change our goddess into the above-mentioned basket-woman. Our intention, in short, is to introduce our heroine with the utmost solemnity in our power, with an elevation of style, and all other circumstances proper to raise the veneration of our reader. Indeed we would, for certain causes, advise those of our male readers who have any hearts, to read no farther, were we not well assured, that how amiable soever the picture of our heroine will appear, as it is really a copy from nature, many of our fair countrywomen will be found worthy to satisfy any passion, and to answer any idea of female perfection which our pencil will be able to raise.

And now, without any further preface, we proceed to our next chapter.

CHAPTER II

HUSHED be every ruder breath. May the heathen ruler of the winds confine in iron chains the boisterous limbs of noisy Boreas, and the sharp-pointed nose of bitter-biting Eurus. Do thou, sweet Zephyrus, rising from thy fragrant bed, mount the western sky, and lead on those delicious gales, the charms of which call forth the lovely Flora from her chamber, perfumed with pearly dews, when on the first of June, her birth-day, the blooming maid, in loose attire, gently trips it over the verdant mead, where every flower rises to do her homage, till the whole field becomes enameled, and colors contend with sweets which shall ravish her most.

So charming may she now appear! and you the feathered choristers of nature, whose sweetest notes not even Handel can excel, tune your melodious throats to celebrate her appearance. From love proceeds your music, and to love it returns. Awaken therefore that gentle passion in every swain: for lo! adorned with all the charms in which nature can array her; bedecked with beauty, youth, sprightliness, innocence, modesty, and ten-

173

derness, breathing sweetness from her rosy lips, and darting brightness from her sparkling eyes, the lovely Sophia comes!

Reader, perhaps thou hast seen the statue of the *Venus de Medicis.* Perhaps, too, thou hast seen the gallery of beauties at Hampton Court. Thou mayest remember each bright Churchill of the galaxy, and all the toasts of the Kit-cat. Or, if their reign was before thy times, at least thou hast seen their daughters, the no less dazzling beauties of the present age; whose names, should we here insert, we apprehend they would fill the whole volume.

Now if thou hast seen all these, be not afraid of the rude answer which Lord Rochester once gave to a man who had seen many things. No. If thou hast seen all these without knowing what beauty is, thou hast no eyes; if without feeling its power, thou hast no heart.

Yet is it possible, my friend, that thou mayest have seen all these without being able to form an exact idea of Sophia; for she did not exactly resemble any of them. She was most like the picture of Lady Ranelagh: and, I have heard, more still to the famous duchess of Mazarine; but most of all she resembled one whose image never can depart from my breast, and whom, if thou dost remember, thou hast then, my friend, an adequate idea of Sophia.

But lest this should not have been thy fortune, we will endeavor with our utmost skill to describe this paragon, though we are sensible that our highest abilities are very inadequate to the task.

Sophia, then, the only daughter of Mr. Western, was a middle-sized woman; but rather inclining to tall. Her shape was not only exact, but extremely delicate: and the nice proportion of her arms promised the truest symmetry in her limbs. Her hair, which was black, was so luxuriant, that it reached her middle, before she cut it to comply with the modern fashion; and it was now curled so gracefully in her neck, that few could believe it to be her own. If envy could find any part of the face which demanded less commendation than the rest, it might possibly think her forehead might have been higher without prejudice to her. Her eyebrows were full, even, and arched beyond the power of art to imitate. Her black eyes had a luster in them, which all her softness could not extinguish. Her nose was exactly regular, and her mouth, in which were two rows of ivory, exactly answered Sir John Suckling's description in those lines:—

> Her lips were red, and one was thin,
> Compar'd to that was next her chin.
> Some bee had stung it newly.

Her cheeks were of the oval kind; and in her right she had a dimple, which the least smile discovered. Her chin had certainly its share in forming the beauty of her face; but it was difficult to say it was either large or small, though perhaps it was rather of the former kind. Her complexion had rather more of the lily than of the rose; but when exercise or modesty increased her natural color, no vermilion could equal it. Then one might indeed cry out with the celebrated Dr. Donne:

>——Her pure and eloquent blood
>Spoke in her cheeks, and so distinctly wrought
>That one might almost say her body thought.

Her neck was long and finely turned: and here, if I was not afraid of offending her delicacy, I might justly say, the highest beauties of the famous *Venus de Medicis* were outdone. Here was whiteness which no lilies, ivory, nor alabaster could match. The finest cambric might indeed be supposed from envy to cover that bosom which was much whiter than itself.—It was indeed,

>*Nitor splendens Pario marmore purius.*
>A gloss shining beyond the purest brightness of Parian marble.

Such was the outside of Sophia; nor was this beautiful frame disgraced by an inhabitant unworthy of it. Her mind was every way equal to her person; nay, the latter borrowed some charms from the former; for when she smiled, the sweetness of her temper diffused that glory over her countenance which no regularity of features can give. But as there are no perfections of the mind which do not discover themselves in that perfect intimacy to which we intend to introduce our reader with this charming young creature, so it is needless to mention them here: nay, it is a kind of tacit affront to our reader's understanding, and may also rob him of that pleasure which he will receive in forming his own judgment of her character.

It may, however, be proper to say, that whatever mental accomplishments she had derived from nature, they were somewhat improved and cultivated by art: for she had been educated under the care of an aunt, who was a lady of great discretion, and was thoroughly acquainted with the world, having lived in her youth about the court, whence she had retired some years since into the country. By her conversation and instructions, Sophia was perfectly well bred, though perhaps she wanted a little of that ease in her behavior which is to be acquired only by habit, and living within what is called the polite circle. But this, to say the truth, is often too dearly purchased; and though it hath charms so inexpressible, that the French, perhaps, among other qualities, mean to express this, when they declare they know not what it is; yet its absence is well compensated by innocence; nor can good sense and a natural gentility ever stand in need of it.

CHAPTER III

Wherein the history goes back to commemorate a trifling incident that happened some years since; but which, trifling as it was, had some future consequences.

THE amiable Sophia was now in her eighteenth year, when she is introduced into this history. Her father, as hath been said, was fonder of her than of any other human creature. To her, therefore, Tom Jones applied, in order to engage her interest on the behalf of his friend the gamekeeper.

But before we proceed to this business, a short recapitulation of some previous matters may be necessary.

Though the different tempers of Mr. Allworthy and of Mr. Western did not admit of a very intimate correspondence, yet they lived upon what is called a decent footing together; by which means the young people of both families had been acquainted from their infancy; and as they were all near of the same age, had been frequent playmates together.

The gayety of Tom's temper suited better with Sophia, than the grave and sober disposition of Master Blifil. And the preference which she gave the former of these, would often appear so plainly, that a lad of a more passionate turn than Master

178

Blifil was, might have shown some displeasure
at it.

As he did not, however, outwardly express any
such disgust, it would be an ill office in us to pay
a visit to the inmost recesses of his mind, as some
scandalous people search into the most secret affairs of their friends, and often pry into their
closets and cupboards, only to discover their
poverty and meanness to the world.

However, as persons who suspect they have
given others cause of offense, are apt to conclude
they are offended; so Sophia imputed an action
of Master Blifil to his anger, which the superior
sagacity of Thwackum and Square discerned to
have arisen from a much better principle.

Tom Jones, when very young, had presented
Sophia with a little bird, which he had taken from
the nest, had nursed up, and taught to sing.

Of this bird, Sophia, then about thirteen years
old, was so extremely fond, that her chief business
was to feed and tend it, and her chief pleasure to
play with it. By these means little Tommy, for
so the bird was called, was become so tame, that
it would feed out of the hand of its mistress, would
perch upon the finger, and lie contented in her
bosom, where it seemed almost sensible of its own
happiness; though she always kept a small string
about its leg, nor would ever trust it with the
liberty of flying away.

One day, when Mr. Allworthy and his whole
family dined at Mr. Western's, Master Blifil, being in the garden with little Sophia, and observing

the extreme fondness that she showed for her little bird, desired her to trust it for a moment in his hands.   Sophia presently complied with the young gentleman's request, and after some previous caution, delivered him her bird; of which he was no sooner in possession, than he slipped the string from its leg and tossed it into the air.

The foolish animal no sooner perceived itself at liberty, than forgetting all the favors it had received from Sophia, it flew directly from her, and perched on a bough at some distance.

Sophia, seeing her bird gone, screamed out so loud, that Tom Jones, who was at a little distance, immediately ran to her assistance.

He was no sooner informed of what had happened, than he cursed Blifil for a pitiful malicious rascal; and then immediately stripping off his coat he applied himself to climbing the tree to which the bird escaped.

Tom had almost recovered his little namesake, when the branch on which it was perched, and that hung over a canal, broke, and the poor lad plumped over head and ears into the water.

Sophia's concern now changed its object.   And as she apprehended the boy's life was in danger, she screamed ten times louder than before; and indeed Master Blifil himself now seconded her with all the vociferation in his power.

The company, who were sitting in a room next the garden, were instantly alarmed, and came all forth; but just as they reached the canal, Tom (for the water was luckily pretty shallow in that part) arrived safely on shore.

Thwackum fell violently on poor Tom, who stood dropping and shivering before him, when Mr. Allworthy desired him to have patience; and turning to Master Blifil, said, "Pray, child, what is the reason of all this disturbance?"

Master Blifil answered, "Indeed, uncle, I am very sorry for what I have done; I have been unhappily the occasion of it all. I had Miss Sophia's bird in my hand, and thinking the poor creature languished for liberty, I own I could not forbear giving it what it desired; for I always thought there was something very cruel in confining anything. It seemed to be against the law of nature, by which everything hath a right to liberty; nay, it is even unchristian, for it is not doing what we would be done by; but if I had imagined Miss Sophia would have been so much concerned at it, I am sure I never would have done it; nay, if I had known what would have happened to the bird itself: for when Master Jones, who climbed up that tree after it, fell into the water, the bird took a second flight, and presently a nasty hawk carried it away."

Poor Sophia, who now first heard of her little Tommy's fate (for her concern for Jones had prevented her perceiving it when it happened), shed a shower of tears. These Mr. Allworthy endeavored to assuage, promising her a much finer bird: but she declared she would never have another. Her father chid her for crying so for a foolish bird; but could not help telling young Blifil, if he was a son of his, his backside should be well flayed.

Sophia now returned to her chamber, the two young gentlemen were sent home, and the rest of the company returned to their bottle; where a conversation ensued on the subject of the bird, so curious, that we think it deserves a chapter by itself.

CHAPTER IV

Containing such very deep and grave matters, that some readers, perhaps, may not relish it.

SQUARE had no sooner lighted his pipe, than, addressing himself to Allworthy, he thus began: "Sir, I cannot help congratulating you on your nephew; who, at an age when few lads have any ideas but of sensible objects, is arrived at a capacity of distinguishing right from wrong. To confine anything, seems to me against the law of nature, by which everything hath a right to liberty. These were his words; and the impression they have made on me is never to be eradicated. Can any man have a higher notion of the rule of right, and the eternal fitness of things? I cannot help promising myself, from such a dawn, that the meridian of this youth will be equal to that of either the elder or the younger Brutus."

Here Thwackum hastily interrupted, and spilling some of his wine, and swallowing the rest with great eagerness, answered, "From another expression he made use of, I hope he will resemble much better men. The law of nature is a jargon of words, which means nothing. I know not of any such law, nor of any right which can be derived from it. To do as we would be done by, is indeed a Christian motive, as the boy well ex-

183

pressed himself; and I am glad to find my instructions have borne such good fruit."

"If vanity was a thing fit," says Square, "I might indulge some on the same occasion; for whence only he can have learned his notions of right or wrong, I think is pretty apparent. If there be no law of nature, there is no right nor wrong."

"How!" says the parson, "do you then banish revelation? Am I talking with a deist or an atheist?"

"Drink about," says Western. "Pox of your laws of nature! I don't know what you mean, either of you, by right and wrong. To take away my girl's bird was wrong, in my opinion; and my neighbor Allworthy may do as he pleases; but to encourage boys in such practices, is to breed them up to the gallows."

Allworthy answered, "That he was sorry for what his nephew had done, but could not consent to punish him, as he acted rather from a generous than unworthy motive." He said, "If the boy had stolen the bird, none would have been more ready to vote for a severe chastisement than himself; but it was plain that was not his design:" and, indeed, it was as apparent to him, that he could have no other view but what he had himself avowed. (For as to that malicious purpose which Sophia suspected, it never once entered into the head of Mr. Allworthy.) He at length concluded with again blaming the action as inconsiderate, and which, he said, was pardonable only in a child.

Square had delivered his opinion so openly,

that if he was now silent, he must submit to have his judgment censured. He said, therefore, with some warmth, "That Mr. Allworthy had too much respect to the dirty consideration of property. That in passing our judgments on great and mighty actions, all private regards should be laid aside; for by adhering to those narrow rules, the younger Brutus had been condemned of ingratitude, and the elder of parricide."

"And if they had been hanged too for those crimes," cried Thwackum, "they would have had no more than their deserts. A couple of heathenish villains! Heaven be praised we have no Brutuses now-a-days! I wish, Mr. Square, you would desist from filling the minds of my pupils with such anti-christian stuff; for the consequence must be, while they are under my care, its being well scourged out of them again. There is your disciple Tom almost spoiled already. I overheard him the other day disputing with Master Blifil that there was no merit in faith without works. I know that is one of your tenets, and I suppose he had it from you."

"Don't accuse me of spoiling him," says Square. "Who taught him to laugh at whatever is virtuous and decent, and fit and right in the nature of things? He is your own scholar, and I disclaim him. No, no, Master Blifil is my boy. Young as he is, that lad's notions of moral rectitude I defy you ever to eradicate."

Thwackum put on a contemptuous sneer at this, and replied, "Ay, ay, I will venture him with you. He is too well grounded for all your philosophical cant to hurt. No, no, I have taken care to instil such principles into him——''

''And I have instilled principles into him too,'' cries Square. ''What but the sublime idea of virtue could inspire a human mind with the generous thought of giving liberty? And I repeat to you again, if it was a fit thing to be proud, I might claim the honor of having infused that idea.''——

''And if pride was not forbidden,'' said Thwackum, ''I might boast of having taught him that duty which he himself assigned as his motive.''

''So between you both,'' says the squire, ''the young gentleman hath been taught to rob my daughter of her bird. I find I must take care of my partridge-mew. I shall have some virtuous religious man or other set all my partridges at liberty.'' Then slapping a gentleman of the law, who was present, on the back, he cried out, ''What say you to this, Mr. Counselor? Is not this against law?''

The lawyer with great gravity delivered himself as follows:——

''If the case be put of a partridge, there can be no doubt but an action would lie; for though this be *feræ naturæ,* yet being reclaimed, property vests: but being the case of a singing bird, though reclaimed, as it is a thing of base nature, it must be considered as *nullius in bonis.* In this case, therefore, I conceive the plaintiff must be nonsuited; and I should disadvise the bringing any such action.''

''Well,'' says the squire, ''if it be *nullus bonus,*

let us drink about, and talk a little of the state
of the nation, or some such discourse that we all
understand; for I am sure I don't understand a
word of this. It may be learning and sense for
aught I know: but you shall never persuade me
into it. Pox! you have neither of you mentioned
a word of that poor lad who deserves to be commended: to venture breaking his neck to oblige
my girl was a generous-spirited action: I have
learning enough to see that. D—n me, here's
Tom's health! I shall love the boy for it the
longest day I have to live.''

Thus was the debate interrupted; but it would
probably have been soon resumed, had not Mr.
Allworthy presently called for his coach and
carried off the two combatants.

Such was the conclusion of this adventure of
the bird, and of the dialogue occasioned by it;
which we could not help recounting to our reader,
though it happened some years before that stage
or period of time at which our history is now arrived.

CHAPTER V

Containing matter accommodated to every taste.

"PARVA leves capiunt animos—Small things affect light minds," was the sentiment of a great master of the passion of love. And certain it is, that from this day Sophia began to have some little kindness for Tom Jones, and no little aversion for his companion.

Many accidents from time to time improved both these passions in her breast; which, without our recounting, the reader may well conclude, from what we have before hinted of the different tempers of these lads, and how much the one suited with her own inclinations more than the other. To say the truth, Sophia, when very young, discerned that Tom, though an idle, thoughtless, rattling rascal, was nobody's enemy but his own; and that Master Blifil, though a prudent, discreet, sober young gentleman, was at the same time strongly attached to the interest only of one single person; and who that single person was the reader will be able to divine without any assistance of ours.

These two characters are not always received in the world with the different regard which seems severally due to either; and which one would imagine mankind, from self-interest, should show

towards them. But perhaps there may be a political reason for it: in finding one of a truly
benevolent disposition, men may very reasonably
suppose they have found a treasure, and be desirous of keeping it, like all other good things, to
themselves. Hence they may imagine, that to
trumpet forth the praises of such a person, would,
in the vulgar phrase, be crying Roast-meat, and
calling in partakers of what they intend to apply
solely to their own use. If this reason does not
satisfy the reader, I know no other means of accounting for the little respect which I have commonly seen paid to a character which really does
great honor to human nature, and is productive
of the highest good to society. But it was otherwise with Sophia. She honored Tom Jones, and
scorned Master Blifil, almost as soon as she knew
the meaning of those two words.

Sophia had been absent upwards of three years
with her aunt; during all which time she had seldom seen either of these young gentlemen. She
dined, however, once, together with her aunt, at
Mr. Allworthy's. This was a few days after the
adventure of the partridge, before commemorated.
Sophia heard the whole story at table, where she
said nothing: nor indeed could her aunt get many
words from her as she returned home; but her
maid, when undressing her, happening to say,
"Well, miss, I suppose you have seen young Master Blifil to-day?" she answered with much passion, "I hate the name of Master Blifil, as I do
whatever is base and treacherous: and I wonder
Mr. Allworthy would suffer that old barbarous

schoolmaster to punish a poor boy so cruelly for what was only the effect of his good-nature.'' She then recounted the story to her maid, and concluded with saying, ''Don't you think he is a boy of noble spirit?''

This young lady was now returned to her father; who gave her the command of his house, and placed her at the upper end of his table, where Tom (who for his great love of hunting was become a great favorite of the squire) often dined. Young men of open, generous dispositions are naturally inclined to gallantry, which, if they have good understandings, as was in reality Tom's case, exerts itself in an obliging complacent behavior to all women in general. This greatly distinguished Tom from the boisterous brutality of mere country squires on the one hand, and from the solemn and somewhat sullen deportment of Master Blifil on the other; and he began now, at twenty, to have the name of a pretty fellow among all the women in the neighborhood.

Tom behaved to Sophia with no particularity, unless perhaps by showing her a higher respect than he paid to any other. This distinction her beauty, fortune, sense, and amiable carriage, seemed to demand; but as to design upon her person he had none; for which we shall at present suffer the reader to condemn him of stupidity; but perhaps we shall be able indifferently well to account for it hereafter.

Sophia, with the highest degree of innocence and modesty, had a remarkable sprightliness in her temper. This was so greatly increased when-

ever she was in company with Tom, that had he
not been very young and thoughtless, he must
have observed it: or had not Mr. Western's
thoughts been generally either in the field, the
stable, or the dog-kennel, it might have perhaps
created some jealousy in him: but so far was the
good gentleman from entertaining any such suspicions, that he gave Tom every opportunity
with his daughter which any lover could have
wished; and this Tom innocently improved to better advantage, by following only the dictates of
his natural gallantry and good-nature, than he
might perhaps have done had he had the deepest
designs on the young lady.

But indeed it can occasion little wonder that
this matter escaped the observation of others,
since poor Sophia herself never remarked it; and
her heart was irretrievably lost before she suspected it was in danger.

Matters were in this situation, when Tom, one
afternoon, finding Sophia alone, began, after a
short apology, with a very serious face, to acquaint her that he had a favor to ask of her which
he hoped her goodness would comply with.

Though neither the young man's behavior, nor
indeed his manner of opening this business, were
such as could give her any just cause of suspecting he intended to make love to her; yet whether
Nature whispered something into her ear, or from
what cause it arose I will not determine; certain
it is, some idea of that kind must have intruded
itself; for her color forsook her cheeks, her limbs
trembled, and her tongue would have faltered,

had Tom stopped for an answer; but he soon
relieved her from her perplexity, by proceeding to inform her of his request; which was
to solicit her interest on behalf of the gamekeeper, whose own ruin, and that of a large
family, must be, he said, the consequence of
Mr. Western's pursuing his action against him.

Sophia presently recovered her confusion, and,
with a smile full of sweetness, said, "Is this the
mighty favor you asked with so much gravity?
I will do it with all my heart. I really pity the
poor fellow, and no longer ago than yesterday
sent a small matter to his wife." This small
matter was one of her gowns, some linen, and ten
shillings in money, of which Tom had heard, and
it had, in reality, put this solicitation into his head.

Our youth, now, emboldened with his success,
resolved to push the matter farther, and ventured
even to beg her recommendation of him to her
father's service; protesting that he thought him
one of the honestest fellows in the country, and
extremely well qualified for the place of a gamekeeper, which luckily then happened to be vacant.

Sophia answered, "Well, I will undertake this
too; but I cannot promise you as much success as
in the former part, which I assure you I will not
quit my father without obtaining. However, I
will do what I can for the poor fellow; for I sincerely look upon him and his family as objects
of great compassion. And now, Mr. Jones, I
must ask you a favor."

"A favor, madam!" cries Tom: "if you knew

the pleasure you have given me in the hopes of receiving a command from you, you would think by mentioning it you did confer the greatest favor on me; for by this dear hand I would sacrifice my life to oblige you.''

He then snatched her hand and eagerly kissed it, which was the first time his lips had ever touched her. The blood which before had forsaken her cheeks, now made her sufficient amends, by rushing all over her face and neck with such violence, that they became all of a scarlet color. She now first felt a sensation to which she had been before a stranger, and which, when she had leisure to reflect on it, began to acquaint her with some secrets, which the reader, if he doth not already guess them, will know in due time.

Sophia, as soon as she could speak (which was not instantly), informed him that the favor she had to desire of him was, not to lead her father through so many dangers in hunting; for that, from what she had heard, she was terribly frightened every time they went out together, and expected some day or other to see her father brought home with broken limbs. She therefore begged him, for her sake, to be more cautious; and as he well knew Mr. Western would follow him, not to ride so madly, nor to take those dangerous leaps for the future.

Tom promised faithfully to obey her commands; and after thanking her for her kind compliance with his request, took his leave, and departed highly charmed with his success.

Poor Sophia was charmed too, but in a very dif-

I—13

ferent way. Her sensations, however, the reader's heart (if he or she have any) will better represent than I can, if I had as many mouths as ever poet wished for, to eat, I suppose, those many dainties with which he was so plentifully provided.

It was Mr. Western's custom every afternoon, as soon as he was drunk, to hear his daughter play on the harpsichord; for he was a great lover of music, and perhaps, had he lived in town, might have passed for a connoisseur; for he always excepted against the finest compositions of Mr. Handel. He never relished any music but what was light and airy; and indeed his most favorite tunes were Old Sir Simon the King, St. George he was for England, Bobbing Joan, and some others.

His daughter, though she was a perfect mistress of music, and would never willingly have played any but Handel's, was so devoted to her father's pleasure, that she learned all those tunes to oblige him. However, she would now and then endeavor to lead him into her own taste; and when he required the repetition of his ballads, would answer with a "Nay, dear sir;" and would often beg him to suffer her to play something else.

This evening, however, when the gentleman was retired from his bottle, she played all his favorites three times over without any solicitation. This so pleased the good squire, that he started from his couch, gave his daughter a kiss, and swore her hand was greatly improved. She took this opportunity to execute her promise to Tom; in which she succeeded so well, that the squire declared, if she would give him t'other bout of Old Sir Simon, he would give the gamekeeper his deputation the next morning. Sir Simon was played again and again, till the charms of the music soothed Mr. Western to sleep. In the morning Sophia did not fail to remind him of his engagement; and his attorney was immediately sent for, ordered to stop any further proceedings in the action, and to make out the deputation.

Tom's success in this affair soon began to ring over the country, and various were the censures passed upon it; some greatly applauding it as an act of good nature; others sneering, and saying, "No wonder that one idle fellow should love another." Young Blifil was greatly enraged at it. He had long hated Black George in the same proportion as Jones delighted in him; not from any offense which he had ever received, but from his great love to religion and virtue;—for Black George had the reputation of a loose kind of a fellow. Blifil therefore represented this as flying in Mr. Allworthy's face; and declared, with great concern, that it was impossible to find any other motive for doing good to such a wretch.

Thwackum and Square likewise sung to the same tune. They were now (especially the latter) become greatly jealous of young Jones with the widow; for he now approached the age of twenty, was really a fine young fellow, and that lady, by her encouragements to him, seemed daily more and more to think him so.

Allworthy was not, however, moved with their malice. He declared himself very well satisfied with what Jones had done. He said the perseverance and integrity of his friendship was highly commendable, and he wished he could see more frequent instances of that virtue.

But Fortune, who seldom greatly relishes such sparks as my friend Tom, perhaps because they do not pay more ardent addresses to her, gave now a very different turn to all his actions, and showed them to Mr. Allworthy in a light far less agreeable than that gentleman's goodness had hitherto seen them in.

CHAPTER VI

An apology for the insensibility of Mr. Jones to all the charms of the lovely Sophia; in which possibly we may, in a considerable degree, lower his character in the estimation of those men of wit and gallantry who approve the heroes in most of our modern comedies.

THERE are two sorts of people, who, I am afraid, have already conceived some contempt for my hero, on account of his behavior to Sophia. The former of these will blame his prudence in neglecting an opportunity to possess himself of Mr. Western's fortune; and the latter will no less despise him for his backwardness to so fine a girl, who seemed ready to fly into his arms, if he would open them to receive her.

Now, though I shall not perhaps be able absolutely to acquit him of either of these charges (for want of prudence admits of no excuse; and what I shall produce against the latter charge will, I apprehend, be scarce satisfactory); yet, as evidence may sometimes be offered in mitigation, I shall set forth the plain matter of fact, and leave the whole to the reader's determination.

Mr. Jones had somewhat about him, which, though I think writers are not thoroughly agreed in its name, doth certainly inhabit some human breasts; whose use is not so properly to distinguish right from wrong, as to prompt and incite them to the former, and to restrain and withhold them from the latter.

This somewhat may be indeed resembled to the famous trunk-maker in the playhouse; for, whenever the person who is possessed of it doth what is right, no ravished or friendly spectator is so eager or so loud in his applause: on the contrary, when he doth wrong, no critic is so apt to hiss and explode him.

To give a higher idea of the principle I mean, as well as one more familiar to the present age; it may be considered as sitting on its throne in the mind, like the Lord High Chancellor of this kingdom in his court; where it presides, governs, directs, judges, acquits, and condemns according to merit and justice, with a knowledge which nothing escapes, a penetration which nothing can deceive, and an integrity which nothing can corrupt.

This active principle may perhaps be said to constitute the most essential barrier between us and our neighbors the brutes; for if there be some in the human shape who are not under any such dominion, I choose rather to consider them as deserters from us to our neighbors; among whom they will have the fate of deserters, and not be placed in the first rank.

Our hero, whether he derived it from Thwackum or Square I will not determine, was very strongly under the guidance of this principle; for though he did not always act rightly, yet he never did otherwise without feeling and suffering for it.

It was this which taught him, that to repay the civilities and little friendships of hospitality by robbing the house where you have received them, is to be the basest and meanest of thieves. He did not think the baseness of this offense lessened by the height of the injury committed; on the contrary, if to steal another's plate deserved death and infamy, it seemed to him difficult to assign a punishment adequate to the robbing a man of his whole fortune, and of his child into the bargain.

This principle, therefore, prevented him from any thought of making his fortune by such means (for this, as I have said, is an active principle, and doth not content itself with knowledge or belief only). Had he been greatly enamored of Sophia, he possibly might have thought otherwise; but give me leave to say, there is great difference between running away with a man's daughter from the motive of love, and doing the same thing from the motive of theft.

Now, though this young gentleman was not insensible of the charms of Sophia; though he greatly liked her beauty, and esteemed all her other qualifications, she had made, however, no deep impression on his heart; for which, as it renders him liable to the charge of stupidity, or at least of want of taste, we shall now proceed to account.

The truth then is, his heart was in the possession of another woman. Here I question not but the reader will be surprised at our long taciturnity as to this matter; and quite at a loss to divine who this woman was, since we have hitherto not dropped a hint of any one likely to be a rival to Sophia; for as to Mrs. Blifil, though we have been obliged to mention some suspicions of her affection for Tom, we have not hitherto given the least latitude for imagining that he had any for her; and, indeed, I am sorry to say it, but the youth of both sexes are too apt to be deficient in their gratitude for that regard with which persons more advanced in years are sometimes so kind to honor them.

That the reader may be no longer in suspense, he will be pleased to remember, that we have often mentioned the family of George Seagrim (commonly called Black George, the gamekeeper), which consisted at present of a wife and five children.

The second of these children was a daughter, whose name was Molly, and who was esteemed one of the handsomest girls in the whole country.

Congreve well says there is in true beauty something which vulgar souls cannot admire; so can no dirt or rags hide this something from those souls which are not of the vulgar stamp.

The beauty of this girl made, however, no impression on Tom, till she grew towards the age of sixteen, when Tom, who was near three years older, began first to cast the eyes of affection upon her. And this affection he had fixed on the girl long before he could bring himself to attempt the possession of her person: for though his constitution urged him greatly to this, his principles no less forcibly restrained him. To debauch a young woman, however low her condition was, appeared to him a very heinous crime; and the good-will he bore the father, with the compassion he had for his family, very strongly corroborated all such sober reflections; so that he once resolved to get the better of his inclinations, and he actually abstained three whole months without ever going to Seagrim's house, or seeing his daughter.

Now, though Molly was, as we have said, generally thought a very fine girl, and in reality she was so, yet her beauty was not of the most amiable kind. It had, indeed, very little of feminine in it, and would have become a man at least as well as a woman; for, to say the truth, youth and florid health had a very considerable share in the composition.

Nor was her mind more effeminate than her person. As this was tall and robust, so was that bold and forward. So little had she of modesty, that Jones had more regard for her virtue than she herself. And as most probably she liked Tom as well as he liked her, so when she perceived his backwardness she herself grew proportionably forward; and when she saw he had entirely deserted the house, she found means of throwing herself in his way, and behaved in such a manner that the youth must have had very much or very little of the hero if her endeavors had proved unsuccessful. In a word, she soon triumphed over all the virtuous resolutions of Jones; for though she behaved at last with all decent reluctance, yet I rather choose to attribute the triumph to her, since, in fact, it was her design which succeeded.

In the conduct of this matter, I say, Molly so
well played her part, that Jones attributed the
conquest entirely to himself, and considered the
young woman as one who had yielded to the violent attacks of his passion. He likewise imputed
her yielding to the ungovernable force of her love
towards him; and this the reader will allow to
have been a very natural and probable supposition, as we have more than once mentioned the
uncommon comeliness of his person: and, indeed,
he was one of the handsomest young fellows in
the world.

As there are some minds whose affections, like
Master Blifil's, are solely placed on one single person, whose interest and indulgence alone they consider on every occasion; regarding the good and
ill of all others as merely indifferent, any farther
than as they contribute to the pleasure or advantage of that person: so there is a different temper
of mind which borrows a degree of virtue even
from self-love. Such can never receive any kind
of satisfaction from another, without loving the
creature to whom that satisfaction is owing, and
without making its well-being in some sort necessary to their own ease.

Of this latter species was our hero. He considered this poor girl as one whose happiness or misery he had caused to be dependent on himself.
Her beauty was still the object of desire, though
greater beauty, or a fresher object, might have
been more so; but the little abatement which frui-
tion had occasioned to this was highly overbalanced by the considerations of the affection which

she visibly bore him, and of the situation into
which he had brought her. The former of these
created gratitude, the latter compassion; and both,
together with his desire for her person, raised in
him a passion which might, without any great violence to the word, be called love; though, perhaps,
it was at first not very judiciously placed.

This, then, was the true reason of that insensibility which he had shown to the charms of Sophia, and that behavior in her which might have
been reasonably enough interpreted as an encouragement to his addresses; for as he could not
think of abandoning his Molly, poor and destitute as she was, so no more could he entertain a
notion of betraying such a creature as Sophia.
And surely, had he given the least encouragement
to any passion for that young lady, he must have
been absolutely guilty of one or other of those
crimes; either of which would, in my opinion,
have very justly subjected him to that fate, which,
at his first introduction into this history, I mentioned to have been generally predicted as his
certain destiny.

CHAPTER VII

Being the shortest chapter in this book.

HER mother first perceived the alteration in the shape of Molly; and in order to hide it from her neighbors, she foolishly clothed her in that sack which Sophia had sent her; though, indeed, that young lady had little apprehension that the poor woman would have been weak enough to let any of her daughters wear it in that form.

Molly was charmed with the first opportunity she ever had of showing her beauty to advantage; for though she could very well bear to contemplate herself in the glass, even when dressed in rags; and though she had in that dress conquered the heart of Jones, and perhaps of some others; yet she thought the addition of finery would much improve her charms, and extend her conquests.

Molly therefore, having dressed herself out in this sack, with a new laced cap, and some other ornaments which Tom had given her, repairs to church with her fan in her hand the very next Sunday. The great are deceived if they imagine they have appropriated ambition and vanity to themselves. These noble qualities flourish as notably in a country church and churchyard as in the drawing-room, or in the closet. Schemes have indeed been laid in the vestry which would

204

hardly disgrace the conclave. Here is a minis-
try, and here is an opposition. Here are plots
and circumventions, parties and factions, equal
to those which are to be found in courts.

Nor are the women here less practiced in the
highest feminine arts than their fair superiors
in quality and fortune. Here are prudes and
coquettes. Here are dressing and ogling, falsehood, envy, malice, scandal; in short, everything
which is common to the most splendid assembly,
or politest circle. Let those of high life, therefore, no longer despise the ignorance of their inferiors; nor the vulgar any longer rail at the
vices of their betters.

Molly had seated herself sometime before she
was known by her neighbors. And then a whisper ran through the whole congregation, "Who
is she?" but when she was discovered, such sneering, giggling, tittering, and laughing ensued among
the women, that Mr. Allworthy was obliged to
exert his authority to preserve any decency
among them.

CHAPTER VIII

MR. WESTERN had an estate in this parish; and as his house stood at little greater distance from this church than from his own, he very often came to Divine Service here; and both he and the charming Sophia happened to be present at this time.

Sophia was much pleased with the beauty of the girl, whom she pitied for her simplicity in having dressed herself in that manner, as she saw the envy which it had occasioned among her equals. She no sooner came home than she sent for the gamekeeper, and ordered him to bring his daughter to her; saying she would provide for her in the family, and might possibly place the girl about her own person, when her own maid, who was now going away, had left her.

Poor Seagrim was thunderstruck at this; for he was no stranger to the fault in the shape of his daughter. He answered, in a stammering voice, "That he was afraid Molly would be too awkward to wait on her ladyship, as she had never been at service." "No matter for that," says Sophia; "she will soon improve. I am pleased with the girl, and am resolved to try her."

Black George now repaired to his wife, on

206

whose prudent counsel he depended to extricate him out of this dilemma; but when he came thither he found his house in some confusion. So great envy had this sack occasioned, that when Mr. Allworthy and the other gentry were gone from church, the rage, which had hitherto been confined, burst into an uproar; and, having vented itself at first in opprobrious words, laughs, hisses, and gestures, betook itself at last to certain missile weapons; which, though from their plastic nature they threatened neither the loss of life or of limb, were however sufficiently dreadful to a well-dressed lady. Molly had too much spirit to bear this treatment tamely. Having therefore—but hold, as we are diffident of our own abilities, let us here invite a superior power to our assistance.

Ye Muses, then, whoever ye are, who love to sing battles, and principally thou who whilom didst recount the slaughter in those fields where Hudibras and Trulla fought, if thou wert not starved with thy friend Butler, assist me on this great occasion. All things are not in the power of all.

As a vast herd of cows in a rich farmer's yard, if, while they are milked, they hear their calves at a distance, lamenting the robbery which is then committing, roar and bellow; so roared forth the Somersetshire mob and hallaloo, made up of almost as many squalls, screams, and other different sounds as there were persons, or indeed passions among them: some were inspired by rage, others alarmed by fear, and others had nothing in their heads but the love of fun; but chiefly

Envy, the sister of Satan, and his constant companion, rushed among the crowd, and blew up the fury of the women; who no sooner came up to Molly than they pelted her with dirt and rubbish.

Molly, having endeavored in vain to make a handsome retreat, faced about; and laying hold of ragged Bess, who advanced in front of the enemy, she at one blow felled her to the ground. The whole army of the enemy (though near a hundred in number), seeing the fate of their general, gave back many paces, and retired behind a new-dug grave; for the churchyard was the field of battle, where there was to be a funeral that very evening. Molly pursued her victory, and catching up a skull which lay on the side of the grave, discharged it with such fury, that having hit a taylor on the head, the two skulls sent equally forth a hollow sound at their meeting, and the taylor took presently measure of his length on the ground, where the skulls lay side by side, and it was doubtful which was the more valuable of the two. Molly then taking a thigh-bone in her hand, fell in among the flying ranks, and dealing her blows with great liberality on either side, overthrew the carcass of many a mighty hero and heroine.

Recount, O Muse, the names of those who fell on this fatal day. First, Jemmy Tweedle felt on his hinder head the direful bone. Him the pleasant banks of sweetly-winding Stour had nourished, where he first learned the vocal art, with which, wandering up and down at wakes and fairs, he cheered the rural nymphs and swains, when upon the green they interweaved the sprightly dance; while he himself stood fiddling and jumping to his own music. How little now avails his fiddle! He thumps the verdant floor with his carcass. Next, old Echepole, the sow-gelder, received a blow in his forehead from our Amazonian heroine, and immediately fell to the ground. He was a swinging fat fellow, and fell with almost as much noise as a house. His to-bacco-box dropped at the same time from his pocket, which Molly took up as lawful spoils. Then Kate of the Mill tumbled unfortunately over a tombstone, which catching hold of her ungar-tered stocking inverted the order of nature, and gave her heels the superiority to her head. Betty Pippin, with young Roger her lover, fell both to the ground; where, oh perverse fate! she salutes the earth, and he the sky. Tom Freckle, the smith's son, was the next victim to her rage. He was an ingenious workman, and made excellent pattens; nay, the very patten with which he was knocked down was his own workmanship. Had he been at that time singing psalms in the church, he would have avoided a broken head. Miss Crow, the daughter of a farmer; John Giddish, himself a farmer; Nan Slouch, Esther Codling, Will Spray, Tom Bennet; the three Misses Pot-ter, whose father keeps the sign of the Red Lion; Betty Chambermaid, Jack Ostler, and many others of inferior note, lay rolling among the graves.

I—14

Not that the strenuous arm of Molly reached all these; for many of them in their flight overthrew each other.

But now Fortune, fearing she had acted out of character, and had inclined too long to the same side, especially as it was the right side, hastily turned about: for now Goody Brown—whom Zekiel Brown caressed in his arms; nor he alone, but half the parish besides; so famous was she in the fields of Venus, nor indeed less in those of Mars. The trophies of both these her husband always bore about on his head and face; for if ever human head did by its horns display the amorous glories of a wife, Zekiel's did; nor did his well-scratched face less denote her talents (or rather talons) of a different kind.

No longer bore this Amazon the shameful flight of her party. She stopped short, and, calling aloud to all who fled, spoke as follows: "Ye Somersetshire men, or rather ye Somersetshire women, are ye not ashamed thus to fly from a single woman? But if no other will oppose her, I myself and Joan Top here will have the honor of the victory." Having thus said, she flew at Molly Seagrim, and easily wrenched the thigh-bone from her hand, at the same time clawing off her cap from her head. Then laying hold of the hair of Molly with her left hand, she attacked her so furiously in the face with the right, that the blood soon began to trickle from her nose. Molly was not idle this while. She soon removed the clout from the head of Goody Brown, and then fastening on her hair with one hand, with the other she caused another bloody stream to issue forth from the nostrils of the enemy.

When each of the combatants had borne off sufficient spoils of hair from the head of her antagonist, the next rage was against the garments. In this attack they exerted so much violence, that in a very few minutes they were both naked to the middle.

It is lucky for the women that the seat of fistycuff war is not the same with them as among men; but though they may seem a little to deviate from their sex, when they go forth to battle, yet I have observed, they never so far forget, as to assail the bosoms of each other; where a few blows would be fatal to most of them. This, I know, some derive from their being of a more bloody inclination than the males. On which account they apply to the nose, as to the part whence blood may most easily be drawn; but this seems a far-fetched as well as ill-natured supposition.

Goody Brown had great advantage of Molly in this particular; for the former had indeed no breasts, her bosom (if it may be so called), as well in color as in many other properties, exactly resembling an ancient piece of parchment, upon which any one might have drummed a considerable while without doing her any great damage.

Molly, beside her present unhappy condition, was differently formed in those parts, and might, perhaps, have tempted the envy of Brown to give her a fatal blow, had not the lucky arrival of Tom Jones at this instant put an immediate end to the bloody scene.

This accident was luckily owing to Mr. Square; for he, Master Blifil, and Jones, had mounted their horses, after church, to take the air, and had ridden about a quarter of a mile, when Square, changing his mind (not idly, but for a reason which we shall unfold as soon as we have leisure), desired the young gentlemen to ride with him another way than they had at first purposed. This motion being complied with, brought them of necessity back again to the churchyard.

Master Blifil, who rode first, seeing such a mob assembled, and two women in the posture in which we left the combatants, stopped his horse to inquire what was the matter. A country fellow, scratching his head, answered him: ''I don't know, measter un't I; an't please your honor, here hath been a vight, I think, between Goody Brown and Moll Seagrim.''

''Who, who?'' cries Tom; but without waiting for an answer, having discovered the features of his Molly through all the discomposure in which they now were, he hastily alighted, turned his horse loose, and, leaping over the wall, ran to her. She now first bursting into tears, told him how barbarously she had been treated. Upon which, forgetting the sex of Goody Brown, or perhaps not knowing it in his rage—for, in reality, she had no feminine appearance but a petticoat, which he might not observe—he gave her a lash or two with his horsewhip; and then flying at the mob, who were all accused by Moll, he dealt his blows so profusely on all sides, that unless I would again invoke the muse (which the good-natured reader may think a little too hard upon her, as she hath so lately been violently sweated), it would be impossible for me to recount the horse-whipping of that day.

Having scoured the whole coast of the enemy, as well as any of Homer's heroes ever did, or as Don Quixote or any knight-errant in the world could have done, he returned to Molly, whom he found in a condition which must give both me and my reader pain, was it to be described here. Tom raved like a madman, beat his breast, tore his hair, stamped on the ground, and vowed the utmost vengeance on all who had been concerned. He then pulled off his coat, and buttoned it round her, put his hat upon her head, wiped the blood from her face as well as he could with his handkerchief, and called out to the servant to ride as fast as possible for a side-saddle, or a pillion, that he might carry her safe home.

Master Blifil objected to the sending away the servant, as they had only one with them; but as Square seconded the order of Jones, he was obliged to comply.

The servant returned in a very short time with the pillion, and Molly, having collected her rags as well as she could, was placed behind him. In which manner she was carried home, Square, Blifil, and Jones attending.

Here Jones having received his coat, given her a sly kiss, and whispered her, that he would return in the evening, quitted his Molly, and rode on after his companions.

CHAPTER IX

Containing matter of no very peaceable color.

MOLLY had no sooner appareled herself in her accustomed rags, than her sisters began to fall violently upon her, particularly her eldest sister, who told her she was well enough served. "How had she the assurance to wear a gown which young Madam Western had given to mother! If one of us was to wear it, I think," says she, "I myself have the best right; but I warrant you think it belongs to your beauty. I suppose you think yourself more handsomer than any of us."—"Hand her down the bit of glass from over the cupboard," cries another; "I'd wash the blood from my face before I talked of my beauty."—"You'd better have minded what the parson says," cries the eldest, "and not a harkened after men voke."—"Indeed, child, and so she had," says the mother, sobbing: "she hath brought a disgrace upon us all. She's the vurst of the vamily that ever was a whore."

"You need not upbraid me with that, mother," cries Molly; "you yourself was brought-to-bed of sister there, within a week after you was married."

"Yes, hussy," answered the enraged mother, "so I was, and what was the mighty matter of that? I was made an honest woman then; and if

you was to be made an honest woman, I should not
be angry; but you must have to doing with a gentleman, you nasty slut; you will have a bastard,
hussy, you will; and that I defy any one to say of
me.''

In this situation Black George found his family,
when he came home for the purpose before mentioned. As his wife and three daughters were all
of them talking together, and most of them crying,
it was some time before he could get an opportunity of being heard; but as soon as such an interval
occurred, he acquainted the company with what
Sophia had said to him.

Goody Seagrim then began to revile her
daughter afresh. ''Here,'' says she, ''you have
brought us into a fine quandary indeed. What
will madam say to that big belly? Oh that ever I
should live to see this day!''

Molly answered with great spirit, ''And what is
this mighty place which you have got for me,
father?'' (for he had not well understood the
phrase used by Sophia of being about her person).
''I suppose it is to be under the cook; but I shan't
wash dishes for anybody. My gentleman will provide better for me. See what he hath given me
this afternoon. He hath promised I shall never
want money; and you shan't want money neither,
mother, if you will hold your tongue, and know
when you are well.'' And so saying, she pulled
out several guineas, and gave her mother one of
them.

The good woman no sooner felt the gold within
her palm, than her temper began (such is the effi-

cacy of that panacea) to be mollified. "Why,
husband," says she, "would any but such a blockhead as you not have inquired what place this was
before he had accepted it? Perhaps, as Molly
says, it may be in the kitchen; and truly I don't
care my daughter should be a scullion wench; for,
poor as I am, I am a gentlewoman. And though
I was obliged, as my father, who was a clergyman,
died worse than nothing, and so could not give me
a shilling of potion, to undervalue myself by marrying a poor man; yet I would have you to know,
I have a spirit above all them things. Marry
come up! it would better become Madam Western
to look at home, and remember who her own grandfather was. Some of my family, for aught I know,
might ride in their coaches, when the grandfathers
of some voke walked a-voot. I warrant she
fancies she did a mighty matter, when she sent us
that old gownd; some of my family would not have
picked up such rags in the street; but poor people
are always trampled upon.—The parish need not
have been in such a fluster with Molly. You might
have told them, child, your grandmother wore better things new out of the shop."

"Well, but consider," cried George, "what answer shall I make to madam?"

"I don't know what answer," says she; "you
are always bringing your family into one quandary or other. Do you remember when you shot
the partridge, the occasion of all our misfortunes?
Did not I advise you never to go into Squire Western's manor? Did not I tell you many a good year
ago what would come of it? But you would have

your own headstrong ways; yes, you would, you villain.''

Black George was, in the main, a peaceable kind of fellow, and nothing choleric nor rash; yet did he bear about him something of what the ancients called the irascible, and which his wife, if she had been endowed with much wisdom, would have feared. He had long experienced, that when the storm grew very high, arguments were but wind, which served rather to increase, than to abate it. He was therefore seldom unprovided with a small switch, a remedy of wonderful force, as he had often essayed, and which the word villain served as a hint for his applying.

No sooner, therefore, had this symptom appeared, than he had immediate recourse to the said remedy, which though, as it is usual in all very efficacious medicines, it at first seemed to heighten and inflame the disease, soon produced a total calm, and restored the patient to perfect ease and tranquillity.

This is, however, a kind of horse-medicine, which requires a very robust constitution to digest, and is therefore proper only for the vulgar, unless in one single instance, viz., where superiority of birth breaks out; in which case, we should not think it very improperly applied by any husband whatever, if the application was not in itself so base, that, like certain applications of the physical kind which need not be mentioned, it so much degrades and contaminates the hand employed in it, that no gentleman should endure the thought of anything so low and detestable.

The whole family were soon reduced to a state of perfect quiet; for the virtue of this medicine, like that of electricity, is often communicated through one person to many others, who are not touched by the instrument. To say the truth, as they both operate by friction, it may be doubted whether there is not something analogous between them, of which Mr. Freke would do well to inquire, before he publishes the next edition of his book.

A council was now called, in which, after many debates, Molly still persisting that she would not go to service, it was at length resolved, that Goody Seagrim herself should wait on Miss Western, and endeavor to procure the place for her eldest daughter, who declared great readiness to accept it: but Fortune, who seems to have been an enemy of this little family, afterwards put a stop to her promotion.

CHAPTER X

A story told by Mr. Supple, the curate. The penetration of Squire Western. His great love for his daughter, and the return to it made by her.

THE next morning Tom Jones hunted with Mr. Western, and was at his return invited by that gentleman to dinner.

The lovely Sophia shone forth that day with more gayety and sprightliness than usual. Her battery was certainly leveled at our hero; though, I believe, she herself scarce yet knew her own intention; but if she had any design of charming him, she now succeeded.

Mr. Supple, the curate of Mr. Allworthy's parish, made one of the company. He was a good-natured worthy man; but chiefly remarkable for his great taciturnity at table, though his mouth was never shut at it. In short, he had one of the best appetites in the world. However, the cloth was no sooner taken away, than he always made sufficient amends for his silence: for he was a very hearty fellow; and his conversation was often entertaining, never offensive.

At his first arrival, which was immediately before the entrance of the roast-beef, he had given an intimation that he had brought some news with him, and was beginning to tell, that he came that moment from Mr. Allworthy's, when the sight of

219

the roast-beef struck him dumb, permitting him only to say grace, and to declare he must pay his respect to the baronet, for so he called the sirloin.

When dinner was over, being reminded by Sophia of his news, he began as follows: "I believe, lady, your ladyship observed a young woman at church yesterday at even-song, who was dressed in one of your outlandish garments; I think I have seen your ladyship in such a one. However, in the country, such dresses are

Rara avis in terris, nigroque simillima cygno.

That is, madam, as much as to say, 'A rare bird upon the earth, and very like a black swan.' The verse is in Juvenal. But to return to what I was relating. I was saying such garments are rare sights in the country; and perchance, too, it was thought the more rare, respect being had to the person who wore it, who, they tell me, is the daughter of Black George, your worship's gamekeeper, whose sufferings, I should have opinioned, might have taught him more wit, than to dress forth his wenches in such gaudy apparel. She created so much confusion in the congregation, that if Squire Allworthy had not silenced it, it would have interrupted the service: for I was once about to stop in the middle of the first lesson. Howbeit, nevertheless, after prayer was over, and I was departed home, this occasioned a battle in the churchyard, where, amongst other mischief, the head of a traveling fiddler was very much broken. This morning the fiddler came to Squire

Allworthy for a warrant, and the wench was brought before him. The squire was inclined to have compounded matters; when, lo! on a sudden the wench appeared (I ask your ladyship's pardon) to be, as it were, at the eve of bringing forth a bastard. The squire demanded of her who was the father? But she pertinaciously refused to make any response. So that he was about to make her mittimus to Bridewel when I departed."

"And is a wench having a bastard all your news, doctor?" cries Western; "I thought it might have been some public matter, something about the nation."

"I am afraid it is too common, indeed," answered the parson; "but I thought the whole story altogether deserved commemorating. As to national matters, your worship knows them best. My concerns extend no farther than my own parish."

"Why, ay," says the squire, "I believe I do know a little of that matter, as you say. But, come, Tommy, drink about; the bottle stands with you."

Tom begged to be excused, for that he had particular business; and getting up from table, escaped the clutches of the squire, who was rising to stop him, and went off with very little ceremony.

The squire gave him a good curse at his departure; and then turning to the parson, he cried out, "I smoke it: I smoke it. Tom is certainly the father of this bastard. Zooks, parson, you remember how he recommended the veather o' her to me. D—n un, what a sly b—ch 'tis. Ay, ay, as sure as two-pence, Tom is the veather of the bastard.''

"I should be very sorry for that," says the parson.

"Why sorry," cries the squire: "Where is the mighty matter o't? What, I suppose dost pretend that thee hast never got a bastard? Pox! more good luck's thine? for I warrant hast a done a *therefore* many's the good time and often.''

"Your worship is pleased to be jocular," answered the parson; "but I do not only animadvert on the sinfulness of the action—though that surely is to be greatly deprecated—but I fear his unrighteousness may injure him with Mr. Allworthy. And truly I must say, though he hath the character of being a little wild, I never saw any harm in the young man; nor can I say I have heard any, save what your worship now mentions. I wish, indeed, he was a little more regular in his responses at church; but altogether he seems

Ingenui vultus puer ingenuique pudoris.

That is a classical line, young lady; and, being rendered into English, is, 'a lad of an ingenuous countenance, and of an ingenuous modesty;' for this was a virtue in great repute both among the Latins and Greeks. I must say, the young gentleman (for so I think I may call him, notwithstanding his birth) appears to me a very modest, civil lad, and I should be sorry that he should do himself any injury in Squire Allworthy's opinion.''

"Poogh!" says the squire: "Injury, with All-worthy! Why, Allworthy loves a wench himself. Doth not all the country know whose son Tom is? You must talk to another person in that manner. I remember Allworthy at college."

"I thought," said the parson, "he had never been at the university."

"Yes, yes, he was," says the squire: "and many a wench have we two had together. As arrant a whoremaster as any within five miles o'un. No, no. It will do'n no harm with he, as-sure yourself; nor with anybody else. Ask Sophy there—You have not the worse opinion of a young fellow for getting a bastard, have you, girl? No, no, the women will like un the better for't."

This was a cruel question to poor Sophia. She had observed Tom's color change at the parson's story; and that, with his hasty and abrupt depar-ture, gave her sufficient reason to think her father's suspicion not groundless. Her heart now at once discovered the great secret to her which it had been so long disclosing by little and little; and she found herself highly interested in this matter. In such a situation, her father's malapert question rushing suddenly upon her, produced some symp-toms which might have alarmed a suspicious heart; but, to do the squire justice, that was not his fault. When she rose therefore from her chair, and told him a hint from him was always sufficient to make her withdraw, he suffered her to leave the room, and then with great gravity of countenance remarked, "That it was better to see a daughter over-modest than over-forward;''—a sentiment which was highly applauded by the parson.

There now ensued between the squire and the parson a most excellent political discourse, framed out of newspapers and political pamphlets; in which they made a libation of four bottles of wine to the good of their country: and then, the squire being fast asleep, the parson lighted his pipe, mounted his horse, and rode home.

When the squire had finished his half-hour's nap, he summoned his daughter to her harpsichord; but she begged to be excused that evening, on account of a violent headache. This remission was presently granted; for indeed she seldom had occasion to ask him twice, as he loved her with such ardent affection, that, by gratifying her, he commonly conveyed the highest gratification to himself. She was really, what he frequently called her, his little darling, and she well deserved to be so; for she returned all his affection in the most ample manner. She had preserved the most inviolable duty to him in all things; and this her love made not only easy, but so delightful, that when one of her companions laughed at her for placing so much merit in such scrupulous obedience, as that young lady called it, Sophia answered, ''You mistake me, madam, if you think I value myself upon this account; for besides that I am barely discharging my duty, I am likewise pleasing myself. I can truly say I have no delight equal to that of contributing to my father's happiness; and if I value myself, my dear, it is on having this power, and not on executing it.''

This was a satisfaction, however, which poor Sophia was incapable of tasting this evening. She therefore not only desired to be excused from her attendance at the harpsichord, but likewise begged that he would suffer her to absent herself from supper. To this request likewise the squire agreed, though not without some reluctance; for he scarce ever permitted her to be out of his sight, unless when he was engaged with his horses, dogs, or bottle. Nevertheless he yielded to the desire of his daughter, though the poor man was at the same time obliged to avoid his own company (if I may so express myself), by sending for a neighboring farmer to sit with him.

CHAPTER XI

The narrow escape of Molly Seagrim, with some observations for which we have been forced to dive pretty deep into nature.

TOM Jones had ridden one of Mr. Western's horses that morning in the chase; so that having no horse of his own in the squire's stable, he was obliged to go home on foot: this he did so expeditiously that he ran upwards of three miles within the half-hour.

Just as he arrived at Mr. Allworthy's outward gate, he met the constable and company with Molly in their possession, whom they were conducting to that house where the inferior sort of people may learn one good lesson, viz., respect and deference to their superiors; since it must show them the wide distinction Fortune intends between those persons who are to be corrected for their faults, and those who are not; which lesson if they do not learn, I am afraid they very rarely learn any other good lesson, or improve their morals, at the house of correction.

A lawyer may perhaps think Mr. Allworthy exceeded his authority a little in this instance. And, to say the truth, I question, as here was no regular information before him, whether his conduct was strictly regular. However, as his intention was truly upright, he ought to be excused in *foro conscientiæ;* since so many arbitrary acts are daily, committed by magistrates who have not this excuse to plead for themselves.

Tom was no sooner informed by the constable whither they were proceeding (indeed he pretty well guessed it of himself), than he caught Molly in his arms, and embracing her tenderly before them all, swore he would murder the first man who offered to lay hold of her. He bid her dry her eyes and be comforted; for, wherever she went, he would accompany her. Then turning to the constable, who stood trembling with his hat off, he desired him, in a very mild voice, to return with him for a moment only to his father (for so he now called Allworthy); for he durst, he said, be assured, that, when he had alleged what he had to say in her favor, the girl would be discharged.

The constable, who, I make no doubt, would have surrendered his prisoner had Tom demanded her, very readily consented to this request. So back they all went into Mr. Allworthy's hall; where Tom desired them to stay till his return, and then went himself in pursuit of the good man. As soon as he was found, Tom threw himself at his feet, and having begged a patient hearing, confessed himself to be the father of the child of which Molly was then big. He entreated him to have compassion on the poor girl, and to consider, if there was any guilt in the case, it lay principally at his door.

"If there is any guilt in the case!" answered Allworthy warmly: "Are you then so profligate and abandoned a libertine to doubt whether the

breaking the laws of God and man, the corrupting
and ruining a poor girl be guilt? I own, indeed, it
doth lie principally upon you; and so heavy it is,
that you ought to expect it should crush you.''

"Whatever may be my fate," says Tom, "let
me succeed in my intercessions for the poor girl.
I confess I have corrupted her! but whether she
shall be ruined, depends on you. For Heaven's
sake, sir, revoke your warrant, and do not send
her to a place which must unavoidably prove her
destruction.''

Allworthy bid him immediately call a servant.
Tom answered there was no occasion; for he had
luckily met them at the gate, and relying upon his
goodness, had brought them all back into his hall,
where they now waited his final resolution, which
upon his knees he besought him might be in favor
of the girl; that she might be permitted to go
home to her parents, and not be exposed to a
greater degree of shame and scorn than must necessarily fall upon her. "I know," said he, "that
is too much. I know I am the wicked occasion of
it. I will endeavor to make amends, if possible;
and if you shall have hereafter the goodness to forgive me, I hope I shall deserve it.''

Allworthy hesitated some time, and at last said,
"Well, I will discharge my mittimus.—You may
send the constable to me." He was instantly
called, discharged, and so was the girl.

It will be believed that Mr. Allworthy failed not
to read Tom a very severe lecture on this occasion;
but it is unnecessary to insert it here, as we have
faithfully transcribed what he said to Jenny Jones

in the first book, most of which may be applied to
the men, equally with the women. So sensible an
effect had these reproofs on the young man, who
was no hardened sinner, that he retired to his own
room, where he passed the evening alone, in much
melancholy contemplation.

Allworthy was sufficiently offended by this
transgression of Jones; for notwithstanding the
assertions of Mr. Western, it is certain this worthy
man had never indulged himself in any loose
pleasures with women, and greatly condemned the
vice of incontinence in others. Indeed, there is
much reason to imagine that there was not the
least truth in what Mr. Western affirmed, especially as he laid the scene of those impurities at
the university, where Mr. Allworthy had never
been. In fact, the good squire was a little too
apt to indulge that kind of pleasantry which is
generally called rhodomontade: but which may,
with as much propriety, be expressed by a much
shorter word; and perhaps we too often supply
the use of this little monosyllable by others; since
very much of what frequently passes in the world
for wit and humor, should, in the strictest purity.
of language, receive that short appellation, which,
in conformity to the well-bred laws of custom, I
here suppress.

But whatever detestation Mr. Allworthy had to
this or to any other vice, he was not so blinded by
it but that he could discern any virtue in the guilty
person, as clearly indeed as if there had been no
mixture of vice in the same character. While he
was angry therefore with the incontinence of

Jones, he was no less pleased with the honor and honesty of his self-accusation. He began now to form in his mind the same opinion of this young fellow, which, we hope, our reader may have conceived. And in balancing his faults with his perfections, the latter seemed rather to preponderate.

It was to no purpose, therefore, that Thwackum, who was immediately charged by Mr. Blifil with the story, unbended all his rancor against poor Tom. Allworthy gave a patient hearing to their invectives, and then answered coldly: "That young men of Tom's complexion were too generally addicted to this vice; but he believed that youth was sincerely affected with what he had said to him on the occasion, and he hoped he would not transgress again." So that, as the days of whipping were at an end, the tutor had no other vent but his own mouth for his gall, the usual poor resource of impotent revenge.

But Square, who was a less violent, was a much more artful man; and as he hated Jones more perhaps than Thwackum himself did, so he contrived to do him more mischief in the mind of Mr. Allworthy.

The reader must remember the several little incidents of the partridge, the horse, and the Bible, which were recounted in the second book. By all which Jones had rather improved than injured the affection which Mr. Allworthy was inclined to entertain for him. The same, I believe, must have happened to him with every other person who hath any idea of friendship, generosity, and greatness of spirit, that is to say, who hath any traces of goodness in his mind.

Square himself was not unacquainted with the true impression which those several instances of goodness had made on the excellent heart of All-worthy; for the philosopher very well knew what virtue was, though he was not always perhaps steady in its pursuit; but as for Thwackum, from what reason I will not determine, no such thoughts ever entered into his head: he saw Jones in a bad light, and he imagined Allworthy saw him in the same, but that he was resolved, from pride and stubbornness of spirit, not to give up the boy whom he had once cherished; since by so doing, he must tacitly acknowledge that his former opinion of him had been wrong.

Square therefore embraced this opportunity of injuring Jones in the tenderest part, by giving a very bad turn to all these before-mentioned oc-currences. "I am sorry, sir," said he, "to own I have been deceived as well as yourself. I could not, I confess, help being pleased with what I ascribed to the motive of friendship, though it was carried to an excess, and all excess is faulty and vicious: but in this I made allowance for youth. Little did I suspect that the sacrifice of truth, which we both imagined to have been made to friendship, was in reality a prostitution of it to a depraved and debauched appetite. You now plainly see whence all the seeming generosity of this young man to the family of the gamekeeper proceeded. He supported the father in order to corrupt the daughter, and preserved the family from starving, to bring one of them to shame and ruin. This is friendship! this is generosity! As Sir Richard Steele says, 'Gluttons who give high prices for delicacies, are very worthy to be called generous.' In short I am resolved, from this instance, never to give way to the weakness of human nature more, nor to think anything virtue which doth not exactly quadrate with the unerring rule of right.''

The goodness of Allworthy had prevented those considerations from occurring to himself; yet were they too plausible to be absolutely and hastily rejected, when laid before his eyes by another. Indeed what Square had said sunk very deeply into his mind, and the uneasiness which it there created was very visible to the other; though the good man would not acknowledge this, but made a very slight answer, and forcibly drove off the discourse to some other subject. It was well perhaps for poor Tom, that no such suggestions had been made before he was pardoned; for they certainly stamped in the mind of Allworthy the first bad impression concerning Jones.

CHAPTER XII

THE reader will be pleased, I believe, to return with me to Sophia. She passed the night, after we saw her last, in no very agreeable manner. Sleep befriended her but little, and dreams less. In the morning, when Mrs. Honour, her maid, attended her at the usual hour, she was found already up and dressed.

Persons who live two or three miles' distance in the country, are considered as next-door neighbors, and transactions at the one house fly with incredible celerity to the other. Mrs. Honour, therefore, had heard the whole story of Molly's shame; which she, being of a very communicative temper, had no sooner entered the apartment of her mistress, than she began to relate in the following manner:—

"La, ma'am, what doth your la'ship think? the girl that your la'ship saw at church on Sunday, whom you thought so handsome; though you would not have thought her so handsome neither, if you had seen her nearer, but to be sure she hath been carried before the justice for being big with child. She seemed to me to look like a confident slut: and to be sure she hath laid the child to young Mr. Jones. And all the parish says Mr. Allworthy

233

is so angry with young Mr. Jones, that he won't
see him. To be sure, one can't help pitying the
poor young man, and yet he doth not deserve much
pity neither, for demeaning himself with such kind
of trumpery. Yet he is so pretty a gentleman, I
should be sorry to have him turned out of doors.
I dares to swear the wench was as willing as he;
for she was always a forward kind of body. And
when wenches are so coming, young men are not
so much to be blamed neither; for to be sure they
do no more than what is natural. Indeed it is beneath them to meddle with such dirty draggle-
tails; and whatever happens to them, it is good
enough for them. And yet, to be sure, the vile
baggages are most in fault. I wishes, with all my
heart, they were well to be whipped at the cart's
tail; for it is pity they should be the ruin of a
pretty young gentleman; and nobody can deny
but that Mr. Jones is one of the most handsomest
young men that ever——"

She was running on thus, when Sophia, with a
more peevish voice than she had ever spoken to
her in before, cried, "Prithee, why dost thou
trouble me with all this stuff? What concern have
I in what Mr. Jones doth? I suppose you are all
alike. And you seem to me to be angry it was not
your own case."

"I, ma'am!" answered Mrs. Honour, "I am
sorry your ladyship should have such an opinion
of me. I am sure nobody can say any such thing
of me. All the young fellows in the world may go
to the divil for me. Because I said he was a handsome man? Everybody says it as well as I. To

be sure, I never thought as it was any harm to say a young man was handsome; but to be sure I shall never think him so any more now; for handsome is that handsome does. A beggar wench!——"

"Stop thy torrent of impertinence," cries Sophia, "and see whether my father wants me at breakfast."

Mrs. Honour then flung out of the room, muttering much to herself, of which "Marry come up, I assure you," was all that could be plainly distinguished.

Whether Mrs. Honour really deserved that suspicion, of which her mistress gave her a hint, is a matter which we cannot indulge our reader's curiosity by resolving. We will, however, make him amends in disclosing what passed in the mind of Sophia.

The reader will be pleased to recollect, that a secret affection for Mr. Jones had insensibly stolen into the bosom of this young lady. That it had there grown to a pretty great height before she herself had discovered it. When she first began to perceive its symptoms, the sensations were so sweet and pleasing, that she had not resolution sufficient to check or repel them; and thus she went on cherishing a passion of which she never once considered the consequences.

This incident relating to Molly first opened her eyes. She now first perceived the weakness of which she had been guilty; and though it caused the utmost perturbation in her mind, yet it had the effect of other nauseous physic, and for the time expelled her distemper. Its operation indeed was most wonderfully quick; and in the short interval, while her maid was absent, so entirely removed all symptoms, that when Mrs. Honour returned with a summons from her father, she was become perfectly easy, and had brought herself to a thorough indifference for Mr. Jones.

The diseases of the mind do in almost every particular imitate those of the body. For which reason, we hope, that learned faculty, for whom we have so profound a respect, will pardon us the violent hands we have been necessitated to lay on several words and phrases, which of right belong to them, and without which our descriptions must have been often unintelligible.

Now there is no one circumstance in which the distempers of the mind bear a more exact analogy to those which are called bodily, than that aptness which both have to a relapse. This is plain in the violent diseases of ambition and avarice. I have known ambition, when cured at court by frequent disappointments (which are the only physic for it), to break out again in a contest for foreman of the grand jury at an assizes; and have heard of a man who had so far conquered avarice, as to give away many a sixpence, that comforted himself, at last, on his deathbed, by making a crafty and advantageous bargain concerning his ensuing funeral, with an undertaker who had married his only child.

In the affair of love, which, out of strict conformity with the Stoic philosophy, we shall here treat as a disease, this proneness to relapse is no less conspicuous. Thus it happened to poor

Sophia; upon whom, the very next time she saw young Jones, all the former symptoms returned, and from that time cold and hot fits alternately seized her heart.

The situation of this young lady was now very different from what it had ever been before. That passion which had formerly been so exquisitely delicious, became now a scorpion in her bosom. She resisted it therefore with her utmost force, and summoned every argument her reason (which was surprisingly strong for her age) could suggest, to subdue and expel it. In this she so far succeeded, that she began to hope from time and absence a perfect cure. She resolved therefore to avoid Tom Jones as much as possible; for which purpose she began to conceive a design of visiting her aunt, to which she made no doubt of obtaining her father's consent.

But Fortune, who had other designs in her head, put an immediate stop to any such proceeding, by introducing an accident, which will be related in the next chapter.

CHAPTER XIII

A dreadful accident which befel Sophia. The gallant behavior of Jones, and the more dreadful consequence of
that behavior to the young lady; with a snort digression
in favor of the female sex.

MR. Western grew every day fonder and
and fonder of Sophia, insomuch that his
beloved dogs themselves almost gave
place to her in his affections; but as he could not
prevail on himself to abandon these, he contrived .
very cunningly to enjoy their company, together
with that of his daughter, by insisting on her riding a hunting with him.

Sophia, to whom her father's word was a law,
readily complied with his desires, though she had
not the least delight in a sport, which was of too
rough and masculine a nature to suit with her disposition. She had however another motive, beside her obedience, to accompany the old gentleman in the chase; for by her presence she hoped
in some measure to restrain his impetuosity, and
to prevent him from so frequently exposing his
neck to the utmost hazard.

The strongest objection was that which would
have formerly been an inducement to her, namely,
the frequent meeting with young Jones, whom she
had determined to avoid; but as the end of the
hunting season now approached, she hoped, by a

238

short absence with her aunt, to reason herself entirely out of her unfortunate passion; and had not any doubt of being able to meet him in the field the subsequent season without the least danger.

On the second day of her hunting, as she was returning from the chase, and was arrived within a little distance from Mr. Western's house, her horse, whose mettlesome spirit required a better rider, fell suddenly to prancing and capering in such a manner that she was in the most imminent peril of falling. Tom Jones, who was at a little distance behind, saw this, and immediately galloped up to her assistance. As soon as he came up, he leaped from his own horse, and caught hold of hers by the bridle. The unruly beast presently reared himself an end on his hind legs, and threw his lovely burden from his back, and Jones caught her in his arms.

She was so affected with the fright, that she was not immediately able to satisfy Jones, who was very solicitous to know whether she had received any hurt. She soon after, however, recovered her spirits, assured him she was safe, and thanked him for the care he had taken of her. Jones answered, "If I have preserved you, madam, I am sufficiently repaid; for I promise you, I would have secured you from the least harm at the expense of a much greater misfortune to myself than I have suffered on this occasion."

"What misfortune?" replied Sophia eagerly; "I hope you have come to no mischief?"

"Be not concerned, madam," answered Jones. "Heaven be praised you have escaped so well, considering the danger you was in. If I have broke my arm, I consider it as a trifle, in comparison of what I feared upon your account.''

Sophia then screamed out, ''Broke your arm! Heaven forbid.''

''I am afraid I have, madam,'' says Jones: ''but I beg you will suffer me first to take care of you. I have a right hand yet at your service, to help you into the next field, whence we have but a very little walk to your father's house.''

Sophia seeing his left arm dangling by his side, while he was using the other to lead her, no longer doubted of the truth. She now grew much paler than her fears for herself had made her before. All her limbs were seized with a trembling, insomuch that Jones could scarce support her; and as her thoughts were in no less agitation, she could not refrain from giving Jones a look so full of tenderness, that it almost argued a stronger sensation in her mind, than even gratitude and pity united can raise in the gentlest female bosom, without the assistance of a third more powerful passion.

Mr. Western, who was advanced at some distance when this accident happened, was now returned, as were the rest of the horsemen. Sophia immediately acquainted them with what had befallen Jones, and begged them to take care of him. Upon which Western, who had been much alarmed by meeting his daughter's horse without its rider, and was now overjoyed to find her unhurt, cried out, ''I am glad it is no worse. If Tom hath

broken his arm, we will get a joiner to mend un
again.''

The squire alighted from his horse, and proceeded to his house on foot, with his daughter and
Jones. An impartial spectator, who had met
them on the way, would, on viewing their several
countenances, have concluded Sophia alone to
have been the object of compassion: for as to
Jones, he exulted in having probably saved the
life of the young lady, at the price only of a
broken bone; and Mr. Western, though he was not
unconcerned at the accident which had befallen
Jones, was, however, delighted in a much higher
degree with the fortunate escape of his daughter.

The generosity of Sophia's temper construed
this behavior of Jones into great bravery; and it
made a deep impression on her heart: for certain
it is, that there is no one quality which so generally
recommends men to women as this; proceeding,
if we believe the common opinion, from that
natural timidity of the sex, which is, says Mr.
Osborne, ''so great, that a woman is the most
cowardly of all the creatures God ever made;''—
a sentiment more remarkable for its bluntness
than for its truth. Aristotle, in his Politics, doth
them, I believe, more justice, when he says, ''The
modesty and fortitude of men differ from those
virtues in women; for the fortitude which becomes
a woman, would be cowardice in a man; and the
modesty which becomes a man, would be pertness
in a woman.'' Nor is there, perhaps, more of
truth in the opinion of those who derive the par-

I—16

tiality which women are inclined to show to the brave, from this excess of their fear. Mr. Bayle (I think, in his article of Helen) imputes this, and with greater probability, to their violent love of glory; for the truth of which, we have the authority of him who of all others saw farthest into human nature, and who introduces the heroine of his Odyssey, the great pattern of matrimonial love and constancy, assigning the glory of her husband as the only source of her affection towards him.[1]

However this be, certain it is that the accident operated very strongly on Sophia; and, indeed, after much inquiry into the matter, I am inclined to believe, that, at this very time, the charming Sophia made no less impression on the heart of Jones; to say truth, he had for some time become sensible of the irresistible power of her charms.

---

[1] The English reader will not find this in the poem; for the sentiment is entirely left out in the translation.

CHAPTER XIV

The arrival of a surgeon.—His operations, and a long dialogue between Sophia and her maid.

WHEN they arrived at Mr. Western's hall, Sophia, who had tottered along with much difficulty, sunk down in her chair; but by the assistance of hartshorn and water, she was prevented from fainting away, and had pretty well recovered her spirits, when the surgeon who was sent for to Jones appeared. Mr. Western, who imputed these symptoms in his daughter to her fall, advised her to be presently blooded by way of prevention. In this opinion he was seconded by the surgeon, who gave so many reasons for bleeding, and quoted so many cases where persons had miscarried for want of it, that the squire became very importunate, and indeed insisted peremptorily that his daughter should be blooded.

Sophia soon yielded to the commands of her father, though entirely contrary to her own inclinations, for she suspected, I believe, less danger from the fright, than either the squire or the surgeon. She then stretched out her beautiful arm, and the operator began to prepare for his work.

While the servants were busied in providing materials, the surgeon, who imputed the backwardness which had appeared in Sophia to her

243

fears, began to comfort her with assurances that
there was not the least danger; for no accident, he
said, could ever happen in bleeding, but from the
monstrous ignorance of pretenders to surgery,
which he pretty plainly insinuated was not at present to be apprehended. Sophia declared she was
not under the least apprehension; adding, "If you
open an artery, I promise you I'll forgive you."
"Will you?" cries Western: "D—n me, if I will.
If he does thee the least mischief, d—n me if I
don't ha' the heart's blood o'un out." The surgeon assented to bleed her upon these conditions,
and then proceeded to his operation, which he performed with as much dexterity as he had promised; and with as much quickness: for he took but
little blood from her, saying, it was much safer
to bleed again and again, than to take away too
much at once.

Sophia, when her arm was bound up, retired:
for she was not willing (nor was it, perhaps,
strictly decent) to be present at the operation on
Jones. Indeed, one objection which she had to
bleeding (though she did not make it) was the delay which it would occasion to setting the broken
bone. For Western, when Sophia was concerned,
had no consideration but for her; and as for Jones
himself, he "sat like patience on a monument smiling at grief." To say the truth, when he saw the
blood springing from the lovely arm of Sophia,
he scarce thought of what had happened to himself.

The surgeon now ordered his patient to be stripped to his shirt, and then entirely baring the arm,

he began to stretch and examine it, in such a manner that the tortures he put him to caused Jones to make several wry faces; which the surgeon observing, greatly wondered at, crying, "What is the matter, sir? I am sure it is impossible I should hurt you." And then holding forth the broken arm, he began a long and very learned lecture of anatomy, in which simple and double fractures were most accurately considered; and the several ways in which Jones might have broken his arm were discussed, with proper annotations showing how many of these would have been better, and how many worse than the present case.

Having at length finished his labored harangue, with which the audience, though it had greatly raised their attention and admiration, were not much edified, as they really understood not a single syllable of all he had said, he proceeded to business, which he was more expeditious in finishing, than he had been in beginning.

Jones was then ordered into a bed, which Mr. Western compelled him to accept at his own house, and sentence of water-gruel was passed upon him.

Among the good company which had attended in the hall during the bone-setting, Mrs. Honour was one; who being summoned to her mistress as soon as it was over, and asked by her how the young gentleman did, presently launched into extravagant praises on the magnanimity, as she called it, of his behavior, which, she said, "was so charming in so pretty a creature." She then burst forth into much warmer encomiums on the beauty of his person; enumerating many particulars, and ending with the whiteness of his skin.

This discourse had an effect on Sophia's countenance, which would not perhaps have escaped the observance of the sagacious waiting-woman, had she once looked her mistress in the face, all the time she was speaking: but as a looking-glass, which was most commodiously placed opposite to her, gave her an opportunity of surveying those features, in which, of all others, she took most delight; so she had not once removed her eyes from that amiable object during her whole speech.

Mrs. Honour was so entirely wrapped up in the subject on which she exercised her tongue, and the object before her eyes, that she gave her mistress time to conquer her confusion; which having done, she smiled on her maid, and told her, "she was certainly in love with this young fellow."—"I in love, madam!" answers she: "upon my word, ma'am, I assure you, ma'am, upon my soul, ma'am, I am not."—"Why, if you was," cries her mistress, "I see no reason that you should be ashamed of it; for he is certainly a pretty fellow."—"Yes, ma'am, answered the other, "that he is, the most handsomest man I ever saw in my life. Yes, to be sure, that he is, and, as your ladyship says, I don't know why I should be ashamed of loving him, though he is my betters. To be sure, gentlefolks are but flesh and blood no more than us servants. Besides, as for Mr. Jones, thof Squire Allworthy hath made a gentleman of him, he was not so good as myself by birth: for thof I am a poor body, I am an honest person's child, and my father and mother were married, which is more

than some people can say, as high as they hold
their heads. Marry, come up! I assure you, my
dirty cousin! thof his skin be so white, and to
be sure it is the most whitest that ever was seen,
I am a Christian as well as he, and nobody can say
that I am base born: my grandfather was a clergyman,[1] and would have been very angry, I believe,
to have thought any of his family should have
taken up with Molly Seagrim's dirty leavings."

Perhaps Sophia might have suffered her maid
to run on in this manner, from wanting sufficient
spirits to stop her tongue, which the reader may
probably conjecture was no very easy task; for
certainly there were some passages in her speech
which were far from being agreeable to the lady.
However, she now checked the torrent, as there
seemed no end of its flowing. "I wonder," says
she, "at your assurance in daring to talk thus of
one of my father's friends. As to the wench, I
order you never to mention her name to me. And
with regard to the young gentleman's birth, those
who can say nothing more to his disadvantage,
may as well be silent on that head, as I desire you
will be for the future."

"I am sorry I have offended your ladyship,"
answered Mrs. Honour. "I am sure I hate Molly
Seagrim as much as your ladyship can; and as for
abusing Squire Jones, I can call all the servants in
the house to witness, that whenever any talk hath

---

[1] This is the second person of low condition whom we have
recorded in this history to have sprung from the clergy. It is
to be hoped such instances will, in future ages, when some provision is made for the families of the inferior clergy, appear
stranger than they can be thought at present.

been about bastards, I have always taken his part,
for which of you, says I to the footmen, would not
be a bastard, if he could, to be made a gentleman
of? And, says I, I am sure he is a very fine gentleman; and he hath one of the whitest hands in
the world; for to be sure so he hath: and, says I,
one of the sweetest temperedest, best naturedest
men in the world he is; and, says I, all the servants and neighbors all round the country loves
him. And, to be sure, I could tell your ladyship
something, but that I am afraid it would offend
you."—"What could you tell me, Honour?" says
Sophia. "Nay, ma'am, to be sure he meant nothing by it, therefore I would not have your ladyship
be offended."—"Prithee tell me," says Sophia;
"I will know it this instant."—"Why, ma'am,"
answered Mrs. Honour, "he came into the room
one day last week when I was at work, and there
lay your ladyship's muff on a chair, and to be
sure he put his hands into it; that very muff your
ladyship gave me but yesterday. La! says I, Mr.
Jones, you will stretch my lady's muff, and spoil
it: but he still kept his hands in it: and then he
kissed it—to be sure I hardly ever saw such a kiss
in my life as he gave it."—"I suppose he did not
know it was mine," replied Sophia. "Your ladyship shall hear, ma'am. He kissed it again and
again, and said it was the prettiest muff in the
world. La! sir, says I, you have seen it a hundred
times. Yes, Mrs. Honour, cried he; but who can
see anything beautiful in the presence of your
lady but herself?—Nay, that's not all neither; but
I hope your ladyship won't be offended, for to be

sure he meant nothing. One day, as your ladyship was playing on the harpsichord to my master, Mr. Jones was sitting in the next room, and methought he looked melancholy. La! says I, Mr. Jones, what's the matter? a penny for your thoughts, says I. Why, hussy, says he, starting up from a dream, what can I be thinking of, when that angel your mistress is playing? And then squeezing me by the hand, Oh! Mrs. Honour, says he, how happy will that man be!—and then he sighed. Upon my troth, his breath is as sweet as a nosegay.—But to be sure he meant no harm by it. So I hope your ladyship will not mention a word; for he gave me a crown never to mention it, and made me swear upon a book, but I believe, indeed, it was not the Bible.''

Till something of a more beautiful red than vermilion be found out, I shall say nothing of Sophia's color on this occasion. "Ho—nour," says she, "I—if you will not mention this any more to me—nor to anybody else, I will not betray you—I mean, I will not be angry; but I am afraid of your tongue. Why, my girl, will you give it such liberties?"—"Nay, ma'am," answered she, "to be sure, I would sooner cut out my tongue than offend your ladyship. To be sure I shall never mention a word that your ladyship would not have me."—"Why, I would not have you mention this any more," said Sophia, "for it may come to my father's ears, and he would be angry with Mr. Jones; though I really believe, as you say, he meant nothing. I should be very angry myself, if I imagined—" —"Nay, ma'am," says Honour, "I protest I believe he meant nothing. I thought he talked as if he was out of his senses; nay, he said he believed he was beside himself when he had spoken the words. Ay, sir, says I, I believe so too. Yes, says he, Honour.—But I ask your ladyship's pardon; I could tear my tongue out for offending you." "Go on," says Sophia; "you may mention anything you have not told me before."—"Yes, Honour, says he (this was some time afterwards, when he gave me the crown), I am neither such a coxcomb, or such a villain, as to think of her in any other delight but as my goddess; as such I will always worship and adore her while I have breath.—This was all, ma'am, I will be sworn, to the best of my remembrance. I was in a passion with him myself, till I found he meant no harm."—"Indeed, Honour," says Sophia, "I believe you have a real affection for me. I was provoked the other day when I gave you warning; but if you have a desire to stay with me, you shall."—"To be sure, ma'am," answered Mrs. Honour, "I shall never desire to part with your ladyship. To be sure, I almost cried my eyes out when you gave me warning. It would be very ungrateful in me to desire to leave your ladyship; because as why, I should never get so good a place again. I am sure I would live and die with your ladyship; for, as poor Mr. Jones said, happy is the man——"

Here the dinner bell interrupted a conversation which had wrought such an effect on Sophia, that she was, perhaps, more obliged to her bleeding in the morning, than she, at the time, had apprehended she should be. As to the present situation of her mind, I shall adhere to a rule of Horace, by not attempting to describe it, from despair of success. Most of my readers will suggest it easily to themselves; and the few who cannot, would not understand the picture, or at least would deny it to be natural, if ever so well drawn.

BOOK V

CHAPTER I

Of the SERIOUS *in writing, and for what purpose it is introduced.*

PERADVENTURE there may be no parts in this prodigious work which will give the reader less pleasure in the perusing, than those which have given the author the greatest pains in composing. Among these probably may be reckoned those initial essays which we have prefixed to the historical matter contained in every book; and which we have determined to be essentially necessary to this kind of writing, of which we have set ourselves at the head.

For this our determination we do not hold ourselves strictly bound to assign any reason; it being abundantly sufficient that we have laid it down as a rule necessary to be observed in all prosai-comi-epic writing. Who ever demanded the reasons of that nice unity of time or place which is now established to be so essential to dramatic poetry? What critic hath been ever asked, why a play may not contain two days as well as one? Or why the audience (provided they travel, like electors, with-

252

out any expense) may not be wafted fifty miles as well as five? Hath any commentator well accounted for the limitation which an ancient critic hath set to the drama, which he will have contain neither more nor less than five acts? Or hath any one living attempted to explain what the modern judges of our theaters mean by that word *low;* by which they have happily succeeded in banishing all humor from the stage, and have made the theater as dull as a drawing-room! Upon all these occasions the world seems to have embraced a maxim of our law, viz., *cuicunque in arte sua perito credendum est:* for it seems perhaps difficult to conceive that any one should have had enough of impudence to lay down dogmatical rules in any art or science without the least foundation. In such cases, therefore, we are apt to conclude there are sound and good reasons at the bottom, though we are unfortunately not able to see so far.

Now, in reality, the world have paid too great a compliment to critics, and have imagined them men of much greater profundity than they really are. From this complacence, the critics have been emboldened to assume a dictatorial power, and have so far succeeded, that they are now become the masters, and have the assurance to give laws to those authors from whose predecessors they originally received them.

The critic, rightly considered, is no more than the clerk, whose office it is to transcribe the rules and laws laid down by those great judges whose vast strength of genius hath placed them in the light of legislators, in the several sciences over which

they presided. This office was all which the critics of old aspired to; nor did they ever dare to advance a sentence, without supporting it by the authority of the judge from whence it was borrowed.

But in process of time, and in ages of ignorance,
the clerk began to invade the power and assume
the dignity of his master. The laws of writing
were no longer founded on the practice of the author, but on the dictates of the critic. The clerk
became the legislator, and those very peremptorily
gave laws whose business it was, at first, only to
transcribe them.

Hence arose an obvious, and perhaps an unavoidable error; for these critics being men of
shallow capacities, very easily mistook mere form
for substance. They acted as a judge would, who
should adhere to the lifeless letter of law, and reject the spirit. Little circumstances, which were
perhaps accidental in a great author, were by
these critics considered to constitute his chief
merit, and transmitted as essentials to be observed
by all his successors. To these encroachments,
time and ignorance, the two great supporters of
imposture, gave authority; and thus many rules
for good writing have been established, which
have not the least foundation in truth or nature;
and which commonly serve for no other purpose
than to curb and restrain genius, in the same manner as it would have restrained the dancing-master, had the many excellent treatises on that art
laid it down as an essential rule that every man
must dance in chains.

To avoid, therefore, all imputation of laying

down a rule for posterity, founded only on the authority of *ipse dixit*—for which, to say the truth, we have not the profoundest veneration—we shall here waive the privilege above contended for, and proceed to lay before the reader the reasons which have induced us to intersperse these several digressive essays in the course of this work.

And here we shall of necessity be led to open a new vein of knowledge, which if it hath been discovered, hath not, to our remembrance, been wrought on by any ancient or modern writer. This vein is no other than that of contrast, which runs through all the works of the creation, and may probably have a large share in constituting in us the idea of all beauty, as well natural as artificial: for what demonstrates the beauty and excellence of anything but its reverse? Thus the beauty of day, and that of summer, is set off by the horrors of night and winter. And, I believe, if it was possible for a man to have seen only the two former, he would have a very imperfect idea of their beauty.

But to avoid too serious an air; can it be doubted, but that the finest woman in the world would lose all benefit of her charms in the eye of a man who had never seen one of another cast? The ladies themselves seem so sensible of this, that they are all industrious to procure foils: nay, they will become foils to themselves; for I have observed (at Bath particularly) that they endeavor to appear as ugly as possible in the morning, in order to set off that beauty which they intend to show you in the evening.

Most artists have this secret in practice, though some, perhaps, have not much studied the theory. The jeweler knows that the finest brilliant requires a foil; and the painter, by the contrast of his figures, often acquires great applause.

A great genius among us will illustrate this matter fully. I cannot, indeed, range him under any general head of common artists, as he hath a title to be placed among those

Inventas qui vitam excoluere per artes.
Who by invented arts have life improved.

I mean here the inventor of that most exquisite entertainment, called the English Pantomime.

This entertainment consisted of two parts, which the inventor distinguished by the names of the serious and the comic. The serious exhibited a certain number of heathen gods and heroes, who were certainly the worst and dullest company into which an audience was ever introduced; and (which was a secret known to few) were actually intended so to be, in order to contrast the comic part of the entertainment, and to display the tricks of harlequin to the better advantage.

This was, perhaps, no very civil use of such personages: but the contrivance was, nevertheless, ingenious enough, and had its effect. And this will now plainly appear, if, instead of serious and comic, we supply the words duller and dullest; for the comic was certainly duller than anything before shown on the stage, and could be set off only by that superlative degree of dullness which composed the serious. So intolerably serious, indeed, were these gods and heroes, that harlequin (though the English gentleman of that name is not at all related to the French family, for he is of a much more serious disposition) was always welcome on the stage, as he relieved the audience from worse company.

Judicious writers have always practiced this art of contrast with great success. I have been surprised that Horace should cavil at this art in Homer; but indeed he contradicts himself in the very next line:

> *Indignor quandoque bonus dormitat Homerus;*
> *Verum opere in longo fas est obrepere somnum.*
> I grieve if e'er great Homer chance to sleep,
> Yet slumbers on long works have right to creep.

For we are not here to understand, as perhaps some have, that an author actually falls asleep while he is writing. It is true, that readers are too apt to be so overtaken; but if the work was as long as any of Oldmixon, the author himself is too well entertained to be subject to the least drowsiness. He is, as Mr. Pope observes,

> Sleepless himself to give his readers sleep.

To say the truth, these soporific parts are so many scenes of serious artfully interwoven, in order to contrast and set off the rest; and this is the true meaning of a late facetious writer, who told the public that whenever he was dull they might be assured there was a design in it.

In this light, then, or rather in this darkness, I would have the reader to consider these initial es-

J—17

says. And after this warning, if he shall be of opinion that he can find enough of serious in other parts of this history, he may pass over these, in which we profess to be laboriously dull, and begin the following books at the second chapter.

CHAPTER II

In which Mr. Jones receives many friendly visits during his confinement; with some fine touches of the passion of love, scarce visible to the naked eye.

TOM JONES had many visitors during his confinement, though some, perhaps, were not very agreeable to him. Mr. Allworthy saw him almost every day; but though he pitied Tom's sufferings, and greatly approved the gallant behavior which had occasioned them; yet he thought this was a favorable opportunity to bring him to a sober sense of his indiscreet conduct; and that wholesome advice for that purpose could never be applied at a more proper season than at the present, when the mind was softened by pain and sickness, and alarmed by danger; and when its attention was unembarrassed with those turbulent passions which engage us in the pursuit of pleasure.

At all seasons, therefore, when the good man was alone with the youth, especially when the latter was totally at ease, he took occasion to remind him of his former miscarriages, but in the mildest and tenderest manner, and only in order to introduce the caution which he prescribed for his future behavior; "on which alone," he assured him, "would depend his own felicity, and the kindness which he might yet promise himself to re-

259

ceive at the hands of his father by adoption, unless he should hereafter forfeit his good opinion: for as to what had passed," he said, "it should be all forgiven and forgotten. He therefore advised him to make a good use of this accident, that so in the end it might prove a visitation for his own good."

Thwackum was likewise pretty assiduous in his visits; and he too considered a sick-bed to be a convenient scene for lectures. His style, however, was more severe than Mr. Allworthy's: he told his pupil, "That he ought to look on his broken limb as a judgment from heaven on his sins. That it would become him to be daily on his knees, pouring forth thanksgivings that he had broken his arm only, and not his neck; which latter," he said, "was very probably reserved for some future occasion, and that, perhaps, not very remote. For his part," he said, "he had often wondered some judgment had not overtaken him before; but it might be perceived by this, that Divine punishments, though slow, are always sure." Hence likewise he advised him, "to foresee, with equal certainty, the greater evils which were yet behind, and which were as sure as this of overtaking him in his state of reprobacy. These are," said he, "to be averted only by such a thorough and sincere repentance as is not to be expected or hoped for from one so abandoned in his youth, and whose mind, I am afraid, is totally corrupted. It is my duty, however, to exhort you to this repentance, though I too well know all exhortations will be vain and fruitless. But *liberavi animam*

meam. I can accuse my own conscience of no
neglect; though it is at the same time with the
utmost concern I see you traveling on to certain
misery in this world, and to as certain damnation
in the next.''

Square talked in a very different strain; he said,
''Such accidents as a broken bone were below the
consideration of a wise man. That it was abundantly sufficient to reconcile the mind to any of
these mischances, to reflect that they are liable to
befall the wisest of mankind, and are undoubtedly
for the good of the whole.'' He said, ''It was a
mere abuse of words to call those things evils, in
which there was no moral unfitness: that pain,
which was the worst consequence of such accidents,
was the most contemptible thing in the world;''
with more of the like sentences, extracted out of
the second book of Tully's Tusculan questions, and
from the great Lord Shaftesbury. In pronounc-
ing these he was one day so eager, that he unfortunately bit his tongue; and in such a manner, that
it not only put an end to his discourse, but created
much emotion in him, and caused him to mutter an
oath or two: but what was worst of all, this accident gave Thwackum, who was present, and who
held all such doctrine to be heathenish and athe-
istical, an opportunity to clap a judgment on his
back. Now this was done with so malicious a
sneer, that it totally unhinged (if I may so say)
the temper of the philosopher, which the bite of
his tongue had somewhat ruffled; and as he was
disabled from venting his wrath at his lips, he had
possibly found a more violent method of reveng-

ing himself, had not the surgeon, who was then luckily in the room, contrary to his own interest, interposed and preserved the peace.

Mr. Blifil visited his friend Jones but seldom, and never alone. This worthy young man, however, professed much regard for him, and as great concern at his misfortune; but cautiously avoided any intimacy, lest, as he frequently hinted, it might contaminate the sobriety of his own character: for which purpose he had constantly in his mouth that proverb in which Solomon speaks against evil communication. Not that he was so bitter as Thwackum; for he always expressed some hopes of Tom's reformation; "which," he said, "the unparalleled goodness shown by his uncle on this occasion, must certainly effect in one not absolutely abandoned:" but concluded, "if Mr. Jones ever offends hereafter, I shall not be able to say a syllable in his favor."

As to Squire Western, he was seldom out of the sick-room, unless when he was engaged either in the field or over his bottle. Nay, he would sometimes retire hither to take his beer, and it was not without difficulty that he was prevented from forcing Jones from taking his beer too: for no quack ever held his nostrum to be a more general panacea than he did this; which, he said, had more virtue in it than was in all the physic in an apothecary's shop. He was, however, by much entreaty, prevailed on to forbear the application of this medicine; but from serenading his patient every hunting morning with the horn under his window, it was impossible to withhold him; nor did he ever lay aside that hallow, with which he entered into all companies, when he visited Jones, without any regard to the sick person's being at that time either awake or asleep.

This boisterous behavior, as it meant no harm, so happily it effected none, and was abundantly compensated to Jones, as soon as he was able to sit up, by the company of Sophia, whom the squire then brought to visit him; nor was it, indeed, long before Jones was able to attend her to the harpsichord, where she would kindly condescend, for hours together, to charm him with the most delicious music, unless when the squire thought proper to interrupt her, by insisting on Old Sir Simon, or some other of his favorite pieces.

Notwithstanding the nicest guard which Sophia endeavored to set on her behavior, she could not avoid letting some appearances now and then slip forth: for love may again be likened to a disease in this, that when it is denied a vent in one part, it will certainly break out in another. What her lips, therefore, concealed, her eyes, her blushes, and many little involuntary actions, betrayed.

One day, when Sophia was playing on the harpsichord, and Jones was attending, the squire came into the room, crying, "There, Tom, I have had a battle for thee below-stairs with thick parson Thwackum. He hath been atelling Allworthy, before my face, that the broken bone was a judgment upon thee. D—n it, says I, how can that be? Did he not come by it in defense of a young woman? A judgment indeed! Pox, if he never doth anything worse, he will go to heaven sooner

than all the parsons in the country. He hath
more reason to glory in it than to be ashamed of
it."—"Indeed, sir," says Jones, "I have no reason for either; but if it preserved Miss Western,
I shall always think it the happiest accident of my
life."—"And to gu," said the squire, "to zet Allworthy against thee vor it! D—n un, if the parson had unt his petticuoats on, I should have lent
un o flick; for I love thee dearly, my boy, and d—n
me if there is anything in my power which I won't
do for thee. Sha't take thy choice of all the
horses in my stable to-morrow morning, except
only the Chevalier and Miss Slouch." Jones
thanked him, but declined accepting the offer.
"Nay," added the squire, "sha't ha the sorrel
mare that Sophy rode. She cost me fifty guineas,
and comes six years old this grass." "If she had
cost me a thousand," cries Jones passionately, "I
would have given her to the dogs." "Pooh!
pooh!" answered Western; "what! because she
broke thy arm? Shouldst forget and forgive. I
thought hadst been more a man than to bear malice against a dumb creature."—Here Sophia interposed, and put an end to the conversation, by
desiring her father's leave to play to him; a request which he never refused.

The countenance of Sophia had undergone more
than one change during the foregoing speeches;
and probably she imputed the passionate resentment which Jones had expressed against the mare,
to a different motive from that from which her
father had derived it. Her spirits were at this
time in a visible flutter; and she played so intoler-

ably ill, that had not Western soon fallen asleep,
he must have remarked it. Jones, however, who
was sufficiently awake, and was not without an ear
any more than without eyes, made some observations; which being joined to all which the reader
may remember to have passed formerly, gave him
pretty strong assurances, when he came to reflect
on the whole, that all was not well in the tender
bosom of Sophia; an opinion which many young
gentlemen will, I doubt not, extremely wonder at
his not having been well confirmed in long ago.
To confess the truth, he had rather too much diffidence in himself, and was not forward enough in
seeing the advances of a young lady; a misfortune
which can be cured only by that early town education, which is at present so generally in fashion.

When these thoughts had fully taken possession
of Jones, they occasioned a perturbation in his
mind, which, in a constitution less pure and firm
than his, might have been, at such a season, at
tended with very dangerous consequences. He
was truly sensible of the great worth of Sophia.
He extremely liked her person, no less admired
her accomplishments, and tenderly loved her goodness. In reality, as he had never once entertained
any thought of possessing her, nor had ever given
the least voluntary indulgence to his inclinations,
he had a much stronger passion for her than he
himself was acquainted with. His heart now
brought forth the full secret, at the same time that
it assured him the adorable object returned his
affection.

CHAPTER III

*Which all who have no heart will think to contain much
ado about nothing.*

THE reader will perhaps imagine the sensations which now arose in Jones to have been so sweet and delicious, that they would rather tend to produce a cheerful serenity in the mind, than any of those dangerous effects which we have mentioned; but in fact, sensations of this kind, however delicious, are, at their first recognition, of a very tumultuous nature, and have very little of the opiate in them. They were, moreover, in the present case, embittered with certain circumstances, which being mixed with sweeter ingredients, tended altogether to compose a draught that might be termed bittersweet; than which, as nothing can be more disagreeable to the palate, so nothing, in the metaphorical sense, can be so injurious to the mind.

For first, though he had sufficient foundation to flatter himself in what he had observed in Sophia, he was not yet free from doubt of misconstruing compassion, or at best, esteem, into a warmer regard. He was far from a sanguine assurance that Sophia had any such affection towards him, as might promise his inclinations that harvest, which, if they were encouraged and nursed, they would finally grow up to require. Besides, if he could

266

hope to find no bar to his happiness from the
daughter, he thought himself certain of meeting
an effectual bar in the father; who, though he was
a country squire in his diversions, was perfectly
a man of the world in whatever regarded his fortune; had the most violent affection for his only
daughter, and had often signified, in his cups, the
pleasure he proposed in seeing her married to
one of the richest men in the county.   Jones was
not so vain and senseless a coxcomb as to expect,
from any regard which Western had professed for
him, that he would ever be induced to lay aside
these views of advancing his daughter.   He well
knew that fortune is generally the principal, if not
the sole, consideration, which operates on the best
of parents in these matters: for friendship makes
us warmly espouse the interest of others; but it is
very cold to the gratification of their passions.
Indeed, to feel the happiness which may result
from this, it is necessary we should possess the
passion ourselves.   As he had therefore no hopes
of obtaining her father's consent; so he thought to
endeavor to succeed without it, and by such means
to frustrate the great point of Mr. Western's life,
was to make a very ill use of his hospitality, and a
very ungrateful return to the many little favors received (however roughly) at his hands.   If he
saw such a consequence with horror and disdain,
how much more was he shocked with what regarded Mr. Allworthy; to whom, as he had more
than filial obligations, so had he for him more than
filial piety!   He knew the nature of that good man
to be so averse to any baseness or treachery, that

the least attempt of such a kind would make the
sight of the guilty person for ever odious to his
eyes, and his name a detestable sound in his ears.
The appearance of such unsurmountable difficulties was sufficient to have inspired him with despair, however ardent his wishes had been; but
even these were controlled by compassion for another woman. The idea of lovely Molly now intruded itself before him. He had sworn eternal
constancy in her arms, and she had as often vowed
never to out-live his deserting her. He now saw
her in all the most shocking postures of death;
nay, he considered all the miseries of prostitution
to which she would be liable, and of which he
would be doubly the occasion; first by seducing,
and then by deserting her; for he well knew the
hatred which all her neighbors, and even her own
sisters, bore her, and how ready they would all
be to tear her to pieces. Indeed, he had exposed
her to more envy than shame, or rather to the latter by means of the former: for many women
abused her for being a whore, while they envied
her her lover, and her finery, and would have been
themselves glad to have purchased these at the
same rate. The ruin, therefore, of the poor girl
must, he foresaw, unavoidably attend his deserting her; and this thought stung him to the soul.
Poverty and distress seemed to him to give none
a right of aggravating those misfortunes. The
meanness of her condition did not represent her
misery as of little consequence in his eyes, nor
did it appear to justify, or even to palliate, his
guilt, in bringing that misery upon her. But why

do I mention justification? His own heart would
not suffer him to destroy a human creature who,
he thought, loved him, and had to that love sacrificed her innocence. His own good heart pleaded
her cause; not as a cold venal advocate, but as
one interested in the event, and which must itself
deeply share in all the agonies its owner brought
on another.

When this powerful advocate had sufficiently
raised the pity of Jones, by painting poor Molly
in all the circumstances of wretchedness; it artfully called in the assistance of another passion,
and represented the girl in all the amiable colors
of youth, health, and beauty; as one greatly the object of desire, and much more so, at least to a good
mind, from being, at the same time, the object of
compassion.

Amidst these thoughts, poor Jones passed a
long sleepless night, and in the morning the result of the whole was to abide by Molly, and to
think no more of Sophia.

In this virtuous resolution he continued all the
next day till the evening, cherishing the idea of
Molly, and driving Sophia from his thoughts; but
in the fatal evening, a very trifling accident set
all his passions again on float, and worked so total a change in his mind, that we think it decent to
communicate it in a fresh chapter.

CHAPTER IV

A little chapter, in which is contained a little incident.

AMONG other visitants, who paid their compliments to the young gentleman in his confinement, Mrs. Honour was one. The reader, perhaps, when he reflects on some expressions which have formerly dropped from her, may conceive that she herself had a very particular affection for Mr. Jones; but, in reality, it was no such thing. Tom was a handsome young fellow; and for that species of men Mrs. Honour had some regard; but this was perfectly indiscriminate; for having being crossed in the love which she bore a certain nobleman's footman, who had basely deserted her after a promise of marriage, she had so securely kept together the broken remains of her heart, that no man had ever since been able to possess himself of any single fragment. She viewed all handsome men with that equal regard and benevolence which a sober and virtuous mind bears to all the good. She might indeed be called a lover of men, as Socrates was a lover of mankind, preferring one to another for corporeal, as he for mental qualifications; but never carrying this preference so far as to cause any perturbation in the philosophical serenity of her temper.

The day after Mr. Jones had that conflict with himself which we have seen in the preceding chapter, Mrs. Honour came into his room, and finding him alone, began in the following manner:—"La, sir, where do you think I have been? I warrant you, you would not guess in fifty years; but if you did guess, to be sure I must not tell you neither." —"Nay, if it be something which you must not tell me," said Jones, "I shall have the curiosity to inquire, and I know you will not be so barbarous to refuse me."—"I don't know," cries she, "why I should refuse you neither, for that matter; for to be sure you won't mention it any more. And for that matter, if you knew where I have been, unless you knew what I have been about, it would not signify much. Nay, I don't see why it should be kept a secret for my part; for to be sure she is the best lady in the world." Upon this, Jones began to beg earnestly to be let into this secret, and faithfully promised not to divulge it. She then proceeded thus:—"Why, you must know, sir, my young lady sent me to inquire after Molly Seagrim, and to see whether the wench wanted anything; to be sure, I did not care to go, methinks; but servants must do what they are ordered.— How could you undervalue yourself so, Mr. Jones? —So my lady bid me go and carry her some linen, and other things. She is too good. If such forward sluts were sent to Bridewel, it would be better for them. I told my lady, says I, madam, your la'ship is encouraging idleness." —"And was my Sophia so good?" says Jones. "My Sophia! I assure you, marry come up," answered Honour. "And yet if you knew all —indeed, if I was as Mr. Jones, I should

look a little higher than such trumpery as
Molly Seagrim." "What do you mean by these
words," replied Jones, "if I knew all?" "I
mean what I mean," says Honour. "Don't you
remember putting your hands in my lady's muff
once? I vow I could almost find in my heart to
tell, if I was certain my lady would never come to
the hearing on't." Jones then made several solemn protestations. And Honour proceeded—
"Then to be sure my lady gave me that muff; and
afterwards, upon hearing what you had done"——-
"Then you told her what I had done?" interrupted
Jones. "If I did, sir," answered she, "you need
not be angry with me. Many's the man would
have given his head to have had my lady told, if
they had known,—for, to be sure, the biggest lord
in the land might be proud—but, I protest, I have
a great mind not to tell you." Jones fell to entreaties, and soon prevailed on her to go on
thus. "You must know then, sir, that my
lady had given this muff to me; but about
a day or two after I had told her the story, she
quarrels with her new muff, and to be sure it is
the prettiest that ever was seen. Honour, says
she, this is an odious muff; it is too big for me, I
can't wear it: till I can get another, you must let
me have my old one again, and you may have this
in the room on't—for she's a good lady, and
scorns to give a thing and take a thing, I promise
you that. So to be sure I fetched it her back
again, and, I believe, she hath worn it upon her
arm almost ever since, and I warrants hath given
it many a kiss when nobody hath seen her."

Here the conversation was interrupted by Mr. Western himself, who came to summon Jones to the harpsichord; whither the poor young fellow went all pale and trembling. This Western observed, but, on seeing Mrs. Honour, imputed it to a wrong cause; and having given Jones a hearty curse between jests and earnest, he bid him beat abroad, and not poach up the game in his warren.

Sophia looked this evening with more than usual beauty, and we may believe it was no small addition to her charms, in the eye of Mr. Jones, that she now happened to have on her right arm this very muff.

She was playing one of her father's favorite tunes, and he was leaning on her chair, when the muff fell over her fingers, and put her out. This so disconcerted the squire, that he snatched the muff from her, and with a hearty curse threw it into the fire. Sophia instantly started up, and with the utmost eagerness recovered it from the flames.

Though this incident will probably appear of little consequence to many of our readers; yet, trifling as it was, it had so violent an effect on poor Jones, that we thought it our duty to relate it. In reality, there are many little circumstances too often omitted by injudicious historians, from which events of the utmost importance arise. The world may indeed be considered as a vast machine, in which the great wheels are originally set in motion by those which are very minute, and almost imperceptible to any but the strongest eyes.

Thus, not all the charms of the incomparable

I—18

Sophia; not all the dazzling brightness, and languishing softness of her eyes; the harmony of her voice, and of her person; not all her wit, good-humor, greatness of mind, or sweetness of disposition, had been able so absolutely to conquer and enslave the heart of poor Jones, as this little incident of the muff. Thus the poet sweetly sings of Troy—

> ——*Captique dolis lachrymisque coacti*
> *Quos neque Tydides, nec Larissæus Achilles,*
> *Non anni domuere decem, non mille Carinæ.*

> What Diomede or Thetis' greater son,
> A thousand ships, nor ten years' siege had done.
> False tears and fawning words the city won.

The citadel of Jones was now taken by surprise. All those considerations of honor and prudence which our hero had lately with so much military wisdom placed as guards over the avenues of his heart, ran away from their posts, and the god of love marched in, in triumph.

CHAPTER V

A very long chapter, containing a very great incident.

BUT though this victorious deity easily expelled his avowed enemies from the heart of Jones, he found it more difficult to supplant the garrison which he himself had placed there. To lay aside all allegory, the concern for what must become of poor Molly greatly disturbed and perplexed the mind of the worthy youth. The superior merit of Sophia totally eclipsed, or rather extinguished, all the beauties of the poor girl; but compassion instead of contempt succeeded to love. He was convinced the girl had placed all her affections, and all her prospect of future happiness, in him only. For this he had, he knew, given sufficient occasion, by the utmost profusion of tenderness towards her: a tenderness which he had taken every means to persuade her he would always maintain. She, on her side, had assured him of her firm belief in his promise, and had with the most solemn vows declared, that on his fulfilling or breaking these promises, it depended, whether she should be the happiest or most miserable of womankind. And to be the author of this highest degree of misery to a human being, was a thought on which he could not bear to ruminate a single moment. He considered this poor girl as having sacrificed to him everything in

her little power; as having been at her own expense the object of his pleasure; as sighing and
languishing for him even at that very instant.
Shall then, says he, my recovery, for which she
hath so ardently wished; shall my presence, which
she hath so eagerly expected, instead of giving her
that joy with which she hath flattered herself, cast
her at once down into misery and despair? Can
I be such a villain? Here, when the genius of
poor Molly seemed triumphant, the love of Sophia
towards him, which now appeared no longer dubious, rushed upon his mind, and bore away every
obstacle before it.

At length it occurred to him, that he might possibly be able to make Molly amends another way;
namely, by giving her a sum of money. This,
nevertheless, he almost despaired of her accepting,
when he recollected the frequent and vehement assurances he had received from her, that the world
put in balance with him would make her no amends
for his loss. However, her extreme poverty, and
chiefly her egregious vanity (somewhat of which
hath been already hinted to the reader), gave him
some little hope, that, notwithstanding all her
avowed tenderness, she might in time be brought
to content herself with a fortune superior to her
expectation, and which might indulge her vanity,
by setting her above all her equals. He resolved
therefore to take the first opportunity of making
a proposal of this kind.

One day, accordingly, when his arm was so well
recovered that he could walk easily with it slung
in a sash, he stole forth, at a season when the

squire was engaged in his field exercises, and visited his fair one. Her mother and sisters, whom he found taking their tea, informed him first that Molly was not at home; but afterwards the eldest sister acquainted him, with a malicious smile, that she was above stairs a-bed. Tom had no objection to this situation of his mistress, and immediately ascended the ladder which led towards her bed-chamber; but when he came to the top, he, to his great surprise found the door fast; nor could he for some time obtain any answer from within; for Molly, as she herself afterwards informed him, was fast asleep.

The extremes of grief and joy have been remarked to produce very similar effects; and when either of these rushes on us by surprise, it is apt to create such a total perturbation and confusion, that we are often thereby deprived of the use of all our faculties. It cannot therefore be wondered at, that the unexpected sight of Mr. Jones should so strongly operate on the mind of Molly, and should overwhelm her with such confusion, that for some minutes she was unable to express the great raptures, with which the reader will suppose she was affected on this occasion. As for Jones, he was so entirely possessed, and as it were enchanted, by the presence of his beloved object, that he for a while forgot Sophia, and consequently the principal purpose of his visit.

This, however, soon recurred to his memory; and after the first transports of their meeting were over, he found means by degrees to introduce a discourse on the fatal consequences which must at-

tend their amour, if Mr. Allworthy, who had strictly forbidden him ever seeing her more, should discover that he still carried on this commerce. Such
a discovery, which his enemies gave him reason to
think would be unavoidable, must, he said, end in
his ruin, and consequently in hers. Since therefore their hard fates had determined that they
must separate, he advised her to bear it with resolution, and swore he would never omit any opportunity, through the course of his life, of showing
her the sincerity of his affection, by providing for
her in a manner beyond her utmost expectation,
or even beyond her wishes, if ever that should be
in his power; concluding at last, that she might
soon find some man who would marry her, and
who would make her much happier than she could
be by leading a disreputable life with him.

Molly remained a few moments in silence, and
then bursting into a flood of tears, she began to upbraid him in the following words: "And this is
your love for me, to forsake me in this manner,
now you have ruined me! How often, when I
have told you that all men are false and perjury
alike, and grow tired of us as soon as ever they
have had their wicked wills of us, how often have
you sworn you would never forsake me! And
can you be such a perjury man after all? What
signifies all the riches in the world to me without
you, now you have gained my heart, so you have
—you have—? Why do you mention another
man to me? I can never love any other man as
long as I live. All other men are nothing to me.
If the greatest squire in all the country would

come a suiting to me to-morrow, I would not give
my company to him.   No, I shall always hate and
despise the whole sex for your sake.''—

She was proceeding thus, when an accident put
a stop to her tongue, before it had run out half
its career.   The room, or rather garret, in which
Molly lay, being up one pair of stairs, that is to
say, at the top of the house, was of a sloping figure, resembling the great Delta of the Greeks.
The English reader may perhaps form a better
idea of it, by being told that it was impossible to
stand upright anywhere but in the middle.   Now,
as this room wanted the conveniency of a closet,
Molly had, to supply that defect, nailed up an old
rug against the rafters of the house, which enclosed a little hole where her best apparel, such
as the remains of that sack which we have formerly mentioned, some caps, and other things with
which she had lately provided herself, were hung
up and secured from the dust.

This enclosed place exactly fronted the foot of
the bed, to which, indeed, the rug hung so near,
that it served in a manner to supply the want of
curtains.   Now, whether Molly, in the agonies of
her rage, pushed this rug with her feet; or Jones
might touch it; or whether the pin or nail gave
way of its own accord, I am not certain; but as
Molly pronounced those last words, which are recorded above, the wicked rug got loose from its
fastening, and discovered everything hid behind
it; where among other female utensils appeared
—(with shame I write it, and with sorrow will it
be read)—the philosopher Square, in a posture

(for the place would not near admit his standing upright) as ridiculous as can possibly be conceived.

The posture, indeed, in which he stood, was not greatly unlike that of a soldier who is tied neck and heels; or rather resembling the attitude in which we often see fellows in the public streets of London, who are not suffering but deserving punishment by so standing. He had a nightcap belonging to Molly on his head, and his two large eyes, the moment the rug fell, stared directly at Jones; so that when the idea of philosophy was added to the figure now discovered, it would have been very difficult for any spectator to have refrained from immoderate laughter.

I question not but the surprise of the reader will be here equal to that of Jones; as the suspicions which must arise from the appearance of this wise and grave man in such a place, may seem so inconsistent with that character which he hath, doubtless, maintained hitherto, in the opinion of every one.

But to confess the truth, this inconsistency is rather imaginary than real. Philosophers are composed of flesh and blood as well as other human creatures; and however sublimated and refined the theory of these may be, a little practical frailty is as incident to them as to other mortals. It is, indeed, in theory only, and not in practice, as we have before hinted, that consists the difference: for though such great beings think much better and more wisely, they always act exactly like other men. They know very well how to subdue all ap-

petites and passions, and to despise both pain and
pleasure; and this knowledge affords much delightful contemplation, and is easily acquired; but
the practice would be vexatious and troublesome;
and, therefore, the same wisdom which teaches
them to know this, teaches them to avoid carrying
it into execution.

Mr. Square happened to be at church on that
Sunday, when, as the reader may be pleased to
remember, the appearance of Molly in her sack
had caused all that disturbance. Here he first observed her, and was so pleased with her beauty,
that he prevailed with the young gentlemen to
change their intended ride that evening, that he
might pass by the habitation of Molly, and by that
means might obtain a second chance of seeing her.
This reason, however, as he did not at that time
mention to any, so neither did we think proper to
communicate it then to the reader.

Among other particulars which constituted the
unfitness of things in Mr. Square's opinion, danger and difficulty were two. The difficulty therefore which he apprehended there might be in corrupting this young wench, and the danger which
would accrue to his character on the discovery,
were such strong dissuasives, that it is probable
he at first intended to have contented himself with
the pleasing ideas which the sight of beauty fur-
nishes us with. These the gravest men, after a
full meal of serious meditation, often allow themselves by way of dessert: for which purpose, certain books and pictures find their way into the
most private recesses of their study, and a certain

liquorish part of natural philosophy is often the principal subject of their conversation.

But when the philosopher heard, a day or two afterwards, that the fortress of virtue had already been subdued he began to give a large scope to his desires. His appetite was not of that squeamish kind which cannot feed on a dainty because another hath tasted it. In short, he liked the girl the better for the want of that chastity, which, if she had possessed it, must have been a bar to his pleasures; he pursued and obtained her.

The reader will be mistaken, if he thinks Molly gave Square the preference to her younger lover: on the contrary, had she been confined to the choice of one only, Tom Jones would undoubtedly have been, of the two, the victorious person. Nor was it solely the consideration that two are better than one (though this had its proper weight) to which Mr. Square owed his success: the absence of Jones during his confinement was an unlucky circumstance; and in that interval some well-chosen presents from the philosopher so softened and unguarded the girl's heart, that a favorable opportunity became irresistible, and Square triumphed over the poor remains of virtue which subsisted in the bosom of Molly.

It was now about a fortnight since this conquest, when Jones paid the above-mentioned visit to his mistress, at a time when she and Square were in bed together. This was the true reason why the mother denied her as we have seen; for as the old woman shared in the profits arising from the iniquity of her daughter, she encouraged and pro-

tected her in it to the utmost of her power; but
such was the envy and hatred which the elder sister bore towards Molly, that, notwithstanding she
had some part of the booty, she would willingly
have parted with this to ruin her sister and spoil
her trade.   Hence she had acquainted Jones with
her being above-stairs in bed, in hopes that he
might have caught her in Square's arms.   This,
however, Molly found means to prevent, as the
door was fastened; which gave her an opportunity
of conveying her lover behind that rug or blanket
where he now was unhappily discovered.

Square no sooner made his appearance than
Molly flung herself back in her bed, cried out she
was undone, and abandoned herself to despair.
This poor girl, who was yet but a novice in her
business, had not arrived to that perfection of assurance which helps off a town lady in any ex-
tremity; and either prompts her with an excuse,
or else inspires her to brazen out the matter with
her husband, who, from love of quiet, or out of
fear of his reputation—and sometimes, perhaps,
from fear of the gallant, who, like Mr. Constant in
the play, wears a sword—is glad to shut his eyes,
and content to put his horns in his pocket.   Molly,
on the contrary, was silenced by this evidence, and
very fairly gave up a cause which she had hitherto
maintained with so many tears, and with such
solemn and vehement protestations of the purest
love and constancy.

As to the gentleman behind the arras, he was
not in much less consternation.   He stood for a
while motionless, and seemed equally at a loss

what to say, or whither to direct his eyes. Jones,
though perhaps the most astonished of the three,
first found his tongue; and being immediately recovered from those uneasy sensations which Molly
by her upbraidings had occasioned, he burst into
a loud laughter, and then saluting Mr. Square,
advanced to take him by the hand, and to relieve
him from his place of confinement.

Square being now arrived in the middle of the
room, in which part only he could stand upright,
looked at Jones with a very grave countenance,
and said to him, ''Well, sir, I see you enjoy this
mighty discovery, and, I dare swear, take great
delight in the thoughts of exposing me; but if
you will consider the matter fairly, you will find
you are yourself only to blame. I am not guilty
of corrupting innocence. I have done nothing for
which that part of the world which judges of matters by the rule of right, will condemn me. Fitness is governed by the nature of things, and not
by customs, forms, or municipal laws. Nothing
is indeed unfit which is not unnatural.''—''Well
reasoned, old boy,'' answered Jones; ''but why
dost thou think that I should desire to expose
thee? I promise thee, I was never better pleased
with thee in my life; and unless thou hast a mind
to discover it thyself, this affair may remain a
profound secret for me.''—''Nay, Mr. Jones,''
replied Square, ''I would not be thought to undervalue reputation. Good fame is a species of the
Kalon, and it is by no means fitting to neglect it.
Besides, to murder one's own reputation is a kind
of suicide, a detestable and odious vice. If you

think proper, therefore, to conceal any infirmity of mine (for such I may have, since no man is perfectly perfect), I promise you I will not betray myself. Things may be fitting to be done, which are not fitting to be boasted of; for by the perverse judgment of the world, that often becomes the subject of censure, which is, in truth, not only innocent but laudable.''—''Right!'' cries Jones: ''what can be more innocent than the indulgence of a natural appetite? or what more laudable than the propagation of our species?''—''To be serious with you,'' answered Square, ''I profess they always appeared so to me.''—''And yet,'' said Jones, ''you was of a different opinion when my affair with this girl was first discovered.''— ''Why, I must confess,'' says Square, ''as the matter was misrepresented to me, by that parson Thwackum, I might condemn the corruption of innocence: it was that, sir, it was that—and that—: for you must know, Mr. Jones, in the consideration of fitness, very minute circumstances, sir, very minute circumstances cause great alteration.''—''Well,'' cries Jones, ''be that as it will, it shall be your own fault, as I have promised you, if you ever hear any more of this adventure.   Behave kindly to the girl, and I will never open my lips concerning the matter to any one. And, Molly, do you be faithful to your friend, and I will not only forgive your infidelity to me, but will do you all the service I can.'' So saying, he took a hasty leave, and, slipping down the ladder, retired with much expedition.

Square was rejoiced to find this adventure was

likely to have no worse conclusion; and as for Molly, being recovered from her confusion, she began at first to upbraid Square with having been the occasion of her loss of Jones; but that gentleman soon found the means of mitigating her anger, partly by caresses and partly by a small nostrum from his purse, of wonderful and approved efficacy in purging off the ill humors of the mind, and in restoring it to a good temper.

She then poured forth a vast profusion of tenderness towards her new lover; turned all she had said to Jones, and Jones himself, into ridicule; and vowed, though he once had the possession of her person, that none but Square had ever been master of her heart.

CHAPTER VI

By comparing which with the former, the reader may possibly
correct some abuse which he hath formerly been guilty
of in the application of the word love.

THE infidelity of Molly, which Jones had
now discovered, would, perhaps, have vin-
dicated a much greater degree of resentment than he expressed on the occasion; and if
he had abandoned her directly from that moment,
very few, I believe, would have blamed him.

Certain, however, it is, that he saw her in the
light of compassion; and though his love to her
was not of that kind which could give him any
great uneasiness at her inconstancy, yet was he
not a little shocked on reflecting that he had himself originally corrupted her innocence; for to this
corruption he imputed all the vice into which she
appeared now so likely to plunge herself.

This consideration gave him no little uneasiness, till Betty, the elder sister, was so kind,
some time afterwards, entirely to cure him by
hint, that one Will Barnes, and not himself, had
been the first seducer of Molly; and that the little
child, which he had hitherto so certainly concluded to be his own, might very probably have
an equal title, at least, to claim Barnes for its
father.

Jones eagerly pursued this scent when he had

287

first received it; and in a very short time was sufficiently assured that the girl had told him truth, not only by the confession of the fellow, but at last by that of Molly herself.

This Will Barnes was a country gallant, and had acquired as many trophies of this kind as any ensign or attorney's clerk in the kingdom. He had, indeed, reduced several women to a state of utter profligacy, had broke the hearts of some, and had the honor of occasioning the violent death of one poor girl, who had either drowned herself, or, what was rather more probable, had been drowned by him.

Among other of his conquests, this fellow had triumphed over the heart of Betty Seagrim. He had made love to her long before Molly was grown to be a fit object of that pastime; but had afterwards deserted her, and applied to her sister, with whom he had almost immediate success. Now Will had, in reality, the sole possession of Molly's affection, while Jones and Square were almost equally sacrifices to her interest and to her pride.

Hence had grown that implacable hatred which we have before seen raging in the mind of Betty; though we did not think it necessary to assign this cause sooner, as envy itself alone was adequate to all the effects we have mentioned.

Jones was become perfectly easy by possession of this secret with regard to Molly; but as to Sophia, he was far from being in a state of tranquillity; nay, indeed, he was under the most violent perturbation; his heart was now, if I may use the metaphor, entirely evacuated, and Sophia took absolute possession of it. He loved her with an unbounded passion, and plainly saw the tender sentiments she had for him; yet could not this assurance lessen his despair of obtaining the consent of her father, nor the horrors which attended his pursuit of her by any base or treacherous method.

The injury which he must thus do to Mr. Western, and the concern which would accrue to Mr. Allworthy, were circumstances that tormented him all day, and haunted him on his pillow at night. His life was a constant struggle between honor and inclination, which alternately triumphed over each other in his mind. He often resolved, in the absence of Sophia, to leave her father's house, and to see her no more; and as often, in her presence, forgot all those resolutions, and determined to pursue her at the hazard of his life, and at the forfeiture of what was much dearer to him.

This conflict began soon to produce very strong and visible effects: for he lost all his usual sprightliness and gayety of temper, and became not only melancholy when alone, but dejected and absent in company; nay, if ever he put on a forced mirth, to comply with Mr. Western's humor, the constraint appeared so plain, that he seemed to have been giving the strongest evidence of what he endeavored to conceal by such ostentation.

It may, perhaps, be a question, whether the art which he used to conceal his passion, or the means which honest nature employed to reveal it, betrayed him most: for while art made him more than ever reserved to Sophia, and forbade him to address any of his discourse to her, nay, to avoid meeting her eyes, with the utmost caution; nature was no less busy in counter-plotting him. Hence, at the approach of the young lady, he grew pale; and if this was sudden, started. If his eyes accidentally met hers, the blood rushed into his cheeks, and his countenance became all over scarlet. If common civility ever obliged him to speak to her, as to drink her health at table, his tongue was sure to falter. If he touched her, his hand, nay his whole frame, trembled. And if any discourse tended, however remotely, to raise the idea of love, an involuntary sigh seldom failed to steal from his bosom. Most of which accidents nature was wonderfully industrious to throw daily in his way.

All these symptoms escaped the notice of the squire: but not so of Sophia. She soon perceived these agitations of mind in Jones, and was at no loss to discover the cause; for indeed she recognized it in her own breast. And this recognition is, I suppose, that sympathy which hath been so often noted in lovers, and which will sufficiently account for her being so much quicker-sighted than her father.

But, to say the truth, there is a more simple and plain method of accounting for that prodigious superiority of penetration which we must observe in some men over the rest of the human species, and one which will serve not only in the case of lovers, but of all others. From whence is it that the knave is generally so quick-sighted to those symptoms and operations of knavery, which often dupe an honest man of a much better under-

standing? There surely is no general sympathy
among knaves; nor have they, like freemasons,
any common sign of communication. In reality,
it is only because they have the same thing in their
heads, and their thoughts are turned the same
way. Thus, that Sophia saw, and that Western
did not see, the plain symptoms of love in Jones
can be no wonder, when we consider that the idea
of love never entered into the head of the father,
whereas the daughter, at present, thought of
nothing else.

When Sophia was well satisfied of the violent
passion which tormented poor Jones, and no less
certain that she herself was its object, she had not
the least difficulty in discovering the true cause
of his present behavior. This highly endeared
him to her, and raised in her mind two of the best
affections which any lover can wish to raise in a
mistress—these were, esteem and pity—for sure
the most outrageously rigid among her sex will
excuse her pitying a man whom she saw miserable on her own account; nor can they blame her
for esteeming one who visibly, from the most
honorable motives, endeavored to smother a flame
in his own bosom, which, like the famous Spartan
theft, was preying upon and consuming his very
vitals. Thus his backwardness, his shunning her,
his coldness, and his silence, were the forwardest,
the most diligent, the warmest, and most eloquent
advocates; and wrought so violently on her sensible and tender heart, that she soon felt for him all
those gentle sensations which are consistent with
a virtuous and elevated female mind. In short,

all which esteem, gratitude, and pity, can inspire in such towards an agreeable man—indeed, all which the nicest delicacy can allow. In a word, she was in love with him to distraction.

One day this young couple accidentally met in the garden, at the end of the two walks which were both bounded by that canal in which Jones had formerly risked drowning to retrieve the little bird that Sophia had there lost.

This place had been of late much frequented by Sophia. Here she used to ruminate, with a mixture of pain and pleasure, on an incident which, however trifling in itself, had possibly sown the first seeds of that affection which was now arrived to such maturity in her heart.

Here then this young couple met. They were almost close together before either of them knew anything of the other's approach. A bystander would have discovered sufficient marks of confusion in the countenance of each; but they felt too much themselves to make any observation. As soon as Jones had a little recovered his first surprise, he accosted the young lady with some of the ordinary forms of salutation, which she in the same manner returned; and their conversation began, as usual, on the delicious beauty of the morning. Hence they passed to the beauty of the place, on which Jones launched forth very high encomiums. When they came to the tree whence he had formerly tumbled into the canal, Sophia could not help reminding him of that accident, and said, "I fancy, Mr. Jones, you have some little shuddering when you see that water."—"I as-

sure you, madam,'' answered Jones, ''the concern
you felt at the loss of your little bird will always
appear to me the highest circumstance in that adventure. Poor little Tommy! there is the branch
he stood upon. How could the little wretch have
the folly to fly away from that state of happiness
in which I had the honor to place him? His fate
was a just punishment for his ingratitude.''—
''Upon my word, Mr. Jones,'' said she, ''your gallantry very narrowly escaped as severe a fate.
Sure the remembrance must affect you.''—''Indeed, madam,'' answered he, ''if I have any reason to reflect with sorrow on it, it is, perhaps, that
the water had not been a little deeper, by which I
might have escaped many bitter heart-aches that
Fortune seems to have in store for me.''—''Fie,
Mr. Jones!'' replied Sophia; ''I am sure you cannot be in earnest now. This affected contempt of
life is only an excess of your complacence to me.
You would endeavor to lessen the obligation of
having twice ventured it for my sake. Beware
the third time.'' She spoke these last words with
a smile, and a softness inexpressible. Jones answered with a sigh, ''He feared it was already too
late for caution:'' and then looking tenderly and
steadfastly on her, he cried, ''Oh, Miss Western!
can you desire me to live? Can you wish me so
ill?'' Sophia, looking down on the ground, answered with some hesitation, ''Indeed, Mr. Jones,
I do not wish you ill.''—''Oh, I know too well
that heavenly temper,'' cries Jones, ''that divine
goodness, which is beyond every other charm.''—
''Nay, now,'' answered she, ''I understand you

not. I can stay no longer."—"I—I would not be understood!" cries he; "nay, I can't be understood. I know not what I say. Meeting you here so unexpectedly, I have been unguarded: for Heaven's sake pardon me, if I have said anything to offend you. I did not mean it. Indeed, I would rather have died—nay, the very thought would kill me."—"You surprise me," answered she. "How can you possibly think you have offended me?"—"Fear, madam," says he, "easily runs into madness; and there is no degree of fear like that which I feel of offending you. How can I speak then? Nay, don't look angrily at me: one frown will destroy me. I mean nothing. Blame my eyes, or blame those beauties. What am I saying? Pardon me if I have said too much. My heart overflowed. I have struggled with my love to the utmost, and have endeavored to conceal a fever which preys on my vitals, and will, I hope, soon make it impossible for me ever to offend you more."

Mr. Jones now fell a trembling as if he had been shaken with the fit of an ague. Sophia, who was in a situation not very different from his, answered in these words: "Mr. Jones, I will not affect to misunderstand you; indeed, I understand you too well; but, for Heaven's sake, if you have any affection for me, let me make the best of my way into the house. I wish I may be able to support myself thither."

Jones, who was hardly able to support himself, offered her his arm, which she condescended to accept, but begged he would not mention a word more to her of this nature at present. He promised he would not; insisting only on her forgiveness of what love, without the leave of his will, had forced from him: this, she told him, he knew how to obtain by his future behavior; and thus this young pair tottered and trembled along, the lover not once daring to squeeze the hand of his mistress, though it was locked in his.

Sophia immediately retired to her chamber, where Mrs. Honour and the hartshorn were summoned to her assistance. As to poor Jones, the only relief to his distempered mind was an unwelcome piece of news, which, as it opens a scene of different nature from those in which the reader hath lately been conversant, will be communicated to him in the next chapter.

CHAPTER VII

In which Mr. Allworthy appears on a sick-bed.

MR. Western was become so fond of Jones that he was unwilling to part with him, though his arm had been long since cured; and Jones, either from the love of sport, or from some other reason, was easily persuaded to continue at his house, which he did sometimes for a fortnight together without paying a single visit at Mr. Allworthy's; nay, without ever hearing from thence.

Mr. Allworthy had been for some days indisposed with a cold, which had been attended with a little fever. This he had, however, neglected; as it was usual with him to do all manner of disorders which did not confine him to his bed, or prevent his several faculties from performing their ordinary functions;—a conduct which we would by no means be thought to approve or recommend to imitation; for surely the gentlemen of the Æsculapian art are in the right in advising, that the moment the disease has entered at one door, the physician should be introduced at the other: what else is meant by that old adage, *Venienti occurrite morbo?* "Oppose a distemper at its first approach." Thus the doctor and the disease meet in fair and equal conflict; whereas, by giving time to the latter, we often suffer him to fortify and en-

trench himself, like a French army; so that the
learned gentleman finds it very difficult, and sometimes impossible, to come at the enemy. Nay,
sometimes by gaining time the disease applies to
the French military politics, and corrupts nature
over to his side, and then all the powers of physic
must arrive too late. Agreeable to these observations was, I remember, the complaint of the great
Doctor Misaubin, who used very pathetically to
lament the late applications which were made to
his skill, saying, "Bygar, me believe my pation
take me for de undertaker, for dey never send for
me till de physicion have kill dem."

Mr. Allworthy's distemper, by means of this
neglect, gained such ground, that, when the increase of his fever obliged him to send for assistance, the doctor at his first arrival shook his head,
wished he had been sent for sooner, and intimated
that he thought him in very imminent danger. Mr.
Allworthy, who had settled all his affairs in this
world, and was as well prepared as it is possible
for human nature to be for the other, received this
information with the utmost calmness and unconcern. He could, indeed, whenever he laid himself
down to rest, say with Cato in the tragical poem—

> Let guilt or fear
> Disturb man's rest: Cato knows neither of them;
> Indifferent in his choice to sleep or die.

In reality, he could say this with ten times more
reason and confidence than Cato, or any other
proud fellow among the ancient or modern heroes;
for he was not only devoid of fear, but might be

considered as a faithful laborer, when at the end of harvest he is summoned to receive his reward at the hands of a bountiful master.

The good man gave immediate orders for all his family to be summoned round him. None of these were then abroad, but Mrs. Blifil, who had been some time in London, and Mr. Jones, whom the reader hath just parted from at Mr. Western's, and who received this summons just as Sophia had left him.

The news of Mr. Allworthy's danger (for the servant told him he was dying) drove all thoughts of love out of his head. He hurried instantly into the chariot which was sent for him, and ordered the coachman to drive with all imaginable haste; nor did the idea of Sophia, I believe, once occur to him on the way.

And now the whole family, namely, Mr. Blifil, Mr. Jones, Mr. Thwackum, Mr. Square, and some of the servants (for such were Mr. Allworthy's orders) being all assembled round his bed, the good man sat up in it, and was beginning to speak, when Blifil fell to blubbering, and began to express very loud and bitter lamentations. Upon this Mr. Allworthy shook him by the hand, and said, "Do not sorrow thus, my dear nephew, at the most ordinary of all human occurrences. When misfortunes befall our friends we are justly grieved; for those are accidents which might often have been avoided, and which may seem to render the lot of one man more peculiarly unhappy than that of others; but death is certainly unavoidable, and is that common lot in which alone the fortunes of all men agree: nor is the time when this happens to us very material. If the wisest of men hath compared life to a span, surely we may be allowed to consider it as a day. It is my fate to leave it in the evening; but those who are taken away earlier have only lost a few hours, at the best little worth lamenting, and much oftener hours of labor and fatigue, of pain and sorrow. One of the Roman poets, I remember, likens our leaving life to our departure from a feast;—a thought which hath often occurred to me when I have seen men struggling to protract an entertainment, and to enjoy the company of their friends a few moments longer. Alas! how short is the most protracted of such enjoyments! how immaterial the difference between him who retires the soonest, and him who stays the latest! This is seeing life in the best view, and this unwillingness to quit our friends is the most amiable motive from which we can derive the fear of death; and yet the longest enjoyment which we can hope for of this kind is of so trivial a duration, that it is to a wise man truly contemptible. Few men, I own, think in this manner; for, indeed, few men think of death till they are in its jaws. However gigantic and terrible an object this may appear when it approaches them, they are nevertheless incapable of seeing it at any distance; nay, though they have been ever so much alarmed and frightened when they have apprehended themselves in danger of dying, they are no sooner cleared from this apprehension than even the fears of it are erased from their minds.

But, alas! he who escapes from death is not pardoned; he is only reprieved, and reprieved to a short day.

"Grieve, therefore, no more, my dear child, on this occasion: an event which may happen every hour; which every element, nay, almost every particle of matter that surrounds us is capable of producing, and which must and will most unavoidably reach us all at last, ought neither to occasion our surprise nor our lamentation.

"My physician having acquainted me (which I take very kindly of him) that I am in danger of leaving you all very shortly, I have determined to say a few words to you at this our parting, before my distemper, which I find grows very fast upon me, puts it out of my power.

"But I shall waste my strength too much. I intended to speak concerning my will, which, though I have settled long ago, I think proper to mention such heads of it as concern any of you, that I may have the comfort of perceiving you are all satisfied with the provision I have there made for you.

"Nephew Blifil, I leave you the heir to my whole estate, except only £500 a-year, which is to revert to you after the death of your mother, and except one other estate of £500 a-year, and the sum of £6000, which I have bestowed in the following manner:

"The estate of £500 a-year I have given to you, Mr. Jones: and as I know the inconvenience which attends the want of ready money, I have added £1000 in specie. In this I know not whether I have exceeded or fallen short of your expectation. Perhaps you will think I have given you too little, and the world will be as ready to condemn me for giving you too much; but the latter censure I despise; and as to the former, unless you should entertain that common error which I have often heard in my life pleaded as an excuse for a total want of charity, namely, that instead of raising gratitude by voluntary acts of bounty, we are apt to raise demands, which of all others are the most boundless and most difficult to satisfy.—Pardon me the bare mention of this; I will not suspect any such thing.''

Jones flung himself at his benefactor's feet, and taking eagerly hold of his hand, assured him his goodness to him, both now and all other times, had so infinitely exceeded not only his merit but his hopes, that no words could express his sense of it. ''And I assure you, sir,'' said he, ''your present generosity hath left me no other concern than for the present melancholy occasion. Oh, my friend, my father!'' Here his words choked him, and he turned away to hide a tear which was starting from his eyes.

Allworthy then gently squeezed his hand, and proceeded thus: ''I am convinced, my child, that you have much goodness, generosity, and honor, in your temper: if you will add prudence and religion to these, you must be happy; for the three former qualities, I admit, make you worthy of happiness, but they are the latter only which will put you in possession of it.

''One thousand pound I have given to you, Mr.

Thwackum; a sum I am convinced which greatly exceeds your desires, as well as your wants. However, you will receive it as a memorial of my friendship; and whatever superfluities may redound to you, that piety which you so rigidly maintain will instruct you how to dispose of them.

"A like sum, Mr. Square, I have bequeathed to you. This, I hope, will enable you to pursue your profession with better success than hitherto. I have often observed with concern, that distress is more apt to excite contempt than commiseration, especially among men of business, with whom poverty is understood to indicate want of ability. But the little I have been able to leave you will extricate you from those difficulties with which you have formerly struggled; and then I doubt not but you will meet with sufficient prosperity to supply what a man of your philosophical temper will require.

"I find myself growing faint, so I shall refer you to my will for my disposition of the residue. My servants will there find some tokens to remember me by; and there are a few charities which, I trust, my executors will see faithfully performed. Bless you all. I am setting out a little before you."—

Here a footman came hastily into the room, and said there was an attorney from Salisbury who had a particular message, which he said he must communicate to Mr. Allworthy himself: that he seemed in a violent hurry, and protested he had so much business to do, that, if he could cut himself into four quarters, all would not be sufficient.

"Go, child," said Allworthy to Blifil, "see what the gentleman wants. I am not able to do any business now, nor can he have any with me, in which you are not at present more concerned than myself. Besides, I really am—I am incapable of seeing any one at present, or of any longer attention." He then saluted them all, saying, perhaps he should be able to see them again, but he should be now glad to compose himself a little, finding that he had too much exhausted his spirits in discourse.

Some of the company shed tears at their parting; and even the philosopher Square wiped his eyes, albeit unused to the melting mood. As to Mrs. Wilkins, she dropped her pearls as fast as the Arabian trees their medicinal gums; for this was a ceremonial which that gentlewoman never omitted on a proper occasion.

After this Mr. Allworthy again laid himself down on his pillow, and endeavored to compose himself to rest.

CHAPTER VIII

Containing matter rather natural than pleasing.

BESIDES grief for her master, there was another source for that briny stream which so plentifully rose above the two mountainous cheek-bones of the housekeeper. She was no sooner retired, than she began to mutter to herself in the following pleasant strain: "Sure master might have made some difference, methinks, between me and the other servants. I suppose he hath left me mourning; but, i'fackins! if that be all, the devil shall wear it for him, for me. I'd have his worship know I am no beggar. I have saved five hundred pound in his service, and after all to be used in this manner.—It is a fine encouragement to servants to be honest; and to be sure, if I have taken a little something now and then, others have taken ten times as much; and now we are all put in a lump together. If so be that it be so, the legacy may go to the devil with him that gave it. No, I won't give it up neither, because that will please some folks. No, I'll buy the gayest gown I can get, and dance over the old curmudgeon's grave in it. This is my reward for taking his part so often, when all the country have cried shame of him, for breeding up his bastard in that manner; but he is going now where he must pay for all. It would have become him better to

304

have repented of his sins on his deathbed, than to
glory in them, and give away his estate out of his
own family to a misbegotten child. Found in his
bed, forsooth! a pretty story! ay, ay, those that
hide know where to find. Lord forgive him! I
warrant he hath many more bastards to answer
for, if the truth was known. One comfort is, they
will all be known where he is a going now.—'The
servants will find some token to remember me by.'
Those were the very words; I shall never forget
them, if I was to live a thousand years. Ay, ay,
I shall remember you for huddling me among the
servants. One would have thought he might have
mentioned my name as well as that of Square; but
he is a gentleman forsooth, though he had not
clothes on his back when he came hither first.
Marry come up with such gentlemen! though he
hath lived here this many years, I don't believe
there is arrow a servant in the house ever saw
the color of his money. The devil shall wait upon
such a gentleman for me.'' Much more of the like
kind she muttered to herself; but this taste shall
suffice to the reader.

Neither Thwackum nor Square were much better satisfied with their legacies. Though they
breathed not their resentment so loud, yet from
the discontent which appeared in their countenances, as well as from the following dialogue, we
collect that no great pleasure reigned in their
minds.

About an hour after they had left the sick-room,
Square met Thwackum in the hall and accosted
him thus: ''Well, sir, have you heard any news

of your friend since we parted from him?"—"If
you mean Mr. Allworthy," answered Thwackum,
"I think you might rather give him the appellation of your friend; for he seems to me to have
deserved that title."—"The title is as good on
your side," replied Square, "for his bounty, such
as it is, hath been equal to both."—"I should not
have mentioned it first," cries Thwackum, "but
since you begin, I must inform you I am of a different opinion. There is a wide distinction between voluntary favors and rewards. The duty I
have done in his family, and the care I have taken
in the education of his two boys, are services for
which some men might have expected a greater return. I would not have you imagine I am therefore dissatisfied; for St. Paul hath taught me to
be content with the little I have. Had the modi-
cum been less, I should have known my duty.
But though the Scriptures obliges me to remain
contented, it doth not enjoin me to shut my eyes
to my own merit, nor restrain me from seeing
when I am injured by an unjust comparison."—
"Since you provoke me," returned Square, "that
injury is done to me; nor did I ever imagine Mr.
Allworthy had held my friendship so light, as to
put me in balance with one who received his
wages. I know to what it is owing; it proceeds
from those narrow principals which you have been
so long endeavoring to infuse into him, in contempt of everything which is great and noble.
The beauty and loveliness of friendship is too
strong for dim eyes, nor can it be perceived by any

other medium than that unerring rule of right,
which you have so often endeavored to ridicule,
that you have perverted your friend's understanding."—"I wish," cries Thwackum, in a rage, "I
wish, for the sake of his soul, your damnable doctrines have not perverted his faith. It is to this
I impute his present behavior, so unbecoming a
Christian. Who but an atheist could think of leaving the world without having first made up his account? without confessing his sins, and receiving
that absolution which he knew he had one in the
house duly authorized to give him? He will feel
the want of these necessaries when it is too late,
when he is arrived at that place where there is
wailing and gnashing of teeth. It is then he will
find in what mighty stead that heathen goddess,
that virtue, which you and all other deists of the
age adore, will stand him. He will then summon
his priest, when there is none to be found, and
will lament the want of that absolution, without
which no sinner can be safe."—"If it be so material," says Square, "why don't you present
it him of your own accord?" "It hath no virtue," cries Thwackum, "but to those who have
sufficient grace to require it. But why do I talk
thus to a heathen and an unbeliever? It is you
that taught him this lesson, for which you have
been well rewarded in this world, as I doubt not
your disciple will soon be in the other."—"I know
not what you mean by reward," said Square;
"but if you hint at that pitiful memorial of our
friendship, which he hath thought fit to bequeath

me, I despise it; and nothing but the unfortunate situation of my circumstances should prevail on me to accept it.''

The physician now arrived, and began to inquire of the two disputants, how we all did above-stairs? "In a miserable way," answered Thwackum. "It is no more than I expected," cries the doctor: "but pray what symptoms have appeared since I left you?"—"No good ones, I am afraid," replied Thwackum: "after what passed at our departure, I think there were little hopes." The bodily physician, perhaps, misunderstood the curer of souls; and before they came to an explanation, Mr. Blifil came to them with a most melancholy countenance, and acquainted them that he brought sad news, that his mother was dead at Salisbury; that she had been seized on the road home with the gout in her head and stomach, which had carried her off in a few hours. "Good-lack-a-day!" says the doctor. "One cannot answer for events; but I wish I had been at hand, to have been called in. The gout is a distemper which it is difficult to treat; yet I have been remarkably successful in it." Thwackum and Square both condoled with Mr. Blifil for the loss of his mother, which the one advised him to bear like a man, and the other like a Christian. The young gentleman said he knew very well we were all mortal, and he would endeavor to submit to his loss as well as he could. That he could not, however, help complaining a little against the peculiar severity of his fate, which brought the news of so

great a calamity to him by surprise, and that at a
time when he hourly expected the severest blow
he was capable of feeling from the malice of fortune. He said, the present occasion would put to
the test those excellent rudiments which he had
learned from Mr. Thwackum and Mr. Square; and
it would be entirely owing to them, if he was enabled to survive such misfortunes.

It was now debated whether Mr. Allworthy
should be informed of the death of his sister.
This the doctor violently opposed; in which, I believe, the whole college would agree with him:
but Mr. Blifil said, he had received such positive
and repeated orders from his uncle, never to keep
any secret from him for fear of the disquietude
which it might give him, that he durst not think of
disobedience, whatever might be the consequence.
He said, for his part, considering the religious and
philosophic temper of his uncle, he could not agree
with the doctor in his apprehensions. He was
therefore resolved to communicate it to him: for
if his uncle recovered (as he heartily prayed he
might) he knew he would never forgive an endeavor to keep a secret of this kind from him.

The physician was forced to submit to these
resolutions, which the two other learned gentlemen very highly commended. So together moved
Mr. Blifil and the doctor toward the sick-room;
where the physician first entered, and approached
the bed, in order to feel his patient's pulse, which
he had no sooner done, than he declared he was
much better; that the last application had suc-

ceeded to a miracle, and had brought the fever to
intermit: so that, he said, there appeared now to
be as little danger as he had before apprehended
there were hopes.

To say the truth, Mr. Allworthy's situation had
never been so bad as the great caution of the doctor had represented it: but as a wise general never
despises his enemy, however inferior that enemy's
force may be, so neither doth a wise physician
ever despise a distemper, however inconsiderable.
As the former preserves the same strict discipline,
places the same guards, and employs the same
scouts, though the enemy be never so weak; so
the latter maintains the same gravity of countenance, and shakes his head with the same significant air, let the distemper be never so trifling.
And both, among many other good ones, may assign this solid reason for their conduct, that by
these means the greater glory redounds to them if
they gain the victory, and the less disgrace if by
any unlucky accident they should happen to be
conquered.

Mr. Allworthy had no sooner lifted up his
eyes, and thanked Heaven for these hopes of his
recovery, than Mr. Blifil drew near, with a very
dejected aspect, and having applied his handkerchief to his eye, either to wipe away his tears, or
to do as Ovid somewhere expresses himself on another occasion.

Si nullus erit, tamen excute nullum,
If there be none, then wipe away that none,

he communicated to his uncle what the reader
hath been just before acquainted with.

Allworthy received the news with concern, with
patience, and with resignation. He dropped a
tender tear, then composed his countenance, and
at last cried, "The Lord's will be done in everything."

He now inquired for the messenger; but Blifil
told him it had been impossible to detain him a
moment; for he appeared by the great hurry he
was in to have some business of importance on his
hands; that he complained of being hurried and
driven and torn out of his life, and repeated many
times, that if he could divide himself into four
quarters, he knew how to dispose of every one.

Allworthy then desired Blifil to take care of the
funeral. He said, he would have his sister deposited in his own chapel; and as to the particulars, he left them to his own discretion, only mentioning the person whom he would have employed
on this occasion.

CHAPTER IX

Which, among other things, may serve as a comment on that saying of Æschines, that "drunkenness shows the mind of a man, as a mirror reflects his person."

THE reader may perhaps wonder at hearing nothing of Mr. Jones in the last chapter. In fact, his behavior was so different from that of the persons there mentioned, that we chose not to confound his name with theirs.

When the good man had ended his speech, Jones was the last who deserted the room. Thence he retired to his own apartment, to give vent to his concern; but the restlessness of his mind would not suffer him to remain long there; he slipped softly therefore to Allworthy's chamber-door, where he listened a considerable time without hearing any kind of motion within, unless a violent snoring, which at last his fears misrepresented as groans. This so alarmed him, that he could not forbear entering the room; where he found the good man in the bed, in a sweet composed sleep, and his nurse snoring in the above-mentioned hearty manner, at the bed's feet. He immediately took the only method of silencing this thorough bass, whose music he feared might disturb Mr. Allworthy; and then sitting down by the nurse, he remained motionless till Blifil and the doctor came in together and waked the sick

312

man, in order that the doctor might feel his pulse,
and that the other might communicate to him that
piece of news, which, had Jones been apprised of
it, would have had great difficulty of finding its
way to Mr. Allworthy's ear at such a season.

When he first heard Blifil tell his uncle this
story, Jones could hardly contain the wrath which
kindled in him at the other's indiscretion, especially as the doctor shook his head, and declared his unwillingness to have the matter mentioned to his patient. But as his passion did not
so far deprive him of all use of his understanding,
as to hide from him the consequences which any
violent expression towards Blifil might have on
the sick, this apprehension stilled his rage at the
present; and he grew afterwards so satisfied with
finding that this news had, in fact, produced no
mischief, that he suffered his anger to die in his
own bosom, without ever mentioning it to Blifil.

The physician dined that day at Mr. Allworthy's; and having after dinner visited his patient, he returned to the company, and told them,
that he had now the satisfaction to say, with assurance, that his patient was out of all danger:
that he had brought his fever to a perfect intermission, and doubted not by throwing in the bark
to prevent its return.

This account so pleased Jones, and threw him
into such immoderate excess of rapture, that he
might be truly said to be drunk with joy—an in-
toxication which greatly forwards the effects of
wine; and as he was very free too with the bottle
on this occasion (for he drank many bumpers to

the doctor's health, as well as to other toasts) he
became very soon literally drunk.

Jones had naturally violent animal spirits:
these being set on float and augmented by the
spirit of wine, produced most extravagant effects.
He kissed the doctor, and embraced him with the
most passionate endearments; swearing that next
to Mr. Allworthy himself, he loved him of all men
living. "Doctor," added he, "you deserve a
statue to be erected to you at the public expense,
for having preserved a man, who is not only the
darling of all good men who know him, but a blessing to society, the glory of his country, and an
honor to human nature. D—n me if I don't love
him better than my own soul."

"More shame for you," cries Thwackum.
"Though I think you have reason to love him, for
he hath provided very well for you. And perhaps it might have been better for some folks
that he had not lived to see just reason of revok-
ing his gift."

Jones now looking on Thwackum with incon-
ceivable disdain, answered, "And doth thy mean
soul imagine that any such considerations could
weigh with me? No, let the earth open and swallow her own dirt (if I had millions of acres I
would say it) rather than swallow up my dear
glorious friend."

> *Quis desiderio sit pudor aut modus*
> *Tam chari capitis?* [1]

[1] "What modesty or measure can set bounds to our desire
of so dear a friend?" The word *desiderium* here cannot be

The doctor now interposed, and prevented the effects of a wrath which was kindling between Jones and Thwackum; after which the former gave a loose to mirth, sang two or three amorous songs, and fell into every frantic disorder which unbridled joy is apt to inspire; but so far was he from any disposition to quarrel, that he was ten times better humored, if possible, than when he was sober.

To say truth, nothing is more erroneous than the common observation, that men who are ill-natured and quarrelsome when they are drunk, are very worthy persons when they are sober: for drink, in reality, doth not reverse nature, or create passions in men which did not exist in them before. It takes away the guard of reason, and consequently forces us to produce those symptoms, which many, when sober, have art enough to conceal. It heightens and inflames our passions (generally indeed that passion which is uppermost in our mind), so that the angry temper, the amorous, the generous, the good-humored, the avaricious, and all other dispositions of men, are in their cups heightened and exposed.

And yet as no nation produces so many drunken quarrels, especially among the lower people, as England (for indeed, with them, to drink and to fight together are almost synonymous terms), I would not, methinks, have it thence concluded, that the English are the worst-natured people

easily translated. It includes our desire of enjoying our friend again, and the grief which attends that desire.

alive. Perhaps the love of glory only is at the bottom of this; so that the fair conclusion seems to be, that our countrymen have more of that love, and more of bravery, than any other plebeians. And this the rather, as there is seldom anything ungenerous, unfair, or ill-natured, exercised on these occasions: nay, it is common for the combatants to express good-will for each other even at the time of the conflict; and as their drunken mirth generally ends in a battle, so do most of their battles end in friendship.

But to return to our history. Though Jones had shown no design of giving offense, yet Mr. Blifil was highly offended at a behavior which was so inconsistent with the sober and prudent reserve of his own temper. He bore it too with the greater impatience, as it appeared to him very indecent at this season; "When," as he said, "the house was a house of mourning, on the account of his dear mother; and if it had pleased Heaven to give him some prospect of Mr. Allworthy's recovery, it would become them better to express the exultations of their hearts in thanksgiving, than in drunkenness and riots; which were properer methods to increase the Divine wrath, than to avert it." Thwackum, who had swallowed more liquor than Jones, but without any ill effect on his brain, seconded the pious harangue of Blifil; but Square, for reasons which the reader may probably guess, was totally silent.

Wine had not so totally overpowered Jones, as to prevent his recollecting Mr. Blifil's loss, the moment it was mentioned. As no person, therefore, was more ready to confess and condemn his own errors, he offered to shake Mr. Blifil by the hand, and begged his pardon, saying, "His excessive joy for Mr. Allworthy's recovery had driven every other thought out of his mind."

Blifil scornfully rejected his hand; and with much indignation answered, "It was little to be wondered at, if tragical spectacles made no impression on the blind; but, for his part, he had the misfortune to know who his parents were, and consequently must be affected with their loss."

Jones, who, notwithstanding his good humor, had some mixture of the irascible in his constitution, leaped hastily from his chair, and catching hold of Blifil's collar, cried out, "D—n you for a rascal, do you insult me with the misfortune of my birth?" He accompanied these words with such rough actions, that they soon got the better of Mr. Blifil's peaceful temper; and a scuffle immediately ensued, which might have produced mischief, had it not been prevented by the interposition of Thwackum and the physician; for the philosophy of Square rendered him superior to all emotions, and he very calmly smoked his pipe, as was his custom in all broils, unless when he apprehended some danger of having it broke in his mouth.

The combatants being now prevented from executing present vengeance on each other, betook themselves to the common resources of disappointed rage, and vented their wrath in threats and defiance. In this kind of conflict, Fortune, which, in the personal attack, seemed to incline to

Jones, was now altogether as favorable to his enemy.

A truce, nevertheless, was at length agreed on, by the mediation of the neutral parties, and the whole company again sat down at the table; where Jones being prevailed on to ask pardon, and Blifil to give it, peace was restored, and everything seemed *in statu quo.*

But though the quarrel was, in all appearance, perfectly reconciled, the good humor which had been interrupted by it, was by no means restored. All merriment was now at an end, and the subsequent discourse consisted only of grave relations of matters of fact, and of as grave observations upon them; a species of conversation, in which, though there is much of dignity and instruction, there is but little entertainment. As we presume therefore to convey only this last to the reader, we shall pass by whatever was said, till the rest of the company having by degrees dropped off left only Square and the physician together; at which time the conversation was a little heightened by some comments on what had happened between the two young gentlemen; both of whom the doctor declared to be no better than scoundrels; to which appellation the philosopher, very sagaciously shaking his head, agreed.

CHAPTER X

Showing the truth of many observations of Ovid, and of other more grave writers, who have proved beyond contradiction, that wine is often the forerunner of incontinency.

JONES retired from the company, in which we have seen him engaged, into the fields, where he intended to cool himself by a walk in the open air before he attended Mr. Allworthy. There, whilst he renewed those meditations on his dear Sophia, which the dangerous illness of his friend and benefactor had for some time interrupted, an accident happened, which with sorrow we relate, and with sorrow doubtless will it be read; however, that historic truth to which we profess so inviolable an attachment, obliges us to communicate it to posterity.

It was now a pleasant evening in the latter end of June, when our hero was walking in a most delicious grove, where the gentle breezes fanning the leaves, together with the sweet trilling of a murmuring stream, and the melodious notes of nightingales, formed altogether the most enchanting harmony. In this scene, so sweetly accommodated to love, he meditated on his dear Sophia. While his wanton fancy roamed unbounded over all her beauties, and his lively imagination painted the charming maid in various ravishing forms, his warm heart melted with tenderness; and at length,

319

throwing himself on the ground, by the side of a gently murmuring brook, he broke forth into the following ejaculation:

"O Sophia, would Heaven give thee to my arms, how blessed would be my condition! Cursed be that fortune which sets a distance between us. Was I but possessed of thee, one only suit of rags thy whole estate, is there a man on earth whom I would envy! How contemptible would the brightest Circassian beauty, dressed in all the jewels of the Indies, appear to my eyes! But why do I mention another woman? Could I think my eyes capable of looking at any other with tenderness, these hands should tear them from my head. No, my Sophia, if cruel fortune separates us for ever, my soul shall dote on thee alone. The chastest constancy will I ever preserve to thy image. Though I should never have possession of thy charming person, still shalt thou alone have possession of my thoughts, my love, my soul. Oh! my fond heart is so wrapped in that tender bosom, that the brightest beauties would for me have no charms, nor would a hermit be colder in their embraces. Sophia, Sophia alone shall be mine. What raptures are in that name! I will engrave it on every tree."

At these words he started up, and beheld—not his Sophia—no, nor a Circassian maid richly and elegantly attired for the grand Signior's seraglio. No; without a gown, in a shift that was somewhat of the coarsest, and none of the cleanest, bedewed likewise with some odoriferous effluvia, the produce of the day's labor, with a pitchfork in her

hand, Molly Seagrim approached. Our hero had
his penknife in his hand, which he had drawn for
the before-mentioned purpose of carving on the
bark; when the girl coming near him, cried out
with a smile, "You don't intend to kill me, squire,
I hope!"—"Why should you think I would kill
you?" answered Jones. "Nay," replied she, "after your cruel usage of me when I saw you last,
killing me would, perhaps, be too great kindness
for me to expect."

Here ensued a parley, which, as I do not think
myself obliged to relate it, I shall omit. It is sufficient that it lasted a full quarter of an hour, at
the conclusion of which they retired into the thickest part of the grove.

Some of my readers may be inclined to think
this event unnatural. However, the fact is true;
and perhaps may be sufficiently accounted for by
suggesting, that Jones probably thought one
woman better than none, and Molly as probably
imagined two men to be better than one. Besides
the before-mentioned motive assigned to the present behavior of Jones, the reader will be likewise
pleased to recollect in his favor, that he was not at
this time perfect master of that wonderful power
of reason, which so well enables grave and wise
men to subdue their unruly passions, and to decline any of these prohibited amusements. Wine
now had totally subdued this power in Jones. He
was, indeed, in a condition, in which, if reason had
interposed, though only to advise, she might have
received the answer which one Cleostratus gave
many years ago to a silly fellow, who asked him,

if he was not ashamed to be drunk? "Are not you," said Cleostratus, "ashamed to admonish a drunken man?"—To say the truth, in a court of justice drunkenness must not be an excuse, yet in a court of conscience it is greatly so; and therefore Aristotle, who commends the laws of Pittacus, by which drunken men received double punishment for their crimes, allows there is more of policy than justice in that law. Now, if there are any transgressions pardonable from drunkenness, they are certainly such as Mr. Jones was at present guilty of; on which head I could pour forth a vast profusion of learning, if I imagined it would either entertain my reader, or teach him anything more than he knows already. For his sake therefore I shall keep my learning to myself, and return to my history.

It hath been observed, that Fortune seldom doth things by halves. To say truth, there is no end to her freaks whenever she is disposed to gratify or displease. No sooner had our hero retired with his Dido, but

> *Speluncam* Blifil *dux et divinus eandem*
> *Deveniunt——*

the parson and the young squire, who were taking a serious walk arrived at the stile which leads into the grove, and the latter caught a view of the lovers just as they were sinking out of sight.

Blifil knew Jones very well, though he was at above a hundred yards' distance, and he was as positive to the sex of his companion, though not to the individual person. He started, blessed himself, and uttered a very solemn ejaculation.

Thwackum expressed some surprise at these sudden emotions, and asked the reason of them. To which Blifil answered, "He was certain he had seen a fellow and wench retire together among the bushes, which he doubted not was with some wicked purpose." As to the name of Jones, he thought proper to conceal it, and why he did so must be left to the judgment of the sagacious reader; for we never choose to assign motives to the actions of men, when there is any possibility of our being mistaken.

The parson, who was not only strictly chaste in his own person, but a great enemy to the opposite vice in all others, fired at this information. He desired Mr. Blifil to conduct him immediately to the place, which as he approached he breathed forth vengeance mixed with lamentations; nor did he refrain from casting some oblique reflections on Mr. Allworthy; insinuating that the wickedness of the country was principally owing to the encouragement he had given to vice, by having exerted such kindness to a bastard, and by having mitigated that just and wholesome rigor of the law which allots a very severe punishment to loose wenches.

The way through which our hunters were to pass in pursuit of their game was so beset with briars, that it greatly obstructed their walk, and caused besides such a rustling, that Jones had sufficient warning of their arrival before they could surprise him; nay, indeed, so incapable was Thwackum of concealing his indignation, and such vengeance did he mutter forth every step he took, that this alone must have abundantly satisfied Jones that he was (to use the language of sportsmen) found sitting.

CHAPTER XI

In which a simile in Mr. Pope's period of a mile introduces
as bloody a battle as can possibly be fought without the
assistance of steel or cold iron.

AS in the season of *rutting* (an uncouth
phrase, by which the vulgar denote that
gentle dalliance, which in the well-
wooded[1] forest of Hampshire, passes between
lovers of the ferine kind), if, while the lofty·
crested stag meditates the amorous sport, a
couple of puppies, or any other beasts of hostile
note, should wander so near the temple of Venus
Ferina that the fair hind should shrink from the
place, touched with that somewhat, either of fear
or frolic, of nicety or skittishness, with which nature hath bedecked all females, or hath at least instructed them how to put it on; lest, through the
indelicacy of males, the Samean mysteries should
be pryed into by unhallowed eyes: for, at the
celebration of these rites, the female priestess
cries out with her in Virgil (who was then, probably, hard at work on such celebration),

——*Procul, o procul este, profani;*
Proclamat vates, totoque absistite luco.
——Far hence be souls profane,
The sibyl cry'd, and from the grove abstain.—DRYDEN.

If, I say, while these sacred rites, which are in common to *genus omne animantium*, are in agitation

[1] This is an ambiguous phrase, and may mean either a forest
well clothed with wood, or well stripped of it.

between the stag and his mistress, any hostile beasts should venture too near, on the first hint given by the frightened hind, fierce and tremendous rushes forth the stag to the entrance of the thicket; there stands he sentinel over his love, stamps the ground with his foot, and with his horns brandished aloft in air, proudly provokes the apprehended foe to combat.

Thus, and more terrible, when he perceived the enemy's approach, leaped forth our hero. Many a step advanced he forwards, in order to conceal the trembling hind, and, if possible, to secure her retreat. And now Thwackum, having first darted some livid lightning from his fiery eyes, began to thunder forth, "Fie upon it! Fie upon it! Mr. Jones. Is it possible you should be the person?" —"You see," answered Jones, "it is possible I should be here."—"And who," said Thwackum, "is that wicked slut with you?"—"If I have any wicked slut with me," cries Jones, "it is possible I shall not let you know who she is."—"I command you to tell me immediately," says Thwackum: "and I would not have you imagine, young man that your age, though it hath somewhat abridged the purpose of tuition, hath totally taken away the authority of the master. The relation of the master and scholar is indelible; as, indeed, all other relations are; for they all derive their original from heaven. I would have you think yourself, therefore, as much obliged to obey me now, as when I taught you your first rudiments."—"I believe you would," cries Jones; "but that will not happen, unless you had the same birchen argument to convince me."—"Then I must tell you plainly," said Thwackum, "I am resolved to discover the wicked wretch."—"And I must tell you plainly," returned Jones, "I am resolved you shall not." Thwackum then offered to advance, and Jones laid hold of his arms; which Mr. Blifil endeavored to rescue, declaring, "he would not see his old master insulted."

Jones now finding himself engaged with two, thought it necessary to rid himself of one of his antagonists as soon as possible. He therefore applied to the weakest first; and, letting the parson go, he directed a blow at the young squire's breast, which luckily taking place, reduced him to measure his length on the ground.

Thwackum was so intent on the discovery, that, the moment he found himself at liberty, he stepped forward directly into the fern, without any great consideration of what might in the meantime befall his friend; but he had advanced a very few paces into the thicket, before Jones, having defeated Blifil, overtook the parson, and dragged him backward by the skirt of his coat.

This parson had been a champion in his youth, and had won much honor by his fist, both at school and at the university. He had now indeed, for a great number of years, declined the practice of that noble art; yet was his courage full as strong as his faith, and his body no less strong than either. He was moreover, as the reader may perhaps have conceived, somewhat irascible in his nature. When he looked back, therefore, and saw his friend stretched out on the ground, and found himself at the same time so roughly handled by one who had formerly been only passive in all conflicts between them (a circumstance which highly aggravated the whole), his patience at length gave way; he threw himself into a posture of offense; and collecting all his force, attacked Jones in the front with as much impetuosity as he had formerly attacked him in the rear.

Our hero received the enemy's attack with the most undaunted intrepidity, and his bosom resounded with the blow. This he presently returned with no less violence, aiming likewise at the parson's breast; but he dexterously drove down the fist of Jones, so that it reached only his belly, where two pounds of beef and as many of pudding were then deposited, and whence consequently no hollow sound could proceed. Many lusty blows, much more pleasant as well as easy to have seen, than to read or describe, were given on both sides: at last a violent fall, in which Jones had thrown his knees into Thwackum's breast, so weakened the latter, that victory had been no longer dubious, had not Blifil, who had now recovered his strength, again renewed the fight, and by engaging with Jones, given the parson a moment's time to shake his ears, and to regain his breath.

And now both together attacked our hero, whose blows did not retain that force with which they had fallen at first, so weakened was he by his combat with Thwackum; for though the pedagogue chose rather to play *solos* on the human instrument, and had been lately used to those only, yet

he still retained enough of his ancient knowledge
to perform his part very well in a *duet*.

The victory, according to modern custom, was
like to be decided by numbers, when, on a sudden,
a fourth pair of fists appeared in the battle, and
immediately paid their compliments to the parson; and the owner of them at the same time crying out, "Are not you ashamed, and be d—n'd to
you, to fall two of you upon one?"

The battle, which was of the kind that for distinction's sake is called royal, now raged with the
utmost violence during a few minutes; till Blifil
being a second time laid sprawling by Jones,
Thwackum condescended to apply for quarter to
his new antagonist, who was now found to be Mr.
Western himself; for in the heat of the action none
of the combatants had recognized him.

In fact that honest squire, happening, in his
afternoon's walk with some company, to pass
through the field where the bloody battle was
fought, and having concluded, from seeing three
men engaged, that two of them must be on a side,
he hastened from his companions, and with more
gallantry than policy, espoused the cause of the
weaker party.   By which generous proceeding he
very probably prevented Mr. Jones from becoming
a victim to the wrath of Thwackum, and to the
pious friendship which Blifil bore his old master;
for, besides the disadvantage of such odds, Jones
had not yet sufficiently recovered the former
strength of his broken arm.   This reinforcement,
however, soon put an end to the action, and Jones
with his ally obtained the victory.

CHAPTER XII

In which is seen a more moving spectacle than all the blood
in the bodies of Thwackum and Blifil, and of twenty
other such, is capable of producing.

THE rest of Mr. Western's company were
now come up, being just at the instant
when the action was over. These were
the honest clergyman, whom we have formerly
seen at Mr. Western's table; Mrs. Western, the
aunt of Sophia; and lastly, the lovely Sophia herself.

At this time the following was the aspect of the
bloody field. In one place lay on the ground, all
pale, and almost breathless, the vanquished Blifil.
Near him stood the conqueror Jones, almost covered with blood, part of which was naturally his
own, and part had been lately the property of the
Reverend Mr. Thwackum. In the third place
stood the said Thwackum, like King Porus, sul-
lenly submitting to the conqueror. The last figure in the piece was Western the Great, most gloriously forbearing the vanquished foe.

Blifil, in whom there was little sign of life, was at
first the principal object of the concern of every
one, and particularly of Mrs. Western, who had
drawn from her pocket a bottle of hartshorn, and
was herself about to apply it to his nostrils, when
on a sudden the attention of the whole company

was diverted from poor Blifil, whose spirit, if it had any such design, might have now taken an opportunity of stealing off to the other world, without any ceremony.

For now a more melancholy and a more lovely object lay motionless before them. This was no other than the charming Sophia herself, who, from the sight of blood, or from fear for her father, or from some other reason, had fallen down in a swoon, before any one could get to her assistance.

Mrs. Western first saw her and screamed. Immediately two or three voices cried out, "Miss Western in dead." Hartshorn, water, every remedy was called for, almost at one and the same instant.

The reader may remember, that in our description of this grove we mentioned a murmuring brook, which brook did not come there, as such gentle streams flow through vulgar romances, with no other purpose than to murmur. No! Fortune had decreed to ennoble this little brook with a higher honor than any of those which wash the plains of Arcadia ever deserved.

Jones was rubbing Blifil's temples, for he began to fear he had given him a blow too much, when the words, Miss Western and Dead, rushed at once on his ear. He started up, left Blifil to his fate, and flew to Sophia, whom, while all the rest were running against each other, backward and forward, looking for water in the dry paths, he caught up in his arms, and then ran away with her over the field to the rivulet above mentioned; where, plunging himself into the water, he contrived to besprinkle her face, head, and neck very plentifully.

Happy was it for Sophia that the same confusion which prevented her other friends from serving her, prevented them likewise from obstructing Jones. He had carried her half ways before they knew what he was doing, and he had actually restored her to life before they reached the waterside. She stretched out her arms, opened her eyes, and cried, "Oh! heavens!" just as her father, aunt, and the parson came up.

Jones, who had hitherto held this lovely burden in his arms, now relinquished his hold; but gave her at the same instant a tender caress, which, had her senses been then perfectly restored, could not have escaped her observation. As she expressed, therefore no displeasure at this freedom, we suppose she was not sufficiently recovered from her swoon at the time.

This tragical scene was now converted into a sudden scene of joy. In this our hero was certainly the principal character; for as he probably felt more ecstatic delight in having saved Sophia than she herself received from being saved, so neither were the congratulations paid to her equal to what were conferred on Jones, especially by Mr. Western himself, who, after having once or twice embraced his daughter, fell to hugging and kissing Jones. He called him the preserver of Sophia, and declared there was nothing, except her, or his estate, which he would not give him; but upon recollection, he afterwards excepted his fox-hounds, the Chevalier, and Miss Slouch (for so he called his favorite mare).

All fears for Sophia being now removed, Jones became the object of the squire's consideration.—"Come, my lad," says Western, "d'off thy quoat and wash thy feace; for att in a devilish pickle, I promise thee. Come, come, wash thyself, and shat go huome with me; and we'l zee to vind thee another quoat."

Jones immediately complied, threw off his coat, went down to the water, and washed both his face and bosom; for the latter was as much exposed and as bloody as the former. But though the water could clear off the blood, it could not remove the black and blue marks which Thwackum had imprinted on both his face and breast, and which, being discerned by Sophia, drew from her a sigh and a look full of inexpressible tenderness.

Jones received this full in his eyes, and it had infinitely a stronger effect on him than all the contusions which he had received before. An effect, however, widely different; for so soft and balmy was it, that, had all his former blows been stabs, it would for some minutes have prevented his feeling their smart.

The company now moved backwards, and soon arrived where Thwackum had got Mr. Blifil again on his legs. Here we cannot suppress a pious wish, that all quarrels were to be decided by those weapons only with which Nature, knowing what is proper for us, hath supplied us; and that cold iron was to be used in digging no bowels but those of the earth. Then would war, the pastime of monarchs, be almost inoffensive, and battles between great armies might be fought at the particular desire of several ladies of quality; who, together with the kings themselves, might be actual spectators of the conflict. Then might the field be this moment well strewed with human carcasses, and the next, the dead men, or infinitely the greatest part of them, might get up, like Mr. Bayes's troops, and march off either at the sound of a drum or fiddle, as should be previously agreed on.

I would avoid, if possible, treating this matter ludicrously, lest grave men and politicians, whom I know to be offended at a jest, may cry pish at it; but, in reality, might not a battle be as well decided by the greater number of broken heads, bloody noses, and black eyes, as by the greater heaps of mangled and murdered human bodies? Might not towns be contended for in the same manner? Indeed, this may be thought too detrimental a scheme to the French interest, since they would thus lose the advantage they have over other nations in the superiority of their engineers; but when I consider the gallantry and generosity of that people, I am persuaded they would never decline putting themselves upon a par with their adversary; or, as the phrase is, making themselves his match.

But such reformations are rather to be wished than hoped for: I shall content myself, therefore, with this short hint, and return to my narrative.

Western began now to inquire into the original rise of the quarrel. To which neither Blifil nor

Jones gave any answer; but Thwackum said surlily, "I believe the cause is not far off; if you beat the bushes well you may find her."—"Find her?" replied Western: "what! have you been fighting for a wench?"—"Ask the gentleman in his waistcoat there," said Thwackum: "he best knows." "Nay then," cries Western, "it is a wench certainly.—Ah, Tom, Tom, thou art a liquorish dog. But come, gentlemen, be all friends, and go home with me, and make final peace over a bottle." "I ask your pardon, sir," says Thwackum: "it is no such slight matter for a man of my character to be thus injuriously treated, and buffeted by a boy, only because I would have done my duty, in endeavoring to detect and bring to justice a wanton harlot; but, indeed, the principal fault lies in Mr. Allworthy and yourself; for if you put the laws in execution, as you ought to do, you will soon rid the country of these vermin."

"I would as soon rid the country of foxes," cries Western. "I think we ought to encourage the recruiting those numbers which we are every day losing in the war.—But where is she? Prithee, Tom, show me." He then began to beat about, in the same language and in the same manner as if he had been beating for a hare; and at last cried out, "Soho! Puss is not far off. Here's her form, upon my soul; I believe I may cry stole away." And indeed so he might; for he had now discovered the place whence the poor girl had, at the beginning of the fray, stolen away, upon as many feet as a hare generally uses in traveling.

Sophia now desired her father to return home; saying she found herself very faint, and apprehended a relapse. The squire immediately complied with his daughter's request (for he was the fondest of parents). He earnestly endeavored to prevail with the whole company to go and sup with him: but Blifil and Thwackum absolutely refused; the former saying, there were more reasons than he could then mention, why he must decline this honor; and the latter declaring (perhaps rightly) that it was not proper for a person of his function to be seen at any place in his present condition.

Jones was incapable of refusing the pleasure of being with his Sophia; so on he marched with Squire Western and his ladies, the parson bringing up the rear. This had, indeed, offered to tarry with his brother Thwackum, professing his regard for the cloth would not permit him to depart; but Thwackum would not accept the favor, and, with no great civility, pushed him after Mr. Western.

Thus ended this bloody fray; and thus shall end the fifth book of this history.

THE HISTORY OF TOM JONES

VOL. II.

CONTENTS OF VOL. II

BOOK VI.

V.

BOOK VII.

CONTAINING THREE DAYS.

CONTENTS vii

BOOK VIII.

CONTAINING ABOUT TWO DAYS.

CONTENTS

CHAPTER XV.

BOOK IX.

CONTAINING TWELVE HOURS.

THE HISTORY OF TOM JONES,

A FOUNDLING

BOOK VI

CHAPTER I

Of love.

IN our last book we have been obliged to deal
pretty much with the passion of love; and in
our succeeding book shall be forced to handle this subject still more largely. It may not
therefore in this place be improper to apply ourselves to the examination of that modern doctrine,
by which certain philosophers, among many other
wonderful discoveries, pretend to have found out,
that there is no such passion in the human breast.

Whether these philosophers be the same with
that surprising sect, who are honorably mentioned by the late Dr. Swift, as having, by the
mere force of genius alone, without the least assistance of any kind of learning, or even reading,
discovered that profound and invaluable secret
that there is no God; or whether they are not
rather the same with those who some years
since very much alarmed the world, by showing

II—: 1

that there were no such things as virtue or goodness really existing in human nature, and who
deduced our best actions from pride, I will not
here presume to determine. In reality, I am inclined to suspect, that all these several finders of
truth, are the very identical men who are by others called the finders of gold. The method used
in both these searches after truth and after gold,
being indeed one and the same, viz., the searching, rummaging, and examining into a nasty
place; indeed, in the former instances, into the
nastiest of all places, A BAD MIND.

But though in this particular, and perhaps in
their success, the truth-finder and the gold-finder
may very properly be compared together; yet in
modesty, surely, there can be no comparison between the two; for who ever heard of a gold-finder
that had the impudence or folly to assert, from
the ill success of his search, that there was no
such thing as gold in the world? whereas the
truth-finder, having raked out that jakes, his own
mind, and being there capable of tracing no ray
of divinity, nor anything virtuous or good, or
lovely, or loving, very fairly, honestly, and logic-
ally concludes that no such things exist in the
whole creation.

To avoid, however, all contention, if possible,
with these philosophers, if they will be called so;
and to show our own disposition to accommodate
matters peaceably between us, we shall here make
them some concessions, which may possibly put
an end to the dispute.

First, we will grant that many minds, and perhaps those of the philosophers, are entirely free from the least traces of such a passion.

Secondly, that what is commonly called love, namely, the desire of satisfying a voracious appetite with a certain quantity of delicate white human flesh, is by no means that passion for which I here contend. This is indeed more properly hunger; and as no glutton is ashamed to apply the word love to his appetite, and to say he LOVES such and such dishes; so may the lover of this kind, with equal propriety, say, he HUNGERS after such and such women.

Thirdly, I will grant, which I believe will be a most acceptable concession, that this love for which I am an advocate, though it satisfies itself in a much more delicate manner, doth nevertheless seek its own satisfaction as much as the grossest of all our appetites.

And, lastly, that this love, when it operates towards one of a different sex, is very apt, towards its complete gratification, to call in the aid of that hunger which I have mentioned above; and which it is so far from abating, that it heightens all its delights to a degree scarce imaginable by those who have never been susceptible of any other emotions than what have proceeded from appetite alone.

In return to all these concessions, I desire of the philosophers to grant, that there is in some (I believe in many) human breasts a kind and benevolent disposition, which is gratified by contributing to the happiness of others. That in this gratification alone, as in friendship, in parental and filial affection, as indeed in general philanthropy, there is a great and exquisite delight. That if we will not call such disposition love, we have no name for it. That though the pleasures arising from such pure love may be heightened and sweetened by the assistance of amorous desires, yet the former can subsist alone, nor are they destroyed by the intervention of the latter. Lastly, that esteem and gratitude are the proper motives to love, as youth and beauty are to desire, and, therefore, though such desire may naturally cease, when age or sickness overtakes its object; yet these can have no effect on love, nor ever shake or remove, from a good mind, that sensation or passion which hath gratitude and esteem for its basis.

To deny the existence of a passion of which we often see manifest instances, seems to be very strange and absurd; and can indeed proceed only from that self-admonition which we have mentioned above: but how unfair is this! Doth the man who recognizes in his own heart no traces of avarice or ambition, conclude, therefore, that there are no such passions in human nature? Why will we not modestly observe the same rule in judging of the good, as well as the evil of others? Or why, in any case, will we, as Shakespeare phrases it, "put the world in our own person?"

Predominant vanity is, I am afraid, too much concerned here. This is one instance of that adulation which we bestow on our own minds, and this almost universally. For there is scarce any man, how much soever he may despise the character of a flatterer, but will condescend in the meanest manner to flatter himself.

To those therefore I apply for the truth of the above observations, whose own minds can bear testimony to what I have advanced.

Examine your heart, my good reader, and resolve whether you do believe these matters with me. If you do, you may now proceed to their exemplification in the following pages: if you do not, you have, I assure you, already read more than you have understood; and it would be wiser to pursue your business, or your pleasures (such as they are), than to throw away any more of your time in reading what you can neither taste nor comprehend. To treat of the effects of love to you, must be as absurd as to discourse on colors to a man born blind; since possibly your idea of love may be as absurd as that which we are told such blind man once entertained of the color scarlet; that color seemed to him to be very much like the sound of a trumpet: and love probably may, in your opinion, very greatly resemble a dish of soup, or a surloin of roast-beef.

CHAPTER II

The character of Mrs. Western. Her great learning and knowledge of the world, and an instance of the deep penetration which she derived from those advantages.

THE reader hath seen Mr. Western, his sister, and daughter, with young Jones, and the parson, going together to Mr. Western's house, where the greater part of the company spent the evening with much joy and festivity. Sophia was indeed the only grave person; for as to Jones, though love had now gotten entire possession of his heart, yet the pleasing reflection on Mr. Allworthy's recovery, and the presence of his mistress, joined to some tender looks which she now and then could not refrain from giving him, so elevated our hero, that he joined the mirth of the other three, who were perhaps as good-humored people as any in the world.

Sophia retained the same gravity of countenance the next morning at breakfast; whence she retired likewise earlier than usual, leaving her father and aunt together. The squire took no notice of this change in his daughter's disposition. To say the truth, though he was somewhat of a politician, and had been twice a candidate in the country interest at an election, he was a man of no great observation. His sister was a lady of a different turn. She had lived about the court,

and had seen the world. Hence she had acquired
all that knowledge which the said world usually
communicates; and was a perfect mistress of
manners, customs, ceremonies, and fashions.
Nor did her erudition stop here. She had considerably improved her mind by study; she had
not only read all the modern plays, operas, ora-
torios, poems, and romances—in all which she
was a critic; but had gone through Rapin's History of England, Eachard's Roman History, and
many French *Mémoires pour servir à l' Histoire:*
to these she had added most of the political
pamphlets and journals published within the last
twenty years. From which she had attained a
very competent skill in politics, and could discourse very learnedly on the affairs of Europe.
She was, moreover, excellently well skilled in the
doctrine of amour, and knew better than anybody
who and who were together; a knowledge which
she the more easily attained, as her pursuit of it
was never diverted by any affairs of her own; for
either she had no inclinations, or they had never
been solicited; which last is indeed very probable;
for her masculine person, which was near six
foot high, added to her manner and learning, possibly prevented the other sex from regarding her,
notwithstanding her petticoats, in the light of a
woman. However, as she had considered the matter scientifically, she perfectly well knew, though
she had never practiced them, all the arts which
fine ladies use when they desire to give encouragement, or to conceal liking, with all the long
appendage of smiles, ogles, glances, &c., as they

are at present practiced in the beau-monde. To
sum the whole, no species of disguise or affectation had escaped her notice; but as to the plain
simple workings of honest nature, as she had
never seen any such, she could know but little of
them.

By means of this wonderful sagacity, Mrs.
Western had now, as she thought, made a discovery of something in the mind of Sophia. The
first hint of this she took from the behavior of the
young lady in the field of battle; and the suspicion which she then conceived, was greatly corroborated by some observations which she had
made that evening and the next morning. However, being greatly cautious to avoid being found
in a mistake, she carried the secret a whole fortnight in her bosom, giving only some oblique hints,
by simpering, winks, nods, and now and then
dropping an obscure word, which indeed sufficiently alarmed Sophia, but did not at all affect
her brother.

Being at length, however, thoroughly satisfied
of the truth of her observation, she took an opportunity, one morning, when she was alone with
her brother, to interrupt one of his whistles in
the following manner:—

"Pray, brother, have you not observed something very extraordinary in my niece lately?"—
"No, not I," answered Western; "is anything
the matter with the girl?"—"I think there is,"
replied she; "and something of much consequence
too."—"Why, she doth not complain of anything," cries Western; "and she hath had the

small-pox.''—''Brother,'' returned she, ''girls
are liable to other distempers besides the small-
pox, and sometimes possibly to much worse.''
Here Western interrupted her with much earnestness, and begged her, if anything ailed his daughter, to acquaint him immediately; adding, ''she
knew he loved her more than his own soul, and
that he would send to the world's end for the best
physician to her.'' ''Nay, nay,'' answered she,
smiling, ''the distemper is not so terrible; but I
believe, brother, you are convinced I know the
world, and I promise you I was never more deceived in my life, if my niece be not most desper-
ately in love.''—''How! in love!'' cries Western,
in a passion; ''in love, without acquainting me!
I'll disinherit her; I'll turn her out of doors, stark
naked, without a farthing. Is all my kindness
vor 'ur, and vondness o'ur come to this, to fall in
love without asking me leave?''—''But you will
not,'' answered Mrs. Western, ''turn this daughter, whom you love better than your own soul,
out of doors, before you know whether you shall
approve her choice. Suppose she should have
fixed on the very person whom you yourself would
wish, I hope you would not be angry then?''—
''No, no,'' cries Western, ''that would make a difference. If she marries the man I would ha' her,
she may love whom she pleases, I shan't trouble
my head about that.'' ''That is spoken,'' answered the sister, ''like a sensible man; but I believe the very person she hath chosen would be
the very person you would choose for her. I will
disclaim all knowledge of the world, if it is not

so; and I believe, brother, you will allow I have some."—"Why, lookee sister," said Western, "I do believe you have as much as any woman; and to be sure those are women's matters. You know I don't love to hear you talk about politics; they belong to us, and petticoats should not meddle: but come, who is the man?"—"Marry!" said she, "you may find him out yourself if you please. You, who are so great a politician, can be at no great loss. The judgment which can penetrate into the cabinets of princes, and discover the secret springs which move the great state wheels in all the political machines of Europe, must surely, with very little difficulty, find out what passes in the rude uninformed mind of a girl."—"Sister," cries the squire, "I have often warn'd you, not to talk the court gibberish to me. I tell you, I don't understand the lingo: but I can read a journal, or the *London Evening Post*. Perhaps, indeed, there may be now and tan a verse which I can't make much of, because half the letters are left out; yet I know very well what is meant by that, and that our affairs don't go so well as they should do, because of bribery and corruption."—"I pity your country ignorance from my heart," cries the lady.—"Do you?" answered Western; "and I pity your town learning; I had rather be anything than a courtier, and a Presbyterian, and a Hanoverian too, as some people, I believe, are."—"If you mean me," answered she, "you know I am a woman, brother; and it signifies nothing what I am. Besides—"—"I do know you are a woman," cries the squire, "and it's well for thee that art one; if hadst been a man, I promise thee I had lent thee a flick long ago."—"Ay, there," said she, "in that flick lies all your fancied superiority. Your bodies, and not your brains, are stronger than ours. Believe me, it is well for you that you are able to beat us; or, such is the superiority of our understanding, we should make all of you what the brave, and wise, and witty, and polite are already—our slaves."—"I am glad I know your mind," answered the squire. "But we'll talk more of this matter another time. At present, do tell me what man is it you mean about my daughter?"—"Hold a moment," said she, "while I digest that sovereign contempt I have for your sex; or else I ought to be angry too with you. There——I have made a shift to gulp it down. And now, good politic sir, what think you of Mr. Blifil? Did she not faint away on seeing him lie breathless on the ground? Did she not, after he was recovered, turn pale again the moment we came up to that part of the field where he stood? And pray what else should be the occasion of all her melancholy that night at supper, the next morning, and indeed ever since?"—"'Fore George!" cries the squire, "now you mind me on't, I remember it all. It is certainly so, and I am glad on't with all my heart. I knew Sophy was a good girl, and would not fall in love to make me angry. I was never more rejoiced in my life; for nothing can lie so handy together as our two estates. I had this matter in my head some time ago: for certainly the two estates are in a manner

joined together in matrimony already, and it
would be a thousand pities to part them. It is
true, indeed, there be larger estates in the kingdom, but not in this county, and I had rather
bate something, than marry my daughter among
strangers and foreigners. Besides, most o' zuch
great estates be in the hands of lords, and I heate
the very name of *themmun.* Well but, sister,
what would you advise me to do; for I tell you
women know these matters better than we do?''
—''Oh, your humble servant, sir,'' answered the
lady: ''we are obliged to you for allowing us a
capacity in anything. Since you are pleased,
then, most politic sir, to ask my advice, I think
you may propose the match to Allworthy yourself.
There is no indecorum in the proposal's coming
from the parent of either side. King Alcinous,
in Mr. Pope's Odyssey, offers his daughter to
Ulysses. I need not caution so politic a person
not to say that your daughter is in love; that
would indeed be against all rules.''—''Well,''
said the squire, ''I will propose it; but I shall
certainly lend un a flick, if he should refuse me.''
''Fear not,'' cries Mrs. Western; ''the match is
too advantageous to be refused.'' ''I don't know
that,'' answered the squire: ''Allworthy is a
queer b—ch, and money hath no effect o'un.''
''Brother,'' said the lady, ''your politics astonish
me. Are you really to be imposed on by professions? Do you think Mr. Allworthy hath more
contempt for money than other men because he
professes more? Such credulity would better become one of us weak women, than that wise sex

which heaven hath formed for politicians. Indeed, brother, you would make a fine plenipo to negotiate with the French. They would soon persuade you, that they take towns out of mere defensive principles." "Sister," answered the squire, with much scorn, "let your friends at court answer for the towns taken; as you are a woman, I shall lay no blame upon you; for I suppose they are wiser than to trust women with secrets." He accompanied this with so sarcastical a laugh, that Mrs. Western could bear no longer. She had been all this time fretted in a tender part (for she was indeed very deeply skilled in these matters, and very violent in them), and therefore, burst forth in a rage, declared her brother to be both a clown and a blockhead, and that she would stay no longer in his house.

The squire, though perhaps he had never read Machiavel, was, however, in many points, a perfect politician. He strongly held all those wise tenets, which are so well inculcated in that Politico-Peripatetic school of Exchange-alley. He knew the just value and only use of money, viz., to lay it up. He was likewise well skilled in the exact value of reversions, expectations, &c., and had often considered the amount of his sister's fortune, and the chance which he or his posterity had of inheriting it. This he was infinitely too wise to sacrifice to a trifling resentment. When he found, therefore, he had carried matters too far, he began to think of reconciling them; which was no very difficult task, as the lady had great affection for her brother, and still greater for her niece; and though too susceptible of an affront offered to her skill in politics, on which she much valued herself, was a woman of a very extraordinary good and sweet disposition.

Having first, therefore, laid violent hands on the horses, for whose escape from the stable no place but the window was left open, he next applied himself to his sister; softened and soothed her, by unsaying all he had said, and by assertions directly contrary to those which had incensed her. Lastly, he summoned the eloquence of Sophia to his assistance, who, besides a most graceful and winning address, had the advantage of being heard with great favor and partiality by her aunt.

The result of the whole was a kind smile from Mrs. Western, who said, "Brother, you are absolutely a perfect Croat; but as those have their use in the army of the empress queen, so you likewise have some good in you. I will therefore once more sign a treaty of peace with you, and see that you do not infringe it on your side; at least, as you are so excellent a politician, I may expect you will keep your leagues, like the French, till your interest calls upon you to break them."

CHAPTER III

Containing two defiances to the critics.

THE squire having settled matters with his sister, as we have seen in the last chapter, was so greatly impatient to communicate the proposal to Allworthy, that Mrs. Western had the utmost difficulty to prevent him from visiting that gentleman in his sickness, for this purpose.

Mr. Allworthy had been engaged to dine with Mr. Western at the time when he was taken ill. He was therefore no sooner discharged out of the custody of physic, but he thought (as was usual with him on all occasions, both the highest and the lowest) of fulfilling his engagement.

In the interval between the time of the dialogue in the last chapter, and this day of public entertainment, Sophia had, from certain obscure hints thrown out by her aunt, collected some apprehension that the sagacious lady suspected her passion for Jones. She now resolved to take this opportunity of wiping out all such suspicion, and for that purpose to put an entire constraint on her behavior.

First, she endeavored to conceal a throbbing melancholy heart with the utmost sprightliness in her countenance, and the highest gayety in her manner. Secondly, she addressed her whole dis-

15

course to Mr. Blifil, and took not the least notice
of poor Jones the whole day.

The squire was so delighted with this conduct
of his daughter, that he scarce ate any dinner,
and spent almost his whole time in watching opportunities of conveying signs of his approbation
by winks and nods to his sister; who was not at
first altogether so pleased with what she saw
as was her brother.

In short, Sophia so greatly overacted her part,
that her aunt was at first staggered, and began to
suspect some affectation in her niece; but as she
was herself a woman of great art, so she soon
attributed this to extreme art in Sophia. She remembered the many hints she had given her niece
concerning her being in love, and imagined the
young lady had taken this way to rally her out
of her opinion, by an overacted civility: a notion
that was greatly corroborated by the excessive
gayety with which the whole was accompanied.
We cannot here avoid remarking, that this conjecture would have been better founded had Sophia lived ten years in the air of Grosvenor
Square, where young ladies do learn a wonderful
knack of rallying and playing with that passion,
which is a mighty serious thing in woods and
groves an hundred miles distant from London.

To say the truth, in discovering the deceit of
others, it matters much that our own art be wound
up, if I may use the expression, in the same key
with theirs: for very artful men sometimes mis-
carry by fancying others wiser, or, in other words,
greater knaves, than they really are. As this ob-

servation is pretty deep, I will illustrate it by the following short story. Three countrymen were pursuing a Wiltshire thief through Brentford. The simplest of them seeing "The Wiltshire House," written under a sign, advised his companions to enter it, for there most probably they would find their countryman. The second, who was wiser, laughed at this simplicity; but the third, who was wiser still, answered, "Let us go in, however, for he may think we should not suspect him of going amongst his own countrymen." They accordingly went in and searched the house, and by that means missed overtaking the thief, who was at that time but a little way before them; and who, as they all knew, but had never once reflected, could not read.

The reader will pardon a digression in which so invaluable a secret is communicated, since every gamester will agree how necessary it is to know exactly the play of another, in order to countermine him. This will, moreover, afford a reason why the wiser man, as is often seen, is the bubble of the weaker, and why many simple and innocent characters are so generally misunderstood and misrepresented; but what is most material, this will account for the deceit which Sophia put on her politic aunt.

Dinner being ended, and the company retired into the garden, Mr. Western, who was thoroughly convinced of the certainty of what his sister had told him, took Mr. Allworthy aside, and very bluntly proposed a match between Sophia and young Mr. Blifil.

II—2

Mr. Allworthy was not one of those men whose hearts flutter at any unexpected and sudden tidings of worldly profit. His mind was, indeed, tempered with that philosophy which becomes a man and a Christian. He affected no absolute superiority to all pleasure and pain, to all joy and grief; but was not at the same time to be discomposed and ruffled by every accidental blast, by every smile or frown of fortune. He received, therefore, Mr. Western's proposal without any visible emotion, or without any alteration of countenance. He said the alliance was such as he sincerely wished; then launched forth into a very just encomium on the young lady's merit; acknowledged the offer to be advantageous in point of fortune; and after thanking Mr. Western for the good opinion he had professed of his nephew, concluded, that if the young people liked each other, he should be very desirous to complete the affair.

Western was a little disappointed at Mr. Allworthy's answer, which was not so warm as he expected. He treated the doubt whether the young people might like one another with great contempt, saying, "That parents were the best judges of proper matches for their children: that for his part he should insist on the most resigned obedience from his daughter: and if any young fellow could refuse such a bed-fellow, he was his humble servant, and hoped there was no harm done."

Allworthy endeavored to soften this resentment by many eulogiums on Sophia, declaring he had no doubt but that Mr. Blifil would very gladly receive the offer; but all was ineffectual; he could obtain no other answer from the squire but—— "I say no more—I humbly hope there's no harm done—that's all." Which words he repeated at least a hundred times before they parted.

Allworthy was too well acquainted with his neighbor to be offended at this behavior; and though he was so averse to the rigor which some parents exercise on their children in the article of marriage, that he had resolved never to force his nephew's inclinations, he was nevertheless much pleased with the prospect of this union; for the whole country resounded the praises of Sophia, and he had himself greatly admired the uncommon endowments of both her mind and person. To which I believe we may add, the consideration of her vast fortune, which, though he was too sober to be intoxicated with it, he was too sensible to despise.

And here, in defiance of all the barking critics in the world, I must and will introduce a digression concerning true wisdom, of which Mr. Allworthy was in reality as great a pattern as he was of goodness.

True wisdom then, notwithstanding all which Mr. Hogarth's poor poet may have writ against riches, and in spite of all which any rich wellfed divine may have preached against pleasure, consists not in the contempt of either of these. A man may have as much wisdom in the possession of an affluent fortune, as any beggar in the streets; or may enjoy a handsome wife or a hearty

friend, and still remain as wise as any sour popish recluse, who buries all his social faculties, and
starves his belly while he well lashes his back.

To say truth, the wisest man is the likeliest to
possess all worldly blessings in an eminent degree; for as that moderation which wisdom pre-
scribes is the surest way to useful wealth, so
can it alone qualify us to taste many pleasures.
The wise man gratifies every appetite and every
passion, while the fool sacrifices all the rest to
pall and satiate one.

It may be objected, that very wise men have
been notoriously avaricious. I answer, Not wise
in that instance. It may likewise be said, That
the wisest men have been in their youth immoderately fond of pleasure. I answer, They were
not wise then.

Wisdom in short, whose lessons have been represented as so hard to learn by those who never
were at her school, only teaches us to extend
a simple maxim universally known and followed
even in the lowest life, a little farther than that
life carries it. And this is, not to buy at too
dear a price.

Now, whoever takes this maxim abroad with
him into the grand market of the world, and constantly applies it to honors, to riches, to pleasures,
and to every other commodity which that market
affords, is, I will venture to affirm, a wise man,
and must be so acknowledged in the worldly sense
of the word; for he makes the best of bargains,
since in reality he purchases everything at the
price only of a little trouble, and carries home all

the good things I have mentioned, while he keeps his health, his innocence, and his reputation, the common prices which are paid for them by others, entire and to himself.

From this moderation, likewise, he learns two other lessons, which complete his character. First, never to be intoxicated when he hath made the best bargain, nor dejected when the market is empty, or when its commodities are too dear for his purchase.

But I must remember on what subject I am writing, and not trespass too far on the patience of a good-natured critic. Here, therefore, I put an end to the chapter.

CHAPTER IV

Containing sundry curious matters.

AS soon as Mr. Allworthy returned home, he took Mr. Blifil apart, and after some preface, communicated to him the proposal which had been made by Mr. Western, and at the same time informed him how agreeable this match would be to himself.

The charms of Sophia had not made the least impression on Blifil; not that his heart was pre-engaged; neither was he totally insensible of beauty, or had any aversion to women; but his appetites were by nature so moderate, that he was able, by philosophy, or by study, or by some other method, easily to subdue them: and as to that passion which we have treated of in the first chapter of this book, he had not the least tincture of it in his whole composition.

But though he was so entirely free from that mixed passion, of which we there treated, and of which the virtues and beauty of Sophia formed so notable an object; yet was he altogether as well furnished with some other passions, that promised themselves very full gratification in the young lady's fortune. Such were avarice and ambition, which divided the dominion of his mind between them. He had more than once considered the possession of this fortune as a very de-

sirable thing, and had entertained some distant
views concerning it; but his own youth, and that
of the young lady, and indeed principally a reflection that Mr. Western might marry again, and
have more children, had restrained him from too
hasty or eager a pursuit.

This last and most material objection was now
in great measure removed, as the proposal came
from Mr. Western himself. Blifil, therefore,
after a very short hesitation, answered Mr. Allworthy, that matrimony was a subject on which
he had not yet thought; but that he was so sensible of his friendly and fatherly care, that he
should in all things submit himself to his pleasure.

Allworthy was naturally a man of spirit, and
his present gravity arose from true wisdom and
philosophy, not from any original phlegm in his
disposition; for he had possessed much fire in
his youth, and had married a beautiful woman for
love. He was not therefore greatly pleased with
'this cold answer of his nephew; nor could he help
launching forth into the praises of Sophia, and
expressing some wonder that the heart of a young
man could be impregnable to the force of such
charms, unless it was guarded by some prior affection.

Blifil assured him he had no such guard; and
then proceeded to discourse so wisely and reli-
giously on love and marriage, that he would have
stopped the mouth of a parent much less devoutly
inclined than was his uncle. In the end, the good
man was satisfied that his nephew, far from hav-

ing any objections to Sophia, had that esteem for her, which in sober and virtuous minds is the sure foundation of friendship and love. And as he doubted not but the lover would, in a little time, become altogether as agreeable to his mistress, he foresaw great happiness arising to all parties by so proper and desirable an union. With Mr. Blifil's consent therefore he wrote the next morning to Mr. Western, acquainting him that his nephew had very thankfully and gladly received the proposal, and would be ready to wait on the young lady, whenever she should be pleased to accept his visit.

Western was much pleased with this letter, and immediately returned an answer; in which, without having mentioned a word to his daughter, he appointed that very afternoon for opening the scene of courtship.

As soon as he had dispatched this messenger, he went in quest of his sister, whom he found reading and expounding the *Gazette* to parson Supple. To this exposition he was obliged to attend near a quarter of an hour, though with great violence to his natural impetuosity, before he was suffered to speak. At length, however, he found an opportunity of acquainting the lady, that he had business of great consequence to impart to her; to which she answered, "Brother, I am entirely at your service. Things look so well in the north, that I was never in a better humor."

The parson then withdrawing, Western acquainted her with all which had passed, and desired her to communicate the affair to Sophia, which she readily and cheerfully undertook; though perhaps her brother was a little obliged to that agreeable northern aspect which had so delighted her, that he heard no comment on his proceedings; for they were certainly somewhat too hasty and violent.

CHAPTER V

In which is related what passed between Sophia and her aunt.

SOPHIA was in her chamber, reading, when her aunt came in. The moment she saw Mrs. Western, she shut the book with so much eagerness, that the good lady could not forbear asking her, What book that was which she seemed so much afraid of showing? "Upon my word, madam," answered Sophia, "it is a book which I am neither ashamed nor afraid to own I have read. It is the production of a young lady of fashion, whose good understanding, I think, doth honor to her sex, and whose good heart is an honor to human nature." Mrs. Western then took up the book, and immediately after threw it down, saying—"Yes, the author is of a very good family; but she is not much among people one knows. I have never read it; for the best judges say, there is not much in it."—"I dare not, madam, set up my own opinion," says Sophia, "against the best judges, but there appears to me a great deal of human nature in it; and in many parts so much true tenderness and delicacy, that it hath cost me many a tear."—"Ay, and do you love to cry then?" says the aunt. "I love a tender sensation," answered the niece, "and would pay the price of a tear for it at any time."—

"Well, but show me," said the aunt, "what was
you reading when I came in; there was something
very tender in that, I believe, and very loving too.
You blush, my dear Sophia. Ah! child, you
should read books which would teach you a little
hypocrisy, which would instruct you how to hide
your thoughts a little better."—"I hope, madam," answered Sophia, "I have no thoughts
which I ought to be ashamed of discovering."—
"Ashamed! no," cries the aunt, "I don't think
you have any thoughts which you ought to be
ashamed of; and yet, child, you blushed just now
when I mentioned the word loving. Dear Sophy,
be assured you have not one thought which I am
not well acquainted with; as well, child, as the
French are with our motions, long before we put
them in execution. Did you think, child, because
you have been able to impose upon your father,
that you could impose upon me? Do you imagine
I did not know the reason of your overacting
all that friendship for Mr. Blifil yesterday? I
have seen a little too much of the world, to be
so deceived. Nay, nay, do not blush again. I
tell you it is a passion you need not be ashamed
of. It is a passion I myself approve, and have
already brought your father into the approbation of it. Indeed, I solely consider your inclination; for I would always have that gratified, if
possible, though one may sacrifice higher prospects. Come, I have news which will delight
your very soul. Make me your confident, and I
will undertake you shall be happy to the very
extent of your wishes." "La. madam." says

Sophia, looking more foolishly than ever she did in her life, "I know not what to say—why, madam, should you suspect?"—"Nay, no dishonesty," returned Mrs. Western. "Consider, you are speaking to one of your own sex, to an aunt, and I hope you are convinced you speak to a friend. Consider, you are only revealing to me what I know already, and what I plainly saw yesterday, through that most artful of all disguises, which you had put on, and which must have deceived any one who had not perfectly known the world. Lastly, consider it is a passion which I highly approve." "La, madam," says Sophia, "you come upon one so unawares, and on a sudden. To be sure, madam, I am not blind—and certainly, if it be a fault to see all human perfections assembled together—but is it possible my father and you, madam, can see with my eyes?" "I tell you," answered the aunt, "we do entirely approve; and this very afternoon your father hath appointed for you to receive your lover." "My father, this afternoon!" cries Sophia, with the blood starting from her face.—"Yes, child," said the aunt, "this afternoon. You know the impetuosity of my brother's temper. I acquainted him with the passion which I first discovered in you that evening when you fainted away in the field. I saw it in your fainting. I saw it immediately upon your recovery. I saw it that evening at supper, and the next morning at breakfast (you know, child, I have seen the world). Well, I no sooner acquainted my brother, but he immediately wanted to pro-

pose it to Allworthy. He proposed it yesterday, Allworthy consented (as to be sure he
must with joy), and this afternoon, I tell you,
you are to put on all your best airs.'' ''This afternoon!'' cries Sophia. ''Dear aunt, you frighten
me out of my senses.'' ''O, my dear,'' said the
aunt, ''you will soon come to yourself again; for
he is a charming young fellow, that's the truth
on't.'' ''Nay, I will own,'' says Sophia, ''I know
none with such perfections. So brave, and yet
so gentle; so, witty, yet so inoffensive; so humane,
so civil, so genteel, so handsome! What signifies his being base born, when compared with
such qualifications as these?'' ''Base born?
What do you mean?'' said the aunt, ''Mr. Blifil
base born!'' Sophia turned instantly pale at
this name, and faintly repeated it. Upon which
the aunt cried, ''Mr. Blifil—ay, Mr. Blifil, of
whom else have we been talking?'' ''Good
heavens,'' answered Sophia, ready to sink, ''of
Mr. Jones, I thought; I am sure I know no other
who deserves—'' ''I protest,'' cries the aunt,
''you frighten me in your turn. Is it Mr. Jones,
and not Mr. Blifil who is the object of your
affection?'' ''Mr. Blifil!'' repeated Sophia.
''Sure it is impossible you can be in earnest;
if you are, I am the most miserable woman alive.''
Mrs. Western now stood a few moments silent,
while sparks of fiery rage flashed from her eyes.
At length, collecting all her force of voice, she
thundered forth in the following articulate
sounds:

''And is it possible you can think of disgracing

your family by allying yourself to a bastard?
Can the blood of the Westerns submit to such
contamination? If you have not sense sufficient
to restrain such monstrous inclinations, I thought
the pride of our family would have prevented
you from giving the least encouragement to so
base an affection; much less did I imagine you
would ever have had the assurance to own it to
my face."

"Madam," answered Sophia, trembling, "what
I have said you have extorted from me. I do
not remember to have ever mentioned the name
of Mr. Jones with approbation to any one before;
nor should I now had I not conceived he had your
approbation. Whatever were my thoughts of that
poor, unhappy young man, I intended to have
carried them with me to my grave—to that grave
where only now, I find, I am to seek repose."
Here she sunk down in her chair, drowned in
her tears, and, in all the moving silence of un-
utterable grief, presented a spectacle which must
have affected almost the hardest heart.

All this tender sorrow, however, raised no
compassion in her aunt. On the contrary, she
now fell into the most violent rage.—"And I
would rather," she cried, in a most vehement
voice, "follow you to your grave, than I would
see you disgrace yourself and your family by
such a match. O Heavens! could I have ever
suspected that I should live to hear a niece of
mine declare a passion for such a fellow? You
are the first—yes, Miss Western, you are the

first of your name who ever entertained so
groveling a thought. A family so noted for the
prudence of its women"—here she ran on a full
quarter of an hour, till, having exhausted her
breath rather than her rage, she concluded with
threatening to go immediately and acquaint her
brother.

Sophia then threw herself at her feet, and laying hold of her hands, begged her with tears to
conceal what she had drawn from her; urging
the violence of her father's temper, and protesting that no inclinations of hers should ever
prevail with her to do anything which might
offend him.

Mrs. Western stood a moment looking at her,
and then, having recollected herself, said, "That
on one consideration only she would keep the
secret from her brother; and this was, that
Sophia should promise to entertain Mr. Blifil
that very afternoon as her lover, and to regard
him as the person who was to be her husband."

Poor Sophia was too much in her aunt's power
to deny her anything positively; she was obliged
to promise that she would see Mr. Blifil, and be
as civil to him as possible; but begged her aunt
that the match might not be hurried on. She
said, "Mr. Blifil was by no means agreeable to
her, and she hoped her father would be prevailed
on not to make her the most wretched of women."

Mrs. Western assured her, "That the match
was entirely agreed upon, and that nothing could
or should prevent it. I must own," said she, "I

looked. on it as on a matter of indifference; nay,
perhaps, had some scruples about it before,
which were actually got over by my thinking it
highly agreeable to your own inclinations; but
now I regard it as the most eligible thing in the
world: nor shall there be, if I can prevent it, a
moment of time lost on the occasion.''

Sophia replied, ''Delay at least, madam, I may
expect from both your goodness and my father's.
Surely you will give me time to endeavor to get
the better of so strong a disinclination as I have
at present to this person.''

The aunt answered, ''She knew too much of
the world to be so deceived; that as she was
sensible another man had her affections, she
should persuade Mr. Western to hasten the match
as much as possible. It would be bad politics,
indeed,'' added she, ''to protract a siege when
the enemy's army is at hand, and in danger of
relieving it. No, no, Sophy,'' said she, ''as I
am convinced you have a violent passion which
you can never satisfy with honor, I will do all I
can to put your honor out of the care of your
family: for when you are married those matters
will belong only to the consideration of your
husband. I hope, child, you will always have
prudence enough to act as becomes you; but if
you should not, marriage hath saved many a
woman from ruin.''

Sophia well understood what her aunt meant;
but did not think proper to make her an answer.
However, she took a resolution to see Mr. Blifil,
and to behave to him as civilly as she could, for on

that condition only she obtained a promise from her aunt to keep secret the liking which her ill fortune, rather than any scheme of Mrs. Western, had unhappily drawn from her.

II—3

CHAPTER VI

Containing a dialogue between Sophia and Mrs. Honour, which may a little relieve those tender affections which the foregoing scene may have raised in the mind of a good-natured reader.

MRS. WESTERN having obtained that promise from her niece which we have seen in the last chapter, withdrew; and presently after arrived Mrs. Honour. She was at work in a neighboring apartment, and had been summoned to the keyhole by some vociferation in the preceding dialogue, where she had continued during the remaining part of it. At her entry into the room, she found Sophia standing motionless, with the tears trickling from her eyes. Upon which she immediately ordered a proper quantity of tears into her own eyes, and then began, "O Gemini, my dear lady, what is the matter?"—"Nothing," cries Sophia. "Nothing! O dear Madam!" answers Honour, "you must not tell me that, when your ladyship is in this taking, and when there hath been such a preamble between your ladyship and Madam Western."—"Don't tease me," cries Sophia; "I tell you nothing is the matter. Good heavens! why was I born?"—"Nay, madam," says Mrs. Honour, "you shall never persuade me that your la'ship can lament yourself so for nothing. To

34

be sure I am but a servant; but to be sure I have
been always faithful to your la'ship, and to be
sure I would serve your la'ship with my life.''—
"My dear Honour," says Sophia, "'tis not in
thy power to be of any service to me. I am irretrievably undone.''—''Heaven forbid!'' answered
the waiting-woman; "but if I can't be of any
service to you, pray tell me, madam—it will be
some comfort to me to know—pray, dear ma'am,
tell me what's the matter.''—''My father,'' cries
Sophia, "is going to marry me to a man I both
despise and hate.''—''O dear, ma'am,'' answered
the other, "who is this wicked man?" for to
be sure he is very bad, or your la'ship would
not despise him.''—''His name is poison to my
tongue,'' replied Sophia: ''thou wilt know it too
soon.'' Indeed, to confess the truth, she knew
it already, and therefore was not very inquisi-
tive as to that point. She then proceeded thus:
"I don't pretend to give your la'ship advice,
whereof your la'ship knows much better than I
can pretend to, being but a servant; but,
i-fackins! no father in England should marry
me against my consent. And, to be sure, the
'squire is so good, that if he did but know your
la'ship despises and hates the young man, to be
sure he would not desire you to marry him. And
if your la'ship would but give me leave to tell
my master so. To be sure, it would be more
proper to come from your own mouth; but as
your la'ship doth not care to foul your tongue
with his nasty name—''—''You are mistaken,
Honour,'' says Sophia; ''my father was de-

termined before he ever thought fit to mention
it to me.''—''More shame for him,'' cries
Honour: ''you are to go to bed to him and not
master: and thof a man may be a very proper
man, yet every woman mayn't think him handsome alike. I am sure my master would never
act in this manner of his own head. I wish
some people would trouble themselves only with
what belongs to them; they would not, I believe,
like to be served so, if it was their own case; for
though I am a maid, I can easily believe as how
all men are not equally agreeable. And what
signifies your la'ship having so great a fortune,
if you can't please yourself with the man you
think most handsomest? Well, I say nothing; but
to be sure it is a pity some folks had not been
better born; nay, as for that matter, I should not
mind it myself; but then there is not so much
money; and what of that? your la'ship hath
money enough for both; and where can your
la'ship bestow your fortune better? for to be
sure every one must allow that he is the most
handsomest charmingest, finest, tallest, properest
man in the world.''—''What do you mean by
running on in this manner to me?'' cries Sophia,
with a very grave countenance. ''Have I ever
given any encouragement for these liberties?''
—''Nay, ma'am, I ask your pardon; I meant no
harm,'' answered she; ''but to be sure the poor
gentleman hath run in my head ever since I saw
him this morning. To be sure, if your la'ship
had but seen him just now, you must have pitied
him. Poor gentleman! I wishes some misfortune

hath not happened to him; for he hath been walking about with his arms across, and looking so melancholy, all this morning: I vow and protest it made me almost cry to see him."—"To see whom?" says Sophia. "Poor Mr. Jones," answered Honour. "See him! why where did you see him?" cries Sophia. "By the canal, ma'am," says Honour. "There he hath been walking all this morning, and at last there he laid himself down: I believe he lies there still. To be sure, if it had not been for my modesty, being a maid, as I am, I should have gone and spoke to him. Do, ma'am, let me go and see, only for a fancy, whether he is there still."—"Pugh!" says Sophia. "There! no, no: what should he do there? He is gone before this time, to be sure. Besides, why—what—why should you go to see? besides, I want you for something else. Go, fetch me my hat and gloves. I shall walk with my aunt in the grove before dinner." Honour did immediately as she was bid, and Sophia put her hat on; when, looking in the glass, she fancied the ribbon with which her hat was tied did not become her, and so sent her maid back again for a ribbon of a different color; and then giving Mrs. Honour repeated charges not to leave her work on any account, as she said it was in violent haste, and must be finished that very day, she muttered something more about going to the grove, and then sallied out the contrary way, and walked, as fast as her tender trembling limbs could carry her, directly towards the canal.

Jones had been there as Mrs. Honour had told

her; he had indeed spent two hours there that morning in melancholy contemplation on his Sophia, and had gone out from the garden at one door the moment she entered it at another. So that those unlucky minutes which had been spent in changing the ribbons, had prevented the lovers from meeting at this time;—a most unfortunate accident, from which my fair readers will not fail to draw a very wholesome lesson. And here I strictly forbid all male critics to intermeddle with a circumstance which I have recounted only for the sake of the ladies, and upon which they only are at liberty to comment.

CHAPTER VII

A picture of formal courtship in miniature, as it always ought to be drawn, and a scene of a tenderer kind painted at full length.

IT was well remarked by one (and perhaps by more), that misfortunes do not come single. This wise maxim was now verified by Sophia, who was not only disappointed of seeing the man she loved, but had the vexation of being obliged to dress herself out, in order to receive a visit from the man she hated.

That afternoon Mr. Western, for the first time, acquainted his daughter with his intentions; telling her he knew very well that she had heard it before from her aunt. Sophia looked very grave upon this, nor could she prevent a few pearls from stealing into her eyes. "Come, come," says Western, "none of your maidenish airs; I know all; I assure you sister hath told me all."

"Is it possible," says Sophia, "that my aunt can have betrayed me already?"—"Ay, ay," says Western; "betrayed you! ay. Why, you betrayed yourself yesterday at dinner. You showed your fancy very plainly, I think. But you young girls never know what you would be at. So you cry because I am going to marry you to the man you are in love with! Your mother, I remember, whimpered and whined just in the same manner; but it was all over within twenty-four hours after we were married: Mr. Blifil is a brisk young man, and will soon put an end to your squeamishness. Come, cheer up, cheer up; I expect un every minute.''

Sophia was now convinced that her aunt had behaved honorably to her: and she determined to go through that disagreeable afternoon with as much resolution as possible, and without giving the least suspicion in the world to her father.

Mr. Blifil soon arrived; and Mr. Western soon after withdrawing, left the young couple together.

Here a long silence of near a quarter of an hour ensued; for the gentleman who was to begin the conversation had all the unbecoming modesty which consists in bashfulness. He often attempted to speak, and as often suppressed his words just at the very point of utterance. At last out they broke in a torrent of far-fetched and high-strained compliments, which were answered on her side by downcast looks, half bows, and civil monosyllables. Blifil, from his inexperience in the ways of women, and from his conceit of himself, took this behavior for a modest assent to his courtship; and when, to shorten a scene which she could no longer support, Sophia rose up and left the room, he imputed that, too, merely to bashfulness, and comforted himself that he should soon have enough of her company.

He was indeed perfectly well satisfied with his prospect of success; for as to that entire and

absolute possession of the heart of his mistress
which romantic lovers require, the very idea of
it never entered his head. Her fortune and her
person were the sole objects of his wishes, of
which he made no doubt soon to obtain the absolute property; as Mr. Western's mind was so
earnestly bent on the match; and as he well knew
the strict obedience which Sophia was always
ready to pay to her father's will, and the greater
still which her father would exact, if there was
occasion. This authority, therefore, together
with the charms which he fancied in his own
person and conversation, could not fail, he
thought, of succeeding with a young lady, whose
inclinations were, he doubted not, entirely dis-
engaged.

Of Jones he certainly had not even the least
jealousy; and I have often thought it wonderful
that he had not. Perhaps he imagined the character which Jones bore all over the country
(how justly, let the reader determine), of being
one of the wildest fellows in England, might
render him odious to a lady of the most exem-
plary modesty. Perhaps his suspicions might
be laid asleep by the behavior of Sophia, and of
Jones himself, when they were all in company
together. Lastly, and indeed principally, he was
well assured there was not another self in the
case. He fancied that he knew Jones to the
bottom, and had in reality a great contempt for
his understanding, for not being more attached
to his own interest. He had no apprehension
that Jones was in love with Sophia; and as for

any lucrative motives, he imagined they would
sway very little with so silly a fellow. Blifil,
moreover, thought the affair of Molly Seagrim
still went on, and indeed believed it would end in
marriage; for Jones really loved him from his
childhood, and had kept no secret from him, till
his behavior on the sickness of Mr. Allworthy
had entirely alienated his heart; and it was by
means of the quarrel which had ensued on this
occasion, and which was not yet reconciled, that
Mr. Blifil knew nothing of the alteration which
had happened in the affection which Jones had
formerly borne towards Molly.

From these reasons, therefore, Mr. Blifil saw
no bar to his success with Sophia. He concluded
her behavior was like that of all other young
ladies on a first visit from a lover, and it had
indeed entirely answered his expectations.

Mr. Western took care to way-lay the lover at
his exit from his mistress. He found him so
elevated with his success, so enamored with his
daughter, and so satisfied with her reception of
him, that the old gentleman began to caper and
dance about his hall, and by many other antic
actions to express the extravagance of his joy;
for he had not the least command over any of
his passions; and that which had at any time the
ascendant in his mind hurried him to the wildest
excesses.

As soon as Blifil was departed, which was not
till after many hearty kisses and embraces bestowed on him by Western, the good squire went
instantly in quest of his daughter, whom he no

sooner found than he poured forth the most extravagant raptures, bidding her choose what clothes and jewels she pleased; and declaring that he had no other use for fortune but to make her happy. He then caressed her again and again with the utmost profusion of fondness, called her by the most endearing names, and protested she was his only joy on earth. ·

Sophia perceiving her father in this fit of affection, which she did not absolutely know the reason of (for fits of fondness were not unusual to him, though this was rather more violent than ordinary), thought she should never have a better opportunity of disclosing herself than at present, as far at least as regarded Mr. Blifil; and she too well foresaw the necessity which she should soon be under of coming to a full explanation. After having thanked the squire, therefore, for all his professions of kindness, she added, with a look full of inexpressible softness, "And is it possible my papa can be so good to place all his joy in his Sophy's happiness?" which Western having confirmed by a great oath, and a kiss; she then laid hold of his hand, and, falling on her knees, after many warm and passionate declarations of affection and duty, she begged him "not to make her the most miserable creature on earth by forcing her to marry a man whom she detested. This I entreat of you, dear sir," said she, "for your sake, as well as my own, since you are so very kind to tell me your happiness depends on mine."—"How! what!" says Western, staring wildly. "Oh! sir," continued she, "not only your poor Sophy's happiness; her very life, her being, depends upon your granting her request. I cannot live with Mr. Blifil. To force me into this marriage would be killing me."—"You can't live with Mr. Blifil?" says Western. "No, upon my soul I can't," answered Sophia. "Then die and be d—d," cries he, spurning her from him. "Oh! sir," cries Sophia, catching hold of the skirt of his coat, "take pity on me, I beseech you. Don't look and say such cruel——Can you be unmoved while you see your Sophy in this dreadful condition? Can the best of father's break my heart? Will he kill me by the most painful, cruel, lingering death?"—"Pooh! pooh!" cries the squire; "all stuff and nonsense; all maidenish tricks. Kill you indeed! Will marriage kill you?"— "Oh! sir," answered Sophia, "such a marriage is worse than death. He is not even indifferent; I hate and detest him."—"If you detest un never so much," cries Western, "you shall ha'un." This he bound by an oath too shocking to repeat; and after many violent asseverations, concluded in these words: "I am resolved upon the match, and unless you consent to it I will not give you a groat, not a single farthing; no, though I saw you expiring with famine in the street, I would not relieve you with a morsel of bread. This is my fixed resolution, and so I leave you to consider on it." He then broke from her with such violence, that her face dashed against the floor; and he burst directly out of the room, leaving poor Sophia prostrate on the ground.

When Western came into the hall, he there found Jones; who seeing his friend looking wild, pale, and almost breathless, could not forbear enquiring the reason of all these melancholy appearances. Upon which the squire immediately acquainted him with the whole matter, concluding with bitter denunciations against Sophia, and very pathetic lamentations of the misery of all fathers who are so unfortunate to have daughters.

Jones, to whom all the resolutions which had been taken in favor of Blifil were yet a secret, was at first almost struck dead with this relation; but recovering his spirits a little, mere despair, as he afterwards said, inspired him to mention a matter to Mr. Western, which seemed to require more impudence than a human forehead was ever gifted with. He desired leave to go to Sophia, that he might endeavor to obtain her concurrence with her father's inclinations.

If the squire had been as quicksighted as he was remarkable for the contrary, passion might at present very well have blinded him. He thanked Jones for offering to undertake the office, and said, "Go, go, prithee, try what canst do;" and then swore many execrable oaths that he would turn her out of doors unless she consented to the match.

CHAPTER VIII

The meeting between Jones and Sophia.

JONES departed instantly in quest of Sophia, whom he found just risen from the ground, where her father had left her, with the tears trickling from her eyes, and the blood running from her lips. He presently ran to her, and with a voice full at once of tenderness and terror, cried, "O my Sophia, what means this dreadful sight?" She looked softly at him for a moment before she spoke, and then said, "Mr. Jones, for Heaven's sake how came you here?—Leave me, I beseech you, this moment."—"Do not," says he, "impose so harsh a command upon me—my heart bleeds faster than those lips. O Sophia, how easily could I drain my veins to preserve one drop of that dear blood."—"I have too many obligations to you already," answered she, "for sure you meant them such." Here she looked at him tenderly almost a minute, and then bursting into an agony, cried, "Oh, Mr. Jones, why did you save my life? my death would have been happier for us both."—"Happier for us both!" cried he. "Could racks or wheels kill me so painfully as Sophia's—I cannot bear the dreadful sound. Do I live but for her?" Both his voice and looks were full of inexpressible tenderness when he spoke these words; and at the same time he laid gently hold on her hand, which she did not withdraw from him; to say the truth, she hardly knew what she did or suffered. A few moments now passed in silence between these lovers, while his eyes were eagerly fixed on Sophia, and hers declined towards the ground: at last she recovered strength enough to desire him again to leave her, for that her certain ruin would be the consequence of their being found together; adding, "Oh, Mr. Jones, you know not, you know not what hath passed this cruel afternoon."—"I know all, my Sophia," answered he; "your cruel father hath told me all, and he himself hath sent me hither to you."—"My father sent you to me!" replied she, "sure you dream." —"Would to Heaven," cries he, "it was but a dream! Oh, Sophia, your father hath sent me to you, to be an advocate for my odious rival, to solicit you in his favor. I took any means to get access to you. O speak to me, Sophia! comfort my bleeding heart. Sure no one ever loved, ever doted like me. Do not unkindly withhold this dear, this soft, this gentle hand—one moment, perhaps, tears you for ever from me— nothing less than this cruel occasion could, I believe, have ever conquered the respect and awe with which you have inspired me." She stood a moment silent, and covered with confusion; then lifting up her eyes gently towards him, she cried, "What would Mr. Jones have me say?"— "O do but promise," cries he, "that you never will give yourself to Blifil."—"Name not," answered she, "the detested sound. Be assured

I never will give him what is in my power to withhold from him."—"Now then," cries he, "while you are so perfectly kind, go a little farther, and add that I may hope."—"Alas!" says she, "Mr. Jones, whither will you drive me? What hope have I to bestow? You know my father's intentions."—"But I know," answered he, "your compliance with them cannot be compelled."—"What," says she, "must be the dreadful consequence of my disobedience? My own ruin is my least concern. I cannot bear the thoughts of being the cause of my father's misery."—"He is himself the cause," cries Jones, "by exacting a power over you which Nature hath not given him. Think on the misery which I am to suffer if I am to lose you, and see on which side pity will turn the balance."—"Think of it!" replied she: "can you imagine I do not feel the ruin which I must bring on you, should I comply with your desire? It is that thought which gives me resolution to bid you fly from me for ever, and avoid your own destruction."—"I fear no destruction," cries he, "but the loss of Sophia. If you would save me from the most bitter agonies, recall that cruel sentence. Indeed, I can never part with you, indeed I cannot.

The lovers now stood both silent and trembling, Sophia being unable to withdraw her hand from Jones, and he almost as unable to hold it; when the scene, which I believe some of my readers will think had lasted long enough, was interrupted by one of so different a nature, that we shall reserve the relation of it for a different chapter.

CHAPTER IX

Being of a much more tempestuous kind than the former.

BEFORE we proceed with what now happened to our lovers, it may be proper to recount what had passed in the hall during their tender interview.

Soon after Jones had left Mr. Western in the manner above mentioned, his sister came to him, and was presently informed of all that had passed between her brother and Sophia relating to Blifil.

This behavior in her niece the good lady construed to be an absolute breach of the condition on which she had engaged to keep her love for Mr. Jones a secret. She considered herself, therefore, at full liberty to reveal all she knew to the squire, which she immediately did in the most explicit terms, and without any ceremony or preface.

The idea of a marriage between Jones and his daughter, had never once entered into the squire's head, either in the warmest minutes of his affection towards that young man, or from suspicion, or on any other occasion. He did indeed consider a parity of fortune and circumstances to be physically as necessary an ingredient in marriage, as difference of sexes, or any other essential; and had no more apprehension of his daughter's falling in love with a poor man, than with any animal of a different species.

He became, therefore, like one thunderstruck at his sister's relation. He was, at first, incapable of making any answer, having been almost deprived of his breath by the violence of the surprise. This, however, soon returned, and, as is usual in other cases after an intermission, with redoubled force and fury.

The first use he made of the power of speech, after his recovery from the sudden effects of his astonishment, was to discharge a round volley of oaths and imprecations. After which he proceeded hastily to the apartment where he expected to find the lovers, and murmured, or rather indeed roared forth, intentions of revenge every step he went.

As when two doves, or two wood-pigeons, or as when Strephon and Phyllis (for that comes nearest to the mark) are retired into some pleasant solitary grove, to enjoy the delightful conversation of Love, that bashful boy, who cannot speak in public, and is never a good companion to more than two at a time; here, while every object is serene, should hoarse thunder burst suddenly through the shattered clouds, and rumbling roll along the sky, the frightened maid starts from the mossy bank or verdant turf, the pale livery of death succeeds the red regimentals in which Love had before dressed her cheeks, fear shakes her whole frame, and her lover scarce supports her trembling tottering limbs.

Or as when two gentleman, strangers to the wondrous wit of the place, are cracking a bottle

together at some inn or tavern at Salisbury, if
the great Dowdy, who acts the part of a madman
as well as some of his setters-on do that of a fool,
should rattle his chains, and dreadfully hum
forth the grumbling catch along the gallery; the
frighted strangers stand aghast; scared at the
horrid sound, they seek some place of shelter
from the approaching danger; and if the well-
barred windows did admit their exit, would venture their necks to escape the threatening fury
now coming upon them.

So trembled poor Sophia, so turned she pale at
the noise of her father, who, in a voice most
dreadful to hear, came on swearing, cursing, and
vowing the destruction of Jones. To say the
truth, I believe the youth himself would, from
some prudent considerations, have preferred
another place of abode at this time, had his terror
on Sophia's account given him liberty to reflect a
moment on what any otherways concerned himself, than as his love made him partake whatever
affected her.

And now the squire, having burst open the
door, beheld an object which instantly suspended
all his fury against Jones; this was the ghastly
appearance of Sophia, who had fainted away in
her lover's arms. This tragical sight Mr. Western no sooner beheld, than all his rage forsook
him; he roared for help with his utmost violence;
ran first to his daughter, then back to the door
calling for water, and then back again to Sophia,
never considering in whose arms she then was,
nor perhaps once recollecting that there was

such a person in the world as Jones; for indeed I believe the present circumstances of his daughter were now the sole consideration which employed his thoughts.

Mrs. Western and a great number of servants soon came to the assistance of Sophia with water, cordials, and everything necessary on those occasions. These were applied with such success, that Sophia in a very few minutes began to recover, and all the symptoms of life to return. Upon which she was presently led off by her own maid and Mrs. Western: nor did that good lady depart without leaving some wholesome admonitions with her brother, on the dreadful effects of his passion, or, as she pleased to call it, madness.

The squire, perhaps, did not understand this good advice, as it was delivered in obscure hints, shrugs, and notes of admiration: at least, if he did understand it, he profited very little by it; for no sooner was he cured of his immediate fears for his daughter, than he relapsed into his former frenzy, which must have produced an immediate battle with Jones, had not parson Supple, who was a very strong man, been present, and by mere force restrained the squire from acts of hostility.

The moment Sophia was departed, Jones advanced in a very suppliant manner to Mr. Western, whom the parson held in his arms, and begged him to be pacified; for that, while he continued in such a passion, it would be impossible to give him any satisfaction.

"I wull have satisfaction o' thee," answered

the squire; "so doff thy clothes. *At unt* half a man, and I'll lick thee as well as wast ever licked in thy life." He then bespattered the youth with abundance of that language which passes between country gentlemen who embrace opposite sides of the question; with frequent applications to him to salute that part which is generally introduced into all controversies that arise among the lower orders of the English gentry at horse-races, cock-matches, and other public places. Allusions to this part are likewise often made for the sake of the jest. And here, I believe, the wit is generally misunderstood. In reality, it lies in desiring another to kiss your a—— for having just before threatened to kick his; for I have observed very accurately, that no one ever desires you to kick that which belongs to himself, nor offers to kiss this part in another.

It may likewise seem surprising that in the many thousand kind invitations of this sort, which every one who hath conversed with country gentlemen must have heard, no one, I believe, hath ever seen a single instance where the desire hath been complied with;—a great instance of their want of politeness; for in town nothing can be more common than for the finest gentlemen to perform this ceremony every day to their superiors, without having that favor once requested of them.

To all such wit, Jones very calmly answered, "Sir, this usage may perhaps cancel every other obligation you have conferred on me; but there is one you can never cancel: nor will I be provoked

by your abuse to lift my hand against the father
of Sophia.''

At these words the squire grew still more outrageous than before; so that the parson begged
Jones to retire; saying, ''You behold, sir, how he
waxeth wrath at your abode here; therefore let
me pray you not to tarry any longer. His anger
is too much kindled for you to commune with him
at present. You had better, therefore, conclude
your visit, and refer what matters you have to
urge in your behalf to some other opportunity.''

Jones accepted this advice with thanks, and
immediately departed. The squire now regained
the liberty of his hands, and so much temper as to
express some satisfaction in the restraint which
had been laid upon him; declaring that he should
certainly have beat his brains out; and adding,
''It would have vexed one confoundedly to have
been hanged for such a rascal.''

The parson now began to triumph in the success
of his peace-making endeavors, and proceeded to
read a lecture against anger, which might perhaps rather have tended to raise than to quiet that
passion in some hasty minds. This lecture he
enriched with many valuable quotations from the
ancients, particularly from Seneca; who hath indeed so well handled this passion, that none but
a very angry man can read him without great
pleasure and profit. The doctor concluded this
harangue with the famous story of Alexander
and Clitus; but as I find that entered in my com-
mon-place under title Drunkenness, I shall not insert it here.

The squire took no notice of this story, nor perhaps of anything he said; for he interrupted him before he had finished, by calling for a tankard of beer; observing (which is perhaps as true as any observation on this fever of the mind) that anger makes a man dry.

No sooner had the squire swallowed a large draught than he renewed the discourse on Jones, and declared a resolution of going the next morning early to acquaint Mr. Allworthy. His friend would have dissuaded him from this, from the mere motive of good-nature; but his dissuasion had no other effect than to produce a large volley of oaths and curses, which greatly shocked the pious ears of Supple; but he did not dare to remonstrate against a privilege which the squire claimed as a freeborn Englishman. To say truth, the parson submitted to please his palate at the squire's table, at the expense of suffering now and then this violence to his ears. He contented himself with thinking he did not promote this evil practice, and that the squire would not swear an oath the less, if he never entered within his gates. However, though he was not guilty of ill manners by rebuking a gentleman in his own house, he paid him off obliquely in the pulpit: which had not, indeed, the good effect of working a reformation in the squire himself; yet it so far operated on his conscience, that he put the laws very severely in execution against others, and the magistrate was the only person in the parish who could swear with impunity.

CHAPTER X

In which Mr. Western visits Mr. Allworthy.

MR. ALLWORTHY was now retired from breakfast with his nephew, well satisfied with the report of the young gentleman's successful visit to Sophia (for he greatly desired the match, more on account of the young lady's character than of her riches), when Mr. Western broke abruptly in upon them, and without any ceremony began as follows:—

"There, you have done a fine piece of work truly! You have brought up your bastard to a fine purpose; not that I believe you have had any hand in it neither, that is, as a man may say, designedly: but there is a fine kettle-of-fish made on't up at our house." "What can be the matter, Mr. Western?" said Allworthy. "O, matter enow of all conscience: my daughter hath fallen in love with your bastard, that's all; but I won't ge her a hapeny, not the twentieth part of a brass varden. I always thought what would come o' breeding up a bastard like a gentleman, and letting un come about to vok's houses. It's well vor un I could not get at un: I'd a lick'd un; I'd a spoil'd his caterwauling; I'd a taught the son of a whore to meddle with meat for his master. He shan't ever have a morsel of meat of mine, or a varden to buy it: if she will ha un, one

56

smock shall be her portion. I'd sooner ge my
estate to the zinking fund, that it may be sent to
Hanover to corrupt our nation with.'' ''I am
heartily sorry,'' cries Allworthy. ''Pox o' your
sorrow,'' says Western; ''it will do me abundance
of good when I have lost my only child, my poor
Sophy, that was the joy of my heart, and all the
hope and comfort of my age; but I am resolved
I will turn her out o' doors; she shall beg, and
starve, and rot in the streets. Not one hapeny,
not a hapeny shall she ever hae o' mine. The son
of a bitch was always good at finding a hare sit·
ting, an be rotted to'n: I little thought what puss
he was looking after; but it shall be the worst he
ever vound in his life. She shall be no better
than carrion: the skin o'er is all he shall hə,
and zu you may tell un.'' ''I am in amazement,''
cries Allworthy, ''at what you tell me, after what
passed between my nephew and the young lady
no longer ago than yesterday.'' ''Yes, sir,'' an·
swered Western, ''it was after what passed be--
tween your nephew and she that the whole matter came out. Mr. Blifil there was no sooner gone
than the son of a whore came lurching about the
house. Little did I think when I used to love him
for a sportsman that he was all the while a poach-
ing after my daughter.'' ''Why truly,'' says
Allworthy, ''I could wish you had not given him
so many opportunities with her; and you will do
me the justice to acknowledge that I have al·
ways been averse to his staying so much at your
house, though I own I had no suspicion of this
kind.'' ''Why, zounds,'' cries Western, ''who

could have thought it? What the devil had she
to do wi'n? He did not come there a courting
to her; he came there a hunting with me." "But
was it possible," says Allworthy, "that you
should never discern any symptoms of love between them, when you have seen them so often
together?" "Never in my life, as I hope to be
saved," cries Western: "I never so much as zeed
him kiss her in all my life; and so far from courting her, he used rather to be more silent when
she was in company than at any other time; and
as for the girl, she was always less civil to'n than
to any young man that came to the house. As to
that matter, I am not more easy to be deceived
than another; I would not have you think I am,
neighbor." Allworthy could scarce refrain
laughter at this; but he resolved to do a violence
to himself; for he perfectly well knew mankind,
and had too much good-breeding and good-nature
to offend the squire in his present circumstances.
He then asked Western what he would have him
do upon this occasion. To which the other answered, "That he would have him keep the rascal
away from his house, and that he would go and
lock up the wench; for he was resolved to make
her marry Mr. Blifil in spite of her teeth." He
then shook Blifil by the hand, and swore he would
have no other son-in-law. Presently after which
he took his leave; saying his house was in such
disorder that it was necessary for him to make
haste home, to take care his daughter did not give
him the slip; and as for Jones, he swore if he

caught him at his house, he would qualify him to run for the geldings' plate.

When Allworthy and Blifil were again left together, a long silence ensued between them; all which interval the young gentleman filled up with sighs, which proceeded partly from disappointment, but more from hatred; for the success of Jones was much more grievous to him than the loss of Sophia.

At length his uncle asked him what he was determined to do, and he answered in the following words:—"Alas! sir, can it be a question what step a lover will take, when reason and passion point different ways? I am afraid it is too certain he will, in that dilemma, always follow the latter. Reason dictates to me, to quit all thoughts of a woman who places her affections on another; my passion bids me hope she may in time change her inclinations in my favor. Here, however, I conceive an objection may be raised, which, if it could not fully be answered, would totally deter me from any further pursuit. I mean the injustice of endeavoring to supplant another in a heart of which he seems already in possession; but the determined resolution of Mr. Western shows that, in this case, I shall, by so doing, promote the happiness of every party; not only that of the parent, who will thus be preserved from the highest degree of misery, but of both the others, who must be undone by this match. The lady, I am sure, will be undone in every sense; for, besides the loss of most part of her own

fortune, she will be not only married to a beggar, but the little fortune which her father cannot withhold from her will be squandered on that
wench with whom I know he yet converses. Nay,
that is a trifle; for I know him to be one of the
worst men in the world; for had my dear uncle
known what I have hitherto endeavored to conceal, he must have long since abandoned so profligate a wretch." "How!" said Allworthy; "hath
he done anything worse than I already know?
Tell me, I beseech you?" "No," replied Blifil;
"it is now past, and perhaps he may have repented of it." "I command you, on your duty,"
said Allworthy, "to tell me what you mean."
"You know, sir," says Blifil, "I never disobeyed
you; but I am sorry I mentioned it, since it
may now look like revenge, whereas, I thank
Heaven, no such motive ever entered my heart;
and if you oblige me to discover it, I must be his
petitioner to you for your forgiveness." "I will
have no conditions," answered Allworthy; "I
think I have shown tenderness enough towards
him, and more perhaps than you ought to thank
me for." "More, indeed, I fear, than he deserved," cries Blifil; "for in the very day of
your utmost danger, when myself and all the family were in tears, he filled the house with riot and
debauchery. He drank, and sung, and roared;
and when I gave him a gentle hint of the inde-
cency of his actions, he fell into a violent passion,
swore many oaths, called me rascal, and struck
me." "How!" cries Allworthy; "did he dare to
strike you?" "I am sure" cries Blifil. "I have

forgiven him that long ago. I wish I could so easily forget his ingratitude to the best of benefactors; and yet even that I hope you will forgive him, since he must have certainly been possessed with the devil: for that very evening, as Mr. Thwackum and myself were taking the air in the fields, and exulting in the good symptoms which then first began to discover themselves, we unluckily saw him engaged with a wench in a manner not fit to be mentioned. Mr. Thwackum, with more boldness than prudence, advanced to rebuke him, when (I am sorry to say it) he fell upon the worthy man, and beat him so outrageously that I wish he may have yet recovered the bruises. Nor was I without my share of the effects of his malice, while I endeavored to protect my tutor; but that I have long forgiven; nay, I prevailed with Mr. Thwackum to forgive him too, and not to inform you of a secret which I feared might be fatal to him. And now, sir, since I have unadvisedly dropped a hint of this matter, and your commands have obliged me to discover the whole, let me intercede with you for him." "O child!" said Allworthy, "I know not whether I should blame or applaud your goodness, in concealing such villainy a moment: but where is Mr. Thwackum? Not that I want any confirmation of what you say; but I will examine all the evidence of this matter, to justify to the world the example I am resolved to make of such a monster."

Thwackum was now sent for, and presently appeared. He corroborated every circumstance which the other had deposed: nay, he produced the record upon his breast, where the handwriting of Mr. Jones remained very legible in black and blue. He concluded with declaring to Mr. Allworthy, that he should have long since informed him of this matter, had not Mr. Blifil, by the most earnest interpositions, prevented him. "He is," says he, "an excellent youth: though such forgiveness of enemies is carrying the matter too far."

In reality, Blifil had taken some pains to prevail with the parson, and to prevent the discovery at that time; for which he had many reasons. He knew that the minds of men are apt to be softened and relaxed from their usual severity by sickness. Besides, he imagined that if the story was told when the fact was so recent, and the physician about the house, who might have unraveled the real truth, he should never be able to give it the malicious turn which he intended. Again, he resolved to hoard up this business, till the indiscretion of Jones should afford some additional complaints; for he thought the joint weight of many facts falling upon him together, would be the most likely to crush him; and he watched, therefore, some such opportunity as that with which fortune had now kindly presented him. Lastly, by prevailing with Thwackum to conceal the matter for a time, he knew he should confirm an opinion of his friendship to Jones, which he had greatly labored to establish in Mr. Allworthy.

CHAPTER XI

A short chapter; but which contains sufficient matter to affect
the good-natured reader.

IT was Mr. Allworthy's custom never to punish any one, not even to turn away a servant, in a passion. He resolved therefore
to delay passing sentence on Jones till the afternoon.

The poor young man attended at dinner, as
usual; but his heart was too much loaded to suffer
him to eat. His grief too was a good deal aggravated by the unkind looks of Mr. Allworthy;
whence he concluded that Western had discovered
the whole affair between him and Sophia; but as
to Mr. Blifil's story, he had not the least apprehension; for of much the greater part he was entirely innocent; and for the residue, as he had
forgiven and forgotten it himself, so he suspected
no remembrance on the other side. When dinner
was over, and the servants departed, Mr. Allworthy began to harangue. He set forth, in a
long speech, the many iniquities of which Jones
had been guilty, particularly those which this day
had brought to light; and concluded by telling
him, "That unless he could clear himself of the
charge, he was resolved to banish him his sight
for ever."

Many disadvantages attended poor Jones in

making his defense; nay, indeed, he hardly knew
his accusation; for as Mr. Allworthy, in recounting the drunkenness, &c., while he lay ill, out of
modesty sunk everything that related particularly
to himself, which indeed principally constituted
the crime; Jones could not deny the charge. His
heart was, besides, almost broken already; and
his spirits were so sunk, that he could say nothing for himself; but acknowledged the whole, and,
like a criminal in despair, threw himself upon
mercy; concluding, "That though he must own
himself guilty of many follies and inadvertencies,
he hoped he had done nothing to deserve what
would be to him the greatest punishment in the
world."

Allworthy answered, "That he had forgiven
him too often already, in compassion to his youth,
and in hopes of his amendment: that he now
found he was an abandoned reprobate, and such
as it would be criminal in any one to support and
encourage. Nay," said Mr. Allworthy to him,
"your audacious attempt to steal away the young
lady, calls upon me to justify my own character
in punishing you. The world who have already
censured the regard I have shown for you may
think, with some color at least of justice, that I
connive at so base and barbarous an action—an
action of which you must have known my abhorrence: and which, had you had any concern for
my ease and honor, as well as for my friendship,
you would never have thought of undertaking.
Fie upon it, young man! indeed there is scarce
any punishment equal to your crimes, and I can

scarce think myself justifiable in what I am now going to bestow on you. However, as I have educated you like a child of my own, I will not turn you naked into the world. When you open this paper, therefore, you will find something which may enable you, with industry, to get an honest livelihood; but if you employ it to worse purposes, I shall not think myself obliged to supply you farther, being resolved, from this day forward, to converse no more with you on any account. I cannot avoid saying, there is no part of your conduct which I resent more than your illtreatment of that good young man (meaning Blifil) who hath behaved with so much tenderness and honor towards you.''

These last words were a dose almost too bitter to be swallowed. A flood of tears now gushed from the eyes of Jones, and every faculty of speech and motion seemed to have deserted him. It was some time before he was able to obey Allworthy's peremptory commands of departing; which he at length did, having first kissed his hands with a passion difficult to be affected, and as difficult to be described.

The reader must be very weak, if, when he considers the light in which Jones then appeared to Mr. Allworthy, he should blame the rigor of his sentence. And yet all the neighborhood, either from this weakness, or from some worse motive, condemned this justice and severity as the highest cruelty. Nay, the very persons who had before censured the good man for the kindness and tenderness shown to a bastard (his own, accord-

II—5

ing to the general opinion), now cried out as loudly against turning his own child out of doors. The women especially were unanimous in taking the part of Jones, and raised more stories on the occasion than I have room, in this chapter, to set down.

One thing must not be omitted, that, in their censures on this occasion, none ever mentioned the sum contained in the paper which Allworthy gave Jones, which was no less than five hundred pounds; but all agreed that he was sent away penniless, and some said naked, from the house of his inhuman father.

CHAPTER XII

Containing love-letters, &c.

JONES was commanded to leave the house immediately, and told, that his clothes and everything else should be sent to him whithersoever he should order them.

He accordingly set out, and walked above a mile, not regarding, and indeed scarce knowing, whither he went. At length a little brook obstructing his passage, he threw himself down by the side of it; nor could he help muttering with some little indignation, ''Sure my father will not deny me this place to rest in!''

Here he presently fell into the most violent agonies, tearing his hair from his head, and using most other actions which generally accompany fits of madness, rage, and despair.

When he had in this manner vented the first emotions of passion, he began to come a little to himself. His grief now took another turn, and discharged itself in a gentler way, till he became at last cool enough to reason with his passion, and to consider what steps were proper to be taken in his deplorable condition.

And now the great doubt was, how to act with regard to Sophia. The thoughts of leaving her almost rent his heart asunder; but the consideration of reducing her to ruin and beggary still racked him, if possible, more; and if the violent desire of possessing her person could have induced him to listen one moment to this alternative, still he was by no means certain of her resolution to indulge his wishes at so high an expense. The resentment of Mr. Allworthy, and the injury he must do to his quiet, argued strongly against this latter; and lastly, the apparent impossibility of his success, even if he would sacrifice all these considerations to it, came to his assistance; and thus honor at last backed with despair, with gratitude to his benefactor, and with real love to his mistress, got the better of burning desire, and he resolved rather to quit Sophia, than pursue her to her ruin.

It is difficult for any who have not felt it, to conceive the glowing warmth which filled his breast on the first contemplation of this victory over his passion. Pride flattered him so agreeably, that his mind perhaps enjoyed perfect happiness; but this was only momentary: Sophia soon returned to his imagination, and allayed the joy of his triumph with no less bitter pangs than a good-natured general must feel, when he surveys the bleeding heaps, at the price of whose blood he hath purchased his laurels; for thousands of tender ideas lay murdered before our conqueror.

Being resolved, however, to pursue the paths of this giant honor, as the gigantic poet Lee calls it, he determined to write a farewell letter to Sophia; and accordingly proceeded to a house not far off, where, being furnished with proper materials, he wrote as follows:—

"MADAM,

"When you reflect on the situation in which I write, I am sure your good-nature will pardon any inconsistency or absurdity which my letter contains; for everything here flows from a heart so full, that no language can express its dictates.

"I have resolved, madam, to obey your commands, in flying for ever from your dear, your lovely sight. Cruel indeed those commands are; but it is a cruelty which proceeds from fortune, not from my Sophia. Fortune hath made it necessary, necessary to your preservation, to forget there ever was such a wretch as I am.

"Believe me, I would not hint all my sufferings to you, if I imagined they could possibly escape your ears. I know the goodness and tenderness of your heart, and would avoid giving you any of those pains which you always feel for the miserable. O let nothing, which you shall hear of my hard fortune, cause a moment's concern; for, after the loss of you, everything is to me a trifle.

"O Sophia! it is hard to leave you; it is harder still to desire you to forget me; yet the sincerest love obliges me to both. Pardon my conceiving that any remembrance of me can give you disquiet; but if I am so gloriously wretched, sacrifice me every way to your relief. Think I never loved you; or think truly how little I deserve you; and learn to scorn me for a presumption which can never be too severely punished.—I am unable to say more.—May guardian angels protect you for ever!"

He was now searching his pockets for his wax, but found none, nor indeed anything else, therein; for in truth he had, in his frantic disposition, tossed everything from him, and amongst the rest, his pocket-book, which he had received from Mr. Allworthy, which he had never opened, and which now first occurred to his memory.

The house supplied him with a wafer for his present purpose, with which, having sealed his letter, he returned hastily towards the brook side, in order to search for the things which he had there lost. In his way he met his old friend Black George, who heartily condoled with him on his misfortune; for this had already reached his ears, and indeed those of all the neighborhood.

Jones acquainted the gamekeeper with his loss, and he as readily went back with him to the brook, where they searched every tuft of grass in the meadow, as well where Jones had not been as where he had been; but all to no purpose, for they found nothing; for, indeed, though the things were then in the meadow, they omitted to search the only place where they were deposited; to wit, in the pockets of the said George; for he had just before found them, and being luckily apprized of their value, had very carefully put them up for his own use.

The gamekeeper having exerted as much diligence in quest of the lost goods, as if he had hoped to find them, desired Mr. Jones to recollect if he had been in no other place: "For sure," said he, "if you had lost them here so lately, the things must have been here still; for this is a very unlikely place for any one to pass by." And indeed it was by great accident that he himself had passed through that field, in order to lay wires for hares, with which he was to supply a poulterer at Bath the next morning.

Jones now gave over all hopes of recovering his loss, and almost all thoughts concerning it, and turning to Black George, asked him earnestly if he would do him the greatest favor in the world?

George answered with some hesitation, "Sir, you know you may command me whatever is in my power, and I heartily wish it was in my power to do you any service." In fact, the question staggered him; for he had, by selling game, amassed a pretty good sum of money in Mr. Western's service, and was afraid that Jones wanted to borrow some small matter of him; but he was presently relieved from his anxiety, by being desired to convey a letter to Sophia, which with great pleasure he promised to do. And indeed I believe there are few favors which he would not have gladly conferred on Mr. Jones; for he bore as much gratitude towards him as he could, and was as honest as men who love money better than any other thing in the universe, generally are.

Mrs. Honour was agreed by both to be the

proper means by which this letter should pass to
Sophia. They then separated; the gamekeeper
returned home to Mr. Western's, and Jones
walked to an alehouse at half a mile's distance,
to wait for his messenger's return.

George no sooner came home to his master's
house than he met with Mrs. Honour; to whom,
having first sounded her with a few previous
questions, he delivered the letter for her mistress,
and received at the same time another from her,
for Mr. Jones; which Honour told him she had
carried all that day in her bosom, and began to
despair of finding any means of delivering it.

The gamekeeper returned hastily and joyfully
to Jones, who, having received Sophia's letter
from him, instantly withdrew, and eagerly breaking it open, read as follows:—

"Sir,

"It is impossible to express what I have
felt since I saw you. Your submitting, on my account, to such cruel insults from my father, lays
me under an obligation I shall ever own. As you
know his temper, I beg you will, for my sake,
avoid him. I wish I had any comfort to send
you; but believe this, that nothing but the last
violence shall ever give my hand or heart where
you would be sorry to see them bestowed."

Jones read this letter a hundred times over,
and kissed it a hundred times as often. His passion now brought all tender desires back into his
mind. He repented that he had writ to Sophia

in the manner we have seen above; but he repented more that he had made use of the interval of his messenger's absence to write and dispatch a letter to Mr. Allworthy, in which he had faithfully promised and bound himself to quit all thoughts of his love. However, when his cool reflections returned, he plainly perceived that his case was neither mended nor altered by Sophia's billet, unless to give him some little glimpse of hope, from her constancy, of some favorable accident hereafter. He therefore resumed his resolution, and taking leave of Black George, set forward to a town about five miles distant, whither he had desired Mr. Allworthy, unless he pleased to revoke his sentence, to send his things after him.

CHAPTER XIII

The behavior of Sophia on the present occasion; which none of her sex will blame, who are capable of behaving in the same manner. And the discussion of a knotty point in the court of conscience.

SOPHIA had passed the last twenty-four hours in no very desirable manner. During a large part of them she had been entertained by her aunt with lectures of prudence, recommending to her the example of the polite world, where love (so the good lady said) is at present entirely laughed at, and where women consider matrimony, as men do offices of public trust, only as the means of making their fortunes, and of advancing themselves in the world. In commenting on which text Mrs. Western had displayed her eloquence during several hours.

These sagacious lectures, though little suited either to the taste or inclination of Sophia, were, however, less irksome to her than her own thoughts, that formed the entertainment of the night, during which she never once closed her eyes.

But though she could neither sleep nor rest in her bed, yet, having no avocation from it, she was found there by her father at his return from Allworthy's, which was not till past ten o'clock in the morning. He went directly up to her apartment,

74

opened the door, and seeing she was not up cried,
"Oh! you are safe then, and I am resolved to
keep you so." He then locked the door, and delivered the key to Honour, having first given her
the strictest charge, with great promises of rewards for her fidelity, and most dreadful menaces of punishment in case she should betray her
trust.

Honour's orders were, not to suffer her mistress to come out of her room without the authority of the squire himself, and to admit none to her
but him and her aunt; but she was herself to attend her with whatever Sophia pleased, except
only pen, ink, and paper, of which she was forbidden the use.

The squire ordered his daughter to dress herself and attend him at dinner; which she obeyed;
and having sat the usual time, was again conducted to her prison.

In the evening the jailer Honour brought her
the letter which she received from the gamekeeper. Sophia read it very attentively twice or
thrice over, and then threw herself upon the bed,
and burst into a flood of tears. Mrs. Honour expressed great astonishment at this behavior in
her mistress; nor could she forbear very eagerly
begging to know the cause of this passion. Sophia
made her no answer for some time, and then,
starting suddenly up, caught her maid by the hand,
and cried, "O Honour! I am undone." "Marry
forbid," cries Honour: "I wish the letter had
been burned before I had brought it to your la'-
ship. I'm sure I thought it would have com-

forted your la'ship, or I would have seen it at the
devil before I would have touched it." "Honour," says Sophia, "you are a good girl, and it
is vain to attempt concealing longer my weakness from you; I have thrown away my heart on
a man who hath forsaken me." "And is Mr.
Jones," answered the maid, "such a perfidy
man?" "He hath taken his leave of me," says
Sophia, "for ever in that letter. Nay, he hath
desired me to forget him. Could he have desired
that if he had loved me? Could he have borne
such a thought? Could he have written such a
word?" "No, certainly, ma'am," cries Honour;
"and to be sure, if the best man in England was
to desire me to forget him, I'd take him at his
word. Marry, come up! I am sure your la'ship
hath done him too much honor ever to think on
him;—a young lady who may take her choice
of all the young men in the country. And to be
sure, if I may be so presumptuous as to offer my
poor opinion, there is young Mr. Blifil, who, besides that he is come of honest parents, and will
be one of the greatest squires all hereabouts, he
is to be sure, in my poor opinion, a more handsomer and a more politer man by half; and besides, he is a young gentleman of a sober character, and who may defy any of the neighbors to
say black is his eye; he follows no dirty trollops,
nor can any bastards be laid at his door. Forget him, indeed! I thank Heaven I myself am
not so much at my last prayers as to suffer any
man to bid me forget him twice. If the best he
that wears a head was for to go for to offer

to say such an affronting word to me, I would
never give him my company afterwards, if there
was another young man in the kingdom.   And as
I was a saying, to be sure, there is young Mr.
Blifil.''   ''Name not his detested name,'' cries
Sophia.   ''Nay, ma'am,'' says Honour, ''if your
la'ship doth not like him, there be more jolly
handsome young men that would court your la'-
ship, if they had but the least encouragement.   I
don't believe there is arrow young gentleman in
this county, or in the next to it, that if your
la'ship was but to look as if you had a mind to
him, would not come about to make his offers
directly.''   ''What a wretch dost thou imagine
me,'' cries Sophia, ''by affronting my ears with
such stuff!   I detest all mankind.''   ''Nay, to be
sure, ma'am,'' answered Honour, ''your la'ship
hath had enough to give you a surfeit of them.
To be used ill by such a poor, beggarly, bastardly
fellow.''—''Hold your blasphemous tongue,''
cries Sophia: ''how dare you mention his name
with disrespect before me?   He use me ill?   No,
his poor bleeding heart suffered more when he
writ the cruel words than mine from reading
them.   O! he is all heroic virtue and angelic goodness.   I am ashamed of the weakness of my own
passion, for blaming what I ought to admire.   O,
Honour! it is my good only which he consults.
To my interest he sacrifices both himself and me.
The apprehension of ruining me hath driven him
to despair.''   ''I am very glad,'' says Honour,
''to hear your la'ship takes that into your consideration; for to be sure, it must be nothing less

than ruin to give your mind to one that is turned
out of doors, and is not worth a farthing in the
world.'' ''Turned out of doors!'' cries Sophia
hastily: ''how! what dost thou mean?'' ''Why,
to be sure, ma'am, my master no sooner told
Squire Allworthy about Mr. Jones having offered to make love to your la'ship than the squire
stripped him stark naked, and turned him out of
doors!'' ''Ha!'' says Sophia, ''I have been the
cursed, wretched cause of his destruction!
Turned naked out of doors! Here, Honour, take
all the money I have; take the rings from my
fingers. Here, my watch: carry him all. Go find
him immediately.'' ''For Heaven's sake, ma'am,''
answered Mrs. Honour, ''do but consider,
if my master should miss any of these things, I
should be made to answer for them. Therefore
let me beg your la'ship not to part with your
watch and jewels. Besides, the money, I think,
is enough of all conscience; and as for that, my
master can never know anything of the matter.''
''Here, then,'' cries Sophia, ''take every farthing
I am worth, find him out immediately, and give
it him. Go, go, lose not a moment.''

Mrs. Honour departed according to orders, and
finding Black George below-stairs, delivered him
the purse, which contained sixteen guineas, being, indeed, the whole stock of Sophia; for though
her father was very liberal to her, she was much
too generous to be rich.

Black George having received the purse, set
forward towards the alehouse; but in the way a
thought occurred to him, whether he should not

detain this money likewise. His conscience, however, immediately started at this suggestion, and began to upbraid him with ingratitude to his benefactor. To this his avarice answered, That his conscience should have considered the matter before, when he deprived poor Jones of his £500. That having quietly acquiesced in what was of so much greater importance, it was absurd, if not downright hypocrisy, to affect any qualms at this trifle. In return to which, Conscience, like a good lawyer, attempted to distinguish between an absolute breach of trust, as here, where the goods were delivered, and a bare concealment of what was found, as in the former case. Avarice presently treated this with ridicule, called it a distinction without a difference, and absolutely insisted that when once all pretensions of honor and virtue were given up in any one instance, that there was no precedent for resorting to them upon a second occasion. In short, poor Conscience had certainly been defeated in the argument, had not Fear stepped in to her assistance, and very strenuously urged that the real distinction between the two actions, did not lie in the different degrees of honor but of safety: for that the secreting the £500 was a matter of very little hazard; whereas the detaining the sixteen guineas was liable to the utmost danger of discovery.

By this friendly aid of Fear, Conscience obtained a complete victory in the mind of Black George, and, after making him a few compliments on his honesty, forced him to deliver the money to Jones.

CHAPTER XIV

A short chapter, containing a short dialogue between Squire Western and his sister.

MRS. WESTERN had been engaged abroad all that day. The squire met her at her return home; and when she enquired after Sophia, he acquainted her that he had secured her safe enough. "She is locked up in chamber," cries he, "and Honour keeps the key." As his looks were full of prodigious wisdom and sagacity when he gave his sister this information, it is probable he expected much applause from her for what he had done; but how was he disappointed when, with a most disdainful aspect, she cried, "Sure, brother, you are the weakest of all men. Why will you not confide in me for the management of my niece? Why will you interpose? You have now undone all that I have been spending my breath in order to bring about. While I have been endeavoring to fill her mind with maxims of prudence, you have been provoking her to reject them. English women, brother, I thank heaven, are no slaves. We are not to be locked up like the Spanish and Italian wives. We have as good a right to liberty as yourselves. We are to be convinced by reason and persuasion only, and not governed by force. I have seen the world, brother, and know

80

what arguments to make use of; and if your folly had not prevented me, should have prevailed with her to form her conduct by those rules of prudence and discretion which I formerly taught her." "To be sure," said the squire, "I am always in the wrong." "Brother," answered the lady, "you are not in the wrong, unless when you meddle with matters beyond your knowledge. You must agree that I have seen most of the world; and happy had it been for my niece if she had not been taken from under my care. It is by living at home with you that she hath learned romantic notions of love and nonsense." "You don't imagine, I hope," cries the squire, "that I have taught her any such things." "Your ignorance, brother," returned she, "as the great Milton says, almost subdues my patience."[1] "D—n Milton!" answered the squire: "if he had the impudence to say so to my face, I'd lend him a douse, thof he was never so great a man. Patience! An you come to that, sister, I have more occasion of patience, to be used like an overgrown schoolboy, as I am by you. Do you think no one hath any understanding, unless he hath been about at court. Pox! the world is come to a fine pass indeed, if we are all fools, except a parcel of round-heads and Hanover rats. Pox! I hope the times are a coming when we shall make fools of them, and every man shall enjoy his own. That's all, sister; and every man shall enjoy his

[1] The reader may, perhaps, subdue his own patience, if he searches for this in Milton.

II—6

own. I hope to zee it, sister, before the Hanover rats have eat up all our corn, and left us nothing, but turneps to feed upon." "I protest, brother," cries she, "you are now got beyond my understanding. Your jargon of turneps and Hanover rats is to me perfectly unintelligible."—"I believe," cries he, "you don't care to hear o'em; but the country interest may succeed one day or other for all that."—"I wish," answered the lady, "you would think a little of your daughter's interest; for, believe me, she is in greater danger than the nation."—"Just now," said he, "you chid me for thinking on her, and would ha' her left to you."—"And if you will promise to interpose no more," answered she, "I will, out of my regard to my niece, undertake the charge." "Well, do then," said the squire, "for you know I always agreed, that women are the properest to manage women."

Mrs. Western then departed, muttering something with an air of disdain, concerning women and management of the nation. She immediately repaired to Sophia's apartment, who was now, after a day's confinement, released again from her captivity.

BOOK VII

CHAPTER I

A comparison between the world and the stage.

THE world hath been often compared to
the theater; and many grave writers, as
well as the poets, have considered human
life as a great drama, resembling, in almost every
particular, those scenical representations which
Thespis is first reported to have invented, and
which have been since received with so much approbation and delight in all polite countries.

This thought hath been carried so far, and is
become so general, that some words proper to the
theater, and which were at first metaphorically
applied to the world, are now indiscriminately
and literally spoken of both; thus stage and scene
are by common use grown as familiar to us, when
we speak of life in general, as when we confine
ourselves to dramatic performances: and when
transactions behind the curtain are mentioned,
St. James's is more likely to occur to our
thoughts than Drury-lane.

It may seem easy enough to account for all
this, by reflecting that the theatrical stage is
nothing more than a representation, or, as

Aristotle calls it, an imitation of what really exists; and hence, perhaps, we might fairly pay a very high compliment to those who by their writings or actions have been so capable of imitating life, as to have their pictures in a manner confounded with, or mistaken for, the originals.

But, in reality, we are not so fond of paying compliments to these people, whom we use as children frequently do the instruments of their amusement; and have much more pleasure in hissing and buffeting them, than in admiring their excellence. There are many other reasons which have induced us to see this analogy between the world and the stage.

Some have considered the larger part of mankind in the light of actors, as personating characters no more their own, and to which in fact they have no better title, than the player hath to be in earnest thought the king or emperor whom he represents. Thus the hypocrite may be said to be a player; and indeed the Greeks called them both by one and the same name.

The brevity of life hath likewise given occasion to this comparison. So the immortal Shakspear—

> ———Life's a poor player,
> That struts and frets his hour upon the stage,
> And then is heard no more.

For which hackneyed quotation I will make the reader amends by a very noble one, which few, I believe, have read. It is taken from a poem called the Deity, published about nine years ago,

and long since buried in oblivion; a proof that
good books, no more than good men, do always
survive the bad.

> From Thee [1] all human actions take their springs,
> The rise of empires and the fall of kings!
> See the vast Theater of Time display'd!
> While o'er the scene succeeding heroes tread!
> With pomp the shining images succeed,
> What leaders triumph, and what monarchs bleed!
> Perform the parts thy providence assign'd,
> Their pride, their passions, to thy ends inclin'd:
> Awhile they glitter in the face of day,
> Then at thy nod the phantoms pass away;
> No traces left of all the busy scene,
> But that remembrance says—*The things have been!*

In all these, however, and in every other simil-
itude of life to the theater, the resemblance
hath been always taken from the stage only.
None, as I remember, have at all considered the
audience at this great drama.

But as Nature often exhibits some of her best
performances to a very full house, so will the
behavior of her spectators no less admit the
above-mentioned comparison than that of her
actors. In this vast theater of time are seated
the friend and the critic; here are claps and
shouts, hisses and groans; in short, everything
which was ever seen or heard at the Theater-
Royal.

Let us examine this in one example; for instance, in the behavior of the great audience on
that scene which Nature was pleased to exhibit

[1] The Deity.

in the twelfth chapter of the preceding book, where she introduced Black George running away with the £500 from his friend and benefactor.

Those who sat in the world's upper gallery treated that incident, I am well convinced, with their usual vociferation; and every term of scurrilous reproach was most probably vented on that occasion.

If we had descended to the next order of spectators, we should have found an equal degree of abhorrence, though less of noise and scurrility; yet here the good women gave Black George to the devil, and many of them expected every minute that the cloven-footed gentleman would fetch his own.

The pit, as usual, was no doubt divided; those who delight in heroic virtue and perfect character objected to the producing such instances of villainy, without punishing them very severely for the sake of example. Some of the author's friends cried, "Look'e, gentlemen, the man is a villain, but it is nature for all that." And all the young critics of the age, the clerks, apprentices, &c., called it low, and fell a groaning.

As for the boxes, they behaved with their accustomed politeness. Most of them were attending to something else. Some of those few who regarded the scene at all, declared he was a bad kind of man; while others refused to give their opinion, till they had heard that of the best judges.

Now we, who are admitted behind the scenes of this great theater of Nature (and no author

ought to write anything besides dictionaries and
spelling-books who hath not this privilege), can
censure the action, without conceiving any absolute detestation of the person, whom perhaps Nature may not have designed to act an ill part in
all her dramas; for in this instance life most exactly resembles the stage, since it is often the
same person who represents the villain and the
hero; and he who engages your admiration to-
day will probably attract your contempt to-morrow. As Garrick, whom I regard in tragedy
to be the greatest genius the world hath ever produced, sometimes condescends to play the fool;
so did Scipio the Great, and Lælius the Wise, according to Horace, many years ago; nay, Cicero
reports them to have been "incredibly childish."
These, it is true, played the fool, like my friend
Garrick, in jest only; but several eminent characters have, in numberless instances of their lives,
played the fool egregiously in earnest; so far as
to render it a matter of some doubt whether their
wisdom or folly was predominant; or whether
they were better entitled to the applause or censure, the admiration or contempt, the love or
hatred, of mankind.

Those persons, indeed, who have passed any
time behind the scenes of this great theater, and
are thoroughly acquainted not only with the several disguises which are there put on, but also
with the fantastic and capricious behavior of the
Passions, who are the managers and directors of
this theater (for as to Reason, the patentee, he is
known to be a very idle fellow and seldom to

exert himself), may most probably have learned to understand the famous *nil admirari* of Horace, or in the English phrase, to stare at nothing.

A single bad act no more constitutes a villain in life, than a single bad part on the stage. The passions, like the managers of a playhouse, often force men upon parts without consulting their judgment, and sometimes without any regard to their talents. Thus the man, as well as the player, may condemn what he himself acts; nay, it is common to see vice sit as awkwardly on some men, as the character of Iago would on the honest face of Mr. William Mills.

Upon the whole, then, the man of candor and of true understanding is never hasty to condemn. He can censure an imperfection, or even a vice, without rage against the guilty party. In a word, they are the same folly, the same childishness, the same ill-breeding, and the same ill-nature, which raise all the clamors and uproars both in life and on the stage. The worst of men generally have the words rogue and villain most in their mouths, as the lowest of all wretches are the aptest to cry out low in the pit.

CHAPTER II

Containing a conversation which Mr. Jones had with himself.

JONES received his effects from Mr. Allworthy's early in the morning, with the following answer to his letter:—

"SIR,

"I am commanded by my uncle to acquaint you, that as he did not proceed to those measures he had taken with you, without the greatest deliberation, and after the fullest evidence of your unworthiness, so will it be always out of your power to cause the least alteration in his resolution. He expresses great surprise at your presumption in saying you have resigned all pretensions to a young lady, to whom it is impossible you should ever have had any, her birth and fortune having made her so infinitely your superior. Lastly, I am commanded to tell you, that the only instance of your compliance with my uncle's inclinations which he requires, is, your immediately quitting this country. I cannot conclude this without offering you my advice, as a Christian, that you would seriously think of amending your life. That you may be assisted with grace so to do, will be always the prayer of

"Your humble servant,
"W. BLIFIL."

Many contending passions were raised in our hero's mind by this letter; but the tender pre-

vailed at last over the indignant and irascible,
and a flood of tears came seasonably to his as·
sistance, and possibly prevented his misfortunes
from either turning his head, or bursting his
heart.

He grew, however, soon ashamed of indulging
this remedy; and starting up, he cried, "Well,
then, I will give Mr. Allworthy the only instance
he requires of my obedience. I will go this moment—but whither?—why, let Fortune direct;
since there is no other who thinks it of any consequence what becomes of this wretched person,
it shall be a matter of equal indifference to myself. Shall I alone regard what no other—Ha!
have I not reason to think there is another?—one
whose value is above that of the whole world!—
I may, I must imagine my Sophia is not indiffer·
ent to what becomes of me. Shall I then leave
this only friend—and such a friend? Shall I
not stay with her?—Where—how can I stay with
her? Have I any hopes of ever seeing her,
though she was as desirous as myself, without
exposing her to the wrath of her father, and to
what purpose? Can I think of soliciting such a
creature to consent to her own ruin? Shall I indulge any passion of mine at such a price? Shall
I lurk about this country like a thief, with such
intentions?—No, I disdain, I detest the thought.
Farewell, Sophia; farewell, most lovely, most
beloved—" Here passion stopped his mouth,
and found a vent at his eyes.

And now having taken a resolution to leave the
country, he began to debate with himself whither

he should go. The world, as Milton phrases it, lay
all before him; and Jones, no more than Adam,
had any man to whom he might resort for comfort or assistance. All his acquaintance were the
acquaintance of Mr. Allworthy; and he had no
reason to expect any countenance from them, as
that gentleman had withdrawn his favor from
him. Men of great and good characters should
indeed be very cautious how they discard their
dependents; for the consequence to the unhappy
sufferer is being discarded by all others.

What course of life to pursue, or to what business to apply himself, was a second consideration: and here the prospect was all a melancholy
void. Every profession, and every trade, required length of time, and what was worse,
money; for matters are so constituted, that
"nothing out of nothing" is not a truer maxim
in physics than in politics; and every man who is
greatly destitute of money, is on that account entirely excluded from all means of acquiring it.

At last the Ocean, that hospitable friend to the
wretched, opened her capacious arms to receive
him; and he instantly resolved to accept her kind
invitation. To express myself less figuratively,
he determined to go to sea.

This thought indeed no sooner suggested itself,
than he eagerly embraced it; and having presently
hired horses, he set out for Bristol to put it in
execution.

But before we attend him on this expedition,
we shall resort awhile to Mr. Western's, and see
what further happened to the charming Sophia.

CHAPTER III

Containing several dialogues.

THE morning in which Mr. Jones departed, Mrs. Western summoned Sophia into her apartment; and having first acquainted her that she had obtained her liberty of her father, she proceeded to read her a long lecture on the subject of matrimony; which she treated not as a romantic scheme of happiness arising from love, as it hath been described by the poets; nor did she mention any of those purposes for which we are taught by divines to regard it as instituted by sacred authority; she considered it rather as a fund in which prudent women deposit their fortunes to the best advantage, in order to receive a larger interest for them than they could have elsewhere.

When Mrs. Western had finished, Sophia answered, "That she was very incapable of arguing with a lady of her aunt's superior knowledge and experience, especially on a subject which she had so very little considered, as this of matrimony."

"Argue with me, child!" replied the other; "I do not indeed expect it. I should have seen the world to very little purpose truly, if I am to argue with one of your years. I have taken this trouble, in order to instruct you. The ancient philosophers, such as Socrates, Alcibiades, and others,

did not use to argue with their scholars. You
are to consider me, child, as Socrates, not asking
your opinion, but only informing you of mine."
From which last words the reader may possibly
imagine, that this lady had read no more of the
philosophy of Socrates, than she had of that of
Alcibiades; and indeed we cannot resolve his
curiosity as to this point.

"Madam," cries Sophia, "I have never presumed to controvert any opinion of yours; and
this subject, as I said, I have never yet thought
of, and perhaps never may."

"Indeed, Sophy," replied the aunt, "this dis-
simulation with me is very foolish. The French
shall as soon persuade me that they take foreign
towns in defense only of their own country, as
you can impose on me to believe you have never
yet thought seriously of matrimony. How can
you, child, affect to deny that you have considered
of contracting an alliance, when you so well know
I am acquainted with the party with whom you
desire to contract it?—an alliance as unnatural,
and contrary to your interest, as a separate
league with the French would be to the interest
of the Dutch! But however, if you have not hitherto considered of this matter, I promise you it is
now high time, for my brother is resolved immediately to conclude the treaty with Mr. Blifil; and
indeed I am a sort of guarantee in the affair, and
have promised your concurrence."

"Indeed, madam," cries Sophia, "this is the
only instance in which I must disobey both yourself and my father. For this is a match which

requires very little consideration in me to refuse."

"If I was not as great a philosopher as Socrates himself," returned Mrs. Western, "you
would overcome my patience. What objection can
you have to the young gentleman?"

"A very solid objection, in my opinion," says
Sophia—"I hate him."

"Will you never learn a proper use of words?"
answered the aunt. "Indeed, child, you should
consult Bailey's Dictionary. It is impossible you
should hate a man from whom you have received
no injury. By hatred, therefore, you mean no
more than dislike, which is no sufficient objection
against your marrying of him. I have known
many couples, who have entirely disliked each
other, lead very comfortable genteel lives. Believe me, child, I know these things better than
you. You will allow me, I think, to have seen
the world, in which I have not an acquaintance
who would not rather be thought to dislike her
husband than to like him. The contrary is such
out-of-fashion romantic nonsense, that the very
imagination of it is shocking."

"Indeed, madam," replied Sophia, "I shall
never marry a man I dislike. If I promise my
father never to consent to any marriage contrary
to his inclinations, I think I may hope he will
never force me into that state contrary to my
own."

"Inclinations!" cries the aunt, with some
warmth. "Inclinations! I am astonished at your
assurance. A young woman of your age, and un-

married, to talk of inclinations! But whatever
your inclinations may be, my brother is resolved;
nay, since you talk of inclinations, I shall advise
him to hasten the treaty. Inclinations!"

Sophia then flung herself upon her knees, and
tears began to trickle from her shining eyes. She
entreated her aunt, "to have mercy upon her, and
not to resent so cruelly her unwillingness to make
herself miserable;" often urging, "that she alone
was concerned, and that her happiness only was
at stake."

As a bailiff, when well authorized by his writ,
having possessed himself of the person of some
unhappy debtor, views all his tears without concern; in vain the wretched captive attempts to
raise compassion; in vain the tender wife bereft
of her companion, the little prattling boy, or
frighted girl, are mentioned as inducements to
reluctance. The noble bumtrap, blind and deaf
to every circumstance of distress, greatly rises
above all the motives to humanity, and into the
hands of the jailer resolves to deliver his miserable prey.

Not less blind to the tears, or less deaf to every
entreaty of Sophia was the politic aunt, nor less
determined was she to deliver over the trembling
maid into the arms of the jailer Blifil. She answered with great impetuosity, "So far, madam,
from your being concerned alone, your concern is
the least, or surely the least important. It is
the honor of your family which is concerned in
this alliance; you are only the instrument. Do
you conceive, mistress, that in an intermarriage

between kingdoms, as when a daughter of France is married into Spain, the princess herself is alone considered in the match? No! it is a match between two kingdoms, rather than between two persons. The same happens in great families such as ours. The alliance between the families is the principal matter. You ought to have a greater regard for the honor of your family than for your own person; and if the example of a princess cannot inspire you with these noble thoughts, you cannot surely complain at being used no worse than all princesses are used.''

''I hope, madam,'' cries Sophia, with a little elevation of voice, ''I shall never do anything to dishonor my family; but as for Mr. Blifil, whatever may be the consequence, I am resolved against him, and no force shall prevail in his favor.''

Western, who had been within hearing during the greater part of the preceding dialogue, had now exhausted all his patience; he therefore entered the room in a violent passion, crying, ''D—n me then if shatunt ha'un, d—n me if shatunt, that's all—that's all; d—n me if shatunt.''

Mrs. Western had collected a sufficient quantity of wrath for the use of Sophia; but she now transferred it all to the squire. ''Brother,'' said she, ''it is astonishing that you will interfere in a matter which you had totally left to my negotiation. Regard to my family hath made me take upon myself to be the mediating power, in order to rectify those mistakes in policy which you have committed in your daughter's education. For, broth-

er, it is you—it is your preposterous conduct
which hath eradicated all the seeds that I had formerly sown in her tender mind. It is you yourself who have taught her disobedience."—
"Blood!" cries the squire, foaming at the mouth,
"you are enough to conquer the patience of the
devil! Have I ever taught my daughter disobedience?—Here she stands; speak honestly,
girl, did ever I bid you be disobedient to me?
Have not I done every thing to humor and to
gratify you, and to make you obedient to me?
And very obedient to me she was when a little
child, before you took her in hand and spoiled
her, by filling her head with a pack of court
notions. Why—why—why—did I not overhear
you telling her she must behave like a princess?
You have made a Whig of the girl; and how
should her father, or anybody else, expect any
obedience from her?"—"Brother," answered
Mrs. Western, with an air of great disdain, "I
cannot express the contempt I have for your
politics of all kinds; but I will appeal likewise to
the young lady herself, whether I have ever
taught her any principles of disobedience. On
the contrary, niece, have I not endeavored to inspire you with a true idea of the several relations
in which a human creature stands in society?
Have I not taken infinite pains to show you, that
the law of nature hath enjoined a duty on children
to their parents? Have I not told you what
Plato says on that subject?—a subject on which
you was so notoriously ignorant when you came
first under my care, that I verily believe you did

not know the relation between a daughter and a father.''—'''Tis a lie,'' answered Western. ''The girl is no such fool, as to live to eleven years old without knowing that she was her father's relation.''—''O! more than Gothic ignorance,'' answered the lady. ''And as for your manners, brother, I must tell you, they deserve a cane.''—''Why then you may gi' it me, if you think you are able,'' cries the squire; ''nay, I suppose your niece there will be ready enough to help you.''—''Brother,'' said Mrs. Western, ''though I despise you beyond expression, yet I shall endure your insolence no longer; so I desire my coach may be got ready immediately, for I am resolved to leave your house this very morning.''—''And a good riddance too,'' answered he; ''I can bear your insolence no longer, an you come to that. Blood! it is almost enough of itself to make my daughter undervalue my sense, when she hears you telling me every minute you despise me.''—''It is impossible, it is impossible,'' cries the aunt; ''no one can undervalue such a boor.''—''Boar,'' answered the squire, ''I am no boar; no, nor ass; no, nor rat neither, madam. Remember that— I am no rat. I am a true Englishman, and not of your Hanover breed, that have eat up the nation.''—''Thou art one of those wise men,'' cries she, ''whose nonsensical principles have undone the nation; by weakening the hands of our government at home, and by discouraging our friends and encouraging our enemies abroad.'' —''Ho! are you come back to your politics?''

cries the squire: "as for those I despise them as much as I do a f—t." Which last words he accompanied and graced with the very action, which, of all others, was the most proper to it. And whether it was this word or the contempt expressed for her politics, which most affected Mrs. Western, I will not determine; but she flew into the most violent rage, uttered phrases improper to be here related, and instantly burst out of the house. Nor did her brother or her niece think proper either to stop or to follow her; for the one was so much possessed by concern, and the other by anger, that they were rendered almost motionless.

The squire, however, sent after his sister the same holloa which attends the departure of a hare, when she is first started before the hounds! He was indeed a great master of this kind of vociferation, and had a holla proper for most occasions in life.

Women who, like Mrs. Western, know the world, and have applied themselves to philosophy and politics, would have immediately availed themselves of the present disposition of Mr. Western's mind, by throwing in a few artful compliments to his understanding at the expense of his absent adversary; but poor Sophia was all simplicity. By which word we do not intend to insinuate to the reader, that she was silly, which is generally understood as a synonymous term with simple; for she was indeed a most sensible girl, and her understanding was of the first rate; but she wanted all that useful art which females convert to so many good purposes in life, and which, as it rather arises from the heart than from the head, is often the property of the silliest of women.

CHAPTER IV

A picture of a country gentlewoman taken from the life.

MR. WESTERN having finished his holla, and taken a little breath, began to lament, in very pathetic terms, the unfortunate condition of men, who are, says he, "always whipped in by the humors of some d—n'd b— or other. I think I was hard run enough by your mother for one man; but after giving her a dodge, here's another b— follows me upon the foil; but curse my jacket if I will be run down in this manner by any o'um."

Sophia never had a single dispute with her father, till this unlucky affair of Blifil, on any account, except in defense of her mother, whom she had loved most tenderly, though she lost her in the eleventh year of her age. The squire, to whom that poor woman had been a faithful upper-servant all the time of their marriage, had returned that behavior by making what the world calls a good husband. He very seldom swore at her (perhaps not above once a week) and never beat her: she had not the least occasion for jealousy, and was perfect mistress of her time; for she was never interrupted by her husband, who was engaged all the morning in his field exercises, and all the evening with bottle companions. She scarce indeed ever saw him but at meals; where she had the pleasure of carving those dishes which she had before attended at the dressing. From these meals she retired about five minutes after the other servants, having only stayed to drink "the king over the water." Such were, it seems, Mr. Western's orders; for it was a maxim with him, that women should come in with the first dish, and go out after the first glass. Obedience to these orders was perhaps no difficult task; for the conversation (if it may be called so) was seldom such as could entertain a lady. It consisted chiefly of hallowing, singing, relations of sporting adventures, b—d—y, and abuse of women, and of the government.

These, however, were the only seasons when Mr. Western saw his wife; for when he repaired to her bed, he was generally so drunk that he could not see; and in the sporting season he always rose from her before it was light. Thus was she perfect mistress of her time, and had besides a coach and four usually at her command; though unhappily, indeed, the badness of the neighborhood, and of the roads, made this of little use; for none who had set much value on their necks would have passed through the one, or who had set any value on their hours, would have visited the other. Now to deal honestly with the reader, she did not make all the return expected to so much indulgence; for she had been married against her will by a fond father, the match having been rather advantageous on her side; for the squire's estate was upward of

£3000 a year, and her fortune no more than a
bare £8000. Hence perhaps she had contracted
a little gloominess of temper, for she was rather
a good servant than a good wife; nor had she
always the gratitude to return the extraordinary
degree of roaring mirth, with which the squire
received her, even with a good-humored smile.
She would, moreover, sometimes interfere with
matters which did not concern her, as the violent
drinking of her husband, which in the gentlest
terms she would take some of the few opportunities he gave her of remonstrating against.
And once in her life she very earnestly entreated
him to carry her for two months to London,
which he peremptorily denied; nay, was angry
with his wife for the request ever after, being
well assured that all the husbands in London
are cuckolds.

For this last, and many other good reasons,
Western at length heartily hated his wife; and as
he never concealed this hatred before her death,
so he never forgot it afterwards; but when anything in the least soured him, as a bad scenting
day, or a distemper among his hounds, or any
other such misfortune, he constantly vented his
spleen by invectives against the deceased, saying,
"If my wife was alive now, she would be glad of
this."

These invectives he was especially desirous of
throwing forth before Sophia; for as he loved
her more than he did any other, so he was really
jealous that she had loved her mother better
than him. And this jealousy Sophia seldom

failed of heightening on these occasions; for he was not contented with violating her ears with the abuse of her mother, but endeavored to force an explicit approbation of all this abuse; with which desire he never could prevail upon her by any promise or threats to comply.

Hence some of my readers will, perhaps, wonder that the squire had not hated Sophia as much as he had hated her mother; but I must inform them, that hatred is not the effect of love, even through the medium of jealousy. It is, indeed, very possible for jealous persons to kill the objects of their jealousy, but not to hate them. Which sentiment being a pretty hard morsel, and bearing something of the air of a paradox, we shall leave the reader to chew the cud upon it to the end of the chapter.

CHAPTER V

The generous behavior of Sophia towards her aunt.

SOPHIA kept silence during the foregoing speech of her father, nor did she once answer otherwise than with a sigh; but as he understood none of the language, or, as he called it, lingo of the eyes, so he was not satisfied without some further approbation of his sentiments, which he now demanded of his daughter; telling her, in the usual way, "he expected she was ready to take the part of everybody against him, as she had always done that of the b— her mother." Sophia remaining still silent, he cried out, "What, art dumb? why dost unt speak? Was not thy mother a d—d b— to me? answer me that. What, I suppose you despise your father too, and don't think him good enough to speak to?"

"For Heaven's sake, sir," answered Sophia, "do not give so cruel a turn to my silence. I am sure I would sooner die than be guilty of any disrespect towards you; but how can I venture to speak, when every word must either offend my dear papa, or convict me of the blackest ingratitude as well as impiety to the memory of the best of mothers; for such, I am certain, my mamma was always to me?"

"And your aunt, I suppose, is the best of

sisters too!" replied the squire. "Will you be so kind as to allow that she is a b—? I may fairly insist upon that, I think?"

"Indeed, sir," says Sophia, "I have great obligations to my aunt. She hath been a second mother to me."

"And a second wife to me too," returned Western; "so you will take her part too! You won't confess that she hath acted the part of the vilest sister in the world?"

"Upon my word, sir," cries Sophia, "I must belie my heart wickedly if I did. I know my aunt and you differ very much in your ways of thinking; but I have heard her a thousand times express the greatest affection for you; and I am convinced, so far from her being the worst sister in the world, there are very few who love a brother better."

"The English of all which is," answered the squire, "that I am in the wrong. Ay, certainly. Ay, to be sure the woman is in the right, and the man in the wrong always."

"Pardon me, sir," cries Sophia. "I do not say so."

"What don't you say?" answered the father: "you have the impudence to say she's in the right: doth it not follow then of course that I am in the wrong? And perhaps I am in the wrong to suffer such a Presbyterian Hanoverian b— to come into my house. She may 'dite me of a plot for anything I know, and give my estate to the government."

"So far, sir, from injuring you or your estate,"

says Sophia, "if my aunt had died yesterday, I am convinced she would have left you her whole fortune."

Whether Sophia intended it or no, I shall not presume to assert; but certain it is, these last words penetrated very deep into the ears of her father, and produced a much more sensible effect than all she had said before. He received the sound with much the same action as a man receives a bullet in his head. He started, staggered, and turned pale. After which he remained silent above a minute, and then began in the following hesitating manner: "Yesterday! she would have left me her estate yesterday! would she? Why yesterday, of all the days in the year? I suppose if she dies to-morrow, she will leave it to somebody else, and perhaps out of the vamily."—"My aunt, sir," cries Sophia, "hath very violent passions, and I can't answer what she may do under their influence."

"You can't!" returned the father: "and pray who hath been the occasion of putting her into those violent passions? Nay, who hath actually put her into them? Was not you and she hard at it before I came into the room? Besides, was not all our quarrel about you? I have not quarreled with sister this many years but upon your account; and now you would throw the whole blame upon me, as thof I should be the occasion of her leaving the estate out o' the vamily. I could have expected no better indeed; this is like the return you make to all the rest of my fondness."

"I beseech you then," cries Sophia, "upon my knees I beseech you, if I have been the unhappy occasion of this difference, that you will endeavor to make it up with my aunt, and not suffer her to leave your house in this violent rage of anger: she is a very good-natured woman, and a few civil words will satisfy her. Let me entreat you, sir."

"So I must go and ask pardon for your fault, must I?" answered Western. "You have lost the hare and I must draw every way to find her again? Indeed, if I was certain"—Here he stopped, and Sophia throwing in more entreaties, at length prevailed upon him; so that after venting two or three bitter sarcastical expressions against his daughter, he departed as fast as he could to recover his sister, before her equipage could be gotten ready.

Sophia then returned to her chamber of mourning, where she indulged herself (if the phrase may be allowed me) in all the luxury of tender grief. She read over more than once the letter which she had received from Jones; her muff too was used on this occasion; and she bathed both these, as well as herself, with her tears. In this situation the friendly Mrs. Honour exerted her utmost abilities to comfort her afflicted mistress. She ran over the names of many young gentlemen: and having greatly commended their parts and persons, assured Sophia that she might take her choice of any. These methods must have certainly been used with some success in disorders of the like kind, or so skillful a practitioner as Mrs. Honour would never have ventured to apply them; nay, I have heard that the college of chambermaids hold them to be as sovereign remedies as any in the female dispensary; but whether it was that Sophia's disease differed inwardly from those cases with which it agreed in external symptoms, I will not assert; but, in fact, the good waiting-woman did more harm than good, and at last so incensed her mistress (which was no easy matter) that with an angry voice she dismissed her from her presence.

CHAPTER VI

Containing great variety of matter.

THE squire overtook his sister just as she was stepping into the coach, and partly by force, and partly by solicitations, prevailed upon her to order her horses back into their quarters. He succeeded in this attempt without much difficulty; for the lady was, as we have already hinted, of a most placable disposition, and greatly loved her brother, though she despised his parts, or rather his little knowledge of the world.

Poor Sophia, who had first set on foot this reconciliation, was now made the sacrifice to it. They both concurred in their censures on her conduct; jointly declared war against her, and directly proceeded to counsel, how to carry it on in the most vigorous manner. For this purpose, Mrs. Western proposed not only an immediate conclusion of the treaty with Allworthy, but as immediately to carry it into execution; saying, "That there was no other way to succeed with her niece, but by violent methods, which she was convinced Sophia had not sufficient resolution to resist. By violent," says she, "I mean rather, hasty measures; for as to confinement or absolute force, no such things must or can be attempted.

Our plan must be concerted for a surprise, and not for a storm.''

These matters were resolved on, when **Mr.** Blifil came to pay a visit to his mistress. The squire no sooner heard of his arrival, than he stepped aside, by his sister's advice, to give his daughter orders for the proper reception of her lover: which he did with the most bitter execrations and denunciations of judgment on her refusal.

The impetuosity of the squire bore down all before him; and Sophia, as her aunt very wisely foresaw, was not able to resist him. She agreed, therefore, to see Blifil, though she had scarce spirits or strength sufficient to utter her assent. Indeed, to give a peremptory denial to a father whom she so tenderly loved, was no easy task. Had this circumstance been out of the case, much less resolution than what she was really mistress of, would, perhaps, have served her; but it is no unusual thing to ascribe those actions entirely to fear, which are in a great measure produced by love.

In pursuance, therefore, of her father's peremptory command, Sophia now admitted Mr. Blifil's visit. Scenes like this, when painted at large, afford, as we have observed, very little entertainment to the reader. Here, therefore, we shall strictly adhere to a rule of Horace; by which writers are directed to pass over all those matters which they despair of placing in a shining light;—a rule, we conceive, of excellent use as well to the historian as to the poet; and which,

if followed, must at least have this good effect,
that many a great evil (for so all great books
are called) would thus be reduced to a small one.

It is possible the great art used by Blifil at this
interview would have prevailed on Sophia to
have made another man in his circumstances her
confident, and to have revealed the whole secret
of her heart to him; but she had contracted so ill
an opinion of this young gentleman, that she was
resolved to place no confidence in him; for simplicity, when set on its guard, is often a match
for cunning. Her behavior to him, therefore,
was entirely forced, and indeed such as is generally prescribed to virgins upon the second
formal visit from one who is appointed for their
husband.

But though Blifil declared himself to the squire
perfectly satisfied with his reception; yet that
gentleman, who, in company with his sister, had
overheard all, was not so well pleased. He resolved, in pursuance of the advice of the sage
lady, to push matters as forward as possible; and
addressing himself to his intended son-in-law in
the hunting phrase, he cried, after a loud holla,
"Follow her, boy, follow her; run in, run in;
that's it honeys. Dead, dead, dead. Never be
bashful, nor stand shall I, shall I? Allworthy
and I can finish all matters between us this afternoon, and let us ha' the wedding to-morrow."

Blifil having conveyed the utmost satisfaction
into his countenance, answered, "As there is
nothing, sir, in this world which I so eagerly
desire as an alliance with your family, except

my union with the most amiable and deserving
Sophia, you may easily imagine how impatient
I must be to see myself in possession of my two
highest wishes. If I have not therefore impor-
tuned you on this head, you will impute it only to
my fear of offending the lady, by endeavoring
to hurry on so blessed an event faster than a
strict compliance with all the rules of decency
and decorum will permit. But if, by your
interest, sir, she might be induced to dispense
with any formalities—''

"Formalities! with a pox!'' answered the
squire. "Pooh, all stuff and nonsense! I tell
thee, she shall ha' thee to-morrow: you will know
the world better hereafter, when you come to my
age. Women never gi' their consent, man, if they
can help it, 'tis not the fashion. If I had stayed
for her mother's consent, I might have been a
batchelor to this day.—To her, to her, co to her,
that's it, you jolly dog. I tell thee shat ha' her
to-morrow morning.''

Blifil suffered himself to be overpowered by
the forcible rhetoric of the squire; and it being
agreed that Western should close with Allworthy
that very afternoon, the lover departed home,
having first earnestly begged that no violence
might be offered to the lady by this haste, in the
same manner as a popish inquisitor begs the
lay power to do no violence to the heretic delivered over to it, and against whom the church
hath passed sentence.

And, to say the truth, Blifil had passed sentence against Sophia; for, however pleased he

II—8

had declared himself to Western with his reception, he was by no means satisfied, unless it was that he was convinced of the hatred and scorn of his mistress: and this had produced no less reciprocal hatred and scorn in him. It may, perhaps, be asked, Why then did he not put an immediate end to all further courtship? I answer, for that very reason, as well as for several others equally good, which we shall now proceed to open to the reader.

Though Mr. Blifil was not of the complexion of Jones, nor ready to eat every woman he saw; yet he was far from being destitute of that appetite which is said to be the common property of all animals. With this, he had likewise that distinguishing taste, which serves to direct men in their choice of the object or food of their several appetites; and this taught him to consider Sophia as a most delicious morsel, indeed to regard her with the same desires which an ortolan inspires into the soul of an epicure. Now the agonies which affected the mind of Sophia, rather augmented than impaired her beauty; for her tears added brightness to her eyes, and her breasts rose higher with her sighs. Indeed, no one hath seen beauty in its highest luster who hath never seen it in distress. Blifil therefore looked on this human ortolan with greater desire than when he viewed her last; nor was his desire at all lessened by the aversion which he discovered in her to himself. On the contrary, this served rather to heighten the pleasure he proposed in rifling her charms, as it added triumph to lust; nay, he had some further views, from obtaining the absolute possession of her person, which we detest too much even to mention; and revenge itself was not without its share in the gratifications which he promised himself. The rivaling poor Jones, and supplanting him in her affections, added another spur to his pursuit, and promised another additional rapture to his enjoyment.

Besides all these views, which to some scrupulous persons may seem to savor too much of malevolence, he had one prospect, which few readers will regard with any great abhorrence. And this was the estate of Mr. Western; which was all to be settled on his daughter and her issue; for so extravagant was the affection of that fond parent, that, provided his child would but consent to be miserable with the husband he chose, he cared not at what price he purchased him.

For these reasons Mr. Blifil was so desirous of the match that he intended to deceive Sophia, by pretending love to her; and to deceive her father and his own uncle, by pretending he was beloved by her. In doing this he availed himself of the piety of Thwackum, who held, that if the end proposed was religious (as surely matrimony is), it mattered not how wicked were the means. As to other occasions, he used to apply the philosophy of Square, which taught, that the end was immaterial, so that the means were fair and consistent with moral rectitude. To say truth, there were few occurrences in life on which he could not draw advantage from the precepts of one or other of those great masters.

Little deceit was indeed necessary to be practiced on Mr. Western; who thought the inclinations of his daughter of as little consequence as Blifil himself conceived them to be; but as the sentiments of Mr. Allworthy were of a very different kind, so it was absolutely necessary to impose on him. In this, however, Blifil was so well assisted by Western, that he succeeded without difficulty; for as Mr. Allworthy had been assured by her father that Sophia had a proper affection for Blifil, and that all which he had suspected concerning Jones was entirely false, Blifil had nothing more to do than to confirm these assertions; which he did with such equivocations, that he preserved a salvo for his conscience; and had the satisfaction of conveying a lie to his uncle, without the guilt of telling one. When he was examined touching the inclinations of Sophia by Allworthy, who said, "He would on no account be accessory to forcing a young lady into a marriage contrary to her own will;" he answered, "That the real sentiments of young ladies were very difficult to be understood; that her behavior to him was full as forward as he wished it, and that if he could believe her father, she had all the affection for him which any lover could desire. As for Jones," said he, "whom I am loth to call villain, though his behavior to you, sir, sufficiently justifies the appellation, his own vanity, or perhaps some wicked views, might make him boast of a falsehood: for if there had been any reality in Miss Western's love to him, the greatness of her fortune would never have suffered him to desert her, as you are well informed he hath. Lastly, sir, I promise you I would not myself, for any consideration, no, not for the whole world, consent to marry this young lady, if I was not persuaded she had all the passion for me which I desire she should have.''

This excellent method of conveying a falsehood with the heart only, without making the tongue guilty of an untruth, by the means of equivocation and imposture, hath quieted the conscience of many a notable deceiver; and yet, when we consider that it is Omniscience on which these endeavor to impose, it may possibly seem capable of affording only a very superficial comfort; and that this artful and refined distinction between communicating a lie, and telling one, is hardly worth the pains it costs them.

Allworthy was pretty well satisfied with what Mr. Western and Mr. Blifil told him: and the treaty was now, at the end of two days, concluded. Nothing then remained previous to the office of the priest, but the office of the lawyers, which threatened to take up so much time, that Western offered to bind himself by all manner of covenants, rather than defer the happiness of the young couple. Indeed, he was so very earnest and pressing, that an indifferent person might have concluded he was more a principle in this match than he really was; but this eagerness was natural to him on all ocasions: and he conducted every scheme he undertook in such a manner, as if the success of that alone was sufficient to constitute the whole happiness of his life.

The joint importunities of both father and son-in-law would probably have prevailed on Mr. Allworthy, who brooked but ill any delay of giving happiness to others, had not Sophia herself prevented it, and taken measures to put a final end to the whole treaty, and to rob both church and law of those taxes which these wise bodies have thought proper to receive from the propagation of the human species in a lawful manner. Of which in the next chapter.

CHAPTER VII

A strange resolution of Sophia, and a more strange stratagem
of Mrs. Honour.

THOUGH Mrs. Honour was principally attached to her own interest, she was not without some little attachment to Sophia. To say truth, it was very difficult for any one to know that young lady without loving her. She no sooner therefore heard a piece of news, which she imagined to be of great importance to her mistress, than, quite forgetting the anger which she had conceived two days before, at her unpleasant dismission from Sophia's presence, she ran hastily to inform her of the news.

The beginning of her discourse was as abrupt as her entrance into the room. "O dear ma'am!" says she, "what doth your la'ship think? To be sure I am frightened out of my wits; and yet I thought it my duty to tell your la'ship, though perhaps it may make you angry, for we servants don't always know what will make our ladies angry; for, to be sure, everything is always laid to the charge of a servant. When our ladies are out of humor, to be sure we must be scolded; and to be sure I should not wonder if your la'ship should be out of humor; nay, it must surprise you certainly, ay, and shock you too."—"Good Honour, let me know it without any longer preface," says Sophia; "there are few things, I promise you, which will surprise, and fewer which will shock me."—"Dear ma'am," answered Honour, "to be sure, I overheard my master talking to parson Supple about getting a license this very afternoon; and to be sure I heard him say, your la'ship should be married to-morrow morning." Sophia turned pale at these words, and repeated eagerly, "To-morrow morning!" —"Yes, ma'am," replied the trusty waiting-woman, "I will take my oath I heard my master say so."—"Honour," says Sophia, "you have both surprised and shocked me to such a degree that I have scarce any breath or spirits left. What is to be done in my dreadful situation?" —"I wish I was able to advise your la'ship," says she. "Do advise me," cries Sophia; "pray, dear Honour, advise me. Think what you would attempt if it was your own case."—"Indeed, ma'am," cries Honour, "I wish your la'ship and I could change situations; that is, I mean without hurting your la'ship; for to be sure I don't wish you so bad as to be a servant; but because that if so be it was my case, I should find no manner of difficulty in it; for, in my poor opinion, young Squire Blifil is a charming, sweet, handsome man."—"Don't mention such stuff," cries Sophia. "Such stuff!" repeated Honour; "why, there. Well, to be sure, what's one man's meat is another man's poison, and the same is altogether as true of women."—"Honour," says Sophia, "rather than submit to be the wife of that contemptible wretch, I would plunge a dagger into my heart."

—"O lud! ma'am!" answered the other, "I am sure you frighten me out of my wits now. Let me beseech your la'ship not to suffer such wicked thoughts to come into your head. O lud! to be sure I tremble every inch of me. Dear ma'am, consider, that to be denied Christian burial, and to have your corpse buried in the highway, and a stake drove through you, as farmer Halfpenny was served at Ox Cross; and, to be sure, his ghost hath walked there ever since, for several people have seen him. To be sure it can be nothing but the devil which can put such wicked thoughts into the head of anybody; for certainly it is less wicked to hurt all the world than one's own dear self; and so I have heard said by more parsons than one. If your la'ship hath such a violent aversion, and hates the young gentleman so very bad, that you can't bear to think of going into bed to him; for to be sure there may be such antipathies in nature, and one had lieverer touch a toad than the flesh of some people"—

Sophia had been too much wrapped in contemplation to pay any great attention to the foregoing excellent discourse of her maid; interrupting her therefore, without making any answer to it, she said, "Honour, I am come to a resolution. I am determined to leave my father's house this very night; and if you have the friendship for me which you have often professed, you will keep me company."—"That I will, ma'am, to the world's end," answered Honour; "but I beg your la'ship to consider the consequence before you undertake any rash action. Where can your

la'ship possibly go?"—"There is," replied
Sophia, "a lady of quality in London, a relation
of mine, who spent several months with my aunt
in the country; during all which time she treated
me with great kindness, and expressed so much
pleasure in my company, that she earnestly desired my aunt to suffer me to go with her to
London. As she is a woman of very great note,
I shall easily find her out, and I make no doubt
of being very well and kindly received by her."
—"I would not have your la'ship too confident
of that," cries Honour; "for the first lady I lived
with used to invite people very earnestly to her
house; but if she heard afterwards they were
coming, she used to get out of the way. Besides,
though this lady would be very glad to see your
la'ship, as to be sure anybody would be glad to
see your la'ship, yet when she hears your la'ship
is run away from my master—" "You are mistaken, Honour," says Sophia: "she looks upon
the authority of a father in a much lower light
than I do; for she pressed me violently to go
to London with her, and when I refused to go
without my father's consent, she laughed me to
scorn, called me silly country girl, and said, I
should make a pure loving wife, since I could be
so dutiful a daughter. So I have no doubt but
she will both receive me and protect me too, till
my father, finding me out of his power, can be
brought to some reason."

"Well, but ma'am," answered Honour, "how
doth your la'ship think of making your escape?
Where will you get any horses or conveyance?

For as for your own horse, as all the servants know a little how matters stand between my master and your la'ship, Robin will be hanged before he will suffer it to go out of the stable without my master's express orders." "I intend to escape," said Sophia, "by walking out of the doors when they are open. I thank Heaven my legs are very able to carry me. They have supported me many a long evening after a fiddle, with no very agreeable partner; and surely they will assist me in running from so detestable a partner for life."—"Oh Heaven, ma'am! doth your la'ship know what you are saying?" cries Honour; "would you think of walking about the country by night and alone?"—"Not alone," answered the lady; "you have promised to bear me company."—"Yes, to be sure," cries Honour, "I will follow your la'ship through the world; but your la'ship had almost as good be alone: for I should not be able to defend you, if any robbers, or other villains, should meet with you. Nay, I should be in as horrible a fright as your la'ship; for to be certain, they would ravish us both. Besides, ma'am, consider how cold the nights are now; we shall be frozen to death."— "A good brisk pace," answered Sophia, "will preserve us from the cold; and if you cannot defend me from a villain, Honour, I will defend you; for I will take a pistol with me. There are two always charged in the hall."—"Dear ma'am, you frighten me more and more," cries Honour: "sure your la'ship would not venture to fire it off! I had rather run any chance than your

la'ship should do that."—"Why so?" says
Sophia, smiling; "would not you, Honour, fire
a pistol at any one who should attack your
virtue?"—"To be sure ma'am," cries Honour,
"one's virtue is a dear thing, especially to us
poor servants; for it is our livelihood, as a body
may say: yet I mortally hate fire-arms; for so
many accidents happen by them."—"Well, well,"
says Sophia, "I believe I may insure your virtue
at a very cheap rate, without carrying any arms
with us; for I intend to take horses at the very
first town we come to, and we shall hardly be
attacked in our way thither. Look'ee, Honour,
I am resolved to go; and if you will attend me,
I promise you I will reward you to the very
utmost of my power."

This last argument had a stronger effect on
Honour than all the preceding. And since she
saw her mistress so determined, she desisted
from any further dissuasions. They then entered
into a debate on ways and means of executing
their project. Here a very stubborn difficulty
occurred, and this was the removal of their effects,
which was much more easily got over by the
mistress than by the maid; for when a lady hath
once taken a resolution to run to a lover, or to
run from him, all obstacles are considered as
trifles. But Honour was inspired by no such
motive; she had no raptures to expect, nor any
terrors to shun; and besides the real value of her
clothes, in which consisted a great part of her fortune, she had a capricious fondness for several
gowns and other things; either because they be-

came her, or because they were given her by
such a particular person; because she had bought
them lately, or because she had had them long; or
for some other reasons equally good; so that she
could not endure the thoughts of leaving the poor
things behind her exposed to the mercy of Western, who, she doubted not, would in his rage
make them suffer martyrdom.

The ingenious Mrs. Honour having applied all
her oratory to dissuade her mistress from her
purpose, when she found her positively determined, at last started the following expedient to
remove her clothes, viz., to get herself turned out
of doors that very evening. Sophia highly approved this method, but doubted how it might be
brought about. "O, ma'am," cries Honour,
"your la'ship may trust that to me; we servants
very well know how to obtain this favor of our
masters and mistresses; though sometimes, indeed, where they owe us more wages than they can
readily pay, they will put up with all our affronts,
and will hardly take any warning we can give
them; but the squire is none of those; and since
your la'ship is resolved upon setting out to-night,
I warrant I get discharged this afternoon." It
was then resolved that she should pack up some
linen and a night-gown for Sophia, with her own
things; and as for all her other clothes, the young
lady abandoned them with no more remorse than
the sailor feels when he throws over the goods
of others, in order to save his own life.

CHAPTER VIII

Containing scenes of altercation, of no very uncommon kind.

M RS. HONOUR had scarce sooner parted
from her young lady, than something
(for I would not, like the old woman in
Quevedo, injure the devil by any false accusation, and possibly he might have no hand in it)
—but something, I say, suggested itself to her,
that by sacrificing Sophia and all her secrets to
Mr. Western, she might probably make her fortune. Many considerations urged this discovery.
The fair prospect of a handsome reward for so
great and acceptable a service to the squire,
tempted her avarice; and again, the danger of the
enterprise she had undertaken; the uncertainty
of its success; night, cold, robbers, ravishers, all
alarmed her fears. So forcibly did all these
operate upon her, that she was almost determined
to go directly to the squire, and to lay open the
whole affair. She was, however, too upright a
judge to decree on one side, before she had heard
the other. And here, first, a journey to London
appeared very strongly in support of Sophia.
She eagerly longed to see a place in which she
fancied charms short only of those which a rap-
tured saint imagines in heaven. In the next
place, as she knew Sophia to have much more
generosity than her master, so her fidelity prom-

126

ised her a greater reward than she could gain by
treachery. She then cross-examined all the articles which had raised her fears on the other side,
and found, on fairly sifting the matter, that there
was very little in them. And now both scales being reduced to a pretty even balance, her love to
her mistress being thrown into the scale of her
integrity, made that rather preponderate, when a
circumstance struck upon her imagination which
might have had a dangerous effect, had its whole
weight been fairly put into the other scale. This
was the length of time which must intervene before Sophia would be able to fulfill her promises;
for though she was entitled to her mother's fortune at the death of her father, and to the sum of
£3,000 left her by an uncle when she came of age;
yet these were distant days, and many accidents
might prevent the intended generosity of the
young lady; whereas the rewards she might expect from Mr. Western were immediate. But
while she was pursuing this thought the good
genius of Sophia, or that which presided over
the integrity of Mrs. Honour, or perhaps mere
chance, sent an accident in her way, which at once
preserved her fidelity, and even facilitated the intended business.

Mrs. Western's maid claimed great superiority
over Mrs. Honour on several accounts. First, her
birth was higher; for her great-grandmother by
the mother's side was a cousin, not far removed,
to an Irish peer. Secondly, her wages were
greater. And lastly, she had been at London, and
had of consequence seen more of the world. She

had always behaved, therefore, to Mrs. Honour
with that reserve, and had always exacted of her
those marks of distinction, which every order of
females preserves and requires in conversation
with those of an inferior order. Now as Honour
did not at all times agree with this doctrine, but
would frequently break in upon the respect which
the other demanded, Mrs. Western's maid was not
at all pleased with her company; indeed, she
earnestly longed to return home to the house of
her mistress, where she domineered at will over
all the other servants. She had been greatly,
therefore, disappointed in the morning, when Mrs.
Western had changed her mind on the very point
of departure; and had been in what is vulgarly
called a glouting humor ever since.

In this humor, which was none of the sweetest,
she came into the room where Honour was de-
bating with herself in the manner we have above
related. Honour no sooner saw her, than she addressed her in the following obliging phrase:
"Soh, madam, I find we are to have the pleasure
of your company longer, which I was afraid the
quarrel between my master and your lady would
have robbed us of."—"I don't know, madam,''
answered the other, "what you mean by we and
us. I assure you I do not look on any of the servants in this house to be proper company for me.
I am company, I hope, for their betters every day
in the week. I do not speak on your account, Mrs.
Honour; for you are a civilized young woman;
and when you have seen a little more of the world,
I should not be ashamed to walk with you in St.

James's Park.''—''Hoity toity!'' cries Honour,
''madam is in her airs, I protest. Mrs. Honour,
forsooth! sure, madam, you might call me by my
sur-name; for though my lady calls me Honour, I
have a sur-name as well as other folks. Ashamed
to walk with me, quotha! marry, as good as yourself, I hope.''—''Since you make such a return to
my civility,'' said the other, ''I must acquaint you,
Mrs. Honour, that you are not so good as me. In
the country, indeed, one is obliged to take up with
all kind of trumpery; but in town I visit none but
the women of women of quality. Indeed, Mrs.
Honour, there is some difference, I hope, between
you and me.''—''I hope so too,'' answered Honour: ''there is some difference in our ages, and—
I think in our persons.'' Upon speaking which
last words, she strutted by Mrs. Western's maid
with the most provoking air of contempt; turning
up her nose, tossing her head, and violently brush-
ing the hoop of her competitor with her own. The
other lady put on one of her most malicious
sneers, and said, ''Creature! you are below my
anger; and it is beneath me to give ill words to
such an audacious, saucy trollop; but, hussy, I
must tell you, your breeding shows the meanness
of your birth as well as of your education; and
both very properly qualify you to be the mean
serving-woman of a country girl.''—''Don't
abuse my lady,'' cries Honour: ''I won't take
that of you; she's as much better than yours as
she is younger, and ten thousand times more handsome.''

Here ill luck, or rather good luck, sent Mrs.

II—9

Western to see her maid in tears, which began to flow plentifully at her approach; and of which being asked the reason by her mistress, she presently acquainted her that her tears were occasioned by the rude treatment of that creature there— meaning Honour. "And, madam," continued she, "I could have despised all she said to me; but she hath had the audacity to affront your ladyship, and to call you ugly—Yes, madam, she called you ugly old cat to my face. I could not bear to hear your ladyship called ugly."—"Why do you repeat her impudence so often?" said Mrs. Western. And then turning to Mrs. Honour, she asked her "How she had the assurance to mention her name with disrespect?"—"Disrespect, madam!" answered Honour; "I never mentioned your name at all: I said somebody was not as handsome as my mistress, and to be sure you know that as well as I."—"Hussy," replied the lady, "I will make such a saucy trollop as yourself know that I am not a proper subject of your discourse. And if my brother doth not discharge you this moment, I will never sleep in his house again. I will find him out, and have you discharged this moment."—"Discharged!" cries Honour; "and suppose I am: there are more places in the world than one. Thank heaven, good servants need not want places; and if you turn away all who do not think you handsome, you will want servants very soon; let me tell you that."

Mrs. Western spoke, or rather thundered, in answer; but as she was hardly articulate, we can not be very certain of the identical words; we shall therefore omit inserting a speech which at best would not greatly redound to her honor. She then departed in search of her brother, with a countenance so full of rage, that she resembled one of the furies rather than a human creature.

The two chambermaids being again left alone, began a second bout at altercation, which soon produced a combat of a more active kind. In this the victory belonged to the lady of inferior rank, but not without some loss of blood, of hair, and of lawn and muslin.

CHAPTER IX

The wise demeanor of Mr. Western in the character of a magistrate. A hint to justices of peace, concerning the necessary qualifications of a clerk; with extraordinary instances of paternal madness and filial affection.

LOGICIANS sometimes prove too much by an argument, and politicians often overreach themselves in a scheme. Thus had it like to have happened to Mrs. Honour, who, instead of recovering the rest of her clothes, had like to have stopped even those she had on her back from escaping; for the squire no sooner heard of her having abused his sister, than he swore twenty oaths he would send her to Bridewell.

Mrs. Western was a very good-natured woman, and ordinarily of a forgiving temper. She had lately remitted the trespass of a stage-coachman, who had overturned her post-chaise into a ditch; nay, she had even broken the law, in refusing to prosecute a highwayman who had robbed her, not only of a sum of money, but of her ear-rings; at the same time d—ning her, and saying, "Such handsome b—s as you don't want jewels to set them off, and be d—n'd to you." But now, so uncertain are our tempers, and so much do we at different times differ from ourselves, she would hear of no mitigation; nor could all the affected penitence of Honour, nor all the entreaties of Sophia for her own servant, prevail with her to desist from earnestly desiring her brother to execute justiceship (for it was indeed a syllable more than justice) on the wench.

But luckily the clerk had a qualification, which no clerk to a justice of peace ought ever to be without, namely, some understanding in the law of this realm. He therefore whispered in the ear of the justice that he would exceed his authority by committing the girl to Bridewell, as there had been no attempt to break the peace; "for I am afraid, sir," says he, "you cannot legally commit any one to Bridewell only for ill-breeding."

In matters of high importance, particularly in cases relating to the game, the justice was not always attentive to these admonitions of his clerk; for, indeed, in executing the laws under that head, many justices of peace suppose they have a large discretionary power, by virtue of which, under the notion of searching for and taking away engines for the destruction of the game, they often commit trespasses, and sometimes felony, at their pleasure.

But this offense was not of quite so high a nature, nor so dangerous to the society. Here, therefore, the justice behaved with some attention to the advice of his clerk; for, in fact, he had already had two informations exhibited against him in the King's Bench, and had no curiosity to try a third.

The squire, therefore, putting on a most wise and significant countenance, after a preface of several hums and hahs, told his sister, that upon more mature deliberation, he was of opinion, that "as there was no breaking up of the peace, such as the law," says he, "calls breaking open a door, or breaking a hedge, or breaking a head, or any such sort of breaking, the matter did not amount to a felonious kind of a thing, nor trespasses, nor damages, and, therefore, there was no punishment in the law for it."

Mrs. Western said, "she knew the law much better; that she had known servants very severely punished for affronting their masters;" and then named a certain justice of the peace in London, "who," she said, "would commit a servant to Bridewell at any time when a master or mistress desired it."

"Like enough," cries the squire; "it may be so in London; but the law is different in the country." Here followed a very learned dispute between the brother and sister concerning the law, which we would insert, if we imagined many of our readers could understand it. This was, however, at length referred by both parties to the clerk, who decided it in favor of the magistrate; and Mrs. Western was, in the end, obliged to content herself with the satisfaction of having Honour turned away; to which Sophia herself very readily and cheerfully consented.

Thus Fortune, after having diverted herself, according to custom, with two or three frolics, at last disposed all matters to the advantage of our heroine; who indeed succeeded admirably well in her deceit, considering it was the first she had ever practiced.   And, to say the truth, I have often concluded, that the honest part of mankind would be much too hard for the knavish, if they could bring themselves to incur the guilt, or thought it worth their while to take the trouble.

Honour acted her part to the utmost perfection.   She no sooner saw herself secure from all danger of Bridewell, a word which had raised most horrible ideas in her mind, than she resumed those airs which her terrors before had a little abated; and laid down her place, with as much affectation of content, and indeed of contempt, as was ever practiced at the resignation of places of much greater importance. If the reader pleases, therefore, we choose rather to say she resigned—which hath, indeed, been always held a synonymous expression with being turned out, or turned away.

Mr. Western ordered her to be very expeditious in packing; for his sister declared she would not sleep another night under the same roof with so impudent a slut. To work therefore she went, and that so earnestly, that everything was ready early in the evening; when, having received her wages, away packed bag and baggage, to the great satisfaction of every one, but of none more than of Sophia; who, having appointed her maid to meet her at a certain place not far from the house, exactly at the dreadful and ghostly hour of twelve, began to prepare for her own departure.

But first she was obliged to give two painful audiences, the one to her aunt, and the other to

her father. In these Mrs. Western herself began to talk to her in a more peremptory style
than before: but her father treated her in so
violent and outrageous a manner, that he frightened her into an affected compliance with his
will; which so highly pleased the good squire,
that he changed his frowns into smiles, and his
menaces into promises: he vowed his whole soul
was wrapped in hers; that her consent (for so
he construed the words, "You know, sir, I must
not, nor can, refuse to obey any absolute command of yours") had made him the happiest of
mankind. He then gave her a large bank-bill to
dispose of in any trinkets she pleased, and kissed
and embraced her in the fondest manner, while
tears of joy trickled from those eyes which a few
moments before had darted fire and rage against
the dear object of all his affection.

Instances of this behavior in parents are so
common, that the reader, I doubt not, will be
very little astonished at the whole conduct of Mr.
Western. If he should, I own I am not able to
account for it; since that he loved his daughter
most tenderly, is, I think, beyond dispute. So
indeed have many others, who have rendered
their children most completely miserable by the
same conduct; which, though it is almost universal in parents, hath always appeared to me to
be the most unaccountable of all the absurdities
which ever entered into the brain of that strange
prodigious creature man.

The latter part of Mr. Western's behavior had
so strong an effect on the tender heart of Sophia,

that it suggested a thought to her, which not all
the sophistry of her politic aunt, nor all the
menaces of her father, had ever once brought into
her head. She reverenced her father so piously,
and loved him so passionately, that she had scarce
ever felt more pleasing sensations, than what
arose from the share she frequently had of contributing to his amusement, and sometimes, perhaps, to higher gratifications; for he never could
contain the delight of hearing her commended,
which he had the satisfaction of hearing almost
every day of her life. The idea, therefore, of
the immense happiness she should convey to her
father by her consent to this match, made a
strong impression on her mind. Again the extreme piety of such an act of obedience worked
very forcibly, as she had a very deep sense of
religion. Lastly, when she reflected how much
she herself was to suffer, being indeed to become
little less than a sacrifice, or a martyr, to filial
love and duty, she felt an agreeable tickling in a
certain little passion, which though it bears no
immediate affinity either to religion or virtue, is
often so kind as to lend great assistance in executing the purposes of both.

Sophia was charmed with the contemplation of
so heroic an action, and began to compliment herself with much premature flattery, when Cupid,
who lay hid in her muff, suddenly crept out,
and like Punchinello in a puppet-show, kicked
all out before him. In truth (for we scorn to
deceive our reader, or to vindicate the character
of our heroine by ascribing her actions to super-

natural impulse) the thoughts of her beloved Jones, and some hopes (however distant) in which he was very particularly concerned, immediately destroyed all which filial love, piety, and pride had, with their joint endeavors, been laboring to bring about.

But before we proceed any farther with Sophia, we must now look back to Mr. Jones.

CHAPTER X

Containing several matters, natural enough perhaps, but low.

THE reader will be pleased to remember, that we left Mr. Jones, in the beginning of this book, on his road to Bristol; being determined to seek his fortune at sea, or rather, indeed, to fly away from his fortune on shore.

It happened (a thing not very unusual), that the guide who undertook to conduct him on his way, was unluckily unacquainted with the road; so that having missed his right track, and being ashamed to ask information, he rambled about backwards and forwards till night came on, and it began to grow dark. Jones suspecting what had happened, acquainted the guide with his apprehensions; but he insisted on it, that they were in the right road, and added, it would be very strange if he should not know the road to Bristol; though, in reality, it would have been much stranger if he had known it, having never passed through it in his life before.

Jones had not such implicit faith in his guide, but that on their arrival at a village he inquired of the first fellow he saw, whether they were in the road to Bristol. "Whence did you come?" cries the fellow. "No matter," says Jones, a little hastily; "I want to know if this be the road

to Bristol?"—"The road to Bristol!" cries the
fellow, scratching his head: "why, measter, I believe you will hardly get to Bristol this way to-
night."—"Prithee, friend, then," answered
Jones, "do tell us which is the way."—"Why,
measter," cries the fellow, "you must be come
out of your road the Lord knows whither; for
thick way goeth to Glocester."—"Well, and
which way goes to Bristol?" said Jones. "Why,
you be going away from Bristol," answered the
fellow. "Then," said Jones, "we must go back
again?"—"Ay, you must," said the fellow.
"Well, and when we come back to the top of the
hill, which way must we take?"—"Why, you
must keep the straight road."—"But I remember
there are two roads, one to the right and the
other to the left."—"Why, you must keep the
right-hand road, and then gu straight vorwards;
only remember to turn vurst to your right, and
then to your left again, and then to your right,
and that brings you to the squire's; and then
you must keep straight vorwards, and turn to the
left."

Another fellow now came up, and asked which
way the gentlemen were going; of which being informed by Jones, he first scratched his head,
and then leaning upon a pole he had in his hand,
began to tell him, "That he must keep the right-
hand road for about a mile, or a mile and a half,
or such a matter, and then he must turn short to
the left, which would bring him round by Measter
Jin Bearnes's."—"But which is Mr. John
Bearnes's?" says Jones. "O Lord!" cries the

fellow, "why, don't you know Measter Jin
Bearnes? Whence then did you come?"

These two fellows had almost conquered the
patience of Jones, when a plain well-looking man
(who was indeed a Quaker) accosted him thus:
"Friend, I perceive thou hast lost thy way; and
if thou wilt take my advice, thou wilt not attempt
to find it to-night. It is almost dark, and the road
is difficult to hit; besides, there have been several
robberies committed lately between this and Bristol. Here is a very creditable good house just
by, where thou may'st find good entertainment
for thyself and thy cattle till morning." Jones,
after a little persuasion, agreed to stay in this
place till the morning, and was conducted by his
friend to the public-house.

The landlord, who was a very civil fellow, told
Jones, "He hoped he would excuse the badness
of his accommodation; for that his wife was gone
from home, and had locked up almost everything,
and carried the keys along with her." Indeed
the fact was, that a favorite daughter of hers
was just married, and gone that morning home
with her husband; and that she and her mother
together had almost stripped the poor man of
all his goods, as well as money; for though he
had several children, this daughter only, who was
the mother's favorite, was the object of her consideration; and to the humor of this one child she
would with pleasure have sacrificed all the rest,
and her husband into the bargain.

Though Jones was very unfit for any kind of
company, and would have preferred being alone,

yet he could not resist the importunities of the honest Quaker; who was the more desirous of sitting with him, from having remarked the melancholy which appeared both in his countenance and behavior; and which the poor Quaker thought his conversation might in some measure relieve.

After they had passed some time together, in such a manner that my honest friend might have thought himself at one of his silent meetings, the Quaker began to be moved by some spirit or other, probably that of curiosity, and said, "Friend, I perceive some sad disaster hath befallen thee; but pray be of comfort. Perhaps thou hast lost a friend. If so, thou must consider we are all mortal. And why shouldst thou grieve, when thou knowest thy grief will do thy friend no good? We are all born to affliction. I myself have my sorrows as well as thee, and most probably greater sorrows. Though I have a clear estate of £100 a year, which is as much as I want, and I have a conscience, I thank the Lord, void of offense; my constitution is sound and strong, and there is no man can demand a debt of me, nor accuse me of an injury; yet, friend, I should be concerned to think thee as miserable as myself."

Here the Quaker ended with a deep sigh; and Jones presently answered, "I am very sorry, sir, for your unhappiness, whatever is the occasion of it."—"Ah! friend," replied the Quaker, "one only daughter is the occasion; one who was my greatest delight upon earth, and who within this week is run away from me, and is married against

my consent. I had provided her a proper match,
a sober man and one of substance; but she, forsooth, would choose for herself, and away she
is gone with a young fellow not worth a groat.
If she had been dead, as I suppose thy friend is,
I should have been happy."—"That is very
strange, sir," said Jones. "Why, would it not
be better for her to be dead, than to be a beggar?" replied the Quaker: "for, as I told you, the
fellow is not worth a groat; and surely she cannot
expect that I shall ever give her a shilling. No,
as she hath married for love, let her live on love
if she can; let her carry her love to market, and
see whether any one will change it into silver,
or even into halfpence."—"You know your own
concerns best, sir," said Jones. "It must have
been," continued the Quaker, "a long premedi-
tated scheme to cheat me: for they have known
one another from their infancy; and I always
preached to her against love, and told her a thousand times over it was all folly and wickedness.
Nay, the cunning slut pretended to hearken to me,
and to despise all wantonness of the flesh; and
yet at last broke out at a window two pair of
stairs: for I began, indeed, a little to suspect her,
and had locked her up carefully, intending the
very next morning to have married her up to my
liking. But she disappointed me within a few
hours, and escaped away to the lover of her own
choosing; who lost no time, for they were married and bedded and all within an hour. But it
shall be the worst hour's work for them both
that ever they did: for they may starve, or beg,

or steal together, for me. I will never give either
of them a farthing." Here Jones starting up
cried, "I really must be excused: I wish you
would leave me."—"Come, come, friend," said
the Quaker, "don't give way to concern. You
see there are other people miserable besides yourself."—"I see there are madmen, and fools, and
villains in the world," cries Jones. "But let
me give you a piece of advice: send for your
daughter and son-in-law home, and don't be yourself the only cause of misery to one you pretend
to love."—"Send for her and her husband
home!" cries the Quaker loudly; "I would sooner
send for the two greatest enemies I have in the
world!"—"Well, go home yourself, or where you
please," said Jones, "for I will sit no longer in
such company."—"Nay, friend," answered the
Quaker, "I scorn to impose my company on any
one." He then offered to pull money from his
pocket, but Jones pushed him with some violence
out of the room.

The subject of the Quaker's discourse had so
deeply affected Jones, that he stared very wildly
all the time he was speaking. This the Quaker
had observed, and this, added to the rest of his
behavior, inspired honest Broadbrim with a conceit, that his companion was in reality out of his
senses. Instead of resenting the affront, therefore, the Quaker was moved with compassion for
his unhappy circumstances; and having communicated his opinion to the landlord, he desired him
to take great care of his guest, and to treat him
with the highest civility.

"Indeed," says the landlord, "I shall use no such civility towards him; for it seems, for all his laced waistcoat there, he is no more a gentleman than myself, but a poor parish bastard, bred up at a great squire's about thirty miles off, and now turned out of doors (not for any good to be sure). I shall get him out of my house as soon as possible. If I do lose my reckoning, the first loss is always the best. It is not above a year ago that I lost a silver spoon."

"What dost thou talk of a parish bastard, Robin?" answered the Quaker. "Thou must certainly be mistaken in thy man."

"Not at all," replied Robin; "the guide, who knows him very well, told it me." For, indeed, the guide had no sooner taken his place at the kitchen fire, than he acquainted the whole company with all he knew or had ever heard concerning Jones.

The Quaker was no sooner assured by this fellow of the birth and low fortune of Jones, than all compassion for him vanished; and the honest plain man went home fired with no less indignation than a duke would have felt at receiving an affront from such a person.

The landlord himself conceived an equal disdain for his guest; so that when Jones rung the bell in order to retire to bed, he was acquainted that he could have no bed there. Besides disdain of the mean condition of his guest, Robin entertained violent suspicion of his intentions, which were, he supposed, to watch some favorable opportunity of robbing the house. In reality, he

II—10

might have been very well eased of these apprehensions, by the prudent precautions of his wife and daughter, who had already removed every-thing which was not fixed to the freehold; but he was by nature suspicious, and had been more particularly so since the loss of his spoon. In short, the dread of being robbed totally absorbed the comfortable consideration that he had nothing to lose.

Jones being assured that he could have no bed, very contentedly betook himself to a great chair made with rushes, when sleep, which had lately shunned his company in much better apartments, generously paid him a visit in his humble cell.

As for the landlord, he was prevented by his fears from retiring to rest. He returned therefore to the kitchen fire, whence he could survey the only door which opened into the parlor, or rather hole, where Jones was seated; and as for the window to that room, it was impossible for any creature larger than a cat to have made his escape through it.

CHAPTER XI

The adventure of a company of soldiers.

THE landlord having taken his seat directly opposite to the door of the parlor, determined to keep guard there the whole night. The guide and another fellow remained long on duty with him, though they neither knew his suspicions, nor had any of their own. The true cause of their watching did, indeed, at length, put an end to it; for this was no other than the strength and goodness of the beer, of which having tippled a very large quantity, they grew at first very noisy and vociferous, and afterwards fell both asleep.

But it was not in the power of liquor to compose the fears of Robin. He continued still waking in his chair, with his eyes fixed steadfastly on the door which led into the apartment of Mr. Jones, till a violent thundering at his outward gate called him from his seat, and obliged him to open it; which he had no sooner done, than his kitchen was immediately full of gentlemen in red coats, who all rushed upon him in as tumultuous a manner as if they intended to take his little castle by storm.

The landlord was now forced from his post to furnish his numerous guests with beer, which they called for with great eagerness; and upon his second or third return from the cellar, he saw Mr. Jones standing before the fire in the midst of the soldiers; for it may easily be believed, that the arrival of so much good company should put an end to any sleep, unless that from which we are to be awakened only by the last trumpet.

The company having now pretty well satisfied their thirst, nothing remained but to pay the reckoning, a circumstance often productive of much mischief and discontent among the inferior rank of gentry, who are apt to find great difficulty in assessing the sum, with exact regard to distributive justice, which directs that every man shall pay according to the quantity which he drinks. This difficulty occurred upon the present occasion; and it was the greater, as some gentlemen had, in their extreme hurry, marched off, after their first draught, and had entirely forgot to contribute anything towards the said reckoning.

A violent dispute now arose, in which every word may be said to have been deposed upon oath; for the oaths were at least equal to all the other words spoken. In this controversy the whole company spoke together, and every man seemed wholly bent to extenuate the sum which fell to his share; so that the most probable conclusion which could be foreseen was, that a large portion of the reckoning would fall to the landlord's share to pay, or (what is much the same thing) would remain unpaid.

All this while Mr. Jones was engaged in conversation with the sergeant; for that officer was entirely unconcerned in the present dispute, being privileged by immemorial custom from all contribution.

The dispute now grew so very warm that it seemed to draw towards a military decision, when Jones, stepping forward, silenced all their clamors at once, by declaring that he would pay the whole reckoning, which indeed amounted to no more than three shillings and fourpence.

This declaration procured Jones the thanks and applause of the whole company. The terms honorable, noble, and worthy gentleman, resounded through the room; nay, my landlord himself began to have a better opinion of him, and almost to disbelieve the account which the guide had given.

The sergeant had informed Mr. Jones that they were marching against the rebels, and expected to be commanded by the glorious Duke of Cumberland. By which the reader may perceive (a circumstance which we have not thought necessary to communicate before) that this was the very time when the late rebellion was at the highest; and indeed the banditti were now marched into England, intending, as it was thought, to fight the king's forces, and to attempt pushing forward to the metropolis.

Jones had some heroic ingredients in his composition, and was a hearty well-wisher to the glorious cause of liberty, and of the Protestant religion. It is no wonder, therefore, that in circumstances which would have warranted a much more romantic and wild undertaking, it should occur to him to serve as a volunteer in this expedition.

Our commanding officer had said all in his

power to encourage and promote this good disposition, from the first moment he had been acquainted with it. He now proclaimed the noble resolution aloud, which was received with great pleasure by the whole company, who all cried out, "God bless King George and your honor;" and then added, with many oaths, "We will stand by you both to the last drops of our blood."

The gentleman who had been all night tippling at the alehouse, was prevailed on by some arguments which a corporal had put into his hands, to undertake the same expedition. And now the portmanteau belonging to Mr. Jones being put up in the baggage-cart, the forces were about to move forwards; when the guide, stepping up to Jones, said, "Sir, I hope you will consider that the horses have been kept out all night, and we have traveled a great ways out of our way." Jones was surprised at the impudence of this demand, and acquainted the soldiers with the merits of his cause, who were all unanimous in condemning the guide for his endeavors to put upon a gentleman. Some said, he ought to be tied neck and heels; others that he deserved to run the gantlope; and the sergeant shook his cane at him, and wished he had him under his command, swearing heartily he would make an example of him.

Jones contented himself however with a negative punishment, and walked off with his new comrades, leaving the guide to the poor revenge of cursing and reviling him; in which latter the

landlord joined, saying, "Ay, ay, he is a pure
one, I warrant you. A pretty gentleman, indeed,
to go for a soldier! He shall wear a laced waistcoat truly. It is an old proverb and a true one,
all is not gold that glisters. I am glad my house
is well rid of him."

All that day the sergeant and the young soldier
marched together; and the former, who was an
arch fellow, told the latter many entertaining
stories of his campaigns, though in reality he had
never made any; for he was but lately come into
the service, and had, by his own dexterity, so
well ingratiated himself with his officers, that he
had promoted himself to a halberd; chiefly indeed
by his merit in recruiting, in which he was most
excellently well skilled.

Much mirth and festivity passed among the
soldiers during their march. In which the many
occurrences that had passed at their last quarters
were remembered, and every one, with great freedom, made what jokes he pleased on his officers,
some of which were of the coarser kind, and very
near bordering on scandal. This brought to our
hero's mind the custom which he had read of
among the Greeks and Romans, of indulging, on
certain festivals and solemn occasions, the liberty to slaves, of using an uncontrolled freedom
of speech towards their masters.

Our little army, which consisted of two companies of foot, were now arrived at the place
where they were to halt that evening. The sergeant then acquainted his lieutenant, who was the
commanding officer, that they had picked up two

fellows in that day's march, one of which, he said,
was as fine a man as ever he saw (meaning the
tippler), for that he was near six feet, well proportioned, and strongly limbed; and the other
(meaning Jones) would do well enough for the
rear rank.

The new soldiers were now produced before the
officer, who having examined the six-foot man, he
being first produced, came next to survey Jones:
at the first sight of whom, the lieutenant could
not help showing some surprise; for besides that
he was very well dressed, and was naturally genteel, he had a remarkable air of dignity in his
look, which is rarely seen among the vulgar, and
is indeed not inseparably annexed to the features
of their superiors.

"Sir," said the lieutenant, "my sergeant informed me that you are desirous of enlisting
in the company I have at present under my command; if so, sir, we shall very gladly receive a
gentleman who promises to do much honor to the
company by bearing arms in it."

Jones answered: "That he had not mentioned
anything of enlisting himself; that he was most
zealously attached to the glorious cause for which
they were going to fight, and was very desirous
of serving as a volunteer;" concluding with some
compliments to the lieutenant, and expressing the
great satisfaction he should have in being under
his command.

The lieutenant returned his civility, commended
his resolution, shook him by the hand, and invited
him to dine with himself and the rest of the officers.

CHAPTER XII

The adventure of a company of officers.

THE lieutenant, whom we mentioned in the preceding chapter, and who commanded this party, was now near sixty years of age. He had entered very young into the army, and had served in the capacity of an ensign at the battle of Tannieres; here he had received two wounds, and had so well distinguished himself, that he was by the Duke of Marlborough advanced to be a lieutenant, immediately after that battle.

In this commission he had continued ever since, viz., near forty years; during which time he had seen vast numbers preferred over his head, and had now the mortification to be commanded by boys, whose fathers were at nurse when he first entered into the service.

Nor was this ill success in his profession solely owing to his having no friends among the men in power. He had the misfortune to incur the displeasure of his colonel, who for many years continued in the command of this regiment. Nor did he owe the implacable ill-will which this man bore him to any neglect or deficiency as an officer, nor indeed to any fault in himself; but solely to the indiscretion of his wife, who was a very beautiful woman, and who, though she was remarkably

153

fond of her husband, would not purchase his preferment at the expense of certain favors which the colonel required of her.

The poor lieutenant was more peculiarly unhappy in this, that while he felt the effects of the enmity of his colonel, he neither knew, nor suspected, that he really bore him any; for he could not suspect an ill-will for which he was not conscious of giving any cause; and his wife, fearing what her husband's nice regard to his honor might have occasioned, contented herself with preserving her virtue without enjoying the triumphs of her conquest.

This unfortunate officer (for so I think he may be called) had many good qualities besides his merit in his profession; for he was a religious, honest, good-natured man; and had behaved so well in his command, that he was highly esteemed and beloved not only by the soldiers of his own company, but by the whole regiment.

The other officers who marched with him were a French lieutenant, who had been long enough out of France to forget his own language, but not long enough in England to learn ours, so that he really spoke no language at all, and could barely make himself understood on the most ordinary occasions. There were likewise two ensigns, both very young fellows; one of whom had been bred under an attorney, and the other was son to the wife of a nobleman's butler.

As soon as dinner was ended, Jones informed the company of the merriment which had passed among the soldiers upon their march; "and yet,"

says he, "notwithstanding all their vociferation,
I dare swear they will behave more like Grecians
than Trojans when they come to the enemy."—
"Grecians and Trojans!" says one of the ensigns,
"who the devil are they? I have heard of all the
troops in Europe, but never of any such as
these."

"Don't pretend to more ignorance than you
have, Mr. Northerton," said the worthy lieutenant. "I suppose you have heard of the Greeks
and Trojans, though perhaps you never read
Pope's Homer; who, I remember, now the gentleman mentions it, compares the march of the
Trojans to the cackling of geese, and greatly
commends the silence of the Grecians. And upon
my honor there is great justice in the cadet's observation."

"Begar, me remember dem ver well," said the
French lieutenant: "me ave read them at school
in dans Madam Daciere, des Greek, des Trojan,
dey fight for von woman—ouy, ouy, me ave read
all dat."

"D—n Homo with all my heart," says Northerton; "I have the marks of him on my a— yet.
There's Thomas, of our regiment, always carries
a Homo in his pocket; d—n me, if ever I come
at it, if I don't burn it. And there's Corderius,
another d—n'd son of a whore, that hath got me
many a flogging."

"Then you have been at school, Mr. Northerton?" said the lieutenant.

"Ay, d—n me, have I," answered he; "the
devil take my father for sending me thither! The

old put wanted to make a parson of me, but d——n me, thinks I to myself, I'll nick you there, old cull; the devil a smack of your nonsense shall you ever get into me. There's Jemmy Oliver, of our regiment, he narrowly escaped being a pimp too, and that would have been a thousand pities; for d——n me if he is not one of the prettiest fellows in the whole world; but he went farther than I with the old cull, for Jimmey can neither write nor read."

"You give your friend a very good character," said the lieutenant, "and a very deserved one, I dare say. But prithee, Northerton, leave off that foolish as well as wicked custom of swearing; for you are deceived, I promise you, if you think there is wit or politeness in it. I wish, too, you would take my advice, and desist from abusing the clergy. Scandalous names, and reflections cast on any body of men, must be always unjustifiable; but especially so, when thrown on so sacred a function; for to abuse the body is to abuse the function itself; and I leave to you to judge how inconsistent such behavior is in men who are going to fight in defense of the Protestant religion."

Mr. Adderly, which was the name of the other ensign, had sat hitherto kicking his heels and humming a tune, without seeming to listen to the discourse; he now answered, "*O, Monsieur, on me parle pas de la religion dans la guerre.*"—"Well said, Jack," cries Northerton: "if *la religion* was the only matter, the parsons should fight their own battles for me."

"I don't know, gentlemen," said Jones, "what may be your opinion; but I think no man can engage in a nobler cause than that of his religion; and I have observed, in the little I have read of history, that no soldiers have fought so bravely as those who have been inspired with a religious zeal: for my own part, though I love my king and country, I hope, as well as any man in it, yet the Protestant interest is no small motive to my becoming a volunteer in the cause."

Northerton now winked on Adderly, and whispered to him slyly, "Smoke the prig, Adderly, smoke him." Then turning to Jones, said to him, "I am very glad, sir, you have chosen our regiment to be a volunteer in; for if our parson should at any time take a cup too much, I find you can supply his place. I presume, sir, you have been at the university; may I crave the favor to know what college?"

"Sir," answered Jones, "so far from having been at the university, I have even had the advantage of yourself, for I was never at school."

"I presumed," cries the ensign, "only upon the information of your great learning."—"Oh! sir," answered Jones, "it is as possible for a man to know something without having been at school, as it is to have been at school and to know nothing."

"Well said, young volunteer," cries the lieutenant. "Upon my word, Northerton, you had better let him alone; for he will be too hard for you."

Northerton did not very well relish the sar-

casm of Jones; but he thought the provocation
was scarce sufficient to justify a blow, or a rascal,
or scoundrel, which were the only repartees that
suggested themselves. He was, therefore, silent
at present; but resolved to take the first opportunity of returning the jest by abuse.

It now came to the turn of Mr. Jones to give a
toast, as it is called; who could not refrain from
mentioning his dear Sophia. This he did the
more readily, as he imagined it utterly impossible
that any one present should guess the person he
meant.

But the lieutenant, who was the toast-master,
was not contented with Sophia only. He said,
he must have her sur-name; upon which Jones
hesitated a little, and presently after named Miss
Sophia Western. Ensign Northerton declared
he would not drink her health in the same round
with his own toast, unless somebody would vouch
for her. "I knew one Sophy Western," says he,
"that was lain with by half the young fellows
at Bath; and perhaps this is the same woman."
Jones very solemnly assured him of the contrary;
asserting that the young lady he named was one
of great fashion and fortune. "Ay, ay," says
the ensign, "and so she is: d—n me, it is the same
woman; and I'll hold half a dozen of Burgundy,
Tom French of our regiment brings her into company with us at any tavern in Bridges-street."
He then proceeded to describe her person exactly
(for he had seen her with her aunt), and concluded with saying, "that her father had a great
estate in Somersetshire."

The tenderness of lovers can ill brook the
least jesting with the names of their mistresses.
However, Jones, though he had enough of the
lover and of the hero too in his disposition, did
not resent these slanders as hastily as, perhaps,
he ought to have done. To say the truth, having
seen but little of this kind of wit, he did not readily understand it, and for a long time imagined
Mr. Northerton had really mistaken his charmer
for some other. But now, turning to the ensign
with a stern aspect, he said, "Pray, sir, choose
some other subject for your wit; for I promise
you I will bear no jesting with this lady's character." "Jesting!" cries the other, "d—n me
if ever I was more in earnest in my life. Tom
French of our regiment had both her and her aunt
at Bath." "Then I must tell you in earnest,"
cries Jones, "that you are one of the most impudent rascals upon earth."

He had no sooner spoken these words, than the
ensign, together with a volley of curses, discharged a bottle full at the head of Jones, which
hitting him a little above the right temple, brought
him instantly to the ground.

The conqueror perceiving the enemy to lie motionless before him, and blood beginning to flow
pretty plentifully from his wound, began now to
think of quitting the field of battle, where no more
honor was to be gotten; but the lieutenant interposed, by stepping before the door, and thus cut
off his retreat.

Northerton was very importunate with the
lieutenant for his liberty; urging the ill conse-

quences of his stay, asking him, what he could
have done less? "Zounds!" says he, "I was but
in jest with the fellow. I never heard any harm
of Miss Western in my life." "Have not you?"
said the lieutenant; "then you richly deserve to
be hanged, as well for making such jests, as for
using such a weapon: you are my prisoner, sir;
nor shall you stir from hence till a proper guard
comes to secure you."

Such an ascendant had our lieutenant over this
ensign, that all that fervency of courage which
had leveled our poor hero with the floor, would
scarce have animated the said ensign to have
drawn his sword against the lieutenant, had he
then had one dangling at his side: but all the
swords being hung up in the room, were, at the
very beginning of the fray, secured by the French
officer. So that Mr. Northerton was obliged to
attend the final issue of this affair.

The French gentleman and Mr. Adderly, at the
desire of their commanding officer, had raised up
the body of Jones, but as they could perceive but
little (if any) sign of life in him, they again let
him fall, Adderly damning him for having
blooded his waistcoat; and the Frenchman declaring, "Begar, me no tush the Engliseman de mort:
me have heard de Englise ley, law, what you call,
hang up de man dat tush him last."

When the good lieutenant applied himself to the
door, he applied himself likewise to the bell; and
the drawer immediately attending, he dispatched
him for a file of musketeers and a surgeon.
These commands, together with the drawer's re-

port of what he had himself seen, not only produced the soldiers, but presently drew up the landlord of the house, his wife, and servants, and, indeed, every one else who happened at that time to be in the inn.

To describe every particular, and to relate the whole conversation of the ensuing scene, is not within my power, unless I had forty pens, and could, at once, write with them all together, as the company now spoke. The reader must, therefore, content himself with the most remarkable incidents, and perhaps he may very well excuse the rest.

The first thing done was securing the body of Northerton, who being delivered into the custody of six men with a corporal at their head, was by them conducted from a place which he was very willing to leave, but it was unluckily to a place whither he was very unwilling to go. To say the truth, so whimsical are the desires of ambition, the very moment this youth had attained the above-mentioned honor, he would have been well contented to have retired to some corner of the world, where the fame of it should never have reached his ears.

It surprises us, and so perhaps, it may the reader, that the lieutenant, a worthy and good man, should have applied his chief care, rather to secure the offender, than to preserve the life of the wounded person. We mention this observation, not with any view of pretending to account for so odd a behavior, but lest some critic should hereafter plume himself on discovering it.

We would have these gentlemen know we can see what is odd in characters as well as themselves, but it is our business to relate facts as they are; which, when we have done, it is the part of the learned and sagacious reader to consult that original book of nature, whence every passage in our work is transcribed, though we quote not always the particular page for its authority.

The company which now arrived were of a different disposition. They suspended their curiosity concerning the person of the ensign, till they should see him hereafter in a more engaging attitude. At present, their whole concern and attention were employed about the bloody object on the floor; which being placed upright in a chair, soon began to discover some symptoms of life and motion. These were no sooner perceived by the company (for Jones was at first generally concluded to be dead) than they all fell at once to prescribing for him (for as none of the physical order was present, every one there took that office upon him).

Bleeding was the unanimous voice of the whole room; but unluckily there was no operator at hand; every one then cried, "Call the barber;" but none stirred a step. Several cordials was likewise prescribed in the same ineffective manner; till the landlord ordered up a tankard of strong beer, with a toast, which he said was the best cordial in England.

The person principally assistant on this occasion, indeed the only one who did any service, or seemed likely to do any, was the landlady: she cut off some of her hair, and applied it to the wound to stop the blood; she fell to chafing the youth's temples with her hand; and having expressed great contempt for her husband's prescription of beer, she despatched one of her maids to her own closet for a bottle of brandy, of which, as soon as it was brought, she prevailed on Jones, who was just returned to his senses, to drink a very large and plentiful draught.

Soon afterwards arrived the surgeon, who having viewed the wound, having shaken his head, and blamed everything which was done, ordered his patient instantly to bed; in which place we think proper to leave him some time to his repose, and shall here, therefore, put an end to this chapter.

CHAPTER XIII

Containing the great address of the landlady, the great learning of a surgeon, and the solid skill in casuistry of the
worthy lieutenant.

WHEN the wounded man was carried to
his bed, and the house began again to
clear up from the hurry which this accident had occasioned, the landlady thus addressed
the commanding officer: "I am afraid, sir,"
said she, "this young man did not behave himself as well as he should do to your honors; and
if he had been killed, I suppose he had but his
desarts: to be sure, when gentlemen admit inferior parsons into their company, they oft to
keep their distance; but, as my first husband used
to say, few of 'em know how to do it. For my
own part, I am sure I should not have suffered
any fellows to *include* themselves into gentlemen's
company; but I thoft he had been an officer himself, till the sergeant told me he was but a re-
cruit."

"Landlady," answered the lieutenant, "you
mistake the whole matter. The young man behaved himself extremely well, and is, I believe, a
much better gentleman than the ensign who
abused him. If the young fellow dies, the man
who struck him will have most reason to be sorry
for it: for the regiment will get rid of a very

164

troublesome fellow, who is a scandal to the army;
and if he escapes from the hands of justice, blame
me, madam, that's all.''

"Ay! ay! good lack-a-day!" said the landlady;
"who could have thoft it? Ay, ay, ay, I am satisfied your honor will see justice done; and to be
sure it oft to be to every one. Gentlemen oft not
to kill poor folks without answering for it. A
poor man hath a soul to be saved, as well as his
betters.''

"Indeed, madam," said the lieutenant, "you do
the volunteer wrong: I dare swear he is more of
a gentleman than the officer.''

"Ay!" cries the landlady; "why, look you
there, now: well, my first husband was a wise
man; he used to say, you can't always know the
inside by the outside. Nay, that might have been
well enough too; for I never *saw'd* him till he was
all over blood. Who would have thoft it? may-
hap, some young gentleman crossed in love.
Good lack-a-day, if he should die, what a concern
it will be to his parents! why, sure the devil
must possess the wicked wretch to do such an act.
To be sure, he is a scandal to the army, as your
honor says; for most of the gentlemen of the
army that ever I saw, are quite different sort
of people, and look as if they would scorn to
spill any Christian blood as much as any men:
I mean, that is, in a civil way, as my first husband used to say. To be sure, when they come
into the wars, there must be bloodshed: but that
they are not to be blamed for. The more of our
enemies they kill there, the better: and I wish,

with all my heart, they could kill every mother's
son of them."

"O fie, madam!" said the lieutenant, smiling;
"*all* is rather too bloody-minded a wish."

"Not at all, sir," answered she; "I am not at
all bloody-minded, only to our enemies; and there
is no harm in that. To be sure it is natural for
us to wish our enemies dead, that the wars may
be at an end, and our taxes be lowered; for it is
a dreadful thing to pay as we do. Why now,
there is above forty shillings for window-lights,
and yet we have stopped up all we could; we have
almost blinded the house, I am sure. Says I to
the exciseman, says I, I think you oft to favor us;
I am sure we are very good friends to the government: and so we are for sartain, for we pay
a mint of money to 'um. And yet, I often think
to myself the government doth not imagine itself
more obliged to us, than to those that don't pay
'um a farthing. Ay, ay, it is the way of the
world."

She was proceeding in this manner when the
surgeon entered the room. The lieutenant immediately asked how his patient did. But he resolved him only by saying, "Better, I believe,
than he would have been by this time, if I had
not been called; and even as it is, perhaps it
would have been lucky if I could have been called
sooner."—"I hope, sir," said the lieutenant, "the
skull is not fractured."—"Hum," cries the surgeon: "fractures are not always the most dangerous symptoms. Contusions and lacerations
are often attended with worse phenomena, and

with more fatal consequences, than fractures.
People who know nothing of the matter conclude,
if the skull is not fractured, all is well; whereas,
I had rather see a man's skull broke all to pieces,
than some contusions I have met with."—"I
hope," says the lieutenant, "there are no such
symptoms here."—"Symptoms," answered the
surgeon, "are not always regular nor constant.
I have known very unfavorable symptoms in the
morning change to favorable ones at noon, and
return to unfavorable again at night. Of wounds,
indeed, it is rightly and truly said, *Nemo repente
fuit turpissimus.* I was once, I remember, called
to a patient who had received a violent contusion
in his tibia, by which the exterior cutis was
lacerated, so that there was a profuse sanguinary
discharge; and the interior membranes were so
divellicated, that the os or bone very plainly appeared through the aperture of the vulnus or
wound. Some febrile symptoms intervening at
the same time (for the pulse was exuberant and
indicated much phlebotomy), I apprehended an
immediate mortification. To prevent which, I
presently made a large orifice in the vein of the
left arm, whence I drew twenty ounces of blood;
which I expected to have found extremely sizy
and glutinous, or indeed coagulated, as it is in
pleuretic complaints; but, to my surprise, it appeared rosy and florid, and its consistency differed little from the blood of those in perfect
health. I then applied a fomentation to the part,
which highly answered the intention; and after
three or four times dressing, the wound began

to discharge a thick pus or matter, by which means the cohesion——But perhaps I do not make myself perfectly well understood?"—"No, really," answered the lieutenant, "I cannot say I understand a syllable."—"Well, sir," said the surgeon, "then I shall not tire your patience; in short, within six weeks my patient was able to walk upon his legs as perfectly as he could have done before he received the contusion."—"I wish, sir," said the lieutenant, "you would be so kind only to inform me, whether the wound this young gentleman hath had the misfortune to receive, is likely to prove mortal."—"Sir," answered the surgeon, "to say whether a wound will prove mortal or not at first dressing, would be very weak and foolish presumption: we are all mortal, and symptoms often occur in a cure which the greatest of our profession could never foresee."—"But do you think him in danger?" says the other.— "In danger! ay, surely," cries the doctor: "who is there among us, who, in the most perfect health, can be said not to be in danger? Can a man, therefore, with so bad a wound as this be said to be out of danger? All I can say at present is, that it is well I was called as I was, and perhaps it would have been better if I had been called sooner. I will see him again early in the morning; and in the meantime let him be kept extremely quiet, and drink liberally of water-gruel." —"Won't you allow him sack-whey?" said the landlady.—"Ay, ay, sack-whey," cries the doctor, "if you will, provided it be very small."— "And a little chicken broth too?" added she.

—"Yes, yes, chicken broth," said the doctor, "is very good."—"Mayn't I make him some jellies too?" said the landlady.—"Ay, ay," answered the doctor, "jellies are very good for wounds, for they promote cohesion." And indeed it was lucky she had not named soup or high sauces, for the doctor would have complied, rather than have lost the custom of the house.

The doctor was no sooner gone, than the landlady began to trumpet forth his fame to the lieutenant, who had not, from their short acquaintance, conceived quite so favorable an opinion of his physical abilities as the good woman, and all the neighborhood, entertained (and perhaps very rightly); for though I am afraid the doctor was a little of a coxcomb, he might be nevertheless very much of a surgeon.

The lieutenant having collected from the learned discourse of the surgeon that Mr. Jones was in great danger, gave orders for keeping Mr. Northerton under a very strict guard, designing in the morning to attend him to a justice of peace, and to commit the conducting the troops to Gloucester to the French lieutenant, who, though he could neither read, write, nor speak any language, was, however, a good officer.

In the evening, our commander sent a message to Mr. Jones, that if a visit would not be troublesome, he would wait on him. This civility was very kindly and thankfully received by Jones, and the lieutenant accordingly went up to his room, where he found the wounded man much better than he expected; nay, Jones assured his friend, that if he had not received express orders to the contrary from the surgeon, he should have got up long ago; for he appeared to himself to be as well as ever, and felt no other inconvenience from his wound but an extreme soreness on that side of his head.

"I should be very glad," quoth the lieutenant, "if you was as well as you fancy yourself, for then you could be able to do yourself justice immediately; for when a matter can't be made up, as in case of a blow, the sooner you take him out the better; but I am afraid you think yourself better than you are, and he would have too much advantage over you."

"I'll try, however," answered Jones, "if you please, and will be so kind to lend me a sword, for I have none here of my own."

"My sword is heartily at your service, my dear boy," cries the lieutenant, kissing him; "you are a brave lad, and I love your spirit; but I fear your strength; for such a blow, and so much loss of blood, must have very much weakened you; and though you feel no want of strength in your bed, yet you most probably would after a thrust or two. I can't consent to your taking him out to-night; but I hope you will be able to come up with us before we get many days' march advance; and I give you my honor you shall have satisfaction, or the man who hath injured you shan't stay in our regiment."

"I wish," said Jones, "it was possible to decide this matter to-night: now you have mentioned it to me, I shall not be able to rest."

"Oh, never think of it," returned the other: "a few days will make no difference. The wounds of honor are not like those in your body: they suffer nothing by the delay of cure. It will be altogether as well for you to receive satisfaction a week hence as now."

"But suppose," says Jones, "I should grow worse, and die of the consequences of my present wound?"

"Then your honor," answered the lieutenant, "will require no reparation at all. I myself will do justice to your character, and testify to the world your intention to have acted properly, if you had recovered."

"Still," replied Jones, "I am concerned at the delay. I am almost afraid to mention it to you who are a soldier; but though I have been a very wild young fellow, still in my most serious moments, and at the bottom, I am really a Christian."

"So am I too, I assure you," said the officer; "and so zealous a one, that I was pleased with you at dinner for taking up the cause of your religion; and I am a little offended with you now, young gentleman, that you should express a fear of declaring your faith before any one."

"But how terrible must it be," cries Jones, "to any one who is really a Christian, to cherish malice in his breast, in opposition to the command of Him who hath expressly forbid it? How can I bear to do this on a sick-bed? Or how shall I make up my account, with such an article as this in my bosom against me?"

"Why, I believe there is such a command," cries the lieutenant; "but a man of honor can't keep it. And you must be a man of honor, if you will be in the army. I remember I once put the case to our chaplain over a bowl of punch, and he confessed there was much difficulty in it; but he said, he hoped there might be a latitude granted to soldiers in this one instance; and to be sure it is our duty to hope so; for who would bear to live without his honor? No, no, my dear boy, be a good Christian as long as you live; but be a man of honor too, and never put up an affront; not all the books, nor all the parsons in the world, shall ever persuade me to that. I love my re- ligion very well, but I love my honor more. There must be some mistake in the wording the text, or in the translation, or in the understanding it, or somewhere or other. But however that be, a man must run the risk, for he must preserve his honor. So compose yourself to-night, and I promise you you shall have an opportunity of doing yourself justice." Here he gave Jones a hearty buss, shook him by the hand, and took his leave.

But though the lieutenant's reasoning was very satisfactory to himself, it was not entirely so to his friend. Jones therefore, having revolved this matter much in his thoughts, at last came to a resolution, which the reader will find in the next chapter.

CHAPTER XIV

A most dreadful chapter indeed; and which few readers ought
to venture upon in an evening, especially when alone.

JONES swallowed a large mess of chicken, or
rather cock, broth, with a very good appetite, as indeed he would have done the cock
it was made of, with a pound of bacon into the
bargain; and now, finding in himself no deficiency
of either health or spirit, he resolved to get up
and seek his enemy.

But first he sent for the sergeant, who was his
first acquaintance among these military gentlemen. Unluckily that worthy officer having, in a
literal sense, taken his fill of liquor, had been
some time retired to his bolster, where he was
snoring so loud that it was not easy to convey a
noise in at his ears capable of drowning that
which issued from his nostrils.

However, as Jones persisted in his desire of
seeing him, a vociferous drawer at length found
means to disturb his slumbers, and to acquaint
him with the message. Of which the sergeant
was no sooner made sensible, than he arose from
his bed, and having his clothes already on, immediately attended. Jones did not think fit to
acquaint the sergeant with his design; though he
might have done it with great safety, for the
halberdier was himself a man of honor, and had

killed his man. He would therefore have faithfully kept this secret, or indeed any other which no reward was published for discovering. But as Jones knew not those virtues in so short an acquaintance, his caution was perhaps prudent and commendable enough.

He began therefore by acquainting the sergeant, that as he was now entered into the army, he was ashamed of being without what was perhaps the most necessary implement of a soldier; namely, a sword; adding, that he should be infinitely obliged to him, if he could procure one. "For which," says he, "I will give you any reasonable price; nor do I insist upon its being silver-hilted; only a good blade, and such as may become a soldier's thigh."

The sergeant, who well knew what had happened, and had heard that Jones was in a very dangerous condition, immediately concluded, from such a message, at such a time of night, and from a man in such a situation, that he was light-headed. Now as he had his wit (to use that word in its common signification) always ready, he bethought himself of making his advantage of this humor in the sick man. "Sir," says he, "I believe I can fit you. I have a most excellent piece of stuff by me. It is not indeed silver-hilted, which, as you say, doth not become a soldier; but the handle is decent enough, and the blade one of the best in Europe. It is a blade that—a blade that—in short, I will fetch it you this instant, and you shall see it and handle it. I am glad to see your honor so well with all my heart."

Being instantly returned with the sword, he delivered it to Jones, who took it and drew it; and then told the sergeant it would do very well, and bid him name his price.

The sergeant now began to harangue in praise of his goods. He said (nay he swore very heartily), "that the blade was taken from a French officer, of very high rank, at the battle of Dettingen. I took it myself," says he, "from his side, after I had knocked him o' the head. The hilt was a golden one. That I sold to one of our fine gentlemen; for there are some of them, an't please your honor, who value the hilt of a sword more than the blade."

Here the other stopped him, and begged him to name a price. The sergeant, who thought Jones absolutely out of his senses, and very near his end, was afraid lest he should injure his family by asking too little. However, after a moment's hesitation, he contented himself with naming twenty guineas, and swore he would not sell it for less to his own brother.

"Twenty guineas!" says Jones, in the utmost surprise: "sure you think I am mad, or that I never saw a sword in my life. Twenty guineas, indeed! I did not imagine you would endeavor to impose upon me. Here, take the sword—No, now I think on't, I will keep it myself, and show it your officer in the morning, acquainting him, at the same time, what a price you asked me for it."

The sergeant, as we have said, had always his wit (*in sensu prædicto*) about him, and now plainly saw that Jones was not in the condition he had apprehended him to be; he now, therefore, counterfeited as great surprise as the other had shown, and said, "I am certain, sir, I have not asked you so much out of the way. Besides, you are to consider, it is the only sword I have, and I must run the risk of my officer's displeasure, by going without one myself. And truly, putting all this together, I don't think twenty shillings was so much out of the way."

"Twenty shillings!" cries Jones; "why, you just now asked me twenty guineas."—"How!" cries the sergeant, "sure your honor must have mistaken me: or else I mistook myself—and indeed I am but half awake. Twenty guineas, indeed! no wonder your honor flew into such a passion. I say twenty guineas too. No, no, I mean twenty shillings, I assure you. And when your honor comes to consider every thing, I hope you will not think that so extravagant a price. It is indeed true, you may buy a weapon which looks us well for less money. But—"

Here Jones interrupted him, saying, "I will be so far from making any words with you, that I will give you a shilling more than your demand." He then gave him a guinea, bid him return to his bed, and wished him a good march; adding, he hoped to overtake them before the division reached Worcester.

The sergeant very civilly took his leave, fully satisfied with his merchandise, and not a little pleased with his dextrous recovery from that false step into which his opinion of the sick man's light-headedness had betrayed him.

As soon as the sergeant was departed, Jones rose from his bed, and dressed himself entirely, putting on even his coat, which, as its color was white, showed very visibly the streams of blood which had flowed down it; and now, having grasped his new-purchased sword in his hand, he was going to issue forth, when the thought of what he was about to undertake laid suddenly hold of him, and he began to reflect that in a few minutes he might possibly deprive a human being of life, or might lose his own. "Very well," said he, "and in what cause do I venture my life? Why, in that of my honor. And who is this human being? A rascal who hath injured and insulted me without provocation. But is not revenge forbidden by Heaven? Yes, but it is enjoined by the world. Well, but shall I obey the world in opposition to the express commands of Heaven? Shall I incur the Divine displeasure rather than be called—ha—coward—scoundrel? —I'll think no more; I am resolved, and must fight him."

The clock had now struck twelve, and every one in the house were in their beds, except the sentinel who stood to guard Northerton, when Jones softly opening his door, issued forth in pursuit of his enemy, of whose place of confinement he had received a perfect description from the drawer. It is not easy to conceive a much more tremendous figure than he now exhibited. He had on, as we have said, a light-colored coat, covered with streams of blood. His face, which missed that very blood, as well as twenty ounces

II—12

more drawn from him by the surgeon, was pallid.
Round his head was a quantity of bandage, not
unlike a turban. In the right hand he carried a
sword, and in the left a candle. So that the
bloody Banquo was not worthy to be compared
to him. In fact, I believe a more dreadful
apparition was never raised in a church-yard,
nor in the imagination of any good people met
in a winter evening over a Christmas fire in
Somersetshire.

When the sentinel first saw our hero approach,
his hair began gently to lift up his grenadier cap;
and in the same instant his knees fell to blows
with each other. Presently his whole body was
seized with worse than an ague fit. He then
fired his piece, and fell flat on his face.

Whether fear or courage was the occasion of
his firing, or whether he took aim at the object
of his terror, I cannot say. If he did, however,
he had the good fortune to miss his man.

Jones seeing the fellow fall, guessed the cause
of his fright, at which he could not forbear smiling, not in the least reflecting on the danger from
which he had just escaped. He then passed by
the fellow, who still continued in the posture in
which he fell, and entered the room where Northerton, as he had heard, was confined. Here, in
a solitary situation, he found—an empty quart
pot standing on the table, on which some beer
being spilled, it looked as if the room had lately
been inhabited; but at present it was entirely
vacant.

Jones then apprehended it might lead to some

other apartment; but upon searching all round it, he could perceive no other door than that at which he entered, and where the sentinel had been posted. He then proceeded to call Northerton several times by his name; but no one answered; nor did this serve to any other purpose than to confirm the sentinel in his terrors, who was now convinced that the volunteer was dead of his wounds, and that his ghost was come in search of the murderer: he now lay in all the agonies of horror; and I wish, with all my heart, some of those actors who are hereafter to represent a man frightened out of his wits had seen him, that they might be taught to copy nature, instead of performing several antic tricks and gestures, for the entertainment and applause of the galleries.

Perceiving the bird was flown, at least despairing to find him, and rightly apprehending that the report of the firelock would alarm the whole house, our hero now blew out his candle, and gently stole back again to his chamber, and to his bed; whither he would not have been able to have gotten undiscovered, had any other person been on the same staircase, save only one gentleman who was confined to his bed by the gout; for before he could reach the door to his chamber, the hall where the sentinel had been posted was half full of people, some in their shirts, and others not half dressed, all very earnestly enquiring of each other what was the matter.

The soldier was now found lying in the same place and posture in which we just now left him.

Several immediately applied themselves to raise him, and some concluded him dead; but they presently saw their mistake, for he not only struggled with those who laid their hands on him, but fell a roaring like a bull. In reality, he imagined so many spirits or devils were handling him; for his imagination being possessed with the horror of an apparition, converted every object he saw or felt into nothing but ghosts and specters.

At length he was overpowered by numbers, and got upon his legs; when candles being brought, and seeing two or three of his comrades present, he came a little to himself; but when they asked him what was the matter? he answered, "I am a dead man, that's all, I am a dead man, I can't recover it, I have seen him." "What hast thou seen, Jack?" says one of the soldiers. "Why, I have seen the young volunteer that was killed yesterday." He then imprecated the most heavy curses on himself, if he had not seen the volunteer, all over blood, vomiting fire out of his mouth and nostrils, pass by him into the chamber where Ensign Northerton was, and then seizing the ensign by the throat, fly away with him in a clap of thunder.

This relation met with a gracious reception from the audience. All the women present believed it firmly, and prayed Heaven to defend them from murder. Amongst the men, too, many had faith in the story; but others turned it into derision and ridicule; and a sergeant who was present answered very coolly, "Young man, you will hear more of this, for going to sleep and dreaming on your post.''

The soldier replied, ''You may punish me if you please; but I was as broad awake as I am now; and the devil carry me away, as he hath the ensign, if I did not see the dead man, as I tell you, with eyes as big and as fiery as two large flambeaux.''

The commander of the forces, and the commander of the house, were now both arrived; for the former being awake at the time, and hearing the sentinel fire his piece, thought it his duty to rise immediately, though he had no great apprehensions of any mischief; whereas the apprehensions of the latter were much greater, lest her spoons and tankards should be upon the march, without having received any such orders from her.

Our poor sentinel, to whom the sight of this officer was not much more welcome than the apparition, as he thought it, which he had seen before, again related the dreadful story, and with many additions of blood and fire; but he had the misfortune to gain no credit with either of the last-mentioned persons: for the officer, though a very religious man, was free from all terrors of this kind; besides, having so lately left Jones in the condition we have seen, he had no suspicion of his being dead. As for the landlady, though not over religious, she had no kind of aversion to the doctrine of spirits; but there was a circumstance in the tale which she well knew to be false, as we shall inform the reader presently.

But whether Northerton was carried away in thunder or fire, or in whatever other manner he was gone, it was now certain that his body was no longer in custody. Upon this occasion the lieutenant formed a conclusion not very different from what the sergeant is just mentioned to have made before, and immediately ordered the sentinel to be taken prisoner. So that, by a strange reverse of fortune (though not very uncommon in a military life), the guard became the guarded.

CHAPTER XV

The conclusion of the foregoing adventure.

BESIDES the suspicion of sleep, the lieutenant harbored another and worse doubt against the poor sentinel, and this was, that of treachery; for as he believed not one syllable of the apparition, so he imagined the whole to be an invention formed only to impose upon him, and that the fellow had in reality been bribed by Northerton to let him escape. And this he imagined the rather, as the fright appeared to him the more unnatural in one who had the character of as brave and bold a man as any in the regiment, having been in several actions, having received several wounds, and, in a word, having behaved himself always like a good and valiant soldier.

That the reader, therefore, may not conceive the least ill opinion of such a person, we shall not delay a moment in rescuing his character from the imputation of this guilt.

Mr. Northerton then, as we have before observed, was fully satisfied with the glory which he had obtained from this action. He had perhaps seen, or heard, or guessed, that envy is apt to attend fame. Not that I would here insinuate that he was heathenishly inclined to believe in or to worship the goddess Nemesis; for, in fact, I am

convinced he never heard of her name. He was,
besides, of an active disposition, and had a great
antipathy to those close quarters in the castle of
Gloucester, for which a justice of peace might
possibly give him a billet. Nor was he moreover free from some uneasy meditations on a
certain wooden edifice, which I forbear to name,
in conformity to the opinion of mankind, who, I
think, rather ought to honor than to be ashamed
of this building, as it is, or at least might be made,
of more benefit to society than almost any other
public erection. In a word, to hint at no more
reasons for his conduct, Mr. Northerton was desirous of departing that evening, and nothing
remained for him but to contrive the quomodo,
which appeared to be a matter of some difficulty.

Now this young gentleman, though somewhat
crooked in his morals, was perfectly straight in
his person, which was extremely strong and well
made. His face too was accounted handsome by
the generality of women, for it was broad and
ruddy, with tolerably good teeth. Such charms
did not fail making an impression on my landlady, who had no little relish for this kind of
beauty. She had, indeed, a real compassion for
the young man; and hearing from the surgeon
that affairs were like to go ill with the volunteer,
she suspected they might hereafter wear no
benign aspect with the ensign. Having obtained,
therefore, leave to make him a visit, and finding
him in a very melancholy mood, which she considerably heightened by telling him there were scarce
any hopes of the volunteer's life, she proceeded to

throw forth some hints, which the other readily
and eagerly taking up, they soon came to a right
understanding; and it was at length agreed that
the ensign should, at a certain signal, ascend the
chimney, which communicating very soon with
that of the kitchen, he might there again let
himself down; for which she would give him an
opportunity by keeping the coast clear.

But lest our readers, of a different complexion,
should take this occasion of too hastily condemning all compassion as a folly, and pernicious to
society, we think proper to mention another particular which might possibly have some little
share in this action. The ensign happened to
be at this time possessed of the sum of fifty
pounds, which did indeed belong to the whole
company; for the captain having quarreled with
his lieutenant, had entrusted the payment of his
company to the ensign. This money, however,
he thought proper to deposit in my landlady's
hand, possibly by way of bail or security that he
would hereafter appear and answer to the charge
against him; but whatever were the conditions,
certain it is, that she had the money and the
ensign his liberty.

The reader may perhaps expect, from the compassionate temper of this good woman, that when
she saw the poor sentinel taken prisoner for a
fact of which she knew him innocent, she should
immediately have interposed in his behalf; but
whether it was that she had already exhausted all
her compassion in the above mentioned instance,
or that the features of this fellow, though not very

different from those of the ensign, could not raise
it, I will not determine; but, far from being an advocate for the present prisoner, she urged his
guilt to his officer, declaring, with uplifted eyes
and hands, that she would not have had any concern in the escape of a murderer for all the world.

Everything was now once more quiet, and most
of the company returned again to their beds;
but the landlady, either from the natural activity
of her disposition, or from her fear for her plate,
having no propensity to sleep, prevailed with the
officers, as they were to march within little more
than an hour, to spend that time with her over
a bowl of punch.

Jones had lain awake all this while, and had
heard great part of the hurry and bustle that had
passed, of which he had now some curiosity to
know the particulars. He therefore applied to
his bell, which he rung at least twenty times
without any effect: for my landlady was in such
high mirth with her company, that no clapper
could be heard there but her own; and the drawer
and chambermaid, who were sitting together in
the kitchen (for neither durst he sit up nor she
lie in bed alone), the more they heard the bell
ring the more they were frightened, and as it
were nailed down in their places.

At last, at a lucky interval of chat, the sound
reached the ears of our good landlady, who presently sent forth her summons, which both her servants instantly obeyed. "Joe," says the mistress,
"don't you hear the gentleman's bell ring? Why
don't you go up?"—"It is not my business,"

answered the drawer, "to wait upon the chambers
—it is Betty Chambermaid's."—"If you come
to that," answered the maid, "it is not my business to wait upon gentlemen. I have done it
indeed sometimes; but the devil fetch me if ever
I do again, since you make your preambles about
it." The bell still ringing violently, their mistress fell into a passion, and swore, if the drawer
did not go up immediately, she would turn him
away that very morning. "If you do, madam,"
says he, "I can't help it. I won't do another
servant's business." She then applied herself
to the maid, and endeavored to prevail by gentle
means; but all in vain: Betty was as inflexible as
Joe. Both insisted it was not their business, and
they would not do it.

The lieutenant then fell a laughing, and said,
"Come I will put an end to this contention;"
and then turning to the servants, commended
them for their resolution in not giving up the
point; but added, he was sure, if one would consent to go the other would. To which proposal
they both agreed in an instant, and accordingly
went up very lovingly and close together. When
they were gone, the lieutenant appeased the wrath
of the landlady, by satisfying her why they were
both so unwilling to go alone.

They returned soon after, and acquainted their
mistress, that the sick gentleman was so far from
being dead, that he spoke as heartily as if he was
well; and that he gave his service to the captain,
and should be very glad of the favor of seeing
him before he marched.

The good lieutenant immediately complied with his desires, and sitting down by his bed-side, acquainted him with the scene which had happened below, concluding with his intentions to make an example of the sentinel.

Upon this Jones related to him the whole truth, and earnestly begged him not to punish the poor soldier, "who, I am confident," says he, "is as innocent of the ensign's escape, as he is of forging any lie, or of endeavoring to impose on you."

The lieutenant hesitated a few moments, and then answered: "Why, as you have cleared the fellow of one part of the charge, so it will be impossible to prove the other, because he was not the only sentinel. But I have a good mind to punish the rascal for being a coward. Yet who knows what effect the terror of such an apprehension may have? and, to say the truth, he hath always behaved well against an enemy. Come, it is a good thing to see any sign of religion in these fellows; so I promise you he shall be set at liberty when we march. But hark, the general beats. My dear boy, give me another buss. Don't discompose nor hurry yourself; but remember the Christian doctrine of patience, and I warrant you will soon be able to do yourself justice, and to take an honorable revenge on the fellow who hath injured you." The lieutenant then departed, and Jones endeavored to compose himself to rest.

BOOK VIII

CHAPTER I

A wonderful long chapter concerning the marvelous; being
much the longest of all our introductory chapters.

AS we are now entering upon a book in which
the course of our history will oblige us to
relate some matters of a more strange and
surprising kind than any which have hitherto
occurred, it may not be amiss, in the prolegome-
nous or introductory chapter, to say something
of that species of writing which is called the
marvelous. To this we shall, as well for the sake
of ourselves as of others, endeavor to set some
certain bounds, and indeed nothing can be more
necessary, as critics [1] of different complexions
are here apt to run into very different extremes;
for while some are, with M. Dacier, ready to
allow, that the same thing which is impossible
may be yet probable,[2] others have so little historic or poetic faith, that they believe nothing to be either possible or probable, the like
to which hath not occurred to their own observation.

[1] By this word here, and in most other parts of our work,
we mean every reader in the world.
[2] It is happy for M. Dacier that he was not an Irishman.

189

First, then, I think it may very reasonably be required of every writer, that he keeps within the bounds of possibility; and still remembers that what it is not possible for man to perform, it is scare possible for man to believe he did perform. This conviction perhaps gave birth to many stories of the ancient heathen deities (for most of them are of poetical original). The poet, being desirous to indulge a wanton and extravagant imagination, took refuge in that power, of the extent of which his readers were no judges, or rather which they imagined to be infinite, and consequently they could not be shocked at any prodigies related of it. This hath been strongly urged in defense of Homer's miracles; and it is perhaps a defense; not, as Mr. Pope would have it, because Ulysses told a set of foolish lies to the Phæacians, who were a very dull nation; but because the poet himself wrote to heathens, to whom poetical fables were articles of faith. For my own part, I must confess, so compassionate is my temper, I wish Polypheme had confined himself to his milk diet, and preserved his eye; nor could Ulysses be much more concerned than myself, when his companions were turned into swine by Circe, who showed, I think, afterwards, too much regard for man's flesh to be supposed capable of converting it into bacon. I wish, likewise, with all my heart, that Homer could have known the rule prescribed by Horace, to introduce supernatural agents as seldom as possible. We should not then have seen his gods coming on trivial errands, and often behaving themselves so as not only to forfeit all title to respect, but to become the objects of scorn and derision. A conduct which must have shocked the credulity of a pious and sagacious heathen; and which could never have been defended, unless by agreeing with a supposition to which I have been sometimes almost inclined, that this most glorious poet, as he certainly was, had an intent to burlesque the superstitious faith of his own age and country.

But I have rested too long on a doctrine which can be of no use to a Christian writer; for as he cannot introduce into his works any of that heavenly host which make a part of his creed, so it is horrid puerility to search the heathen theology for any of those deities who have been long since dethroned from their immortality. Lord Shaftesbury observes, that nothing is more cold than the invocation of a muse by a modern; he might have added, that nothing can be more absurd. A modern may with much more elegance invoke a ballad, as some have thought Homer did, or a mug of ale, with the author of Hudibras; which latter may perhaps have inspired much more poetry, as well as prose, than all the liquors of Hippocrene or Helicon.

The only supernatural agents which can in any manner be allowed to us moderns, are ghosts; but of these I would advise an author to be extremely sparing. These are indeed, like arsenic, and other dangerous drugs in physic, to be used with the utmost caution; nor would I advise the introduction of them at all in those works, or by those authors, to which, or to whom, a horse-laugh in the reader would be any great prejudice or mortification.

As for elves and fairies, and other such mummery, I purposely omit the mention of them, as I should be very unwilling to confine within any bounds those surprising imaginations, for whose vast capacity the limits of human nature are too narrow; whose works are to be considered as a new creation; and who have consequently just right to do what they will with their own.

Man therefore is the highest subject (unless on, very extraordinary occasions indeed) which presents itself to the pen of our historian, or of our poet; and, in relating his actions, great care is to be taken that we do not exceed the capacity of the agent we describe.

Nor is possibility alone sufficient to justify us; we must keep likewise within the rules of probability. It is, I think, the opinion of Aristotle; or if not, it is the opinion of some wise man, whose authority will be as weighty when it is as old, "That it is no excuse for a poet who relates what is incredible, that the thing related is really matter of fact." This may perhaps be allowed true with regard to poetry, but it may be thought impracticable to extend it to the historian; for he is obliged to record matters as he finds them, though they may be of so extraordinary a nature as will require no small degree of historical faith to swallow them. Such was the successless armament of Xerxes described by Herodotus, or the successful expedition of Alexander related by Arrian. Such of later years was the victory of

Agincourt obtained by Harry the Fifth, or that of Narva won by Charles the Twelfth of Sweden. All which instances, the more we reflect on them, appear still the more astonishing.

Such facts, however, as they occur in the thread of the story, nay, indeed, as they constitute the essential parts of it, the historian is not only justifiable in recording as they really happened, but indeed would be unpardonable should he omit or alter them. But there are other facts not of such consequence nor so necessary, which though ever so well attested, may nevertheless be sacrificed to oblivion in complacence to the skepticism of a reader. Such is that memorable story of the ghost of George Villiers, which might with more propriety have been made a present of to Dr. Drelincourt, to have kept the ghost of Mrs. Veale company, at the head of his Discourse upon Death, than have been introduced into so solemn a work as the History of the Rebellion.

To say the truth, if the historian will confine himself to what really happened, and utterly reject any circumstance, which, though never so well attested, he must be well assured is false, he will sometimes fall into the marvelous, but never into the incredible. He will often raise the wonder and surprise of his reader, but never that incredulous hatred mentioned by Horace. It is by falling into fiction, therefore, that we generally offend against this rule, of deserting probability, which the historian seldom, if ever, quits, till he forsakes his character and commences a writer of romance. In this, however, those historians who relate public transactions, have the advantage of us who confine ourselves to scenes of private life. The credit of the former is by common notoriety supported for a long time; and public records, with the concurrent testimony of many authors, bear evidence to their truth in future ages. Thus a Trajan and an Antoninus, a Nero and a Caligula, have all met with the belief of posterity; and no one doubts but that men so very good, and so very bad, were once the masters of mankind.

But we who deal in private character, who search into the most retired recesses, and draw forth examples of virtue and vice from holes and corners of the world, are in a more dangerous situation. As we have no public notoriety, no concurrent testimony, no records to support and corroborate what we deliver, it becomes us to keep within the limits not only of possibility, but of probability too; and this more especially in painting what is greatly good and amiable. Knavery and folly, though never so exorbitant, will more easily meet with assent; for ill-nature adds great support and strength to faith.

Thus we may, perhaps, with little danger, relate the history of Fisher; who having long owed his bread to the generosity of Mr. Derby, and having one morning received a considerable bounty from his hands, yet, in order to possess himself of what remained in his friend's scrutore, concealed himself in a public office of the Temple, through which there was a passage into Mr. Derby's chambers. Here he overheard Mr. Derby for many hours

solacing himself at an entertainment which he that
evening gave his friends, and to which Fisher had
been invited.   During all this time, no tender, no
grateful reflections arose to restrain his purpose;
but when the poor gentleman had let his company out through the office, Fisher came suddenly
from his lurking-place, and walking softly behind
his friend into his chamber, discharged a pistol-
ball into his head.   This may be believed when the
bones of Fisher are as rotten as his heart.   Nay,
perhaps, it will be credited, that the villain went
two days afterwards with some young ladies to
the play of Hamlet; and with an unaltered countenance heard one of the ladies, who little sus
pected how near she was to the person, cry out,
"Good God! if the man that murdered Mr. Derby
was now present!" manifesting in this a more
seared and callous conscience than even Nero himself; of whom we are told by Suetonius, "that the
consciousness of his guilt, after the death of his
mother, became immediately intolerable, and so
continued; nor could all the congratulations of the
soldiers, of the senate, and the people, allay the
horrors of his conscience."

But now, on the other hand, should I tell my
reader that I had known a man whose penetrating
genius had enabled him to raise a large fortune
in a way where no beginning was chalked out
to him; that he had done this with the most
perfect preservation of his integrity, and not only
without the least injustice or injury to any one
individual person, but with the highest advantage
to trade, and a vast increase of the public rev-

enue; that he had expended one part of the income of this fortune in discovering a taste superior to most, by works where the highest dignity was united with the purest simplicity, and another part in displaying a degree of goodness superior to all men, by acts of charity to objects whose only recommendations were their merits, or their wants; that he was most industrious in searching after merit in distress, most eager to relieve it, and then as careful (perhaps too careful) to conceal what he had done; that his house, his furniture, his gardens, his table, his private hospitality, and his public beneficence, all denoted the mind from which they flowed, and were all intrinsically rich and noble, without tinsel, or external ostentation; that he filled every relation in life with the most adequate virtue; that he was most piously religious to his Creator, most zealously loyal to his sovereign; a most tender husband to his wife, a kind relation, a munificent patron, a warm and firm friend, a knowing and a cheerful companion, indulgent to his servants, hospitable to his neighbors, charitable to the poor, and benevolent to all mankind. Should I add to these the epithets of wise, brave, elegant, and indeed every other amiable epithet in our language, I might surely say,

> —*Quis credet? nemo Hercule! nemo;*
> *Vel duo, vel nemo;*

and yet I know a man who is all I have here described. But a single instance (and I really know not such another) is not sufficient to justify us, while we are writing to thousands who never heard of the person, nor of anything like him. Such *raræ aves* should be remitted to the epitaph writer, or to some poet who may condescend to hitch him in a distich, or to slide him into a rhyme with an air of carelessness and neglect, without giving an offense to the reader.

In the last place, the actions should be such as may not only be within the compass of human agency, and which human agents may probably be supposed to do; but they should be likely for the very actors and characters themselves to have performed; for what may be only wonderful and surprising in one man may become improbable, or indeed impossible, when related of another.

This last requisite is what the dramatic critics call conversation of character; and it requires a very extraordinary degree of judgment, and a most exact knowledge of human nature.

It is admirably remarked by a most excellent writer, that zeal can no more hurry a man to act in direct opposition to itself, than a rapid stream can carry a boat against its own current. I will venture to say, that for a man to act in direct contradiction to the dictates of his nature, is, if not impossible, as improbable and as miraculous as anything which can well be conceived. Should the best parts of the story of M. Antoninus be ascribed to Nero, or should the worst incidents of Nero's life be imputed to Antoninus, what would be more shocking to belief than either instance? whereas both these being related of their proper agent, constitute the truly marvelous.

Our modern authors of comedy have fallen almost universally into the error here hinted at; their heroes generally are notorious rogues, and their heroines abandoned jades, during the first four acts; but in the fifth, the former become very worthy gentlemen, and the latter women of virtue and discretion: nor is the writer often so kind as to give himself the least trouble to reconcile or account for this monstrous change and incongruity. There is, indeed, no other reason to be assigned for it, than because the play is drawing to a conclusion; as if it was no less natural in a rogue to repent in the last act of a play, than in the last of his life; which we perceive to be generally the case at Tyburn, a place which might indeed close the scene of some comedies with much propriety, as the heroes in these are most commonly eminent for those very talents which not only bring men to the gallows, but enable them to make an heroic figure when they are there.

Within these few restrictions, I think, every writer may be permitted to deal as much in the wonderful as he pleases; nay, if he thus keeps within the rules of credibility, the more he can surprise the reader the more he will engage his attention, and the more he will charm him. As a genius of the highest rank observes in his fifth chapter of the Bathos, "The great art of all poetry is to mix truth with fiction, in order to join the credible with the surprising."

For though every good author will confine himself within the bounds of probability, it is by no means necessary that his characters, or his incidents, should be trite, common, or vulgar; such as happen in every street, or in every house, or which may be met with in the home articles of a newspaper. Nor must he be inhibited from showing many persons and things, which may possibly have never fallen within the knowledge of great part of his readers. If the writer strictly observes the rules above-mentioned, he hath discharged his part; and is then entitled to some faith from his reader, who is indeed guilty of critical infidelity if he disbelieves him.

For want of a portion of such faith, I remember the character of a young lady of quality, which was condemned on the stage for being unnatural, by the unanimous voice of a very large assembly of clerks and apprentices; though it had the previous suffrages of many ladies of the first rank; one of whom, very eminent for her understanding, declared it was the picture of half the young people of her acquaintance.

CHAPTER II

WHEN Jones had taken leave of his friend the lieutenant, he endeavored to close his eyes, but all in vain; his spirits were too lively and wakeful to be lulled to sleep. So having amused, or rather tormented, himself with the thoughts of his Sophia till it was open daylight, he called for some tea; upon which occasion my landlady herself vouchsafed to pay him a visit.

This was indeed the first time she had seen him, or at least had taken any notice of him; but as the lieutenant had assured her that he was certainly some young gentleman of fashion, she now determined to show him all the respect in her power; for, to speak truly, this was one of those houses where gentlemen, to use the language of advertisements, meet with civil treatment for their money.

She had no sooner begun to make his tea, than she likewise began to discourse:—"La! sir," said she, "I think it is a great pity that such a pretty young gentleman should undervalue himself so, as to go about with these soldier fellows. They call themselves gentlemen, I warrant you; but, as my first husband used to say, they should remember it is we that pay them. And to be sure it is very hard upon us to be obliged to pay them, and

to keep 'um too, as we publicans are. I had twenty
of 'um last night, besides officers: nay, for matter
o' that, I had rather have the soldiers than
officers: for nothing is ever good enough for
those sparks; and I am sure, if you was to see
the bills; la! sir, it is nothing. I have had less
trouble, I warrant you, with a good squire's
family, where we take forty or fifty shillings of a
night, besides horses. And yet I warrants me,
there is narrow a one of those officer fellows but
looks upon himself to be as good as arrow a squire
of £500 a year. To be sure it doth me good to
hear their men run about after 'um, crying your
honor, and your honor. Marry come up with
such honor, and an ordinary at a shilling a head.
Then there's such swearing among 'um, to be
sure it frightens me out o' my wits: I thinks
nothing can ever prosper with such wicked people.
And here one of 'um has used you in so barbarous
a manner. I thought indeed how well the rest
would secure him; they all hang together; for if
you had been in danger of death, which I am glad
to see you are not, it would have been all as one to
such wicked people. They would have let the
murderer go. Laud have mercy upon 'um; I
would not have such a sin to answer for, for the
whole world. But though you are likely, with the
blessing, to recover, there is laa for him yet; and
if you will employ lawyer Small, I darest be sworn
he'll make the fellow fly the country for him;
though perhaps he'll have fled the country before;
for it is here to-day and gone to-morrow with such
chaps. I hope, however, you will learn more wit

for the future, and return back to your friends;
I warrant they are all miserable for your loss; and
if they was but to know what had happened—La,
my seeming! I would not for the world they
should. Come, come, we know very well what all
the matter is; but if one won't, another will; so
pretty a gentleman need never want a lady. I
am sure, if I was you, I would see the finest she
that ever wore a head hanged, before I would go
for a soldier for her.—Nay, don't blush so'' (for
indeed he did to a violent degree). ''Why, you
thought, sir, I knew nothing of the matter, I warrant you, about Madam Sophia.''—''How,'' says
Jones starting up, ''do you know my Sophia?''—
''Do I! ay marry,'' cries the landlady; ''many's
the time hath she lain in this house.''—''With her
aunt, I suppose,'' says Jones. ''Why, there it is
now,'' cries the landlady. ''Ay, ay, ay, I know
the old lady very well. And a sweet young
creature is madam Sophia, that's the truth on't.''
—''A sweet creature,'' cries Jones; ''O heavens!''

> Angels are painted fair to look like her,
> There's in her all that we believe of heav'n,
> Amazing brightness, purity, and truth,
> Eternal joy and everlasting love.

''And could I ever have imagined that you had
known my Sophia!''—''I wish,'' says the landlady, ''you knew half so much of her. What
would you have given to have sat by her bed-side?
What a delicious neck she hath! Her lovely limbs
have stretched themselves in that very bed you

now lie in."—"Here!" cries Jones: "hath Sophia ever laid here?"—"Ay, ay, here; there, in that very bed," says the landlady; "where I wish you had her this moment; and she may wish so too for anything I know to the contrary, for she hath mentioned your name to me."—"Ha!" cries he; "did she ever mention her poor Jones? You flatter me now: I can never believe so much."— "Why, then," answered she, "as I hope to be saved, and may the devil fetch me if I speak a syllable more than the truth, I have heard her mention Mr. Jones; but in a civil and modest way, I confess; yet I could perceive she thought a great deal more than she said."—"O my dear woman!" cries Jones, "her thoughts of me I shall never be worthy of. Oh, she is all gentleness, kindness, goodness! Why was such a rascal as I born, ever to give her soft bosom a moment's uneasiness? Why am I cursed? I, who would undergo all the plagues and miseries which any demon ever invented for mankind, to procure her any good; nay, torture itself could not be misery to me, did I but know that she was happy."—"Why, look you there now," says the landlady; "I told her you was a constant lover."—"But pray, madam, tell me when or where you knew anything of me; for I never was here before, nor do I remember ever to have seen you."—"Nor is it possible you should," answered she; "for you was a little thing when I had you in my lap at the squire's." —"How, the squire's?" says Jones: "what, do you know that great and good Mr. Allworthy then?"—"Yes, marry, do I," says she: "who in

the country doth not?"—"The fame of his goodness indeed," answered Jones, "must have extended farther than this; but heaven only can
know him—can know that benevolence which it
copied from itself, and sent upon earth as its own
pattern. Mankind are as ignorant of such divine
goodness, as they are unworthy of it; but none
so unworthy of it as myself. I, who was raised
by him to such a height; taken in, as you must
well know, a poor base-born child, adopted by him,
and treated as his own son, to dare by my follies
to disoblige him, to draw his vengeance upon me.
Yes, I deserve it all; for I will never be so ungrateful as ever to think he hath done an act of
injustice by me. No, I deserve to be turned out of
doors, as I am. And now, madam," says he, "I
believe you will not blame me for turning soldier,
especially with such a fortune as this in my pocket." At which words he shook a purse, which
had but very little in it, and which still appeared
to the landlady to have less.

My good landlady was (according to vulgar
phrase) struck all of a heap by this relation. She
answered coldly, "That to be sure people were the
best judges what was most proper for their circumstances. But hark," says she, "I think I hear
somebody call. Coming! coming! the devil's in all
our volk; nobody hath any ears. I must go down-
stairs; if you want any more breakfast the maid
will come up. Coming!" At which words, without taking any leave, she flung out of the room;
for the lower sort of people are very tenacious

of respect; and though they are contented to give this gratis to persons of quality, yet they never confer it on those of their own order without taking care to be well paid for their pains.

CHAPTER III

BEFORE we proceed any farther, that the reader may not be mistaken in imagining the landlady knew more than she did, nor surprised that she knew so much, it may be necessary to inform him that the lieutenant had acquainted her that the name of Sophia had been the occasion of the quarrel; and as for the rest of her knowledge, the sagacious reader will observe how she came by it in the preceding scene. Great curiosity was indeed mixed with her virtues; and she never willingly suffered any one to depart from her house, without enquiring as much as possible into their names, families, and fortunes.

She was no sooner gone than Jones, instead of animadverting on her behavior, reflected that he was in the same bed which he was informed had held his dear Sophia. This occasioned a thousand fond and tender thoughts, which we would dwell longer upon, did we not consider that such kind of lovers will make a very inconsiderable part of our readers. In this situation the surgeon found him, when he came to dress his wound. The doctor perceiving, upon examination, that his pulse was disordered, and hearing that he had not slept, declared that he was in great danger; for he apprehended a fever was coming on, which he would have prevented by bleeding, but Jones would not submit, declaring he would lose no more blood; "and, doctor," says he, "if you will be so kind only to dress my head, I have no doubt of being well in a day or two."

"I wish," answered the surgeon, "I could assure your being well in a month or two. Well, indeed! No, no, people are not so soon well of such contusions; but, sir, I am not at this time of day to be instructed in my operations by a patient, and I insist on making a revulsion before I dress you."

Jones persisted obstinately in his refusal, and the doctor at last yielded; telling him at the same time that he would not be answerable for the ill consequence, and hoped he would do him the justice to acknowledge that he had given him a contrary advice; which the patient promised he would.

The doctor retired into the kitchen, where, addressing himself to the landlady, he complained bitterly of the undutiful behavior of his patient, who would not be blooded, though he was in a fever.

"It is an eating fever then," says the landlady; "for he hath devoured two swinging buttered toasts this morning for breakfast."

"Very likely," says the doctor: "I have known people eat in a fever; and it is very easily accounted for; because the acidity occasioned by the febrile matter may stimulate the nerves of the diaphragm, and thereby occasion a craving which will not be easily distinguishable from a natural

appetite; but the aliment will not be concreted,
nor assimilated into chyle, and so will corrode the
vascular orifices, and thus will aggravate the
febrific symptoms.   Indeed, I think the gentleman
in a very dangerous way, and, if he is not blooded,
I am afraid will die.''

"Every man must die some time or other," answered the good woman; "it is no business of
mine.   I hope, doctor, you would not have me hold
him while you bleed him.   But, hark'ee, a word in
your ear; I would advise you, before you proceed
too far, to take care who is to be your paymaster.''

"Paymaster!" said the doctor, staring; "why,
I've a gentleman under my hands, have I not?''

"I imagined so as well as you," said the landlady; "but, as my first husband used to say, everything is not what it looks to be.   He is an arrant
scrub, I assure you.   However, take no notice
that I mentioned anything to you of the matter;
but I think people in business oft always to let one
another know such things.''

"And have I suffered such a fellow as this?''
cries the doctor, in a passion, "to instruct me?
Shall I hear my practice insulted by one who will
not pay me?   I am glad I have made this discovery in time.   I will see now whether he will be
blooded or no.''   He then immediately went up-
stairs, and flinging open the door of the chamber
with much violence, awaked poor Jones from a
very sound nap, into which he was fallen, and,
what was still worse, from a delicious dream concerning Sophia.

"Will you be blooded or no?" cries the doctor, in a rage. "I have told you my resolution already," answered Jones, "and I wish with all my heart you had taken my answer; for you have awaked me out of the sweetest sleep which I ever had in my life."

"Ay, ay," cries the doctor; "many a man hath dozed away his life. Sleep is not always good, no more than food; but remember, I demand of you for the last time, will you be blooded?"— "I answer you for the last time," said Jones, "I will not."—"Then I wash my hands of you," cries the doctor; "and I desire you to pay me for the trouble I have had already. Two journeys at 5s. each, two dressings at 5s. more, and half a crown for phlebotomy."—"I hope," said Jones, "you don't intend to leave me in this condition." —"Indeed but I shall," said the other. "Then," said Jones, "you have used me rascally, and I will not pay you a farthing."—"Very well," cries the doctor; "the first loss is the best. What a pox did my landlady mean by sending for me to such vagabonds!" At which words he flung out of the room, and his patient turning himself about soon recovered his sleep; but his dream was unfortunately gone.

CHAPTER IV

In which is introduced one of the pleasantest barbers that was ever recorded in history, the barber of Bagdad, or he in Don Quixote, not excepted.

THE clock had now struck five when Jones awaked from a nap of seven hours, so much refreshed, and in such perfect health and spirits, that he resolved to get up and dress himself; for which purpose he unlocked his portmanteau, and took out clean linen, and a suit of clothes; but first he slipped on a frock, and went down into the kitchen to bespeak something that might pacify certain tumults he found rising within his stomach.

Meeting the landlady, he accosted her with great civility, and asked, "What he could have for dinner?"—"For dinner!" says she; "it is an odd time a day to think about dinner. There is nothing dressed in the house, and the fire is almost out."—"Well, but," says he, "I must have something to eat, and it is almost indifferent to me what; for, to tell you the truth, I was never more hungry in my life."—"Then," says she, "I believe there is a piece of cold buttock and carrot, which will fit you."—"Nothing better," answered Jones; "but I should be obliged to you, if you would let it be fried." To which the landlady consented, and said, smiling, "she was glad to see him so well recovered;'' for the sweetness of our hero's temper was almost irresistible; besides, she was really no ill-humored woman at the bottom; but she loved money so much, that she hated everything which had the semblance of poverty.

Jones now returned in order to dress himself, while his dinner was preparing, and was, according to his orders, attended by the barber.

This barber, who went by the name of Little Benjamin, was a fellow of great oddity and humor, which had frequently let him into small inconveniencies, such as slaps in the face, kicks in the breech, broken bones, &c. For every one doth not understand a jest; and those who do are often displeased with being themselves the subjects of it. This vice was, however, incurable in him; and though he had often smarted for it, yet if ever he conceived a joke, he was certain to be delivered of it, without the least respect of persons, time, or place.

He had a great many other particularities in his character, which I shall not mention, as the reader will himself very easily perceive them, on his farther acquaintance with this extraordinary person.

Jones being impatient to be dressed, for a reason which may be easily imagined, thought the shaver was very tedious in preparing his suds, and begged him to make haste; to which the other answered with much gravity, for he never discomposed his muscles on any account, "Festina lentè. is a proverb which I learned long before

I ever touched a razor."—"I find, friend, you are
a scholar," replied Jones. "A poor one," said
the barber, *"non omnia possumus omnes."*—
"Again!" said Jones; "I fancy you are good at
capping verses."—"Excuse me, sir," said the
barber, *"non tanto me dignor honore."* And
then proceeding to his operation, "Sir," said he,
"since I have dealt in suds, I could never discover more than two reasons for shaving; the one
is to get a beard, and the other to get rid of one.
I conjecture, sir, it may not be long since you
shaved from the former of these motives. Upon
my word, you have had good success; for one may
say of your beard, that it is *tondenti gravior."*—
"I conjecture," says Jones, "that thou art a very
comical fellow."—"You mistake me widely, sir,"
said the barber: "I am too much addicted to the
study of philosophy; *hinc illæ lacrymæ,* sir; that's
my misfortune. Too much learning hath been
my ruin."—"Indeed," says Jones, "I confess,
friend, you have more learning than generally
belongs to your trade; but I can't see how it can
have injured you."—"Alas! sir," answered the
shaver, "my father disinherited me for it. He
was a dancing-master; and because I could read
before I could dance, he took an aversion to me,
and left every farthing among his other children.
—Will you please to have your temples—O la!
I ask your pardon, I fancy there is *hiatus in man-
uscriptis.* I heard you was going to the wars;
but I find it was a mistake."—"Why do you
conclude so?" says Jones. "Sure, sir," answered the barber, "you are too wise a man to

carry a broken head thither; for that would be carrying coals to Newcastle."

"Upon my word," cries Jones, "thou art a very odd fellow, and I like thy humor extremely; I shall be very glad if thou wilt come to me after dinner, and drink a glass with me; I long to be better acquainted with thee."

"O dear sir!" said the barber, "I can do you twenty times as great a favor, if you will accept of it."—"What is that, my friend?" cries Jones. "Why, I will drink a bottle with you if you please; for I dearly love good-nature; and as you have found me out to be a comical fellow, so I have no skill in physiognomy, if you are not one of the best-natured gentlemen in the universe." Jones now walked down-stairs neatly dressed, and perhaps the fair Adonis was not a lovelier figure; and yet he had no charms for my landlady; for as that good woman did not resemble Venus at all in her person, so neither did she in her taste. Happy had it been for Nanny the chambermaid, if she had seen with the eyes of her mistress, for that poor girl fell so violently in love with Jones in five minutes, that her passion afterwards cost her many a sigh. This Nanny was extremely pretty, and altogether as coy; for she had refused a drawer, and one or two young farmers in the neighborhood, but the bright eyes of our hero thawed all her ice in a moment.

When Jones returned to the kitchen, his cloth was not yet laid; nor indeed was there any occasion it should, his dinner remaining *in statu quo,* as did the fire which was to dress it. This disappointment might have put many a philosophical temper into a passion; but it had no such effect on Jones. He only gave the landlady a gentle rebuke, saying, "Since it was so difficult to get it heated he would eat the beef cold." But now the good woman, whether moved by compassion, or by shame, or by whatever other motive, I cannot tell, first gave her servants a round scold for disobeying the orders which she had never given, and then bidding the drawer lay a napkin in the Sun, she set about the matter in good earnest, and soon accomplished it.

This Sun, into which Jones was now conducted, was truly named, as *lucus a non lucendo;* for it was an apartment into which the sun had scarce ever looked. It was indeed the worst room in the house; and happy was it for Jones that it was so. However, he was now too hungry to find any fault; but having once satisfied his appetite, he ordered the drawer to carry a bottle of wine into a better room, and expressed some resentment at having been shown into a dungeon.

The drawer having obeyed his commands, he was, after some time, attended by the barber, who would not indeed have suffered him to wait so long for his company had he not been listening in the kitchen to the landlady, who was entertaining a circle that she had gathered round her with the history of poor Jones, part of which she had extracted from his own lips, and the other part was her own ingenious composition; for she said "he was a poor parish boy, taken into the

house of Squire Allworthy, where he was bred
up as an apprentice, and now turned out of doors
for his misdeeds, particularly for making love to
his young mistress, and probably for robbing
the house; for how else should he come by the
little money he hath; and this,'' says she, "is
your gentleman, forsooth!''—''A servant of
Squire Allworthy!'' says the barber; "what's his
name?''—''Why he told me his name was Jones,''
says she: "perhaps he goes by a wrong name.
Nay, and he told me, too, that the squire had
maintained him as his own son, thof he had quarreled with him now.''—''And if his name be
Jones, he told you the truth,'' said the barber;
"for I have relations who live in that country;
nay, and some people say he is his son.''—''Why
doth he not go by the name of his father?''—
''I can't tell that,'' said the barber; "many people's sons don't go by the name of their father.''
—''Nay,'' said the landlady, "if I thought he was
a gentleman's son, thof he was a bye-blow, I
should behave to him in another guess manner;
for many of these bye-blows come to be great
men, and, as my poor first husband used to say,
never affront any customer that's a gentleman.''

CHAPTER V

A dialogue between Mr. Jones and the barber.

THIS conversation passed partly while Jones was at dinner in his dungeon, and partly while he was expecting the barber in the parlor. And, as soon as it was ended, Mr. Benjamin, as we have said, attended him, and was very kindly desired to sit down. Jones then filling out a glass of wine, drank his health by the appellation of *doctissime tonsorum.* *"Ago tibi gratias, domine,"* said the barber; and then looking very steadfastly at Jones, he said, with great gravity, and with a seeming surprise, as if he had recollected a face he had seen before, "Sir, may I crave the favor to know if your name is not Jones?" To which the other answered, "That it was."—*"Proh deum atque hominum fidem!"* says the barber; "how strangely things come to pass! Mr. Jones, I am your most obedient servant. I find you do not know me, which indeed is no wonder, since you never saw me but once, and then you was very young. Pray, sir, how doth the good Squire Allworthy? how doth *ille optimus omnium patronus?"*—"I find," said Jones, "you do indeed know me; but I have not the like happiness of recollecting you."—"I do not wonder at that," cries Benjamin; "but I am surprised I did not know you sooner, for

you are not in the least altered. And pray, sir,
may I, without offense, enquire whither you are
traveling this way?"—"Fill the glass, Mr. Barber," said Jones, "and ask no more questions."
—"Nay, sir," answered Benjamin, "I would not
be troublesome; and I hope you don't think me
a man of an impertinent curiosity, for that is a
vice which nobody can lay to my charge; but I ask
pardon; for when a gentleman of your figure
travels without his servants, we may suppose him
to be, as we say, *in casu incognito,* and perhaps,
I ought not to have mentioned your name."—"I
own," says Jones, "I did not expect to have been
so well known in this country as I find I am; yet,
for particular reasons, I shall be obliged to you if
you will not mention my name to any other person till I am gone from hence."—"*Pauca verba,*"
answered the barber; "and I wish no other here
knew you but myself; for some people have
tongues; but I promise you I can keep a secret.
My enemies will allow me that virtue."—"And
yet that is not the characteristic of your profession, Mr. Barber," answered Jones. "Alas!
sir," replied Benjamin, "*Non si male nunc et
olim sic erit.* I was not born nor bred a barber,
I assure you. I have spent most of my time
among gentlemen, and though I say it, I understand something of gentility. And if you had
thought me as worthy of your confidence as you
have some other people, I should have shown you
I could have kept a secret better. I should not
have degraded your name in a public kitchen;
for indeed, sir, some people have not used you

well; for besides making a public proclamation of what you told them of a quarrel between yourself and Squire Allworthy, they added lies of their own, things which I knew to be lies."—"You surprise me greatly," cries Jones. "Upon my word, sir," answered Benjamin, "I tell the truth, and I need not tell you my landlady was the person. I am sure it moved me to hear the story, and I hope it is all false; for I have a great respect for you, I do assure you I have, and have had ever since the good-nature you showed to Black George, which was talked of all over the country, and I received more than one letter about it. Indeed, it made you beloved by everybody. You will pardon me, therefore; for it was real concern at what I heard made me ask many questions; for I have no impertinent curiosity about me: but I love good-nature and thence became *amoris abundantia erga te.*"

Every profession of friendship easily gains credit with the miserable; it is no wonder therefore, if Jones, who, besides his being miserable, was extremely open-hearted, very readily believed all the professions of Benjamin, and received him into his bosom. The scraps of Latin, some of which Benjamin applied properly enough, though it did not savor of profound literature, seemed yet to indicate something superior to a common barber; and so indeed did his whole behavior. Jones therefore believed the truth of what he had said, as to his original and education; and at length, after much entreaty, he said, "Since you have heard, my friend, so much of my affairs, and seem so desirous to know the truth, if you will have patience to hear it, I will inform you of the whole."—"Patience!" cries Benjamin, "that I will, if the chapter was never so long; and I am very much obliged to you for the honor you do me."

Jones now began, and related the whole history, forgetting only a circumstance or two, namely, everything which passed on that day in which he had fought with Thwackum; and ended with his resolution to go to sea, till the rebellion in the North had made him change his purpose, and had brought him to the place where he then was.

Little Benjamin, who had been all attention, never once interrupted the narrative; but when it was ended he could not help observing, that there must be surely something more invented by his enemies, and told Mr. Allworthy against him, or so good a man would never have dismissed one he had loved so tenderly, in such a manner. To which Jones answered, "He doubted not but such villainous arts had been made use of to destroy him."

And surely it was scarce possible for any one to have avoided making the same remark with the barber, who had not indeed heard from Jones one single circumstance upon which he was condemned; for his actions were not now placed in those injurious lights in which they had been misrepresented to Allworthy; nor could he mention those many false accusations which had been from time to time preferred against him to Allworthy: for with none of these he was himself acquainted. He had likewise, as we have observed, omitted many material facts in his present relation. Upon the whole, indeed, everything now appeared in such favorable colors to Jones, that malice itself would have found it no easy matter to fix any blame upon him.

Not that Jones desired to conceal or to disguise the truth; nay, he would have been more unwilling to have suffered any censure to fall on Mr. Allworthy for punishing him, than on his own actions for deserving it; but, in reality, so it happened, and so it always will happen; for let a man be never so honest, the account of his own conduct will, in spite of himself, be so very favorable, that his vices will come purified through his lips, and, like foul liquors well strained, will leave all their foulness behind. For though the facts themselves may appear, yet so different will be the motives, circumstances, and consequences, when a man tells his own story, and when his enemy tells it, that we scarce can recognize the facts to be one and the same.

Though the barber had drank down this story with greedy ears, he was not yet satisfied. There was a circumstance behind which his curiosity, cold as it was, most eagerly longed for. Jones had mentioned the fact of his amour, and of his being the rival of Blifil, but had cautiously concealed the name of the young lady. The barber, therefore, after some hesitation, and many hums and hahs, at last begged leave to crave the name of the lady, who appeared to be the principal cause of all this mischief. Jones paused a mo-

ment, and then said, "Since I have trusted you
with so much, and since, I am afraid, her name
is become too public already on this occasion, I
will not conceal it from you.   Her name is Sophia
Western."

"*Proh deum atque hominum fidem!* Squire
Western hath a daughter grown a woman!"—
"Ay, and such a woman," cries Jones, "that the
world cannot match.   No eye ever saw anything
so beautiful; but that is her least excellence.
Such sense! such goodness!   Oh, I could praise
her for ever, and yet should omit half her virtues!"—"Mr. Western a daughter grown up!"
cries the barber: "I remember the father a boy;
well, *Tempus edax rerum.*"

The wine being now at an end, the barber
pressed very eagerly to be his bottle; but Jones
absolutely refused, saying, "He had already drank
more than he ought: and that he now chose to retire to his room, where he wished he could procure himself a book."—"A book!" cried Benjamin; "what book would you have? Latin or
English?   I have some curious books in both languages; such as *Erasmi Colloquia, Ovid de Tristi-
bus, Gradus ad Parnassum;* and in English I have
several of the best books, though some of them
are a little torn; but I have a great part of Stowe's
Chronicle; the sixth volume of Pope's Homer; the
third volume of the Spectator; the second volume
of Echard's Roman History; the Craftsman; Rob-
inson Crusoe; Thomas à Kempis; and two volumes of Tom Brown's Works."

"Those last," cries Jones, "are books I never

saw, so if you please lend me one of those volumes.'' The barber assured him he would be highly entertained, for he looked upon the author to have been one of the greatest wits that ever the nation produced. He then stepped to his house, which was hard by, and immediately returned; after which, the barber having received very strict injunctions of secrecy from Jones, and having sworn inviolably to maintain it, they separated; the barber went home, and Jones retired to his chamber.

CHAPTER VI

In which more of the talents of Mr. Benjamin will appear, as well as who this extraordinary person was.

IN the morning Jones grew a little uneasy at the desertion of his surgeon, as he apprehended some inconvenience, or even danger, might attend the not dressing his wound; he enquired therefore of the drawer, what other surgeons were to be met with in that neighborhood. The drawer told him, there was one not far off, but he had known him often refuse to be concerned after another had been sent for before him; "but, sir," says he, "if you will take my advice, there is not a man in the kingdom can do your business better than the barber who was with you last night. We look upon him to be one of the ablest men at a cut in all this neighborhood. For though he hath not been here above three months, he hath done several great cures."

The drawer was presently dispatched for Little Benjamin, who being acquainted in what capacity he was wanted, prepared himself accordingly, and attended; but with so different an air and aspect from that which he wore when his basin was under his arm, that he could scarce be known to be the same person.

"So, tonsor," says Jones, "I find you have more trades than one; how came you not to in-

223

form me of this last night?"—"A surgeon,"
answered Benjamin, with great gravity, "is a
profession, not a trade. The reason why I did
not acquaint you last night that I professed this
art, was, that I then concluded you was under
the hands of another gentleman, and I never love
to interfere with my brethren in their business.
Ars omnibus communis. But now, sir, if you
please, I will inspect your head, and when I see
into your skull, I will give my opinion of your
case."

Jones had no great faith in this new professor;
however, he suffered him to open the bandage and
to look at his wound; which as soon as he had
done, Benjamin began to groan and shake his
head violently. Upon which Jones, in a peevish
manner, bid him not play the fool, but tell him in
what condition he found him. "Shall I answer
you as a surgeon, or a friend?" said Benjamin.
"As a friend, and seriously," said Jones. "Why
then, upon my soul," cries Benjamin, "it would
require a great deal of art to keep you from
being well after a very few dressings; and if you
will suffer me to apply some salve of mine, I will
answer for the success." Jones gave his consent,
and the plaster was applied accordingly.

"There, sir," cries Benjamin: "now I will, if
you please, resume my former self; but a man is
obliged to keep up some dignity in his countenance whilst he is performing these operations,
or the world will not submit to be handled by him.
You can't imagine, sir, of how much consequence
a grave aspect is to a grave character. A barber

may make you laugh, but a surgeon ought rather to make you cry.''

''Mr. Barber, or Mr. Surgeon, or Mr. Barber-surgeon,'' said Jones. ''O dear sir!'' answered Benjamin, interrupting him, *''Infandum, regina, jubes renovare dolorem.* You recall to my mind that cruel separation of the united fraternities, so much to the prejudice of both bodies, as all separations must be, according to the old adage, *Vis unita fortior;* which to be sure there are not wanting some of one or of the other fraternity who are able to construe. What a blow was this to me, who unite both in my own person!'' ''Well, by whatever name you please to be called,'' continued Jones, ''you certainly are one of the oddest, most comical fellows I ever met with, and must have something very surprising in your story, which you must confess I have a right to hear.''—''I do confess it,'' answered Benjamin, ''and will very readily acquaint you with it, when you have sufficient leisure, for I promise you it will require a good deal of time.'' Jones told him, he could never be more at leisure than at present. ''Well, then,'' said Benjamin, ''I will obey you; but first I will fasten the door, that none may interrupt us.'' He did so, and then advancing with a solemn air to Jones, said: ''I must begin by telling you, sir, that you yourself have been the greatest enemy I ever had.'' Jones was a little startled at this sudden declaration. ''I your enemy, sir!'' says he, with much amazement, and some sternness in his look. ''Nay, be not angry,'' said Benjamin, ''for I promise you

I am not. You are perfectly innocent of having intended me any wrong; for you was then an infant: but I shall, I believe, unriddle all this the moment I mention my name. Did you never hear, sir, of one Partridge, who had the honor of being reputed your father, and the misfortune of being ruined by that honor?'' ''I have, indeed, heard of that Partridge,'' says Jones, ''and have always believed myself to be his son.'' ''Well, sir,'' answered Benjamin, ''I am that Partridge; but I here absolve you from all filial duty, for I do assure you, you are no son of mine.'' ''How!'' replied Jones, ''and is it possible that a false suspicion should have drawn all the ill consequences upon you, with which I am too well acquainted?'' ''It is possible,'' cries Benjamin, ''for it is so: but though it is natural enough for men to hate even the innocent causes of their sufferings, yet I am of a different temper. I have loved you ever since I heard of your behavior to Black George, as I told you; and I am convinced, from this extraordinary meeting, that you are born to make me amends for all I have suffered on that account. Besides, I dreamed, the night before I saw you, that I stumbled over a stool without hurting myself; which plainly showed me something good was towards me: and last night I dreamed again, that I rode behind you on a milk-white mare, which is a very excellent dream, and betokens much good fortune, which I am resolved to pursue unless you have the cruelty to deny me.''

''I should be very glad, Mr. Partridge,'' answered Jones, "to have it in my power to make you amends for your sufferings on my account, though at present I see no likelihood of it; however, I assure you I will deny you nothing which is in my power to grant."

"It is in your power sure enough," replied Benjamin; "for I desire nothing more than leave to attend you in this expedition. Nay, I have so entirely set my heart upon it, that if you should refuse me, you will kill both a barber and a surgeon in one breath."

Jones answered, smiling, that he should be very sorry to be the occasion of so much mischief to the public. He then advanced many prudential reasons, in order to dissuade Benjamin (whom we shall hereafter call Partridge) from his purpose; but all were in vain. Partridge relied strongly on his dream of the milk-white mare. "Besides, sir," says he, "I promise you I have as good an inclination to the cause as any man can possibly have; and go I will, whether you admit me to go in your company or not."

Jones, who was as much pleased with Partridge as Partridge could be with him, and who had not consulted his own inclination but the good of the other in desiring him to stay behind, when he found his friend so resolute, at last gave his consent; but then recollecting himself, he said, "Perhaps, Mr. Partridge, you think I shall be able to support you, but I really am not;" and then taking out his purse, he told out nine guineas, which he declared were his whole fortune.

Partridge answered, "That his dependence was

only on his future favor; for he was thoroughly convinced he would shortly have enough in his power. At present, sir," said he, "I believe I am rather the richer man of the two; but all I have is at your service, and at your disposal. I insist upon your taking the whole, and I beg only to attend you in the quality of your servant; *Nil desperandum est Teucro duce et auspice Teucro:* but to this generous proposal concerning the money, Jones would by no means submit.

It was resolved to set out the next morning, when a difficulty arose concerning the baggage; for the portmanteau of Mr. Jones was too large to be carried without a horse.

"If I may presume to give my advice," says Partridge, "this portmanteau, with everything in it, except a few shirts, should be left behind. Those I shall be easily able to carry for you, and the rest of your clothes will remain very safe locked up in my house."

This method was no sooner proposed than agreed to; and then the barber departed, in order to prepare everything for his intended expedition.

CHAPTER VII

Containing better reasons than any which have yet appeared
for the conduct of Partridge; an apology for the weakness of Jones; and some further anecdotes concerning
my landlady.

THOUGH Partridge was one of the most
superstitious of men, he would hardly
perhaps have desired to accompany
Jones on his expedition merely from the omens
of the joint-stool and white mare, if his prospect
had been no better than to have shared the
plunder gained in the field of battle. In fact,
when Partridge came to ruminate on the relation
he had heard from Jones, he could not reconcile
to himself that Mr. Allworthy should turn his son
(for so he most firmly believed him to be) out
of doors, for any reason which he had heard assigned. He concluded, therefore, that the whole
was a fiction, and that Jones, of whom he had
often from his correspondents heard the wildest
character, had in reality run away from his
father. It came into his head, therefore, that if
he could prevail with the young gentleman to return back to his father, he should by that means
render a service to Allworthy, which would oblit-
erate all his former anger; nay, indeed, he conceived that very anger was counterfeited, and that
Allworthy had sacrificed him to his own reputa-

tion. And this suspicion indeed he well accounted
for, from the tender behavior of that excellent
man to the foundling child; from his great severity to Partridge, who, knowing himself to be innocent, could not conceive that any other should
think him guilty; lastly, from the allowance which
he had privately received long after the annuity
had been publicly taken from him, and which he
looked upon as a kind of smart-money, or rather
by way of atonement for injustice; for it is very
uncommon, I believe, for men to ascribe the benefactions they receive to pure charity, when they
can possibly impute them to any other motive.
If he could by any means therefore persuade the
young gentleman to return home, he doubted not
but that he should again be received into the favor
of Allworthy, and well rewarded for his pains;
nay, and should be again restored to his native
country; a restoration which Ulysses himself
never wished more heartily than poor Partridge.

As for Jones, he was well satisfied with the
truth of what the other had asserted, and believed that Partridge had no other inducements
but love to him, and zeal for the cause; a blamable want of caution and diffidence in the veracity
of others, in which he was highly worthy of censure. To say the truth, there are but two ways
by which men become possessed of this excellent
quality. The one is from long experience, and
the other is from nature; which last, I presume,
is often meant by genius, or great natural parts;
and it is infinitely the better of the two, not only
as we are masters of it much earlier in life, but

as it is much more infallible and conclusive; for a man who hath been imposed on by ever so many, may still hope to find others more honest; whereas he who receives certain necessary admonitions from within, that this is impossible, must have very little understanding indeed, if he ever renders himself liable to be once deceived. As Jones had not this gift from nature, he was too young to have gained it by experience; for at the diffident wisdom which is to be acquired this way, we seldom arrive till very late in life; which is perhaps the reason why some old men are apt to despise the understandings of all those who are a little younger than themselves.

Jones spent most part of the day in the company of a new acquaintance. This was no other than the landlord of the house, or rather the husband of the landlady. He had but lately made his descent down-stairs, after a long fit of the gout, in which distemper he was generally confined to his room during one half of the year; and during the rest, he walked about the house, smoked his pipe, and drank his bottle with his friends, without concerning himself in the least with any kind of business. He had been bred, as they call it, a gentleman; that is, bred up to do nothing; and had spent a very small fortune, which he inherited from an industrious farmer his uncle, in hunting, horse-racing, and cock-fighting, and had been married by my landlady for certain purposes, which he had long since desisted from answering; for which she hated him heartily. But as he was a surly kind of fellow, so she contented herself with frequently upbraiding him by disadvantageous comparisons with her first husband, whose praise she had eternally in her mouth; and as she was for the most part mistress of the profit, so she was satisfied to take upon herself the care and government of the family, and, after a long successless struggle, to suffer her husband to be master of himself.

In the evening, when Jones retired to his room, a small dispute arose between this fond couple concerning him:—"What," says the wife, "you have been tippling with the gentleman, I see?"—"Yes," answered the husband, "we have cracked a bottle together, and a very gentlemanlike man he is, and hath a very pretty notion of horse-flesh. Indeed, he is young, and hath not seen much of the world; for I believe he hath been at very few horse-races."—"Oho! he is one of your order, is he?" replies the landlady: "he must be a gentleman to be sure, if he is a horse-racer. The devil fetch such gentry! I am sure I wish I had never seen any of them. I have reason to love horse-racers truly!"—"That you have," says the husband; "for I was one, you know."—"Yes," answered she, "you are a pure one indeed. As my first husband used to say, I may put all the good I have ever got by you in my eyes, and see never the worse."—"D—n your first husband!" cries he. "Don't d—n a better man than yourself," answered the wife: "if he had been alive, you durst not have done it."—"Then you think," says he, "I have not so much courage as yourself; for you have d—n'd him often in my hearing."

—"If I did," says she, "I have repented of it many's the good time and oft. And if he was so good to forgive me a word spoken in haste or so, it doth not become such a one as you to twitter me. He was a husband to me, he was; and if ever I did make use of an ill word or so in a passion, I never called him rascal; I should have told a lie, if I had called him rascal." Much more she said, but not in his hearing; for having lighted his pipe, he staggered off as fast as he could. We shall therefore transcribe no more of her speech, as it approached still nearer and nearer to a subject too indelicate to find any place in this history.

Early in the morning Partridge appeared at the bedside of Jones, ready equipped for the journey, with his knapsack at his back. This was his own workmanship; for besides his other trades, he was no indifferent tailor. He had already put up his whole stock of linen in it, consisting of four shirts, to which he now added eight for Mr. Jones; and then packing up the portmanteau, he was departing with it towards his own house, but was stopped in his way by the landlady, who refused to suffer any removals till after the payment of the reckoning.

The landlady was, as we have said, absolute governess in these regions; it was therefore necessary to comply with her rules; so the bill was presently writ out, which amounted to a much larger sum than might have been expected, from the entertainment which Jones had met with. But here we are obliged to disclose some maxims,

which publicans hold to be the grand mysteries
of their trade. The first is, If they have anything good in their house (which indeed very seldom happens) to produce it only to persons who
travel with great equipages. Secondly, To charge
the same for the very worst provisions, as if they
were the best. And lastly, If any of their guests
call but for little, to make them pay a double price
for everything they have; so that the amount by
the head may be much the same.

The bill being made and discharged, Jones set
forward with Partridge, carrying his knapsack;
nor did the landlady condescend to wish him a
good journey; for this was, it seems, an inn frequented by people of fashion; and I know not
whence it is, but all those who get their livelihood
by people of fashion, contract as much insolence
to the rest of mankind, as if they really belonged
to that rank themselves.

CHAPTER VIII

MR. JONES and Partridge, or Little Benjamin (which epithet of Little was perhaps given him ironically, he being in reality near six feet high), having left their last quarters in the manner before described, traveled on to Gloucester without meeting any adventure worth relating.

Being arrived here, they chose for their house of entertainment the sign of the Bell, an excellent house indeed, and which I do most seriously recommend to every reader who shall visit this ancient city. The master of it is brother to the great preacher Whitefield; but is absolutely untainted with the pernicious principles of Methodism, or of any other heretical sect. He is indeed a very honest plain man, and, in my opinion, not likely to create any disturbance either in church or state. His wife hath, I believe, had much pretension to beauty, and is still a very fine woman. Her person and deportment might have made a shining figure in the politest assemblies; but though she must be conscious of this and many other perfections, she seems perfectly contented with, and resigned to, that state of life to which

235

she is called; and this resignation is entirely owing to the prudence and wisdom of her temper;
for she is at present as free from any Methodist-
ical notions as her husband: I say at present; for
she freely confesses that her brother's documents
made at first some impression upon her, and that
she had put herself to the expense of a long hood,
in order to attend the extraordinary emotions of
the Spirit; but having found, during an experiment of three weeks, no emotions, she says, worth
a farthing, she very wisely laid by her hood, and
abandoned the sect.   To be concise, she is a very
friendly good-natured woman; and so industrious
to oblige, that the guests must be of a very mo-
rose disposition who are not extremely well satisfied in her house.

Mrs. Whitefield happened to be in the yard
when Jones and his attendant marched in.   Her
sagacity soon discovered in the air of our hero
something which distinguished him from the vulgar.   She ordered her servants, therefore, immediately to show him into a room, and presently
afterwards invited him to dinner with herself;
which invitation he very thankfully accepted; for
indeed much less agreeable company than that of
Mrs. Whitefield, and a much worse entertainment
than she had provided, would have been welcome
after so long fasting and so long a walk.

Besides Mr. Jones and the good governess of
the mansion, there sat down at table an attorney
of Salisbury, indeed the very same who had
brought the news of Mrs. Blifil's death to Mr.
Allworthy, and whose name, which I think we did

not before mention, was Dowling: there was likewise present another person, who styled himself a lawyer, and who lived somewhere near Linlinch, in Somersetshire. This fellow, I say, styled himself a lawyer, but was indeed a most vile pettifogger, without sense or knowledge of any kind; one of those who may be termed train-bearers to the law; a sort of supernumeraries in the profession, who are the hackneys of attorneys, and will ride more miles for half-a-crown than a postboy.

During the time of dinner, the Somersetshire lawyer recollected the face of Jones, which he had seen at Mr. Allworthy's; for he had often visited in that gentleman's kitchen. He therefore took occasion to inquire after the good family there with that familiarity which would have become an intimate friend or acquaintance of Mr. Allworthy; and indeed he did all in his power to insinuate himself to be such, though he had never had the honor of speaking to any person in that family higher than the butler. Jones answered all his questions with much civility, though he never remembered to have seen the pettifogger before; and though he concluded, from the outward appearance and behavior of the man, that he usurped a freedom with his betters, to which he was by no means entitled.

As the conversation of fellows of this kind is of all others the most detestable to men of any sense, the cloth was no sooner removed than Mr. Jones withdrew, and a little barbarously left poor Mrs. Whitefield to do a penance, which I have often heard Mr. Timothy Harris, and other publicans of good taste, lament, as the severest lot annexed to their calling, namely, that of being obliged to keep company with their guests.

Jones had no sooner quitted the room, than the pettifogger, in a whispering tone, asked Mrs. Whitefield, "If she knew who that fine spark was?" She answered, "She had never seen the gentleman before."—"The gentleman, indeed!" replied the pettifogger; "a pretty gentleman, truly! Why, he's the bastard of a fellow who was hanged for horse-stealing. He was dropped at Squire Allworthy's door, where one of the servants found him in a box so full of rain-water, that he would certainly have been drowned, had he not been reserved for another fate."—"Ay, ay, you need not mention it, I protest: we understand what that fate is very well," cries Dowling, with a most facetious grin.—"Well," continued the other, "the squire ordered him to be taken in; for he is a timbersome man everybody knows, and was afraid of drawing himself into a scrape; and there the bastard was bred up, and fed, and clothified all to the world like any gentleman; and there he got one of the servant-maids with child, and persuaded her to swear it to the squire himself; and afterwards he broke the arm of one Mr. Thwackum a clergyman, only because he reprimanded him for following whores; and afterwards he snapped a pistol at Mr. Blifil behind his back; and once, when Squire Allworthy was sick, he got a drum, and beat it all over the house to prevent him from sleeping; and twenty other pranks he hath played, for all which, about four or five days ago, just before I left the country, the squire stripped him stark naked, and turned him out of doors.''

"And very justly too, I protest," cries Dowling; "I would turn my own son out of doors, if he was guilty of half as much. And pray what is the name of this pretty gentleman?"

"The name o' un?" answered Pettifogger; "why, he is called Thomas Jones."

"Jones!" answered Dowling a little eagerly; "what, Mr. Jones that lived at Mr. Allworthy's? was that the gentleman that dined with us?"— "The very same," said the other. "I have heard of the gentleman," cries Dowling, "often; but I never heard any ill character of him."—"And I am sure," says Mrs. Whitefield, "if half what this gentleman hath said be true, Mr. Jones hath the most deceitful countenance I ever saw; for sure his looks promise something very different; and I must say, for the little I have seen of him, he is as civil a well-bred man as you would wish to converse with."

Pettifogger calling to mind that he had not been sworn, as he usually was, before he gave his evidence, now bound what he had declared with so many oaths and imprecations that the landlady's ears were shocked, and she put a stop to his swearing, by assuring him of her belief. Upon which he said, "I hope, madam, you imagine I would scorn to tell such things of any man, unless I knew them to be true. What interest have I in taking away the reputation of a man who never injured me? I promise you every syllable of what I have said is fact, and the whole country knows it.''

As Mrs. Whitefield had no reason to suspect that the pettifogger had any motive or temptation to abuse Jones, the reader cannot blame her for believing what he so confidently affirmed with many oaths. She accordingly gave up her skill in physiognomy, and henceforward conceived so ill an opinion of her guest, that she heartily wished him out of her house.

This dislike was now further increased by a report which Mr. Whitefield made from the kitchen, where Partridge had informed the company, ''That though he carried the knapsack, and contented himself with staying among servants, while Tom Jones (as he called him) was regaling in the parlor, he was not his servant, but only a friend and companion, and as good a gentleman as Mr. Jones himself.''

Dowling sat all this while silent, biting his fingers, making faces, grinning, and looking wonderfully arch; at last he opened his lips, and protested that the gentleman looked like another sort of man. He then called for his bill with the utmost haste, declared he must be at Hereford that evening, lamented his great hurry of business, and wished he could divide himself into twenty pieces, in order to be at once in twenty places.

The pettifogger now likewise departed, and then Jones desired the favor of Mrs. Whitefield's company to drink tea with him; but she refused, and with a manner so different from that with which she had received him at dinner, that it a little surprised him. And now he soon perceived her behavior totally changed; for instead of that natural affability which we have before celebrated, she wore a constrained severity on her countenance, which was so disagreeable to Mr. Jones, that he resolved, however late, to quit the house that evening.

He did indeed account somewhat unfairly for this sudden change; for besides some hard and unjust surmises concerning female fickleness and mutability, he began to suspect that he owed this want of civility to his want of horses; a sort of animals which, as they dirty no sheets, are thought in inns to pay better for their beds than their riders, and are therefore considered as the more desirable company; but Mrs. Whitefield, to do her justice, had a much more liberal way of thinking. She was perfectly well-bred, and could be very civil to a gentleman, though he walked on foot. In reality, she looked on our hero as a sorry scoundrel, and therefore treated him as such, for which not even Jones himself, had he known as much as the reader, could have blamed her; nay, on the contrary, he must have approved her conduct, and have esteemed her the more for the disrespect shown towards himself. This is indeed a most aggravating circumstance, which attends depriving men unjustly of their reputation; for a man who is conscious of having an ill character, cannot justly be angry with those who neglect and slight him; but ought rather to despise such as affect his conversation, unless where

II—16

a perfect intimacy must have convinced them that
their friend's character hath been falsely and injuriously aspersed.

This was not, however, the case of Jones; for
as he was a perfect stranger to the truth, so he
was with good reason offended at the treatment
he received. He therefore paid his reckoning and
departed, highly against the will of Mr. Partridge,
who having remonstrated much against it to no
purpose, at last condescended to take up his knapsack and to attend his friend.

CHAPTER IX

Containing several dialogues between Jones and Partridge, concerning love, cold, hunger, and other matters; with the lucky and narrow escape of Partridge, as he was on the very brink of making a fatal discovery to his friend.

THE shadows began now to descend larger from the high mountains; the feathered creation had betaken themselves to their rest. Now the highest order of mortals were sitting down to their dinners, and the lowest order to their suppers. In a word, the clock struck five just as Mr. Jones took his leave of Gloucester; an hour at which (as it was now mid-winter) the dirty fingers of Night would have drawn her sable curtain over the universe, had not the moon forbid her, who now, with a face as broad and as red as those of some jolly mortals, who, like her, turn night into day, began to rise from her bed, where she had slumbered away the day, in order to sit up all night. Jones had not traveled far before he paid his compliments to that beautiful planet, and, turning to his companion, asked him if he had ever beheld so delicious an evening? Partridge making no ready answer to his question, he proceeded to comment on the beauty of the moon, and repeated some passages from Milton, who hath certainly excelled all other poets

243

in his description of the heavenly luminaries. He
then told Partridge the story from the Spectator,
of two lovers who had agreed to entertain themselves when they were at a great distance from
each other, by repairing, at a certain fixed hour,
to look at the moon; thus pleasing themselves
with the thought that they were both employed
in contemplating the same object at the same time.
"Those lovers," added he, "must have had souls
truly capable of feeling all the tenderness of the
sublimest of all human passions."—"Very probably," cries Partridge: "but I envy them more,
if they had bodies incapable of feeling cold; for
I am almost frozen to death, and am very much
afraid I shall lose a piece of my nose before we
get to another house of entertainment. Nay,
truly, we may well expect some judgment should
happen to us for our folly in running away so by
night from one of the most excellent inns I ever
set my foot into. I am sure I never saw more
good things in my life, and the greatest lord in
the land cannot live better in his own house than
he may there. And to forsake such a house, and
go a rambling about the country, the Lord knows
whither, *per devia rura viarum,* I say nothing for
my part; but some people might not have charity
enough to conclude we were in our sober senses."
—"Fie upon it, Mr. Partridge!" says Jones,
"have a better heart; consider you are going to
face an enemy; and are you afraid of facing a
little cold? I wish, indeed, we had a guide to
advise which of these roads we should take."—
"May I be so bold," says Partridge, "to offer

my advice? *Interdum stultus opportuna loqui-
tur.*"—"Why, which of them," cries Jones,
"would you recommend?"—"Truly neither of
them," answered Partridge. "The only road we
can be certain of finding, is the road we came.
A good hearty pace will bring us back to Gloucester in an hour; but if we go forward, the Lord
Harry knows when we shall arrive at any place;
for I see at least fifty miles before me, and no
house in all the way."—"You see, indeed, a very
fair prospect," says Jones, "which receives great
additional beauty from the extreme luster of the
moon. However, I will keep the left-hand track,
as that seems to lead directly to those hills, which
we were informed lie not far from Worcester.
And here, if you are inclined to quit me, you may,
and return back again; but for my part, I am
resolved to go forward."

"It is unkind in you, sir," says Partridge, "to
suspect me of any such intention. What I have
advised hath been as much on your account as on
my own: but since you are determined to go on,
I am as much determined to follow. *I præ sequar
te.*"

They now traveled some miles without speaking
to each other, during which suspense of discourse
Jones often sighed, and Benjamin groaned as bitterly, though from a very different reason. At
length Jones made a full stop, and turning about,
cries, "Who knows, Partridge, but the loveliest
creature in the universe may have her eyes now
fixed on that very moon which I behold at this
instant?" "Very likely, sir," answered Par-

tridge; "and if my eyes were fixed on a good sirloin of roast beef, the devil might take the moon and her horns into the bargain." "Did ever Tramontane make such an answer?" cries Jones. "Prithee, Partridge, wast thou ever susceptible of love in thy life, or hath time worn away all the traces of it from thy memory?" "Alack-a-day!" cries Partridge, "well would it have been for me if I had never known what love was. *Infandum regina jubes renovare dolorem.* I am sure I have tasted all the tenderness, and sublimities, and bitternesses of the passion." "Was your mistress unkind, then?" says Jones. "Very unkind, indeed, sir," answered Partridge; "for she married me, and made one of the most confounded wives in the world. However, heaven be praised, she's gone; and if I believed she was in the moon, according to a book I once read, which teaches that to be the receptacle of departed spirits, I would never look at it for fear of seeing her; but I wish, sir, that the moon was a looking-glass for your sake, and that Miss Sophia Western was now placed before it." "My dear Partridge," cries Jones, "what a thought was there! A thought which I am certain could never have entered into any mind but that of a lover. O Partridge! could I hope once again to see that face; but, alas! all those golden dreams are vanished for ever, and my only refuge from future misery is to forget the object of all my former happiness." "And do you really despair of ever seeing Miss Western again?" answered Partridge; "if you will follow my advice I will engage you shall not only see her but have her in your arms.'' ''Ha! do not awaken a thought of that nature,'' cries Jones: ''I have struggled sufficiently to conquer all such wishes already.'' ''Nay,'' answered Partridge, ''if you do not wish to have your mistress in your arms you are a most extraordinary lover indeed.'' ''Well, well,'' says Jones, ''let us avoid this subject; but pray what is your advice?'' ''To give it you in the military phrase, then,'' says Partridge, ''as we are soldiers, 'To the right about.' Let us return the way we came; we may yet reach Gloucester to-night, though late; whereas, if we proceed, we are likely, for aught I see, to ramble about for ever without coming either to house or home.'' ''I have already told you my resolution is to go on,'' answered Jones; ''but I would have you go back. I am obliged to you for your company hither; and I beg you to accept a guinea as a small instance of my gratitude. Nay, it would be cruel in me to suffer you to go any farther; for, to deal plainly with you, my chief end and desire is a glorious death in the service of my king and country.'' ''As for your money,'' replied Partridge, ''I beg, sir, you will put it up; I will receive none of you at this time; for at present I am, I believe, the richer man of the two. And as your resolution is to go on, so mine is to follow you if you do. Nay, now my presence appears absolutely necessary to take care of you, since your intentions are so desperate; for I promise you my views are much more prudent; as you are resolved to fall in battle if you can, so I am resolved as firmly to come to no hurt if I can help it. And, indeed, I have the comfort to think there will be but little danger; for a popish priest told me the other day the business would soon be over, and he believed without a battle." "A popish priest!" cries Jones, "I have heard is not always to be believed when he speaks in behalf of his religion." "Yes, but so far," answered the other, "from speaking in behalf of his religion, he assured me the Catholics did not expect to be any gainers by the change; for that Prince Charles was as good a Protestant as any in England; and that nothing but regard to right made him and the rest of the popish party to be Jacobites."—"I believe him to be as much a Protestant as I believe he hath any right," says Jones; "and I make no doubt of our success, but not without a battle. So that I am not so sanguine as your friend the popish priest." "Nay, to be sure, sir," answered Partridge, "all the prophecies I have ever read speak of a great deal of blood to be spilled in the quarrel, and the miller with three thumbs, who is now alive, is to hold the horses of three kings, up to his knees in blood. Lord, have mercy upon us all, and send better times!" "With what stuff and nonsense hast thou filled thy head!" answered Jones: "this too, I suppose, comes from the popish priest. Monsters and prodigies are the proper arguments to support monstrous and absurd doctrines. The cause of King George is the cause of liberty and true religion. In other words, it is the cause of common sense, my boy, and I warrant you will

succeed, though Briarius himself was to rise
again with his hundred thumbs, and to turn miller.'' Partridge made no reply to this. He was,
indeed, cast into the utmost confusion by this
declaration of Jones. For, to inform the reader
of a secret, which he had no proper opportunity
of revealing before, Partridge was in truth a
Jacobite, and had concluded that Jones was of
the same party, and was now proceeding to join
the rebels. An opinion which was not without
foundation. For the tall, long-sided dame, mentioned by Hudibras—that many-eyed, many-ton-
gued, many-mouthed, many-eared monster of
Virgil, had related the story of the quarrel between Jones and the officer, with the usual regard
to truth. She had, indeed, changed the name of
Sophia into that of the Pretender, and had reported, that drinking his health was the cause
for which Jones was knocked down. This Partridge had heard, and most firmly believed. 'Tis
no wonder, therefore, that he had thence entertained the above-mentioned opinion of Jones; and
which he had almost discovered to him before
he found out his own mistake. And at this
the reader will be the less inclined to wonder, if
he pleases to recollect the doubtful phrase in
which Jones first communicated his resolution to
Mr. Partridge; and, indeed, had the words been
less ambiguous, Partridge might very well have
construed them as he did; being persuaded as he
was that the whole nation were of the same inclination in their hearts; nor did it stagger him that
Jones had traveled in the company of soldiers;

for he had the same opinion of the army which he had of the rest of the people.

But however well affected he might be to James or Charles, he was still much more attached to Little Benjamin than to either; for which reason he no sooner discovered the principles of his fellow-traveler than he thought proper to conceal and outwardly give up his own to the man on whom he depended for the making his fortune, since he by no means believed the affairs of Jones to be so desperate as they really were with Mr. Allworthy; for as he had kept a constant correspondence with some of his neighbors since he left that country, he had heard much, indeed more than was true, of the great affection Mr. Allworthy bore this young man, who, as Partridge had been instructed, was to be that gentleman's heir, and whom, as we have said, he did not in the least doubt to be his son.

He imagined therefore that whatever quarrel was between them, it would be certainly made up at the return of Mr. Jones; an event from which he promised great advantages, if he could take this opportunity of ingratiating himself with that young gentleman; and if he could by any means be instrumental in procuring his return, he doubted not, as we have before said, but it would as highly advance him in the favor of Mr. Allworthy.

We have already observed, that he was a very good-natured fellow, and he hath himself declared the violent attachment he had to the person and character of Jones; but possibly the views which

I have just before mentioned, might likewise have some little share in prompting him to undertake this expedition, at least in urging him to continue it, after he had discovered that his master and himself, like some prudent fathers and sons, though they traveled together in great friendship, had embraced opposite parties. I am led into this conjecture, by having remarked, that though love, friendship, esteem, and such like, have very powerful operations in the human mind; interest, however, is an ingredient seldom omitted by wise men, when they would work others to their own purposes. This is indeed a most excellent medicine, and, like Ward's pill, flies at once to the particular part of the body on which you desire to operate, whether it be the tongue, the hand, or any other member, where it scarce ever fails of immediately producing the desired effect.

CHAPTER X

In which our travelers meet with a very extraordinary
adventure.

JUST as Jones and his friend came to the end of their dialogue in the proceeding chapter, they arrived at the bottom of a very steep hill. Here Jones stopped short, and directing his eyes upwards, stood for a while silent. At length he called to his companion, and said, "Partridge, I wish I was at the top of this hill; it must certainly afford a most charming prospect, especially by this light; for the solemn gloom which the moon casts on all objects, is beyond expression beautiful, especially to an imagination which is desirous of cultivating melancholy ideas."— "Very probably," answered Partridge; "but if the top of the hill be properest to produce melancholy thoughts, I suppose the bottom is the likeliest to produce merry ones, and these I take to be much the better of the two. I protest you have made my blood run cold with the very mentioning the top of the mountain; which seems to me to be one of the highest in the world. No, no, if we look for anything, let it be for a place under ground, to screen ourselves from the frost."—"Do so," said Jones; "let it be but within hearing of this place, and I will hallow to you at my return back."—"Surely, sir, you are not mad," said

Partridge.—"Indeed, I am," answered Jones, "if ascending this hill be madness; but as your complain so much of the cold already, I would have you stay below. I will certainly return to you within an hour."—"Pardon me, sir," cries Partridge; "I have determined to follow you wherever you go." Indeed he was now afraid to stay behind; for though he was coward enough in all respects, yet his chief fear was that of ghosts, with which the present time of night, and the wildness of the place, extremely well suited.

At this instant Partridge espied a glimmering light through some trees, which seemed very near to them. He immediately cried out in a rapture, "Oh, sir! Heaven hath at last heard my prayers, and hath brought us to a house; perhaps it may be an inn. Let me beseech you, sir, if you have any compassion either for me or yourself, do not despise the goodness of Providence, but let us go directly to yon light. Whether it be a public-house or no, I am sure if they be Christians that dwell there, they will not refuse a little house-room to persons in our miserable condition." Jones at length yielded to the earnest supplications of Partridge, and both together made directly towards the place whence the light issued.

They soon arrived at the door of this house, or cottage, for it might be called either, without much impropriety. Here Jones knocked several times without receiving any answer from within; at which Partridge, whose head was full of nothing but of ghosts, devils, witches, and such like,

began to tremble, crying, "Lord have mercy upon
'us! surely the people must be all dead. I can
see no light neither now, and yet I am certain I
saw a candle burning but a moment before.—
Well! I have heard of such things."—"What
hast thou heard of?" said Jones. "The people
are either fast asleep, or probably, as this is a
lonely place, are afraid to open their door." He
then began to vociferate pretty loudly, and at
last an old woman, opening an upper casement,
asked, Who they were, and what they wanted?
Jones answered, They were travelers who had
lost their way, and having seen a light in the
window, had been led thither in hopes of finding
some fire to warm themselves. "Whoever you
are," cries the woman, "you have no business
here; nor shall I open the door to any one at
this time of night." Partridge, whom the sound
of a human voice had recovered from his fright,
fell to the most earnest supplications to be admitted for a few minutes to the fire, saying, he
was almost dead with the cold; to which fear had
indeed contributed equally with the frost. He
assured her that the gentleman who spoke to her
was one of the greatest squires in the country;
and made use of every argument, save one, which
Jones afterwards effectually added; and this was,
the promise of half-a-crown;—a bribe too great
to be resisted by such a person, especially as the
genteel appearance of Jones, which the light of
the moon plainly discovered to her, together with
his affable behavior, had entirely subdued those
apprehensions of thieves which she had at first

conceived. She agreed therefore, at last, to let them in; where Partridge, to his infinite joy, found a good fire ready for his reception.

The poor fellow, however, had no sooner warmed himself, than those thoughts which were always uppermost in his mind, began a little to disturb his brain. There was no article of his creed in which he had a stronger faith than he had in witchcraft, nor can the reader conceive a figure more adapted to inspire this idea, than the old woman who now stood before him. She answered exactly to that picture drawn by Otway in his Orphan. Indeed, if this woman had lived in the reign of James the First, her appearance alone would have hanged her, almost without any evidence.

Many circumstances likewise conspired to confirm Partridge in his opinion. Her living, as he then imagined, by herself in so lonely a place; and in a house, the outside of which seemed much too good for her, but its inside was furnished in the most neat and elegant manner. To say the truth, Jones himself was not a little surprised at what he saw; for, besides the extraordinary neatness of the room, it was adorned with a great number of nicknacks and curiosities, which might have engaged the attention of a virtuoso.

While Jones was admiring these things, and Partridge sat trembling with the firm belief that he was in the house of a witch, the old woman said, ''I hope, gentlemen, you will make what haste you can; for I expect my master presently, and I would not for double the money he should

find you here."—"Then you have a master?"
cries Jones. "Indeed, you will excuse me, good
woman, but I was surprised to see all those fine
things in your house."—"Ah, sir," said she, "if
the twentieth part of these things were mine, I
should think myself a rich woman. But pray,
sir, do not stay much longer, for I look for him in
every minute."—"Why, sure he would not be
angry with you," said Jones, "for doing a common act of charity?"—"Alack-a-day, sir!" said
she, "he is a strange man, not at all like other
people. He keeps no company with anybody, and
seldom walks out but by night, for he doth not
care to be seen; and all the country people are as
much afraid of meeting him; for his dress is
enough to frighten those who are not used to it.
They call him, the Man of the Hill (for there he
walks by night), and the country people are not,
I believe, more afraid of the devil himself. He
would be terribly angry if he found you here."—
"Pray, sir," says Partridge, "don't let us offend
the gentleman; I am ready to walk, and was
never warmer in my life. Do pray, sir, let us
go. Here are pistols over the chimney: who
knows whether they be charged or no, or what
he may do with them?"—"Fear nothing, Partridge," cries Jones; "I will secure thee from
danger."—"Nay, for matter o' that, he never
doth any mischief," said the woman; "but to be
sure it is necessary he should keep some arms
for his own safety; for his house hath been beset
more than once; and it is not many nights ago
that we thought we heard thieves about it: for

my own part, I have often wondered that he is not
murdered by some villain or other, as he walks
out by himself at such hours; but then, as I said,
the people are afraid of him; and besides, they
think, I suppose, he hath nothing about him worth
taking.''—''I should imagine, by this collection of
rarities,'' cries Jones, ''that your master had
been a traveler.''—''Yes, sir,'' answered she,
''he hath been a very great one: there be few
gentlemen that know more of all matters than
he. I fancy he hath been crossed in love, or whatever it is I know not; but I have lived with him
above these thirty years, and in all that time he
hath hardly spoke to six living people.'' She
then again solicited their departure, in which she
was backed by Partridge; but Jones purposely
protracted the time, for his curiosity was greatly
raised to see this extraordinary person. Though
the old woman, therefore, concluded every one of
her answers with desiring him to be gone, and
Partridge proceeded so far as to pull him by the
sleeve, he still continued to invent new questions,
till the old woman with an affrighted countenance,
declared she heard her master's signal; and at
the same instant more than one voice was heard
without the door, crying, ''D—n your blood, show
us your money this instant. Your money, you
villain, or we will blow your brains about your
ears.''

''O, good heaven!'' cries the old woman, ''some
villains, to be sure, have attacked my master. O
la! what shall I do? what shall I do?''—''How!''
cries Jones, ''how!—Are these pistols loaded?''

II—17

—"O, good sir, there is nothing in them, indeed. O pray don't murder us, gentlemen!" (for in reality she now had the same opinion of those within as she had of those without). Jones made her no answer; but snatching an old broad sword which hung in the room, he instantly sallied out, where he found the old gentleman struggling with two ruffians, and begging for mercy. Jones asked no questions, but fell so briskly to work with his broad sword, that the fellows immediately quitted their hold; and without offering to attack our hero, betook themselves to their heels and made their escape; for he did not attempt to pursue them, being contented with having delivered the old gentleman; and indeed he concluded he had pretty well done their business, for both of them, as they ran off, cried out with bitter oaths that they were dead men.

Jones presently ran to lift up the old gentleman, who had been thrown down in the scuffle, expressing at the same time great concern lest he should have received any harm from the villains. The old man stared a moment at Jones, and then cried, "No, sir, no, I have very little harm, I thank you. Lord have mercy upon me!"—"I see, sir," said Jones, "you are not free from apprehensions even of those who have had the happiness to be your delivers; nor can I blame any suspicions which you may have; but indeed you have no real occasion for any; here are none but your friends present. Having missed our way this cold night, we took the liberty of warming ourselves at your fire, whence we were just departing when we heard you call for assistance, which, I must say, Providence alone seems to have sent you."—"Providence, indeed," cries the old gentleman, "if it be so."—"So it is, I assure you," cries Jones. "Here is your own sword, sir; I have used it in your defense, and I now return it into your hand." The old man having received the sword, which was stained with the blood of his enemies, looked steadfastly at Jones during some moments, and then with a sigh cried out, "You will pardon me, young gentleman; I was not always of a suspicious temper, nor am I a friend to ingratitude."

"Be thankful then," cries Jones, "to that Providence to which you owe your deliverance: as to my part, I have only discharged the common duties of humanity, and what I would have done for any fellow-creature in your situation."— "Let me look at you a little longer," cries the old gentleman. "You are a human creature then? Well, perhaps you are. Come pray walk into my little hut. You have been my deliverer indeed."

The old woman was distracted between the fears which she had of her master, and for him; and Partridge was, if possible, in a greater fright. The former of these, however, when she heard her master speak kindly to Jones, and perceived what had happened, came again to herself; but Partridge no sooner saw the gentleman, than the strangeness of his dress infused greater terrors into that poor fellow than he had before felt, either from the strange description which he had

heard, or from the uproar which had happened at
the door.

To say the truth, it was an appearance which
might have affected a more constant mind than
that of Mr. Partridge. This person was of the
tallest size, with a long beard as white as snow.
His body was clothed with the skin of an ass, made
something into the form of a coat. He wore likewise boots on his legs, and a cap on his head,
both composed of the skin of some other animals.

As soon as the old gentleman came into his
house, the old woman began her congratulations
on his happy escape from the ruffians. "Yes,"
cried he, "I have escaped, indeed, thanks to my
preserver."—"O the blessing on him!" answered
she: "he is a good gentleman, I warrant him. I
was afraid your worship would have been angry
with me for letting him in; and to be certain
I should not have done it, had not I seen by the
moon-light, that he was a gentleman, and almost
frozen to death. And to be certain it must have
been some good angel that sent him hither, and
tempted me to do it."

"I am afraid, sir," said the old gentleman to
Jones, "that I have nothing in this house which
you can either eat or drink, unless you will accept a dram of brandy; of which I can give you
some most excellent, and which I have had by me
these thirty years." Jones declined this offer in
a very civil and proper speech, and then the
other asked him, "Whither he was traveling
when he missed his way?" saying, "I must own
myself surprised to see such a person as you

appear to be, journeying on foot at this time of night. I suppose, sir, you are a gentleman of these parts; for you do not look like one who is used to travel far without horses?"

"Appearances," cried Jones, "are often deceitful; men sometimes look what they are not. I assure you I am not of this country; and whither I am traveling, in reality I scarce know myself."

"Whoever you are, or whithersoever you are going," answered the old man, "I have obligations to you which I can never return."

"I once more," replied Jones, "affirm that you have none; for there can be no merit in having hazarded that in your service on which I set no value; and nothing is so contemptible in my eyes as life."

"I am sorry, young gentleman," answered the stranger, "that you have any reason to be so unhappy at your years."

"Indeed I am, sir," answered Jones, "the most unhappy of mankind."—"Perhaps you have had a friend or a mistress?" replied the other. "How could you," cries Jones, "mention two words sufficient to drive me to distraction?"—"Either of them are enough to drive any man to distraction," answered the old man. "I enquire no farther, sir; perhaps my curiosity hath led me too far already."

"Indeed, sir," cries Jones, "I cannot censure a passion which I feel at this instant in the highest degree. You will pardon me when I assure you, that everything which I have seen or heard since I first entered this house hath conspired to raise the greatest curiosity in me. Something very extraordinary must have determined you to this course of life, and I have reason to fear your own history is not without misfortunes."

Here the old gentleman again sighed, and remained silent for some minutes: at last, looking earnestly on Jones, he said, "I have read that a good countenance is a letter of recommendation; if so, none ever can be more strongly recommended than yourself. If I did not feel some yearnings towards you from another consideration, I must be the most ungrateful monster upon earth; and I am really concerned it is no otherwise in my power than by words to convince you of my gratitude."

Jones after a moment's hesitation, answered, "That it was in his power by words to gratify him extremely. I have confessed a curiosity," said he, "sir; need I say how much obliged I should be to you, if you would condescend to gratify it? Will you suffer me therefore to beg, unless any consideration restrains you, that you would be pleased to acquaint me what motives have induced you thus to withdraw from the society of mankind, and to betake yourself to a course of life to which it sufficiently appears you were not born?"

"I scarce think myself at liberty to refuse you anything after what hath happened," replied the old man. "If you desire therefore to hear the story of an unhappy man, I will relate it to you. Indeed you judge rightly, in thinking there is commonly something extraordinary in the fortunes of those who fly from society; for however it may seem a paradox, or even a contradiction, certain it is, that great philanthropy chiefly inclines us to avoid and detest mankind; not on account so much of their private and selfish vices, but for those of a relative kind; such as envy, malice, treachery, cruelty, with every other species of malevolence. These are the vices which true philanthropy abhors, and which rather than see and converse with, she avoids society itself. However, without a compliment to you, you do not appear to me one of those whom I should shun or detest; nay, I must say, in what little hath dropped from you, there appears some parity in our fortunes: I hope, however, yours will conclude more successfully.''

Here some compliments passed between our hero and his host, and then the latter was going to begin his history, when Partridge interrupted him. His apprehensions had now pretty well left him, but some effects of his terrors remained; he therefore reminded the gentleman of that excellent brandy which he had mentioned. This was presently brought, and Partridge swallowed a large bumper.

The gentleman then, without any farther preface began as you may read in the next chapter.

CHAPTER XI

"I WAS born in a village of Somersetshire, called Mark, in the year 1657. My father was one of those whom they call gentlemen farmers. He had a little estate of about £300 a year of his own, and rented another estate of near the same value. He was prudent and industrious, and so good a husbandman, that he might have led a very easy and comfortable life, had not an arrant vixen of a wife soured his domestic quiet. But though this circumstance perhaps made him miserable, it did not make him poor; for he confined her almost entirely at home, and rather chose to bear eternal upbraidings in his own house, than to injure his fortune by indulging her in the extravagances she desired abroad.

"By this Xanthippe" (so was the wife of Socrates called, said Partridge)—"by this Xanthippe he had two sons, of which I was the younger. He designed to give us both good education; but my elder brother, who, unhappily for him, was the favorite of my mother, utterly neglected his learning; insomuch that, after having been five or six years at school with little or no improvement, my father, being told by his master that it would be to no purpose to keep him longer there, at last complied with my mother in taking him

264

home from the hands of that tyrant, as she called
his master; though indeed he gave the lad much
less correction than his idleness deserved, but
much more, it seems, than the young gentleman
liked, who constantly complained to his mother
of his severe treatment, and she as constantly
gave him a hearing.''

''Yes, yes,'' cries Partridge, ''I have seen such
mothers; I have been abused myself by them, and
very unjustly; such parents deserve correction as
much as their children.''

Jones chid the pedagogue for his interruption,
and then the stranger proceeded.

''My brother now, at the age of fifteen, bade
adieu to all learning, and to everything else but
to his dog and gun; with which latter he became
so expert, that, though perhaps you may think it
incredible, he could not only hit a standing mark
with great certainty, but hath actually shot a
crow as it was flying in the air. He was likewise
excellent at finding a hare sitting, and was soon
reputed one of the best sportsmen in the country;
a reputation which both he and his mother enjoyed as much as if he had been thought the finest
scholar.

''The situation of my brother made me at
first think my lot the harder, in being continued
at school: but I soon changed my opinion; for as
I advanced pretty fast in learning, my labors became easy, and my exercise so delightful, that
holidays were my most unpleasant time; for my
mother, who never loved me, now apprehending
that I had the greater share of my father's affec-

tion, and finding, or at least thinking, that I was more taken notice of by some gentlemen of learning, and particularly by the parson of the parish, than my brother, she now hated my sight, and made home so disagreeable to me, that what is called by school-boys Black Monday, was to me the whitest in the whole year.

"Having at length gone through the school at Taunton, I was thence removed to Exeter College in Oxford, where I remained four years; at the end of which an accident took me off entirely from my studies; and hence I may truly date the rise of all which happened to me afterwards in life.

"There was at the same college with myself one Sir George Gresham, a young fellow who was entitled to a very considerable fortune, which he was not, by the will of his father, to come into full possession of till he arrived at the age of twenty-five. However, the liberality of his guardians gave him little cause to regret the abundant caution of his father; for they allowed him five hundred pounds a year while he remained at the university, where he kept his horses and his whore, and lived as wicked and as profligate a life as he could have done had he been never so entirely master of his fortune; for besides the five hundred a year which he received from his guardians, he found means to spend a thousand more. He was above the age of twenty-one, and had no difficulty in gaining what credit he pleased.

"This young fellow, among many other tolerable bad qualities, had one very diabolical. He had a great delight in destroying and ruining

the youth of inferior fortune, by drawing them
into expenses which they could not afford so well
as himself; and the better, and worthier, and
soberer any young man was, the greater pleasure
and triumph had he in his destruction. Thus
acting the character which is recorded of the
devil, and going about seeking whom he might devour.

"It was my misfortune to fall into an acquaintance and intimacy with this gentleman. My
reputation of diligence in my studies made me
a desirable object of his mischievous intention;
and my own inclination made it sufficiently easy
for him to effect his purpose; for though I had
applied myself with much industry to books, in
which I took great delight, there were other pleasures in which I was capable of taking much
greater; for I was high-mettled, had a violent flow
of animal spirits, was a little ambitious, and extremely amorous.

"I had not long contracted an intimacy with
Sir George before I became a partaker of all his
pleasures; and when I was once entered on that
scene, neither my inclination nor my spirit would
suffer me to play an under part. I was second to
none of the company in any acts of debauchery;
nay, I soon distinguished myself so notably in
all riots and disorders, that my name generally
stood first in the roll of delinquents; and instead
of being lamented as the unfortunate pupil of
Sir George, I was now accused as the person who
had misled and debauched that hopeful young
gentleman; for though he was the ringleader and

promoter of all the mischief, he was never so considered. I fell at last under the censure of the vice-chancellor, and very narrowly escaped expulsion.

"You will easily believe, sir, that such a life as I am now describing must be incompatible with my further progress in learning; and that in proportion as I addicted myself more and more to loose pleasure, I must grow more and more remiss in application to my studies. This was truly the consequence; but this was not all. My expenses now greatly exceeded not only my former income, but those additions which I extorted from my poor generous father, on pretenses of sums being necessary for preparing for my approaching degree of bachelor of arts. These demands, however, grew at last so frequent and exorbitant, that my father by slow degrees opened his ears to the accounts which he received from many quarters of my present behavior, and which my mother failed not to echo very faithfully and loudly; adding, 'Ay, this is the fine gentleman, the scholar who doth so much honor to his family, and is to be the making of it. I thought what all this learning would come to. He is to be the ruin of us all, I find, after his elder brother hath been denied necessaries for his sake, to perfect his education forsooth, for which he was to pay us such interest: I thought what the interest would come to,' with much more of the same kind; but I have, I believe, satisfied you with this taste.

"My father, therefore, began now to return re-monstrances instead of money to my demands, which brought my affairs perhaps a little sooner to a crisis; but had he remitted me his whole income, you will imagine it could have sufficed a very short time to support one who kept pace with the expenses of Sir George Gresham.

"It is more than possible that the distress I was now in for money, and the impracticability of going on in this manner, might have restored me at once to my senses and to my studies, had I opened my eyes before I became involved in debts from which I saw no hopes of ever extricating myself. This was indeed the great art of Sir George, and by which he accomplished the ruin of many, whom he afterwards laughed at as fools and coxcombs, for vying, as he called it, with a man of his fortune. To bring this about, he would now and then advance a little money himself, in order to support the credit of the unfortunate youth with other people; till, by means of that very credit, he was irretrievably undone.

"My mind being by these means grown as desperate as my fortune, there was scarce a wickedness which I did not meditate, in order for my relief. Self-murder itself became the subject of my serious deliberation; and I had certainly resolved on it, had not a more shameful, though perhaps less sinful, thought expelled it from my head."—Here he hesitated a moment, and then cried out, "I protest, so many years have not washed away the shame of this act, and I shall blush while I relate it." Jones desired him to pass over anything that might give him pain in

the relation; but Partridge eagerly cried out
"Oh, pray, sir, let us hear this; I had rather hear
this than all the rest; as I hope to be saved, I will
never mention a word of it." Jones was going
to rebuke him, but the stranger prevented it by
proceeding thus: "I had a chum, a very prudent,
frugal young lad, who, though he had no very large
allowance, had by his parsimony heaped up upwards of forty guineas, which I knew he kept in
his escritoire. I took therefore an opportunity of
purloining his key from his breeches-pocket, while
he was asleep, and thus made myself master of all
his riches: after which I again conveyed his key
into his pocket and counterfeiting sleep—though
I never once closed my eyes, lay in bed till after
he arose and went to prayers—an exercise to
which I had long been unaccustomed.

"Timorous thieves, by extreme caution, often
subject themselves to discoveries, which those of
a bolder kind escape. Thus it happened to me;
for had I boldly broken open his escritoire, I had,
perhaps, escaped even his suspicion; but as it
was plain that the person who robbed him had
possessed himself of his key, he had no doubt,
when he first missed his money, but that his chum
was certainly the thief. Now as he was of a fear-
ful disposition, and much my inferior in strength,
and I believe in courage, he did not dare to con-
front me with my guilt, for fear of worse bodily
consequences which might happen to him. He
repaired therefore immediately to the vice-chancellor, and upon swearing to the robbery, and to
the circumstances of it, very easily obtained a

warrant against one who had now so bad a character through the whole university.

"Luckily for me, I lay out of the college the next evening; for that day I attended a young lady in a chaise to Witney, where we stayed all night, and in our return, the next morning, to Oxford, I met one of my cronies, who acquainted me with sufficient news concerning myself to make me turn my horse another way."

"Pray, sir, did he mention anything of the warrant?" said Partridge. But Jones begged the gentleman to proceed without regarding any impertinent questions; which he did as follows:—

"Having now abandoned all thoughts of returning to Oxford, the next thing which offered itself was a journey to London. I imparted this intention to my female companion, who at first remonstrated against it; but upon producing my wealth, she immediately consented. We then struck across the country, into the great Cirencester road, and made such haste, that we spent the next evening, save one, in London.

"When you consider the place where I now was, and the company with whom I was, you will, I fancy, conceive that a very short time brought me to an end of that sum of which I had so iniquitously possessed myself.

"I was now reduced to a much higher degree of distress than before: the necessaries of life began to be numbered among my wants; and what made my case still the more grievous was, that my paramour, of whom I was now grown immoderately fond, shared the same distresses with myself. To see a woman you love in distress; to be unable to relieve her, and at the same time to reflect that you have brought her into this situation, is perhaps a curse of which no imagination can represent the horrors to those who have not felt it.''—''I believe it from my soul,'' cries Jones, ''and I pity you from the bottom of my heart:'' he then took two or three disorderly turns about the room, and at last begged pardon, and flung himself into his chair, crying, ''I thank Heaven, I have escaped that!''

''This circumstance,'' continued the gentleman, ''so severely aggravated the horrors of my present situation, that they became absolutely intolerable. I could with less pain endure the raging in my own natural unsatisfied appetites, even hunger or thirst, than I could submit to leave ungratified the most whimsical desires of a woman on whom I so extravagantly doted, that, though I knew she had been the mistress of half my acquaintance, I firmly intended to marry her. But the good creature was unwilling to consent to an action which the world might think so much to my disadvantage. And as, possibly, she compassionated the daily anxieties which she must have perceived me suffer on her account, she resolved to put an end to my distress. She soon, indeed, found means to relieve me from my troublesome and perplexed situation; for while I was distracted with various inventions to supply her with pleasures, she very kindly—betrayed me to one of her former lovers at Oxford, by whose care and diligence I was immediately apprehended and committed to jail.

"Here I first began seriously to reflect on the miscarriages of my former life; on the errors I had been guilty of; on the misfortunes which I had brought on myself; and on the grief which I must have occasioned to one of the best of fathers. When I added to all these the perfidy of my mistress, such was the horror of my mind, that life, instead of being longer desirable, grew the object of my abhorrence; and I could have gladly embraced death as my dearest friend, if it had offered itself to my choice unattended by shame.

"The time of the assizes soon come, and I was removed by habeas corpus to Oxford, where I expected certain conviction and condemnation; but, to my great surprise, none appeared against me, and I was, at the end of the session, discharged for want of prosecution. In short, my chum had left Oxford, and whether from indolence, or from what other motive I am ignorant, had declined concerning himself any farther in the affair."

"Perhaps," cries Partridge, "he did not care to have your blood upon his hands; and he was in the right on't. If any person was to be hanged upon my evidence, I should never be able to lie alone afterwards, for fear of seeing his ghost."

"I shall shortly doubt, Partridge," says Jones, "whether thou art more brave or wise."—"You may laugh at me, sir, if you please," answered Partridge; "but if you will hear a very short

II—18

story which I can tell, and which is most certainly true, perhaps you may change your opinion. In the parish where I was born——'' Here Jones would have silenced him; but the stranger interceded that he might be permitted to tell his story, and in the meantime promised to recollect the remainder of his own.

Partridge then proceeded thus: ''In the parish where I was born, there lived a farmer whose name was Bridle, and he had a son named Francis, a good hopeful young fellow: I was at the grammar-school with him, where I remember he was got into Ovid's Epistles, and he could construe you three lines together sometimes without looking into a dictionary. Besides all this, he was a very good lad, never missed church o' Sundays, and was reckoned one of the best psalm-singers in the whole parish. He would indeed now and then take a cup too much, and that was the only fault he had.''—''Well, but come to the ghost,'' cries Jones. ''Never fear, sir; I shall come to him soon enough,'' answered Partridge. ''You must know, then, that farmer Bridle lost a mare, a sorrel one, to the best of my remembrance; and so it fell out that this young Francis shortly afterward being at a fair at Hindon, and as I think it was on——, I can't remember the day; and being as he was, what should he happen to meet but a man upon his father's mare. Frank called out presently, Stop thief; and it being in the middle of the fair, it was impossible, you know, for the man to make his escape. So they apprehended him and carried him before the justice: I remem-

ber it was Justice Willoughby, of Noyle, a very
worthy good gentleman; and he committed him
to prison, and bound Frank in a recognizance, I
think they call it—a hard word compounded of
re and *cognosco;* but it differs in its meaning from
the use of the simple, as many other compounds
do. Well, at last down came my Lord Justice
Page to hold the assizes; and so the fellow was
had up, and Frank was had up for a witness. To
be sure, I shall never forget the face of the judge,
when he began to ask him what he had to say
against the prisoner. He made poor Frank tremble and shake in his shoes. 'Well you, fellow,'
says my lord, 'what have you to say? Don't
stand humming and hawing, but speak out.' But
however, he soon turned altogether as civil
to Frank, and began to thunder at the fellow;
and when he asked him if he had anything to say
for himself, the fellow said, he had found the
horse. 'Ay!' answered the judge, 'thou art a
lucky fellow: I have traveled the circuit these
forty years, and never found a horse in my life:
but I'll tell thee what, friend, thou wast more lucky
than thou didst know of; for thou didst not only
find a horse, but a halter too, I promise thee.' To
be sure, I shall never forget the word. Upon
which everybody fell a laughing, as how could
they help it? Nay, and twenty other jests he
made, which I can't remember now. There was
something about his skill in horse-flesh which
made all the folks laugh. To be certain, the judge
must have been a very brave man, as well as a
man of much learning. It is indeed charming

sport to hear trials upon life and death. One
thing I own I thought a little hard, that the prisoner's counsel was not suffered to speak for him,
though he desired only to be heard one very
short word, but my lord would not hearken to him,
though he suffered a counselor to talk against
him for above half-an-hour. I thought it hard, I
own, that there should be so many of them; my
lord, and the court, and the jury, and the coun-
selors, and the witnesses, all upon one poor man,
and he too in chains. Well, the fellow was
hanged, as to be sure it could be no otherwise, and
poor Frank could never be easy about it. He
never was in the dark alone, but he fancied he
saw the fellow's spirit."—"Well, and is this thy
story?" cries Jones. "No, no," answered Partridge. "O Lord have mercy upon me! I am
just now coming to the matter; for one night,
coming from the alehouse, in a long, narrow, dark
lane, there he ran directly up against him; and
the spirit was all in white, and fell upon Frank;
and Frank, who was a sturdy lad, fell upon the
spirit again, and there they had a tussle together,
and poor Frank was dreadfully beat: indeed he
made a shift at last to crawl home; but what with
the beating, and what with the fright, he lay ill
about a fortnight; and all this is most certainly
true, and the whole parish will bear witness to it."

The stranger smiled at this story, and Jones
burst into a loud fit of laughter; upon which
Partridge cried, "Ay, you may laugh, sir; and
so did some others, particularly a squire, who is
thought to be no better than an atheist; who, for-

sooth, because there was a calf with a white face found dead in the same lane the next morning, would fain have it that the battle was between Frank and that, as if a calf would set upon a man. Besides, Frank told me he knew it to be a spirit, and could swear to him in any court in Christendom; and he had not drank above a quart or two or such a matter of liquor, at the time. Lud have mercy upon us, and keep us all from dipping our hands in blood, I say!''

''Well, sir,'' said Jones to the stranger, ''Mr. Partridge hath finished his story, and I hope will give you no future interruption, if you will be so kind to proceed.'' He then resumed his narration; but as he hath taken breath for a while, we think proper to give it to our reader, and shall therefore put an end to this chapter.

CHAPTER XII

In which the Man of the Hill continues his history.

"I HAD now regained my liberty," said the stranger; "but I had lost my reputation; for there is a wide difference between the case of a man who is barely acquitted of a crime in a court of justice, and of him who is acquitted in his own heart, and in the opinion of the people. I was conscious of my guilt, and ashamed to look any one in the face; so resolved to leave Oxford the next morning, before the daylight discovered me to the eyes of any beholders.

"When I had got clear of the city, it first entered into my head to return home to my father, and endeavor to obtain his forgiveness; but as I had no reason to doubt his knowledge of all which had passed, and as I was well assured of his great aversion to all acts of dishonesty, I could entertain no hopes of being received by him, especially since I was too certain of all the good offices in the power of my mother; nay, had my father's pardon been as sure, as I conceived his resentment to be, I yet question whether I could have had the assurance to behold him, or whether I could, upon any terms, have submitted to live and converse with those who, I was convinced, knew me to have been guilty of so base an action.

"I hastened therefore back to London, the best

278

retirement of either grief or shame, unless for
persons of a very public character; for here you
have the advantage of solitude without its disadvantage, since you may be alone and in company
at the same time; and while you walk or sit unobserved, noise, hurry, and a constant succession
of objects, entertain the mind, and prevent the
spirits from preying on themselves, or rather on
grief or shame, which are the most unwholesome
diet in the world; and on which (though there are
many who never taste either but in public) there
are some who can feed very plentifully and very
fatally when alone.

"But as there is scarce any human good without its concomitant evil, so there are people who
find an inconvenience in this unobserving temper
of mankind; I mean persons who have no money;
for as you are not put out of countenance, so
neither are you clothed or fed by those who do
not know you. And a man may be as easily
starved in Leadenhall-market as in the deserts of
Arabia.

"It was at present my fortune to be destitute of
that great evil, as it is apprehended to be by several writers, who I suppose were overburdened
with it, namely, money."—"With submission,
sir," said Partridge, "I do not remember any
writers who have called it *malorum;* but *irritamenta malorum. Effodiuntur opes, irritamenta
malorum.*"—"Well, sir," continued the stranger,
"whether it be an evil, or only the cause of evil,
I was entirely void of it, and at the same time of
friends, and, as I thought, of acquaintance; when

one evening, as I was passing through the Inner Temple, very hungry, and very miserable, I heard a voice on a sudden hailing me with great familiarity by my Christian name; and upon my turning about, I presently recollected the person who so saluted me to have been my fellow-collegiate; one who had left the university above a year, and long before any of my misfortunes had befallen me. This gentleman, whose name was Watson, shook me heartily by the hand; and expressing great joy at meeting me, proposed our immediately drinking a bottle together. I first declined the proposal, and pretended business, but as he was very earnest and pressing, hunger at last overcame my pride, and I fairly confessed to him I had no money in my pocket; yet not without framing a lie for an excuse, and imputing it to my having changed my breeches that morning. Mr. Watson answered, 'I thought, Jack, you and I had been too old acquaintance for you to mention such a matter.' He then took me by the arm, and was pulling me along; but I gave him very little trouble, for my own inclinations pulled me much stronger than he could do.

"We then went into the Friars, which you know is the scene of all mirth and jollity. Here, when we arrived at the tavern, Mr. Watson applied himself to the drawer only, without taking the least notice of the cook; for he had no suspicion but that I had dined long since. However, as the case was really otherwise, I forged another falsehood, and told my companion I had been at the further end of the city on business of consequence,

and had snapped up a mutton-chop in haste; so
that I was again hungry, and wished he would add
a beef-steak to his bottle."—"Some people,"
cries Partridge, "ought to have good memories;
or did you find just money enough in your
breeches to pay for the mutton-chop?"—"Your
observation is right," answered the stranger,
"and I believe such blunders are inseparable from
all dealing in untruth.—But to proceed—I began
now to feel myself extremely happy. The meat
and wine soon revived my spirits to a high pitch,
and I enjoyed much pleasure in the conversation
of my old acquaintance, the rather as I thought
him entirely ignorant of what had happened at the
university since his leaving it.

"But he did not suffer me to remain long in
this agreeable delusion; for taking a bumper in
one hand, and holding me by the other, 'Here, my
boy,' cries he, 'here's wishing you joy of your
being so honorably acquitted of that affair laid
to your charge.' I was thunderstruck with confusion at those words, which Watson observing,
proceeded thus: 'Nay, never be ashamed, man;
thou hast been acquitted, and no one now dares
call thee guilty; but, prithee, do tell me, who am
thy friend—I hope thou didst really rob him? for
rat me if it was not a meritorious action to strip
such a sneaking, pitiful rascal; and instead of the
two hundred guineas, I wish you had taken as
many thousand. Come, come, my boy, don't be
shy of confessing to me: you are not now brought
before one of the pimps. D—n me if I don't
honor you for it; for, as I hope for salvation, I

would have made no manner of scruple of doing the same thing.'

"This declaration a little relieved my abashment; and as wine had now somewhat opened my heart, I very freely acknowledged the robbery, but acquainted him that he had been misinformed as to the sum taken, which was little more than a fifth part of what he had mentioned.

" 'I am sorry for it with all my heart,' quoth he, 'and I wish thee better success another time. Though, if you will take my advice, you shall have no occasion to run any such risk. Here,' said he, taking some dice out of his pocket, 'here's the stuff. Here are the implements; here are the little doctors which cure the distempers of the purse. Follow but my counsel, and I will show you a way to empty the pocket of a queer cull without any danger of the nubbing cheat.' "

"Nubbing cheat!" cries Partridge: "pray, sir, what is that?"

"Why that, sir," says the stranger, "is a cant phrase for the gallows; for as gamesters differ little from highwaymen in their morals, so do they very much resemble them in their language.

"We had now each drank our bottle, when Mr. Watson said, the board was sitting, and that he must attend, earnestly pressing me at the same time to go with him and try my fortune. I answered he knew that was at present out of my power, as I had informed him of the emptiness of my pocket. To say the truth, I doubted not from his many strong expressions of friendship, but that he would offer to lend me a small sum for that purpose, but he answered, 'Never mind that, man; e'en boldly run a levant' (Partridge was going to inquire the meaning of that word, but Jones stopped his mouth): 'but be circumspect as to the man. I will tip you the proper person, which may be necessary, as you do not know the town, nor can distinguish a rum cull from a queer one.'

"The bill was now brought, when Watson paid his share, and was departing. I reminded him, not without blushing, of my having no money. He answered, 'That signifies nothing; score it behind the door, or make a bold brush and take no notice.—Or—stay,' says he; 'I will go downstairs first, and then do you take up my money, and score the whole reckoning at the bar, and I will wait for you at the corner.' I expressed some dislike at this, and hinted my expectations that he would have deposited the whole; but he swore he had not another sixpence in his pocket.

"He then went down, and I was prevailed on to take up the money and follow him, which I did close enough to hear him tell the drawer the reckoning was upon the table. The drawer passed by me up-stairs; but I made such haste into the street, that I heard nothing of his disappointment, nor did I mention a syllable at the bar, according to my instructions.

"We now went directly to the gaming-table, where Mr. Watson, to my surprise, pulled out a large sum of money and placed it before him, as did many others; all of them, no doubt, considering their own heaps as so many decoy birds.

which were to entice and draw over the heaps of their neighbors.

"Here it would be tedious to relate all the freaks which Fortune, or rather the dice, played in this her temple. Mountains of gold were in a few moments reduced to nothing at one part of the table, and rose as suddenly in another. The rich grew in a moment poor, and the poor as suddenly became rich; so that it seemed a philosopher could nowhere have so well instructed his pupils in the contempt of riches, at least he could nowhere have better inculcated the uncertainty of their duration.

"For my own part, after having considerably improved my small estate, I at last entirely demolished it. Mr. Watson too, after much variety of luck, rose from the table in some heat, and declared he had lost a cool hundred, and would play no longer. Then coming up to me, he asked me to return with him to the tavern; but I positively refused, saying, I would not bring myself a second time into such a dilemma, and especially as he had lost all his money and was now in my own condition. 'Pooh!' says he, 'I have just borrowed a couple of guineas of a friend, and one of them is at your service.' He immediately put one of them into my hand, and I no longer resisted his inclination.

"I was at first a little shocked at returning to the same house whence we had departed in so unhandsome a manner; but when the drawer, with very civil address, told us, 'he believed we had forgot to pay our reckoning,' I became perfectly easy, and very readily gave him a guinea, bid him pay himself, and acquiesced in the unjust charge which had been laid on my memory.

"Mr. Watson now bespoke the most extravagant supper he could well think of; and though he had contented himself with simple claret before, nothing now but the most precious Burgundy would serve his purpose.

"Our company was soon increased by the addition of several gentlemen from the gaming-table; most of whom, as I afterwards found, came not to the tavern to drink, but in the way of business; for the true gamesters pretended to be ill, and refused their glass, while they piled heartily two young fellows, who were to be afterwards pillaged, as indeed they were without mercy. Of this plunder I had the good fortune to be a sharer, though I was not yet let into the secret.

"There was one remarkable accident attended this tavern play; for the money by degrees totally disappeared; so that though at the beginning the table was half covered with gold, yet before the play ended, which it did not till the next day, being Sunday, at noon, there was scarce a single guinea to be seen on the table; and this was the stranger as every person present, except myself, declared he had lost; and what was become of the money, unless the devil himself carried it away, is difficult to determine."

"Most certainly he did," says Partridge, "for evil spirits can carry away anything without being seen, though there were never so many folk

in the room; and I should not have been surprised
if he had carried away all the company of a set
of wicked wretches, who were at play in sermon
time. And I could tell you a true story, if I
would, where the devil took a man out of bed from
another man's wife, and carried him away
through the keyhole of the door. I've seen the
very house where it was done, and nobody hath
lived in it these thirty years."

Though Jones was a little offended by the impertinence of Partridge, he could not however
avoid smiling at his simplicity. The stranger did
the same, and then proceeded with his story, as
will be seen in the next chapter.

CHAPTER XIII

In which the foregoing story is farther continued.

"MY fellow-collegiate had now entered me in a new scene of life. I soon became acquainted with the whole fraternity of sharpers, and was let into their secrets; I mean, into the knowledge of those gross cheats which are proper to impose upon the raw and unexperienced; for there are some tricks of a finer kind, which are known only to a few of the gang, who are at the head of their profession; a degree of honor beyond my expectation; for drink, to which I was immoderately addicted, and the natural warmth of my passions, prevented me from arriving at any great success in an art which requires as much coolness as the most austere school of philosophy.

"Mr. Watson, with whom I now lived in the closest amity, had unluckily the former failing to a very great excess; so that instead of making a fortune by his profession, as some others did, he was alternately rich and poor, and was often obliged to surrender to his cooler friends, over a bottle which they never tasted, that plunder that he had taken from culls at the public table.

"However, we both made a shift to pick up an uncomfortable livelihood; and for two years I continued of the calling; during which time I tasted all the varieties of fortune, sometimes flourishing in affluence, and at others being obliged to struggle with almost incredible difficulties. Today wallowing in luxury, and to-morrow reduced to the coarsest and most homely fare. My fine clothes being often on my back in the evening, and at the pawn-shop the next morning.

"One night, as I was returning penniless from the gaming-table, I observed a very great disturbance, and a large mob gathered together in the street. As I was in no danger from pick-pockets, I ventured into the crowd, where upon inquiry I found that a man had been robbed and very ill used by some ruffians. The wounded man appeared very bloody, and seemed scarce able to support himself on his legs. As I had not there-fore been deprived of my humanity by my present life and conversation, though they had left me very little of either honesty or shame, I imme-diately offered my assistance to the unhappy per-son, who thankfully accepted it, and, putting him-self under my conduct, begged me to convey him to some tavern, where he might send for a sur-geon, being, as he said, faint with loss of blood. He seemed indeed highly pleased at finding one who appeared in the dress of a gentleman; for as to all the rest of the company present, their out-side was such that he could not wisely place any confidence in them.

"I took the poor man by the arm, and led him to the tavern where we kept our rendezvous, as it happened to be the nearest at hand. A sur-geon happening luckily to be in the house, immediately attended, and applied himself to dressing his wounds, which I had the pleasure to hear were not likely to be mortal.

"The surgeon having very expeditiously and dextrously finished his business, began to inquire in what part of the town the wounded man lodged; who answered, 'That he was come to town that very morning; that his horse was at an inn in Piccadilly, and that he had no other lodging, and very little or no acquaintance in town.'

"This surgeon, whose name I have forgot, though I remember it began with an R, had the first character in his profession, and was ser- geant-surgeon to the king. He had moreover many good qualities, and was a very generous good-natured man, and ready to do any service to his fellow-creatures. He offered his patient the use of his chariot to carry him to his inn, and at the same time whispered in his ear, 'That if he wanted any money, he would furnish him.'

"The poor man was not now capable of return- ing thanks for this generous offer; for having had his eyes for some time steadfastly on me, he threw himself back in his chair, crying, 'Oh, my son! my son!' and then fainted away.

"Many of the people present imagined this ac- cident had happened through his loss of blood; but I, who at the same time began to recollect the features of my father, was now confirmed in my suspicion, and satisfied that it was he himself who appeared before me. I presently ran to him, raised him in my arms, and kissed his cold lips with the utmost eagerness. Here I must draw

II—19

a curtain over a scene which I cannot describe; for though I did not lose my being, as my father for a while did, my senses were however so over-powered with affright and surprise, that I am a stranger to what passed during some minutes, and indeed till my father had again recovered from his swoon, and I found myself in his arms, both tenderly embracing each other, while the tears trickled a-pace down the cheeks of each of us.

"Most of those present seemed affected by this scene, which we, who might be considered as the actors in it, were desirous of removing from the eyes of all spectators as fast as we could; my father therefore accepted the kind offer of the surgeon's chariot, and I attended him in it to his inn.

"When we were alone together, he gently up-braided me with having neglected to write to him during so long a time, but entirely omitted the mention of that crime which had occasioned it. He then informed me of my mother's death, and insisted on my returning home with him, saying, 'That he had long suffered the greatest anxiety on my account; that he knew not whether he had most feared my death or wished it, since he had so many more dreadful apprehensions for me. At last, he said, a neighboring gentleman, who had just recovered a son from the same place, in-formed him where I was; and that to reclaim me from this course of life was the sole cause of his journey to London.' He thanked Heaven he had succeeded so far as to find me out by means of an accident which had like to have proved fatal to

him; and had the pleasure to think he partly
owed his preservation to my humanity, with which
he professed himself to be more delighted than
he should have been with my filial piety, if I had
known that the object of all my care was my own
father.

"Vice had not so depraved my heart as to excite in it an insensibility of so much paternal affection, though so unworthily bestowed. I presently promised to obey his commands in my return home with him, as soon as he was able to
travel, which indeed he was in a very few days,
by the assistance of that excellent surgeon who
had undertaken his cure.

"The day preceding my father's journey (before which time I scarce ever left him), I went to
take my leave of some of my most intimate acquaintance, particularly of Mr. Watson, who dissuaded me from burying myself, as he called it,
out of a simple compliance with the fond desires
of a foolish old fellow. Such solicitations, however, had no effect, and I once more saw my own
home. My father now greatly solicited me to
think of marriage; but my inclinations were utterly averse to any such thoughts. I had tasted
of love already, and perhaps you know the extravagant excesses of that most tender and most
violent passion."——Here the old gentleman
paused, and looked earnestly at Jones; whose
countenance, within a minute's space, displayed
the extremities of both red and white. Upon
which the old man, without making any observations, renewed his narrative.

"Being now provided with all the necessaries of life, I betook myself once again to study, and that with a more inordinate application than I had ever done formerly. The books which now employed my time solely were those, as well ancient as modern, which treat of true philosophy, a word which is by many thought to be the subject only of farce and ridicule. I now read over the works of Aristotle and Plato, with the rest of those inestimable treasures which ancient Greece had bequeathed to the world.

"These authors, though they instructed me in no science by which men may promise to themselves to acquire the least riches or worldly power, taught me, however, the art of despising the highest acquisitions of both. They elevate the mind, and steel and harden it against the capricious invasions of fortune. They not only instruct in the knowledge of Wisdom, but confirm men in her habits, and demonstrate plainly, that this must be our guide, if we propose ever to arrive at the greatest worldly happiness, or to defend ourselves, with any tolerable security, against the misery which everywhere surrounds and invests us.

"To this I added another study, compared to which, all the philosophy taught by the wisest heathens is little better than a dream, and is indeed as full of vanity as the silliest jester ever pleased to represent it. This is that Divine wisdom which is alone to be found in the Holy Scriptures; for they impart to us the knowledge and assurance of things much more worthy our attention than all which this world can offer to our acceptance; of things which Heaven itself hath condescended to reveal to us, and to the smallest knowledge of which the highest human wit unassisted could never ascend. I began now to think all the time I had spent with the best heathen writers was little more than labor lost: for, however pleasant and delightful their lessons may be, or however adequate to the right regulation of our conduct with respect to this world only; yet, when compared with the glory revealed in Scripture, their highest documents will appear as trifling, and of as little consequence, as the rules by which children regulate their childish little games and pastime. True it is, that philosophy makes us wiser, but Christianity makes us better men. Philosophy elevates and steels the mind, Christianity softens and sweetens it. The former makes us the objects of human admiration, the latter of Divine love. That insures us a temporal, but this an eternal happiness.—But I am afraid I tire you with my rhapsody.''

''Not at all,'' cries Partridge; ''Lud forbid we should be tired with good things!''

''I had spent,'' continued the stranger, ''about four years in the most delightful manner to myself, totally given up to contemplation, and entirely unembarrassed with the affairs of the world, when I lost the best of fathers, and one whom I so entirely loved, that my grief at his loss exceeds all description. I now abandoned my books, and gave myself up for a whole month to the effects of melancholy and despair. Time, how-

ever, the best physician of the mind, at length
brought me relief."—"Ay, ay; *Tempus edax
rerum,*" said Partridge.—"I then," continued the
stranger, "betook myself again to my former
studies, which I may say perfected my cure; for
philosophy and religion may be called the exercises of the mind, and when this is disordered,
they are as wholesome as exercise can be to a distempered body. They do indeed produce similar
effects with exercise; for they strengthen and confirm the mind, till man becomes, in the noble strain
of Horace—

> *Fortis, et in seipso totus teres atque rotundus,*
> *Externi ne quid valeat per læve morari;*
> *In quem manca ruit semper Fortuna."* [1]

Here Jones smiled at some conceit which intruded itself into his imagination; but the stranger, I believe, perceived it not, and proceeded
thus:—

"My circumstances were now greatly altered
by the death of that best of men; for my brother,
who was now become master of the house, differed
so widely from me in his inclinations, and our
pursuits in life had been so very various, that we
were the worst of company to each other: but
what made our living together still more disagreeable, was the little harmony which could subsist
between the few who resorted to me, and the numerous train of sportsmen who often attended my

[1] Firm in himself, who on himself relies,
Polish'd and round, who runs his proper course
And breaks misfortunes with superior force.— MR. FRANCIS.

brother from the field to the table; for such fellows, besides the noise and nonsense with which they persecute the ears of sober men, endeavor always to attack them with affront and contempt. This was so much the case, that neither I myself, nor my friends, could ever sit down to a meal with them without being treated with derision, because we were unacquainted with the phrases of sportsmen. For men of true learning, and almost universal knowledge, always compassionate the ignorance of others; but fellows who excel in some little, low, contemptible art, are always certain to despise those who are unacquainted with that art.

"In short, we soon separated, and I went, by the advice of a physician, to drink the Bath waters; for my violent affliction, added to a sedentary life, had thrown me into a kind of paralytic disorder, for which those waters are accounted an almost certain cure. The second day after my arrival, as I was walking by the river, the sun shone so intensely hot (though it was early in the year), that I retired to the shelter of some willows, and sat down by the river side. Here I had not been seated long before I heard a person on the other side of the willows sighing and bemoaning himself bitterly. On a sudden, having uttered a most impious oath, he cried, 'I am resolved to bear it no longer,' and directly threw himself into the water. I immediately started, and ran towards the place, calling at the same time as loudly as I could for assistance. An angler happened luckily to be a-fishing a little

below me, though some very high sedge had hid
him from my sight. He immediately came up,
and both of us together, not without some hazard
of our lives, drew the body to the shore. At first
we perceived no sign of life remaining; but having held the body up by the heels (for we soon had
assistance enough), it discharged a vast quantity
of water at the mouth, and at length began to discover some symptoms of breathing, and a little
afterwards to move both its hands and its legs.

"An apothecary, who happened to be present
among others, advised that the body, which
seemed now to have pretty well emptied itself of
water, and which began to have many convulsive
motions, should be directly taken up, and carried
into a warm bed. This was accordingly performed, the apothecary and myself attending.

"As we were going towards an inn, for we knew
not the man's lodgings, luckily a woman met us,
who, after some violent screaming, told us that
the gentleman lodged at her house.

"When I had seen the man safely deposited
there, I left him to the care of the apothecary;
who, I suppose, used all the right methods with
him, for the next morning I heard he had perfectly
recovered his senses.

"I then went to visit him, intending to search
out, as well as I could, the cause of his having
attempted so desperate an act, and to prevent, as
far as I was able, his pursuing such wicked intentions for the future. I was no sooner admitted
into his chamber, than we both instantly knew
each other; for who should this person be but my

good friend Mr. Watson.   Here I will not trouble
you with what passed at our first interview; for
I would avoid prolixity as much as possible.''—
"Pray let us hear all,'' cries Partridge; "I want
mightily to know what brought him to Bath.''

"You shall hear everything material,'' answered the stranger; and then proceeded to relate
what we shall proceed to write, after we have
given a short breathing time to both ourselves and
the reader.

CHAPTER XIV

In which the Man of the Hill concludes his history.

"MR. WATSON," continued the stranger, "very freely acquainted me, that the unhappy situation of his circumstances, occasioned by a tide of ill luck, had in a manner forced him to a resolution of destroying himself.

"I now began to argue very seriously with him, in opposition to this heathenish, or indeed diabolical, principle of the lawfulness of self-murder; and said everything which occurred to me on the subject; but, to my great concern, it seemed to have very little effect on him. He seemed not at all to repent of what he had done, and gave me reason to fear he would soon make a second attempt of the like horrible kind.

"When I had finished my discourse, instead of endeavoring to answer my arguments, he looked me steadfastly in the face, and with a smile said, 'You are strangely altered, my good friend, since I remember you. I question whether any of our bishops could make a better argument against suicide than you have entertained me with; but unless you can find somebody who will lend me a cool hundred, I must either hang, or drown, or starve; and, in my opinion, the last death is the most terrible of the three.'

"I answered him very gravely that I was indeed altered since I had seen him last. That I had found leisure to look into my follies and to repent of them. I then advised him to pursue the same steps; and at last concluded with an assurance that I myself would lend him a hundred pound, if it would be of any service to his affairs, and he would not put it into the power of a die to deprive him of it.

"Mr. Watson, who seemed almost composed in slumber by the former part of my discourse, was roused by the latter. He seized my hand eagerly, gave me a thousand thanks, and declared I was a friend indeed; adding that he hoped I had a better opinion of him than to imagine he had profited so little by experience, as to put any confidence in those damned dice which had so often deceived him. 'No, no,' cries he; 'let me but once handsomely be set up again, and if ever Fortune makes a broken merchant of me afterwards, I will forgive her.'

"I very well understood the language of setting up, and broken merchant. I therefore said to him, with a very grave face, Mr. Watson, you must endeavor to find out some business or employment, by which you may procure yourself a livelihood; and I promise you, could I see any probability of being repaid hereafter, I would advance a much larger sum than what you have mentioned, to equip you in any fair and honorable calling; but as to gaming, besides the baseness and wickedness of making it a profession, you are really, to my own knowledge, unfit for it, and it will end in your certain ruin.

" 'Why now, that's strange,' answered he; 'neither you, nor any of my friends, would ever allow me to know anything of the matter, and yet I believe I am as good a hand at every game as any of you all; and I heartily wish I was to play with you only for your whole fortune: I should desire no better sport, and I would let you name your game into the bargain: but come, my dear boy, have you the hundred in your pocket?'

"I answered I had only a bill for £50, which I delivered him, and promised to bring him the rest next morning; and after giving him a little more advice, took my leave.

"I was indeed better than my word; for I returned to him that very afternoon. When I entered the room, I found him sitting up in his bed at cards with a notorious gamester. This sight, you will imagine, shocked me not a little; to which I may add the mortification of seeing my bill delivered by him to his antagonist, and thirty guineas only given in exchange for it.

"The other gamester presently quitted the room, and then Watson declared he was ashamed to see me; 'but,' says he, 'I find luck runs so damnably against me, that I will resolve to leave off play for ever. I have thought of the kind proposal you made me ever since, and I promise you there shall be no fault in me, if I do not put it in execution.'

"Though I had no great faith in his promises, I produced him the remainder of the hundred in consequence of my own; for which he gave me a note, which was all I ever expected to see in return for my money.

"We were prevented from any further discourse at present by the arrival of the apothecary; who, with much joy in his countenance, and without even asking his patient how he did, proclaimed there was great news arrived in a letter to himself, which he said would shortly be public, 'That the Duke of Monmouth was landed in the west with a vast army of Dutch; and that another vast fleet hovered over the coast of Norfolk, and was to make a descent there, in order to favor the duke's enterprise with a diversion on that side.'

"This apothecary was one of the greatest politicians of his time. He was more delighted with the most paltry packet, than with the best patient, and the highest joy he was capable of, he received from having a piece of news in his possession an hour or two sooner than any other person in the town. His advices, however, were seldom authentic; for he would swallow almost anything as a truth—a humor which many made use of to impose upon him.

"Thus it happened with what he at present communicated; for it was known within a short time afterwards that the duke was really landed, but that his army consisted only of a few attendants; and as to the diversion in Norfolk, it was entirely false.

"The apothecary stayed no longer in the room than while he acquainted us with his news; and then, without saying a syllable to his patient on any other subject, departed to spread his advices all over the town.

"Events of this nature in the public are generally apt to eclipse all private concerns. Our discourse therefore now became entirely political. For my own part, I had been for some time very seriously affected with the danger to which the Protestant religion was so visibly exposed under a Popish prince, and thought the apprehension of it alone sufficient to justify that insurrection; for no real security can ever be found against the persecuting spirit of Popery, when armed with power, except the depriving it of that power, as woeful experience presently showed. You know how King James behaved after getting the better of this attempt; how little he valued either his royal word, or coronation oath, or the liberties and rights of his people. But all had not the sense to foresee this at first; and therefore the Duke of Monmouth was weakly supported; yet all could feel when the evil came upon them; and therefore all united, at last, to drive out that king, against whose exclusion a great party among us had so warmly contended during the reign of his brother, and for whom they now fought with such zeal and affection."

"What you say," interrupted Jones, "is very true; and it has often struck me, as the most wonderful thing I ever read of in history, that so soon after this convincing experience which brought our whole nation to join so unanimously in expelling King James, for the preservation of our religion and liberties, there should be a party among us mad enough to desire the placing his family again on the throne." "You are not in earnest!" answered the old man; "there can be no such party. As bad an opinion as I have of mankind, I cannot believe them infatuated to such a degree. There may be some hot-headed Papists led by their priests to engage in this desperate cause, and think it a holy war; but that Protestants, that are members of the Church of England, should be such apostates, such *felos de se,* I cannot believe it; no, no, young man, unacquainted as I am with what has passed in the world for these last thirty years, I cannot be so imposed upon as to credit so foolish a tale; but I see you have a mind to sport with my ignorance."—"Can it be possible," replied Jones, "that you have lived so much out of the world as not to know that during that time there have been two rebellions in favor of the son of King James, one of which is now actually raging in the very heart of the kingdom." At these words the old gentleman started up, and in a most solemn tone of voice, conjured Jones by his Maker to tell him if what he said was really true; which the other as solemnly affirming, he walked several turns about the room in a profound silence, then cried, then laughed, and at last fell down on his knees, and blessed God, in a loud thanksgiving prayer, for having delivered him from all society with human nature, which could be capable of such monstrous extravagances. After which, being reminded by Jones that he had broke off his story, he resumed it again in this manner:—

"As mankind in the days I was speaking of, was not yet arrived at that pitch of madness which I find they are capable of now, and which, to be sure, I have only escaped by living alone, and at a distance from the contagion, there was a considerable rising in favor of Monmouth; and my principles strongly inclining me to take the same part, I determined to join him; and Mr. Watson, from different motives concurring in the same resolution (for the spirit of a gamester will carry a man as far upon such an occasion as the spirit of patriotism), we soon provided ourselves with all necessaries, and went to the duke at Bridgewater.

"The unfortunate event of this enterprise, you are, I conclude, as well acquainted with as myself. I escaped, together with Mr. Watson, from the battle at Sedgemore, in which action I received a slight wound. We rode near forty miles together on the Exeter road, and then abandoning our horses, scrambled as well as we could through the fields and by-roads, till we arrived at a little wild hut on a common, where a poor old woman took all the care of us she could, and dressed my wound with salve, which quickly healed it."

"Pray, sir, where was the wound?" says Partridge. The stranger satisfied him it was in his arm, and then continued his narrative. "Here, sir," said he, "Mr. Watson left me the next morning in order, as he pretended, to get us some provision from the town of Collumpton; but—can I relate it, or can you believe it?—this Mr. Watson, this friend, this base, barbarous, treacherous villain, betrayed me to a party of horse belonging to King James, and at his return delivered me into their hands.

"The soldiers, being six in number, had now seized me, and were conducting me to Taunton jail; but neither my present situation, nor the apprehensions of what might happen to me, were half so irksome to my mind as the company of my false friend, who, having surrendered himself, was likewise considered as a prisoner, though he was better treated, as being to make his peace at my expense. He at first endeavored to excuse his treachery; but when he received nothing but scorn and upbraiding from me, he soon changed his note, abused me as the most atrocious and malicious rebel, and laid all his own guilt to my charge, who, as he declared, had solicited, and even threatened him, to make him take up arms against his gracious as well as lawful sovereign.

"This false evidence (for in reality he had been much the forwarder of the two) stung me to the quick, and raised an indignation scarce conceivable by those who have not felt it. However, fortune at length took pity on me; for as we were got a little beyond Wellington, in a narrow lane, my guards received a false alarm, that near fifty of the enemy were at hand; upon which they shifted for themselves, and left me and my betrayer to do the same. That villain immediately ran from me, and I am glad he did, or I should have certainly endeavored, though I had no arms, to have executed vengeance on his baseness.

II—20

"I was now once more at liberty; and immediately withdrawing from the highway into the fields, I traveled on, scarce knowing which way I went, and making it my chief care to avoid all public roads and all towns—nay, even the most homely houses; for I imagined every human creature whom I saw desirous of betraying me.

"At last, after rambling several days about the country, during which the fields afforded me the same bed and the same food which nature bestows on our savage brothers of the creation, I at length arrived at this place, where the solitude and wildness of the country invited me to fix my abode. The first person with whom I took up my habitation was the mother of this old woman, with whom I remained concealed till the news of the glorious revolution put an end to all my apprehensions of danger, and gave me an opportunity of once more visiting my own home, and of inquiring a little into my affairs, which I soon settled as agreeably to my brother as to myself; having resigned everything to him, for which he paid me the sum of a thousand pounds, and settled on me an annuity for life.

"His behavior in this last instance, as in all others, was selfish and ungenerous. I could not look on him as my friend, nor indeed did he desire that I should; so I presently took my leave of him, as well as of my other acquaintance; and from that day to this, my history is little better than a blank."

"And is it possible, sir," said Jones, "that you can have resided here from that day to this?"—

"O no, sir," answered the gentleman; "I have been a great traveler, and there are few parts of Europe with which I am not acquainted." "I have not, sir," cried Jones, "the assurance to ask it of you now; indeed it would be cruel, after so much breath as you have already spent: but you will give me leave to wish for some further opportunity of hearing the excellent observations which a man of your sense and knowledge of the world must have made in so long a course of travels."—"Indeed, young gentleman," answered the stranger, "I will endeavor to satisfy your curiosity on this head likewise, as far as I am able." Jones attempted fresh apologies, but was prevented; and while he and Partridge sat with greedy and impatient ears, the stranger proceeded as in the next chapter.

CHAPTER XV

"IN Italy the landlords are very silent. In France they are more talkative, but yet civil. In Germany and Holland they are generally very impertinent. And as for their honesty, I believe it is pretty equal in all those countries. The *laquais à louange* are sure to lose no opportunity of cheating you; and as for the postilions, I think they are pretty much alike all the world over. These, sir, are the observations on men which I made in my travels; for these were the only men I ever conversed with. My design, when I went abroad, was to divert myself by seeing the wondrous variety of prospects, beasts, birds, fishes, insects, and vegetables, with which God has been pleased to enrich the several parts of this globe; a variety which, as it must give great pleasure to a contemplative beholder, so doth it admirably display the power, and wisdom, and goodness of the Creator. Indeed, to say the truth, there is but one work in his whole creation that doth him any dishonor, and with that I have long since avoided holding any conversation."

"You will pardon me," cries Jones; "but I have always imagined that there is in this very work you mention as great variety as in all the rest; for, besides the difference of inclination, customs and climates have, I am told, introduced the utmost diversity into human nature.''

''Very little indeed,'' answered the other: ''those who travel in order to acquaint themselves with the different manners of men might spare themselves much pains by going to a carnival at Venice; for there they will see at once all which they can discover in the several courts of Europe. The same hypocrisy, the same fraud; in short, the same follies and vices dressed in different habits. In Spain, these are equipped with much gravity; and in Italy, with vast splendor. In France, a knave is dressed like a fop; and in the northern countries, like a sloven. But human nature is everywhere the same, everywhere the object of detestation and scorn.

''As for my own part, I passed through all these nations as you perhaps may have done through a crowd at a show—jostling to get by them, holding my nose with one hand, and defending my pockets with the other, without speaking a word to any of them, while I was pressing on to see what I wanted to see; which, however entertaining it might be in itself, scarce made me amends for the trouble the company gave me.''

''Did not you find some of the nations among which you traveled less troublesome to you than others?'' said Jones. ''O yes,'' replied the old man: ''the Turks were much more tolerable to me than the Christians; for they are men of profound taciturnity, and never disturb a stranger with questions. Now and then indeed they be-

stow a short curse upon him, or spit in his face
as he walks the streets, but then they have done
with him; and a man may live an age in their
country without hearing a dozen words from them.
But of all the people I ever saw, heaven defend
me from the French! With their damned prate
and civilities, and doing the honor of their nation
to strangers (as they are pleased to call it), but
indeed setting forth their own vanity; they are
so troublesome, that I had infinitely rather pass
my life with the Hottentots than set my foot in
Paris again. They are a nasty people, but their
nastiness is mostly without; whereas, in France,
and some other nations that I won't name, it is
all within, and makes them stink much more to
my reason than that of Hottentots does to my
nose.

"Thus, sir, I have ended the history of my life;
for as to all that series of years during which I
have lived retired here, it affords no variety to
entertain you, and may be almost considered as
one day. The retirement has been so complete,
that I could hardly have enjoyed a more absolute
solitude in the deserts of the Thebais than here
in the midst of this populous kingdom. As I have
no estate, I am plagued with no tenants or stew-
ards: my annuity is paid me pretty regularly, as
indeed it ought to be; for it is much less than what
I might have expected in return for what I gave
up. Visits I admit none; and the old woman who
keeps my house knows that her place entirely depends upon her saving me all the trouble of buy-
ing the things that I want, keeping off all solicita-

tion or business from me, and holding her tongue
whenever I am within hearing. As my walks are
all by night, I am pretty secure in this wild un-
frequented place from meeting any company.
Some few persons I have met by chance, and sent
them home heartily frighted, as from the oddness
of my dress and figure they took me for a ghost
or a hobgoblin. But what has happened to-night
shows that even here I cannot be safe from the
villainy of men; for without your assistance I had
not only been robbed, but very probably murdered.''

Jones thanked the stranger for the trouble he
had taken in relating his story, and then expressed
some wonder how he could possibly endure a life
of such solitude; ''in which,'' says he, ''you may
well complain of the want of variety. Indeed I
am astonished how you have filled up, or rather
killed, so much of your time.''

''I am not at all surprised,'' answered the
other, ''that to one whose affections and thoughts
are fixed on the world my hours should appear to
have wanted employment in this place: but there
is one single act, for which the whole life of man
is infinitely too short: what time can suffice for
the contemplation and worship of that glorious,
immortal, and eternal Being, among the works of
whose stupendous creation not only this globe, but
even those numberless luminaries which we may
here behold spangling all the sky, though they
should many of them be suns lighting different
systems of worlds, may possibly appear but as a
few atoms opposed to the whole earth which we

inhabit? Can a man who by divine meditations is admitted as it were into the conversation of this ineffable, incomprehensible Majesty, think days, or years, or ages, too long for the continuance of so ravishing an honor? Shall the trifling amusements, the palling pleasures, the silly business of the world, roll away our hours too swiftly from us; and shall the pace of time seem sluggish to a mind exercised in studies so high, so important, and so glorious? As no time is sufficient, so no place is improper, for this great concern. On what object can we cast our eyes which may not inspire us with ideas of his power, of his wisdom, and of his goodness? It is not necessary that the rising sun should dart his fiery glories over the eastern horizon; nor that the boisterous winds should rush from their caverns, and shake the lofty forest; nor that the opening clouds should pour their deluges on the plains: it is not necessary, I say, that any of these should proclaim his majesty: there is not an insect, not a vegetable, of so low an order in the creation as not to be honored with bearing marks of the attributes of its great Creator; marks not only of his power, but of his wisdom and goodness. Man alone, the king of this globe, the last and greatest work of the Supreme Being, below the sun; man alone hath basely dishonored his own nature; and by dishonesty, cruelty, ingratitude, and treachery, hath called his Maker's goodness in question, by puzzling us to account how a benevolent being should form so foolish and so vile an animal. Yet this is the being from whose conversation you think,

I suppose, that I have been unfortunately restrained, and without whose blessed society, life, in your opinion, must be tedious and insipid.''

"In the former part of what you said,'' replied Jones, "I most heartily and readily concur; but I believe, as well as hope, that the abhorrence which you express for mankind in the conclusion, is much too general. Indeed, you here fall into an error, which in my little experience I have observed to be a very common one, by taking the character of mankind from the worst and basest among them; whereas, indeed, as an excellent writer observes, nothing should be esteemed as characteristical of a species, but what is to be found among the best and most perfect individuals of that species. This error, I believe, is generally committed by those who from want of proper caution in the choice of their friends and acquaintance, have suffered injuries from bad and worthless men; two or three instances of which are very unjustly charged on all human nature.''

"I think I had experience enough of it,'' answered the other: "my first mistress and my first friend betrayed me in the basest manner, and in matters which threatened to be of the worst of consequences—even to bring me to a shameful death.''

"But you will pardon me,'' cries Jones, "if I desire you to reflect who that mistress and who that friend were. What better, my good sir, could be expected in love derived from the stews, or in friendship first produced and nourished at the gaming-table? To take the characters of women from the former instance, or of men from the latter, would be as unjust as to assert that air is a nauseous and unwholesome element, because we find it so in a jakes. I have lived but a short time in the world, and yet have known men worthy of the highest friendship, and women of the highest love."

"Alas! young man," answered the stranger, "you have lived, you confess, but a very short time in the world: I was somewhat older than you when I was of the same opinion."

"You might have remained so still," replies Jones, "if you had not been unfortunate, I will venture to say incautious, in the placing your affections. If there was, indeed, much more wickedness in the world than there is, it would not prove such general assertions against human nature, since much of this arrives by mere accident, and many a man who commits evil is not totally bad and corrupt in his heart. In truth, none seem to have any title to assert human nature to be necessarily and universally evil, but those whose own minds afford them one instance of this natural depravity; which is not, I am convinced, your case."

"And such," said the stranger, "will be always the most backward to assert any such thing. Knaves will no more endeavor to persuade us of the baseness of mankind, than a highwayman will inform you that there are thieves on the road. This would, indeed, be a method to put you on your guard, and to defeat their own purposes. For which reason, though knaves, as I remember, are very apt to abuse particular persons, yet they never cast any reflection on human nature in general.'' The old gentleman spoke this so warmly, that as Jones despaired of making a convert, and was unwilling to offend, he returned no answer.

The day now began to send forth its first streams of light, when Jones made an apology to the stranger for having stayed so long, and perhaps detained him from his rest. The stranger answered, ''He never wanted rest less than at present; for that day and night were indifferent seasons to him; and that he commonly made use of the former for the time of his repose and of the latter for his walks and lucubrations. However,'' said he, ''it is now a most lovely morning, and if you can bear any longer to be without your own rest or food, I will gladly entertain you with the sight of some very fine prospects which I believe you have not yet seen.''

Jones very readily embraced this offer, and they immediately set forward together from the cottage. As for Partridge, he had fallen into a profound repose just as the stranger had finished his story; for his curiosity was satisfied, and the subsequent discourse was not forcible enough in its operation to conjure down the charms of sleep. Jones therefore left him to enjoy his nap; and as the reader may perhaps be at this season glad of the same favor, we will here put an end to the eighth book of our history.

BOOK IX

CHAPTER I

Of those who lawfully may, and of those who may not, write
such histories as this.

AMONG other good uses for which I have
thought proper to institute these several
introductory chapters, I have considered
them as a kind of mark or stamp, which may
hereafter enable a very indifferent reader to distinguish what is true and genuine in this historic
kind of writing, from what is false and counter-
feit. Indeed, it seems likely that some such mark
may shortly become necessary, since the favorable reception which two or three authors have
lately procured for their works of this nature
from the public, will probably serve as an encouragement to many others to undertake the like.
Thus a swarm of foolish novels and monstrous
romances will be produced, either to the great
impoverishing of booksellers, or to the great loss
of time and depravation of morals in the reader;
nay, often to the spreading of scandal and calum-
ny, and to the prejudice of the characters of many
worthy and honest people.

I question not but the ingenious author of the

Spectator was principally induced to prefix Greek and Latin mottoes to every paper, from the same consideration of guarding against the pursuit of those scribblers, who having no talents of a writer but what is taught by the writing-master, are yet nowise afraid nor ashamed to assume the same titles with the greatest genius, than their good brother in the fable was of braying in the lion's skin.

By the device therefore of his motto, it became impracticable for any man to presume to imitate the Spectators, without understanding at least one sentence in the learned languages. In the same manner I have now secured myself from the imitation of those who are utterly incapable of any degree of reflection, and whose learning is not equal to an essay.

I would not be here understood to insinuate, that the greatest merit of such historical productions can ever lie in these introductory chapters; but, in fact, those parts which contain mere narrative only, afford much more encouragement to the pen of an imitator, than those which are composed of observation and reflection. Here I mean such imitators as Rowe was of Shakespear, or as Horace hints some of the Romans were of Cato, by bare feet and sour faces.

To invent good stories, and to tell them well, are possibly very rare talents, and yet I have observed few persons who have scrupled to aim at both: and if we examine the romances and novels with which the world abounds, I think we may fairly conclude, that most of the authors would not have attempted to show their teeth (if the expression may be allowed me) in any other way of writing; nor could indeed have strung together a dozen sentences on any other subject whatever. *Scribimus indocti doctique passim,*[1] may be more truly said of the historian and biographer, than of any other species of writing; for all the arts and sciences (even criticism itself) require some little degree of learning and knowledge. Poetry, indeed, may perhaps be thought an exception; but then it demands numbers, or something like numbers: whereas, to the composition of novels and romances, nothing is necessary but paper, pens, and ink, with the manual capacity of using them. This, I conceive, their productions show to be the opinion of the authors themselves: and this must be the opinion of their readers, if indeed there be any such.

Hence we are to derive that universal contempt which the world, who always denominate the whole from the majority, have cast on all historical writers who do not draw their materials from records. And it is the apprehension of this contempt that hath made us so cautiously avoid the term romance, a name with which we might otherwise have been well enough contented. Though, as we have good authority for all our characters, no less indeed than the vast authentic doomsday-book of nature, as is elsewhere hinted, our labors have sufficient title to the name of history. Certainly they deserve some distinction from those

----

[1] —— Each desperate blockhead dares to write:
Verse is the trade of every living wight.— FRANCIS.

works, which one of the wittiest of men regarded only as proceeding from a *pruritus,* or indeed rather from a looseness of the brain.

But besides the dishonor which is thus cast on one of the most useful as well as entertaining of all kinds of writing, there is just reason to apprehend, that by encouraging such authors we shall propagate much dishonor of another kind; I mean to the characters of many good and valuable members of society; for the dullest writers, no more than the dullest companions, are always inoffensive.   They have both enough of language to be indecent and abusive.   And surely if the opinion just above cited be true, we cannot wonder that works so nastily derived should be nasty themselves, or have a tendency to make others so.

To prevent therefore, for the future, such intemperate abuses of leisure, of letters, and of the liberty of the press, especially as the world seems at present to be more than usually threatened with them, I shall here venture to mention some qualifications, every one of which are in a pretty high degree necessary to this order of historians.

The first is, genius, without a full vein of which no study, says Horace, can avail us.   By genius I would understand that power or rather those powers of the mind, which are capable of penetrating into all things within our reach and knowledge, and of distinguishing their essential differences.   These are no other than invention and judgment; and they are both called by the collective name of genius, as they are of those gifts of nature which we bring with us into the world.

Concerning each of which many seem to have
fallen into very great error; for by invention, I
believe, is generally understood a creative faculty,
which would indeed prove most romance writers
to have the highest pretensions to it; whereas by
invention is really meant no more (and so the
word signifies) than discovery, or finding out; or
to explain it at large, a quick and sagacious penetration into the true essence of all the objects
of our contemplation. This, I think, can rarely
exist without the concomitancy of judgment; for
how we can be said to have discovered the true
essence of two things, without discerning their
difference, seems to me hard to conceive. Now
this last is the undisputed province of judgment,
and yet some few men of wit have agreed with
all the dull fellows in the world in representing
these two to have been seldom or never the prop·
erty of one and the same person.

But though they should be so, they are not suf·
ficient for our purpose, without a good share of
learning; for which I could again cite the authority of Horace, and of many others, if any was
necessary to prove that tools are of no service
to a workman, when they are not sharpened by
art, or when he wants rules to direct him in his
work, or hath no matter to work upon. All these
uses are supplied by learning; for nature can
only furnish us with capacity; or, as I have chose
to illustrate it, with the tools of our profession;
learning must fit them for use, must direct them
in it, and, lastly, must contribute part at least of
the materials. A competent knowledge of his-

tory and of the belles-lettres is here absolutely necessary; and without this share of knowledge at least, to affect the character of an historian, is as vain as to endeavor at building a house without timber or mortar, or brick or stone. Homer and Milton, who, though they added the ornament of numbers to their works, were both historians of our order, were masters of all the learning of their times.

Again, there is another sort of knowledge, beyond the power of learning to bestow, and this is to be had by conversation. So necessary is this to the understanding the characters of men, that none are more ignorant of them than those learned pedants whose lives have been entirely consumed in colleges and among books; for however exquisitely human nature may have been described by writers, the true practical system can be learned only in the world. Indeed the like happens in every other kind of knowledge. Neither physic nor law are to be practically known from books. Nay, the farmer, the planter, the gardener, must perfect by experience what he hath acquired the rudiments of by reading. How accurately soever the ingenious Mr. Miller may have described the plant, he himself would advise his disciple to see it in the garden. As we must perceive, that after the nicest strokes of a Shakespeare or a Jonson. of a Wycherly or an Otway, some touches of nature will escape the reader, which the judicious action of a Garrick, of a Cibber, or a Clive[1] can

---

[1] There is a peculiar propriety in mentioning this great actor, and these two most justly celebrated actresses, in this

II—21

convey to him; so, on the real stage, the character shows himself in a stronger and bolder light than he can be described. And if this be the case in those fine and nervous descriptions which great authors themselves have taken from life, how much more strongly will it hold when the writer himself takes his lines not from nature, but from books? Such characters are only the faint copy of a copy, and can have neither the justness nor spirit of an original.

Now this conversation in our historian must be universal, that is, with all ranks and degrees of men; for the knowledge of what is called high life will not instruct him in low; nor *è converso*, will his being acquainted with the inferior part of mankind teach him the manners of the superior. And though it may be thought that the knowledge of either may sufficiently enable him to describe at least that in which he hath been conversant, yet he will even here fall greatly short of perfection; for the follies of either rank do in reality illustrate each other. For instance, the affectation of high life appears more glaring and ridiculous from the simplicity of the low; and again, the rudeness and barbarity of this latter, strikes with much stronger ideas of absurdity, when contrasted with, and opposed to, the politeness which controls the former. Besides, to say the truth, the manners of our historian will be

place, as they have all formed themselves on the study of nature only, and not on the imitation of their predecessors. Hence they have been able to excel all who have gone before them; a degree of merit which the servile herd of imitators can never possibly arrive at.

improved by both these conversations; for in the one he will easily find examples of plainness, honesty, and sincerity; in the other of refinement, elegance, and a liberality of spirit; which last quality I myself have scarce ever seen in men of low birth and education.

Nor will all the qualities I have hitherto given my historian avail him, unless he have what is generally meant by a good heart, and be capable of feeling. The author who will make me weep, says Horace, must first weep himself. In reality, no man can paint a distress well which he doth not feel while he is painting it; nor do I doubt, but that the most pathetic and affecting scenes have been writ with tears. In the same manner it is with the ridiculous. I am convinced I never make my reader laugh heartily but where I have laughed before him; unless it should happen at any time, that instead of laughing with me he should be inclined to laugh at me. Perhaps this may have been the case at some passages in this chapter, from which apprehension I will here put an end to it.

CHAPTER II

Containing a very surprising adventure indeed, which Mr. Jones met with in his walk with the Man of the Hill.

AURORA now first opened her casement, *Anglicè* the day began to break, when Jones walked forth in company with the stranger, and mounted Mazard Hill; of which they had no sooner gained the summit than one of the most noble prospects in the world presented itself to their view, and which we would likewise present to the reader, but for two reasons: first, we despair of making those who have seen this prospect admire our description; secondly, we very much doubt whether those who have not seen it would understand it.

Jones stood for some minutes fixed in one posture, and directing his eyes towards the south; upon which the old gentleman asked, What he was looking at with so much attention? "Alas! sir," answered he with a sigh, "I was endeavoring to trace out my own journey hither. Good heavens! what a distance is Gloucester from us! What a vast track of land must be between me and my own home!"—"Ay, ay, young gentleman," cries the other, "and by your sighing, from what you love better than your own home, or I am mistaken. I perceive now the object of your contemplation is not within your sight, and yet I

324

fancy you have a pleasure in looking that way." Jones answered with a smile, "I find, old friend, you have not yet forgot the sensations of your youth. I own my thoughts were employed as you have guessed."

They now walked to that part of the hill which looks to the north-west, and which hangs over a vast and extensive wood. Here they were no sooner arrived than they heard at a distance the most violent screams of a woman, proceeding from the wood below them. Jones listened a moment, and then, without saying a word to his companion (for indeed the occasion seemed sufficiently pressing), ran, or rather slid, down the hill, and, without the least apprehension or concern for his own safety, made directly to the thicket, whence the sound had issued.

He had not entered far into the wood before he beheld a most shocking sight indeed, a woman stripped half naked, under the hands of a ruffian, who had put his garter round her neck, and was endeavoring to draw her up to a tree. Jones asked no questions at this interval, but fell instantly upon the villain, and made such good use of his trusty oaken stick that he laid him sprawling on the ground before he could defend himself, indeed almost before he knew he was attacked; nor did he cease the prosecution of his blows till the woman herself begged him to forbear, saying, she believed he had sufficiently done his business.

The poor wretch then fell upon her knees to Jones, and gave him a thousand thanks for her deliverance. He presently lifted her up, and told

her he was highly pleased with the extraordinary
accident which had sent him thither for her relief, where it was so improbable she should find
any; adding, that Heaven seemed to have designed him as the happy instrument of her protection. "Nay," answered she, "I could almost
conceive you to be some good angel; and, to say
the truth, you look more like an angel than a man
in my eye." Indeed he was a charming figure;
and if a very fine person, and a most comely set
of features, adorned with youth, health, strength,
freshness, spirit, and good-nature, can make a
man resemble an angel, he certainly had that resemblance.

The redeemed captive had not altogether so
much of the human-angelic species: she seemed to
be at least of the middle age, nor had her face
much appearance of beauty; but her clothes being
torn from all the upper part of her body, her
breasts, which were well formed and extremely
white, attracted the eyes of her deliverer, and
for a few moments they stood silent, and gazing
at each other; till the ruffian on the ground beginning to move, Jones took the garter which
had been intended for another purpose, and
bound both his hands behind him. And now, on
contemplating his face, he discovered, greatly to
his surprise, and perhaps not a little to his satisfaction, this very person to be no other than
ensign Northerton. Nor had the ensign forgotten his former antagonist, whom he knew the
moment he came to himself. His surprise was

equal to that of Jones; but I conceive his pleasure
was rather less on this occasion.

Jones helped Northerton upon his legs, and
then looking him steadfastly in the face, "I fancy,
sir," said he, "you did not expect to meet me
any more in this world, and I confess I had as
little expectation to find you here. However,
fortune, I see, hath brought us once more together, and hath given me satisfaction for the
injury I have received, even without my own
knowledge."

"It is very much like a man of honor, indeed,"
answered Northerton, "to take satisfaction by
knocking a man down behind his back. Neither
am I capable of giving you satisfaction here, as
I have no sword; but if you dare behave like a
gentleman, let us go where I can furnish myself
with one, and I will do by you as a man of honor
ought."

"Doth it become such a villain as you are,"
cries Jones, "to contaminate the name of honor
by assuming it? But I shall waste no time in
discourse with you. Justice requires satisfaction of you now, and shall have it." Then turning to the woman, he asked her, if she was
near her home; or if not, whether she was
acquainted with any house in the neighborhood,
where she might procure herself some decent
clothes, in order to proceed to a justice of the
peace.

She answered she was an entire stranger in
that part of the world. Jones then recollecting

himself; said, he had a friend near who would direct them; indeed, he wondered at his not following; but, in fact, the good Man of the Hill, when our hero departed, sat himself down on the brow, where, though he had a gun in his hand, he with great patience and unconcern had attended the issue.

Jones then stepping without the wood, perceived the old man sitting as we have just described him; he presently exerted his utmost agility, and with surprising expedition ascended the hill.

The old man advised him to carry the woman to Upton, which, he said, was the nearest town, and there he would be sure of furnishing her with all manner of conveniencies. Jones having received his direction to the place, took his leave of the Man of the Hill, and, desiring him to direct Partridge the same way, returned hastily to the wood.

Our hero, at his departure to make this inquiry of his friend, had considered, that as the ruffian's hands were tied behind him, he was incapable of executing any wicked purposes on the poor woman. Besides, he knew he should not be beyond the reach of her voice, and could return soon enough to prevent any mischief. He had moreover declared to the villain, that if he attempted the least insult, he would be himself immediately the executioner of vengeance on him. But Jones unluckily forgot, that though the hands of Northerton were tied, his legs were at liberty; nor did he lay the least injunction on

the prisoner that he should not make what use
of these he pleased. Northerton therefore having given no parole of that kind, thought he
might without any breach of honor depart; not
being obliged, as he imagined, by any rules, to
wait for a formal discharge. He therefore took
up his legs, which were at liberty, and walked off
through the wood, which favored his retreat; nor
did the woman, whose eyes were perhaps rather
turned toward her deliver, once think of his escape, or give herself any concern or trouble to
prevent it.

Jones therefore, at his return, found the
woman alone. He would have spent some time
in searching for Northerton, but she would not
permit him; earnestly entreating that he would
accompany her to the town whither they had been
directed. "As to the fellow's escape," said she,
"it gives me no uneasiness; for philosophy and
Christianity both preach up forgiveness of injuries. But for you, sir, I am concerned at the
trouble I give you; nay, indeed, my nakedness
may well make me ashamed to look you in the
face; and if it was not for the sake of your protection, I should wish to go alone."

Jones offered her his coat; but, I know not for
what reason, she absolutely refused the most
earnest solicitations to accept it. He then
begged her to forget both the causes of her confusion. "With regard to the former," says he,
"I have done no more than my duty in protecting
you; and as for the latter, I will entirely remove
it, by walking before you all the way; for I would

not have my eyes offend you, and I could not answer for my power of resisting the attractive charms of so much beauty.''

Thus our hero and the redeemed lady walked in the same manner as Orpheus and Eurydice marched heretofore; but though I cannot believe that Jones was designedly tempted by his fair one to look behind him, yet as she frequently wanted his assistance to help her over stiles, and had besides many trips and other accidents, he was often obliged to turn about. However, he had better fortune than what attended poor Orpheus, for he brought his companion, or rather follower, safe into the famous town of Upton.

CHAPTER III

The arrival of Mr. Jones with his lady at the inn; with a very full description of the battle of Upton.

THOUGH the reader, we doubt not, is very eager to know who this lady was, and how she fell into the hands of Mr. Northerton, we must beg him to suspend his curiosity for a short time, as we are obliged, for some very good reasons which hereafter perhaps he may guess, to delay his satisfaction a little longer.

Mr. Jones and his fair companion no sooner entered the town, than they went directly to that inn which in their eyes presented the fairest appearance to the street. Here Jones, having ordered a servant to show a room above stairs, was ascending, when the disheveled fair, hastily following, was laid hold on by the master of the house, who cried, "Heyday, where is that beggar wench going? Stay below stairs, I desire you." But Jones at that instant thundered from above, "Let the lady come up," in so authoritative a voice, that the good man instantly withdrew his hands, and the lady made the best of her way to the chamber.

Here Jones wished her joy of her safe arrival, and then departed, in order, as he promised, to send the landlady up with some clothes. The poor woman thanked him heartily for all his kind-

331

ness, and said, she hoped she should see him again soon, to thank him a thousand times more. During this short conversation, she covered her white bosom as well as she could possibly with her arms; for Jones could not avoid stealing a sly peep or two, though he took all imaginable care to avoid giving any offense.

Our travelers had happened to take up their residence at a house of exceeding good repute, whither Irish ladies of strict virtue, and many northern lasses of the same predicament, were accustomed to resort in their way to Bath. The landlady therefore would by no means have admitted any conversation of a disreputable kind to pass under her roof. Indeed, so foul and contagious are all such proceedings, that they contaminate the very innocent scenes where they are committed, and give the name of a bad house, or of a house of ill repute, to all those where they are suffered to be carried on.

Not that I would intimate that such strict chastity as was preserved in the temple of Vesta can possibly be maintained at a public inn. My good landlady did not hope for such a blessing, nor would any of the ladies I have spoken of, or indeed any others of the most rigid note, have expected or insisted on any such thing. But to exclude all vulgar concubinage, and to drive all whores in rags from within the walls, is within the power of every one. This my landlady very strictly adhered to, and this her virtuous guests, who did not travel in rags, would very reasonably have expected of her.

Now it required no very blamable degree of suspicion to imagine that Mr. Jones and his ragged companion had certain purposes in their intention, which, though tolerated in some Christian countries, connived at in others, and practiced in all, are however as expressly forbidden as murder, or any other horrid vice, by that religion which is universally believed in those countries. The landlady, therefore, had no sooner received an intimation of the entrance of the above-said persons than she began to meditate the most expeditious means for their expulsion. In order to this, she had provided herself with a long and deadly instrument, with which, in times of peace, the chambermaid was wont to demolish the labors of the industrious spider. In vulgar phrase, she had taken up the broomstick, and was just about to sally from the kitchen, when Jones accosted her with a demand of a gown and other vestments, to cover the half-naked woman upstairs.

Nothing can be more provoking to the human temper, nor more dangerous to that cardinal virtue, patience, than solicitations of extraordinary offices of kindness on behalf of those very persons with whom we are highly incensed. For this reason Shakespeare hath artfully introduced his Desdemona soliciting favors for Cassio of her husband, as the means of inflaming, not only his jealousy, but his rage, to the highest pitch of madness; and we find the unfortunate Moor less able to command his passion on this occasion, than even when he beheld his valued present to his wife in the hands of his supposed rival. In fact, we regard these efforts as insults on our understanding, and to such the pride of man is very difficultly brought to submit.

My landlady, though a very good-tempered woman, had, I suppose, some of this pride in her composition, for Jones had scarce ended his request, when she fell upon him with a certain weapon, which, though it be neither long, nor sharp, nor hard, nor indeed threatens from its appearance with either death or wound, hath been however held in great dread and abhorrence by many wise men—nay, by many brave ones; insomuch, that some who have dared to look into the mouth of a loaded cannon, have not dared to look into a mouth where this weapon was brandished; and rather than run the hazard of its execution, have contented themselves with making a most pitiful and sneaking figure in the eyes of all their acquaintance.

To confess the truth, I am afraid Mr. Jones was one of these; for though he was attacked and violently belabored with the aforesaid weapon, he could not be provoked to make any resistance; but in a most cowardly manner applied, with many entreaties, to his antagonist to desist from pursuing her blows; in plain English, he only begged her with the utmost earnestness to hear him; but before he could obtain his request, my landlord himself entered into the fray, and embraced that side of the cause which seemed to stand very little in need of assistance.

There are a sort of heroes who are supposed

to be determined in their choosing or avoiding a
conflict by the character and behavior of the person whom they are to engage. These are said
to know their men, and Jones, I believe, knew
his woman; for though he had been so submissive
to her, he was no sooner attacked by her husband, than he demonstrated an immediate spirit
of resentment, and enjoined him silence under a
very severe penalty; no less than that, I think,
of being converted into fuel for his own fire.

The husband, with great indignation, but with
a mixture of pity, answered, "You must pray
first to be made able. I believe I am a better man
than yourself; ay, every way, that I am;" and
presently proceeded to discharge half-a-dozen
whores at the lady above stairs, the last of which
had scarce issued from his lips, when a-swinging
blow from the cudgel that Jones carried in his
hand assaulted him over the shoulders.

It is a question whether the landlord or the
landlady was the most expeditious in returning
this blow. My landlord, whose hands were
empty, fell to with his fist, and the good wife,
uplifting her broom and aiming at the head of
Jones, had probably put an immediate end to the
fray, and to Jones likewise, had not the descent
of this broom been prevented—not by the miraculous intervention of any heathen deity, but by a
very natural though fortunate accident, viz., by
the arrival of Partridge; who entered the house
at that instant (for fear had caused him to run
every step from the hill), and who, seeing the
danger which threatened his master or com-

panion (which you choose to call him), prevented
so sad a catastrophe, by catching hold of the landlady's arm, as it was brandished aloft in the air.

The landlady soon perceived the impediment
which prevented her blow; and being unable to
rescue her arm from the hands of Partridge, she
let fall the broom; and then leaving Jones to the
discipline of her husband, she fell with the utmost
fury on that poor fellow, who had already given
some intimation of himself, by crying, "Zounds!
do you intend to kill my friend?"

Partridge, though not much addicted to battle, would not however stand still when his friend
was attacked; nor was he much displeased with
that part of the combat which fell to his share;
he therefore returned my landlady's blows as
soon as he received them: and now the fight was
obstinately maintained on all parts, and it seemed
doubtful to which side Fortune would incline,
when the naked lady, who had listened at the top
of the stairs to the dialogue which preceded the
engagement, descended suddenly from above, and
without weighing the unfair inequality of two to
one, fell upon the poor woman who was boxing
with Partridge; nor did that great champion desist, but rather redoubled his fury, when he
found fresh succors were arrived to his assistance.

Victory must now have fallen to the side of the
travelers (for the bravest troops must yield to
numbers) had not Susan the chambermaid come
luckily to support her mistress. This Susan was
as two-handed a wench (according to the phrase)

as any in the country, and would, I believe, have
beat the famed Thalestris herself, or any of her
subject Amazons; for her form was robust and
man-like, and every way made for such encounters.   As her hands and arms were formed
to give blows with great mischief to an enemy, so
was her face as well contrived to receive blows
without any great injury to herself, her nose being already flat to her face; her lips were so
large, that no swelling could be perceived in them,
and moreover they were so hard, that a fist could
hardly make any impression on them.   Lastly,
her cheek-bones stood out, as if nature had intended them for two bastions to defend her eyes
in those encounters for which she seemed so well
calculated, and to which she was most wonderfully well inclined.

This fair creature entering the field of battle,
immediately filed to that wing where her mistress maintained so unequal a fight with one of
either sex.   Here she presently challenged Partridge to single combat.   He accepted the challenge, and a most desperate fight began between
them.

Now the dogs of war being let loose, began to
lick their bloody lips; now Victory, with golden
wings, hung hovering in the air; now Fortune,
taking her scales from her shelf began to weigh
the fates of Tom Jones, his female companion,
and Partridge, against the landlord, his wife, and
maid; all which hung in exact balance before her;
when a good-natured accident put suddenly an
end to the bloody fray, with which half of the

II—22

combatants had already sufficiently feasted. This accident was the arrival of a coach and four; upon which my landlord and landlady immediately desisted from fighting, and at their entreaty obtained the same favor of their antagonists, but Susan was not so kind to Partridge; for that Amazonian fair having overthrown and bestrid her enemy, was now cuffing him lustily with both her hands, without any regard to his request of a cessation of arms, or to those loud exclamations of murder which he roared forth.

No sooner, however, had Jones quitted the landlord, than he flew to the rescue of his defeated companion, from whom he with much difficulty drew off the enraged chambermaid: but Partridge was not immediately sensible of his deliverance, for he still lay flat on the floor, guarding his face with his hands; nor did he cease roaring till Jones had forced him to look up, and to perceive that the battle was at an end.

The landlord, who had no visible hurt, and the landlady, hiding her well-scratched face with her handkerchief, ran both hastily to the door to attend the coach, from which a young lady and her maid now alighted. These the landlady presently ushered into that room where Mr. Jones had at first deposited his fair prize, as it was the best apartment in the house. Hither they were obliged to pass through the field of battle, which they did with the utmost haste, covering their faces with their handkerchiefs, as desirous to avoid the notice of any one. Indeed their caution was quite unnecessary; for the poor unfortunate Helen, the fatal cause of all the bloodshed, was entirely taken up in endeavoring to conceal her own face, and Jones was no less occupied in rescuing Partridge from the fury of Susan; which being happily effected, the poor fellow immediately departed to the pump to wash his face, and to stop that bloody torrent which Susan had plentifully set a-flowing from his nostrils.

CHAPTER IV

In which the arrival of a man of war puts a final end to hostilities, and causes the conclusion of a firm and lasting peace between all parties.

A SERGEANT and a file of musketeers, with a deserter in their custody, arrived about this time. The sergeant presently inquired for the principal magistrate of the town, and was informed by my landlord, that he himself was vested in that office. He then demanded his billets, together with a mug of beer, and complaining it was cold, spread himself before the kitchen fire.

Mr. Jones was at this time comforting the poor distressed lady, who sat down at a table in the kitchen, and leaning her head upon her arm, was bemoaning her misfortunes; but lest my fair readers should be in pain concerning a particular circumstance, I think proper here to acquaint them, that before she had quitted the room above stairs, she had so well covered herself with a pillowbeer which she there found, that her regard to decency was not in the least violated by the presence of so many men as were now in the room.

One of the soldiers now went up to the sergeant, and whispered something in his ear; upon which he steadfastly fixed his eyes on the lady, and having looked at her for near a minute, he came up to her, saying, "I ask pardon, madam; but I am certain I am not deceived; you can be no other person than Captain Waters's lady?"

The poor woman, who in her present distress had very little regarded the face of any person present, no sooner looked at the sergeant than she presently recollected him, and calling him by his name, answered, "That she was indeed the unhappy person he imagined her to be;" but added, "I wonder any one should know me in this disguise." To which the sergeant replied, "He was very much surprised to see her ladyship in such a dress, and was afraid some accident had happened to her."—"An accident hath happened to me, indeed," says she, "and I am highly obliged to this gentleman" (pointing to Jones) "that it was not a fatal one, or that I am now living to mention it."—"Whatever the gentleman hath done," cries the sergeant, "I am sure the captain will make him amends for it; and if I can be of any service, your ladyship may command me, and I shall think myself very happy to have it in my power to serve your ladyship; and so indeed may any one, for I know the captain will well reward them for it."

The landlady, who heard from the stairs all that passed between the sergeant and Mrs. Waters, came hastily down, and running directly up to her, began to ask pardon for the offenses she had committed, begging that all might be imputed to ignorance of her quality: for, "Lud! madam," says she, "how should I have imagined that a lady of your fashion would appear in such a dress? I am sure, madam, if I had once suspected that your ladyship was your ladyship, I would sooner have burned my tongue out, than have said what I have said; and I hope your ladyship will accept of a gown, till you can get your own clothes.''

''Prithee, woman,'' says Mrs. Waters, ''cease your impertinence: how can you imagine I should concern myself about anything which comes from the lips of such low creatures as yourself? But I am surprised at your assurance in thinking, after what is past, that I will condescend to put on any of your dirty things. I would have you know, creature, I have a spirit above that.''

Here Jones interfered, and begged Mrs. Waters to forgive the landlady, and to accept her gown: ''for I must confess,'' cries he, ''our appearance was a little suspicious when first we came in; and I am well assured all this good woman did was, as she professed, out of regard to the reputation of her house.''

''Yes, upon my truly was it,'' says she: ''the gentleman speaks very much like a gentleman, and I see very plainly is so; and to be certain the house is well known to be a house of as good reputation as any on the road, and though I say it, is frequented by gentry of the best quality, both Irish and English. I defy anybody to say black is my eye, for that matter. And, as I was saying, if I had known your ladyship to be your ladyship, I would as soon have burned my fingers as have affronted your ladyship; but truly where

gentry come and spend their money, I am not
willing that they should be scandalized by a set
of poor shabby vermin, that, wherever they go,
leave more lice than money behind them; such
folks never raise my compassion, for to be certain it is foolish to have any for them; and if our
justices did as they ought, they would be all
whipped out of the kingdom, for to be certain
it is what is most fitting for them. But as for
your ladyship, I am heartily sorry your ladyship
hath had a misfortune, and if your ladyship
will do me the honor to wear my clothes till you
can get some of your ladyship's own, to be certain the best I have is at your ladyship's service.''

Whether cold, shame, or the persuasions of Mr.
Jones prevailed most on Mrs. Waters, I will not
determine, but she suffered herself to be pacified
by this speech of my landlady, and retired with
that good woman, in order to apparel herself in
a decent manner.

My landlord was likewise beginning his oration
to Jones, but was presently interrupted by that
generous youth, who shook him heartily by the
hand, and assured him of entire forgiveness, saying, ''If you are satisfied, my worthy friend, I
promise you I am;'' and indeed, in one sense, the
landlord had the better reason to be satisfied;
for he had received a bellyfull of drubbing,
whereas Jones had scarce felt a single blow.

Partridge, who had been all this time washing
his bloody nose at the pump, returned into the
kitchen at the instant when his master and the

landlord were shaking hands with each other.
As he was of a peaceable disposition, he was
pleased with those symptoms of reconciliation;
and though his face bore some marks of Susan's
fist, and many more of her nails, he rather chose
to be contented with his fortune in the last battle
than to endeavor at bettering it in another.

The heroic Susan was likewise well contented
with her victory, though it had cost her a black
eye, which Partridge had given her at the first
onset. Between these two, therefore, a. league
was struck, and those hands which had been the
instruments of war became now the mediators
of peace.

Matters were thus restored to a perfect calm;
at which the sergeant, though it may seem so
contrary to the principles of his profession,
testified his approbation. "Why now, that's
friendly," said he; "d—n me, I hate to see two
people bear ill-will to one another after they
have had a tussle. The only way when friends
quarrel is to see it out fairly in a friendly manner, as a man may call it, either with a fist, or
sword, or pistol, according as they like, and then
let it be all over; for my own part, d—n me if
ever I love my friend better than when I am
fighting with him! To bear malice is more like
a Frenchman than an Englishman."

He then proposed a libation as a necessary
part of the ceremony at all treaties of this kind.
Perhaps the reader may here conclude that he
was well versed in ancient history; but this,
though highly probable, as he cited no authority

to support the custom, I will not affirm with any confidence. Most likely indeed it is, that he founded his opinion on very good authority, since he confirmed it with many violent oaths.

Jones no sooner heard the proposal than, immediately agreeing with the learned sergeant, he ordered a bowl, or rather a large mug, filled with the liquor used on these occasions, to be brought in, and then began the ceremony himself. He placed his right hand in that of the landlord, and, seizing the bowl with his left, uttered the usual words, and then made his libation. After which, the same was observed by all present. Indeed, there is very little need of being particular in describing the whole form, as it differed so little from those libations of which so much is recorded in ancient authors and their modern transcribers. The principal difference lay in two instances; for, first, the present company poured the liquor only down their throats; and secondly, the sergeant, who officiated as priest, drank the last; but he preserved, I believe, the ancient form, in swallowing much the largest draught of the whole company, and in being the only person present who contributed nothing towards the libation besides his good offices in assisting at the performance.

The good people now ranged themselves round the kitchen fire, where good humor seemed to maintain an absolute dominion; and Partridge not only forgot his shameful defeat, but converted hunger into thirst, and soon became extremely facetious. We must however quit this agreeable assembly for a while, and attend Mr. Jones to Mrs. Waters's apartment, where the dinner which he had bespoke was now on the table. Indeed, it took no long time in preparing, having been all dressed three days before, and required nothing more from the cook than to warm it over again.

END OF VOL. II

Printed in the United Kingdom
by Lightning Source UK Ltd.
125387UK00001B/249/A